LONDON BRIDGE DOWN

WHISKEY WITCHES PARA WARS BOOK 2

S.S. WOLFRAM

Whistling Book Press

Alaska

Printed in the United States of America

Published by Whistling Book Press

Whistling Book Press
Alaska
Visit our web site at:
www.whistlingbooks.com

WHISKEY MAGICK & MENTAL HEALTH

Sign up to learn more about our books and receive this free e-zine about Whiskey Magick and Mental Health.
https://www.fjblooding.com/books-lp

There are too many people to list. The top of the list, however, belongs to my wife. She has superpower levels of everything. I can only sometimes spin a yarn.

Oh, and my kids. Love those little turds.

1

Ooooh, paperwork! Actually, it was a bit more toward *eww*. Dexx slid the paper to the done stack and pulled another one off the too-tall pile.

If he looked real hard at himself, not even the paperwork was the real problem. That would be frustration and anger. At Paige.

He stopped and stared in stupefied wonder at the next report. "Bow," he called through the door.

A few seconds later, Rainbow Blu stuck her head through the door. Her afro came in first, followed by beautiful brown skin and childlike enthusiasm. "Yes, boss?" Her deep brown eyes twinkled.

He wasn't angry per se, but Rainbow had been told—asked to take a *little* more time and to fill out more of the blanks on her reports. Which, in her defense, she *had*. "Could you, oh, I don't know, put a bit more *description* on a few of these?"

"I filled all the blanks, didn't I?"

Dexx suppressed a laugh somewhere between genuine

humor and actual exasperation. "*Coloring in the boxes* isn't filling it out. Words and stuff. I can't decipher the colors."

"Isn't that what you said? White is yours, gold is Tuck's, and pink is—"

This time Dexx did chuckle. "That's the 'in triplicate' part. You know, carbon copy without all the *carbon paper.*"

"What's that?" Rainbow pushed the door further open and entered the office.

Dexx pressed his lips together and counted. "You're special. Short-bus special with a twist. Okay. I need you actually to write words. With a subject, predicate, noun, and verbs. You know, to add more *actual* color."

"That's it." Rainbow poked a finger toward Dexx excitedly. "You said to add more color."

So literal. "Yeah, okay. So, for example, on Tuesday the twenty-fourth, you *red* at location— I'm calling it periwinkle —and green *detailed description.* Is that how it happened? Exactly *as* it happened?"

A grin split Rainbow's face.

A couple of months ago, he would have just laughed, but he was starting to get this was serious. "You could face an internal investigation if you left out any of the *brown*, but don't forget grey. I know red is still important, though."

Rainbow giggled. She sat in the chair across from the desk. "You know those things don't mean much. How many times have you said the mundane's laws didn't really apply to us?"

That was before he had the hot seat. "You're right. We *do* have a different set of laws, but it's *inside* the mundane's laws." Wait. That sounded familiar. Hadn't Paige said something like that?

Hattie stirred in the back of his mind. *Yes, cub. She told you almost precisely in those words.* His spirit animal was bored out of her skull, and not happy about it.

Well, shit. *Who asked you anyway?*

Hattie returned to her boredom, her spirit form rolling over and batting at imaginary butterflies.

Life had decidedly become less exciting since he had the reins. Why had Paige and Tony had to leave? Oh yeah, they'd either moved on or had been forced out. "Come on, Bow. Please, for the sake of my sanity and your safety, use complete sentences and descriptions. You don't have to write an encyclopedia but make a complete statement."

Rainbow sat in her chair with her hands pressed between her knees and just smiled expectantly.

He tilted his head. "Something you want to add?" He waited for something, anything, but Rainbow just smiled. "Bow?"

Nothing.

"Hey." He rapped his knuckles on the desk.

Rainbow jumped a little and blinked rapidly as though waking up. "Huh, what happened?"

Dexx let his head fall. Her being unable to concentrate through a conversation was so typically Rainbow. "Can you please start using words on your reports? Personally, I don't care if you use different colored ink to make it mean more to *you* but write words. Real words."

Rainbow saluted with that smile plastered to her face. "Sure, boss. Full assimilation."

"Are you... okay?" Dexx couldn't have Rainbow flaking. She was the little sister of the whole department, and she was the best detective they had. Better than Michelle or Tarik. If she flaked, they would all suffer.

"Oh, I'm fine." She fluttered her eyelashes and tipped her head to the side. "I just got lost in your eyes."

Dexx couldn't tell if she was exaggerating or serious. "Sometimes, I just want to throttle you."

"Why?" She looked as vacant as a deer in the headlights.

"So, I can use your neck to warm my hands up."

"Actually, if they're cold, you can just stick them up in your pits. It's okay if you shower. They won't stink or anything."

Dexx dropped his head. "I'm going to kill whoever you learned that from."

Wide-eyed innocence answered. "Learned what from?"

"Bow, go back to your desk before you leave on a stretcher."

"Kay, boss. Anything else I can help you with?"

"Find a store with all the color pens, then buy them."

She wiggled her eyebrows in challenge. "I bet I can do that before you can."

"It's a race." Dexx showed teeth. She'd probably think he smiled.

Rainbow popped out of her chair and flung the door open, then jumped back with a squeak.

Mario Kester stood in the doorway, his hand raised to knock.

She slipped past the DoDO agent.

Fuck. What did that *asshat* want? Sounded good in his head, so... "What the fuck do you want, asshat?"

Mario didn't even flinch, his pale blond eyebrows not even twitching. "Charming as ever, Colt," he said in his slight British accent. "I came by to see how things are going."

"Things are going smashingly. That's how you say that, right? Smashingly?"

"I think the word you're looking for is bollocks." His alarmingly bright blue eyes almost radiated something probably unpleasant. "It's a steaming pile of bollocks, and you've got to take a big bite from it." Mario took the seat Rainbow vacated, but he leaned back, almost lounging.

He didn't even ask. Limey bastich. "I'm pretty sure it might be closer to 'You've bollocksed up my day.'"

Mario's eye tightened a fraction. "Too right. But I didn't come out to offer a lesson in language."

"And there goes the rest of *my* day." Dexx collected the done pile and tapped them together in a neat stack, turning the top page over so Mario couldn't read it. Not that he'd get much out of it, since Rainbow had only colored in the boxes. Mario didn't need to know that, though.

"I came with an offer. No games, no hidden hooks. That's how you say it, right?"

What was he talking about? "I'm sure there's plenty of fine print you'll forget to share."

"Clean offer. My people were very impressed with your performance under my leadership when you helped us. We'd like you to come be an apprentice seeker."

A few months back, Red Star had teamed up with DoDO temporarily to take out Sven's hideout.

Dexx'd led the operation, which was why it'd been such a success, so being an apprentice to this ass wipe? Probably not. "Seeker?" Dexx leaned back, tapping his lip with a pen. "Apprentice? You fish and chip turds are the *apprentices* if anyone is."

"Over here, you call yourselves *hunters*. Not the best descriptor since you don't eat what you kill."

This guy really knew how to get under Dexx's skin. The sleazy tone, the calm as fuck body language. Maybe it was that sneer. Whatever it was, Dexx just wanted to punch him in his smug face. "But *seeker* is so much better? Look but don't kill? Tag and bag for later? I think I like *hunter* better."

"Call it what you will. Hunter, seeker, doesn't matter. We want you to work for us. Oh, I'm sure this place will be here to check in on in between missions."

This guy wanted Dexx—a shifter—to work for DoDO?

They'd made their stance pretty clear on shifter kind. DoDO wanted them all in collars and chains. "Have you looked around lately? Things between my people— *our people,* and you are a bit strained."

"What if they didn't have to be? If you remember, one call can make things quite warm for you." Mario shrugged with a hand. "Or they can be comfortable. We have a surprising amount of pull with your president."

"This is your *clean offer*? Innuendo and veiled threats? You've got to read more books about selling yourself. 'Cause what you're doing here—" Dexx swirled his hand in the air. "—isn't the way to do it." He stood and leaned on his knuckles. "Counteroffer. You get the hell out of my office and keep going until you get of town, or I'm going to let Hattie eat what she kills."

Mario stood, staring Dexx in the eyes, and slipped his hand into his jacket pocket. He pulled a card out and slid it across the desk.

Dexx didn't twitch. He did, however, bring Hattie out a bit, enough to change his features and turn his eyes a flame green.

Mario didn't rush from the office, but he didn't take his time either. He shut the door behind him.

Dexx pushed Hattie back and slumped in his chair. How did Paige get everyone to do what she wanted without threatening? He felt like he was herding cats.

Apprenticing to DoDO? As though he didn't have more experience than the whole *Department of Delicate Operations* combined?

Mario had a point, though. If they had a line to the president, then things could be pretty hostile for any paranormal without protection, like having powerful wards around their town or a supernatural police force like Red Star.

Dexx ran his hands through his hair and blew out his

cheeks, scratching his head. One stack to review, and another, much shorter, that was finished.

His vision swam for a second, then solidified.

This was no fun at *all*. "Enough of this shit. Let's go out."

Hattie turned over, her ears flicking forward in excitement. Days, weeks of sitting in that chair doing nothing wasn't her idea of fun. Hunting demons and other bad guys with liberal doses of play definitely were. *We cannot stay healthy if we lay down to hunt.*

Damn straight. Dexx flipped his jacket from the hook and left the office.

The bullpen was *alive*. Well, when compared to his office.

Michelle entertained Tarik and Frey. Something was worthwhile on the computer screen, but when they saw Dexx, they filtered back to their desks and sat.

Rainbow furiously tapped at her computer.

Ethel sat on a taller stool and watched.

Dexx's desk, which *had* been Quinn Winters's before she'd disappeared, was empty. The thing was cursed. Anyone who sat in it was destined to be replaced.

"Who wants to find something to break?" Dexx gave the bullpen a mischievous sidelong look.

Blank stares met his.

Were they *all* a bunch of adults? "Nobody?"

Michelle used her pencil to point at her keyboard nonverbally, stating she was busy. Police work.

Tarik didn't move.

Frey crossed her arms.

"Hey, I'm not the bad guy. Let's break some shit. Bow? You want to see what we can scare up?"

"Can't. I'm trying to snipe this two hundred color painter's pen set."

"What?" Of course, she'd taken him literally.

Rainbow already had her attention back on her screen.

Michelle finally released a frustrated sigh and looked up from her computer. "The wards, Dexx."

"Yeah? What about 'em?"

She gave him a long, hard stare as if waiting for him to remember something.

Okay. Yeah. He did. Paige'd told him that the wards would keep DoDO from doing anything overtly stupid, like coming into town and pointing guns at their kids. That was probably why the crime rate was down all over town, too.

Damn, he was bored.

Bored, bored, bored, bored, *bored.*

Fuck it. *Let's go, cat.*

We can patrol the border.

Maybe. We could go to work on Jackie.

Hattie didn't think that was nearly as fun.

Dexx opened the door on Leah's '72 Ranchero and plopped into the seat, wondering what he should do. Responsibilities pulled at him, but that just wasn't him. He wanted to play—needed to play.

The exhaust burbled robust without crackles or pops. Caballo, as Leah had named him, had come a long way since his junkyard refugee days. He and Leah had given the car a Krylon makeover to make him a single color. Road warrior black in satin. He looked pretty menacing now, with chrome highlights.

Thinking about cars made him feel more in control, but it wasn't helping the current restlessness.

Where should he go? Hattie voted to patrol the border, his own was to work on Jackie, his '70 Dodge Challenger, but he couldn't do either. This excess energy wouldn't let him.

Paige had taken his kids to D.C. against his wishes. She'd taken all of his kids—well, except little Bobby. Leah was his adopted—not officially—teenage daughter and the twins were weeks old. Dexx wanted to throttle her.

But he was frustrated with himself, too, for getting himself into a situation like this one. He was a demon hunter. He saved people and hunted things. That's just what he did.

And now, he herded babies.

That didn't sit well with him.

The car stopped in the sheriff's parking lot, and Dexx had no clue how'd he'd gotten there. Driven, obviously, but intentionally?

Sheriff Tuck's old beat-up truck added a spot of happy orange color in the black and white lot. Rust and orange.

Dexx shut the car off and pulled the keys. Why would he come here?

Probably because Sheriff Tuck, for all his ear-pulling, was someone Dexx looked up to. Not just as a boss, but as a man. He opened the door and headed inside.

Tuck had a largish office with pressed texture walls. The walls separating him from his bullpen had glass halfway up with slatted blinds for privacy.

Dexx stopped, trying to figure out what he wanted to say. That he didn't like the big chair, or he *did* like the big chair, but not all the responsibilities that came with it? He definitely didn't want the pencil-pushing.

He was *really* livid about the kids. He was *trying* not to let it show, trying not to let it get to him.

But if he was supposed to be Paige's partner, if he was supposed to be handling things she couldn't, then shouldn't she *not* immediately dismiss what he had to say just because *he'd* been the one to say it? Dexx inhaled deeply and let it go slow.

Before he was ready, he knocked on the open door.

"What's up, Colt?" Tuck looked like a mix between the Most Interesting Man in the World and Sam Elliot. Damn, he looked *competent* behind the desk.

"Gotta minute?" Dexx felt himself say. Had Hattie taken over somehow?

"No, but since you're here, I'll push the mayor back a little." The corner of his mouth went up in a smirk behind his mustache.

"Ha, ha. You funny guy." Cop humor. He didn't get it. Or was he really pushing the mayor back? It didn't matter anyway since the city was walled off from the world.

"What's on your mind, Dexx? I hope it's not to tell me you're planning on breaking more of the city because you and Sven did a pretty good job of it already. The good news is there's less to break now. And—" Tuck held up a piece of paper. "—they're sending me bartering invoices since everyone knows we're outta money."

Dexx had never *once* intentionally destroyed *any* part of the city. *That* had always been bad people doing bad shit. "Always got to get another dig in, don't ya?"

Tuck smiled broad, without teeth. "If I didn't, how would you know you're alive?"

"Pea and Les keep me on my toes often enough."

"How are things on your side of town?"

That felt like the reason he was there. "I don't know. I'm the boss now, *really* the boss…"

"And you don't know if you're cut out for it? Maybe you thought you'd have more tee times and less seat time? I thought that too, but it goes away after a while."

Did it? "How long does this last?"

"Not long. Say, a day or two after you die." Tuck grinned at him again. The mentor was teasing the apprentice.

"Hm." Situation normal, all fucked up. "So, I have *that* to look forward to. Can't we get rid of the never-ending rain of procedural writing? We're on our own now."

"Look, Dexx. I want to say it's all fun and games, and you'll be out with your guys, crackin' heads and blasting demons, and the truth is, you have a hell of a team, but they need your guidance. I know you want to lead from the front, but sometimes you have to push from the rear. The best generals of all time lead the charge. The other best generals lead from smoke-filled rooms. You may be one of the best. You'll have an easier time of it if you find the balance of pushing and pulling."

"How do *you* do it?" Tuck seemed the most level-headed man Dexx'd ever known.

"I trust my guys. I give them the discipline I need in them and trust that they'll do the right thing."

That sounded good, but there was always the desk in front of him. That sucked royally. "I hate paperwork."

"At the end of every good job is paperwork." Tuck's face pulled up in another smirk.

The end of every good job? "The shitty kind, right?"

"Yeah, that kind," Tuck said through a chuckle. "Dexx, I want you to know I'm here for you when you need help. Sometimes I have doubts too, but don't let your people know. The face you show them is the strength they'll take out there." He waved a hand toward the walls. *Beyond* the walls.

That felt right.

Hattie nodded at the truth of it.

"Go home. Relax. Recharge and come at it again tomorrow. It gets easier, even if it doesn't get any more exciting."

Dexx stood up, and half turned. "You sound a lot like Alma but without swearing or cookies."

Tuck barked a laugh. "She was an amazing woman."

"Yes, yes, she was." Dexx missed her more than he thought he should.

Dexx left the office and drove home to recharge. He had an idea of what might help, but Hattie might not.

Jackie had a real shot at firing up tonight.

He just needed the world to not fall apart before then. Or maybe that's what he wanted. He didn't know.

2

After playing around with Bobby for a bit and eating dinner—and doing the dishes, again, with his toddler stepson, Dexx cracked open a beer and leaned over Jackie's engine. A brand new Hellcat crate motor nestled beautifully between her shock towers. Who knew back then that they'd build over seven hundred horse production engines?

"Hey, baby, you ready to return to service?" He took a sip and patted Jackie's fender.

Jackie said nothing, of course, but he talked like she might. Never know, he heard other voices in his head all the time.

Hattie growled lightly.

Paige had taken Leah and the twins with her to D.C. How had he converted into a family man? A woman. It always came back to a woman.

She left Bobby because the few angels and demons still on Earth would hunt him down if they got wind of his existence, so taking him outside the protections of the Troutdale wards as an absolute no But the toddler didn't like working on cars, not like his teenaged daughter did. So, Margo and the rest of the pack probably had him out somewhere, teaching him pack stuff. Or rolling him around, but he was safe. Mostly. He felt them out far away with his alpha senses, but they were still on the property.

He couldn't feel Paige or Leah or the twins.

Why? Was everything okay?

Dexx reached down and pulled the cloth covering the intake where the missing supercharger would fit, concentrating on what he had control over. The hole seemed gigantic, and it was. The old Jackie had been fun and had been everything he'd ever wanted. The new Jackie represented everything that could be new, exciting, and uncharted.

Bolting the supercharger on would only take a few minutes. Maybe. Most of the new build was 'modify and fabricate,' since nobody in the manufacturing business had paved the way with explicit pics and step by step instructions.

He stood and went to the bench with the new aluminum lung and spun the pulley. The internals were still stiff. The break-in would cure that.

Finishing up the engine, and then the new grille and lights, and bolting on the hood should take ten hours or so. He had the time.

The phone rang in his pocket. Witchy Woman sang out. Paige, the almighty Whiskey witch, wanted to talk.

But did he? He swiped the ignore button.

No. He didn't.

She sent him a message to call her when he got her message.

He rolled his eyes and ignored it. Why did she want to hear what he had to say now?

The next couple of hours went to installing equipment on Jackie as he chewed on his anger. Bobby'd come to "help" him a few times, only to be chased out by Clem, one of Dexx's wolves. Bobby was into using his magick to blow stuff up, which wasn't great when trying to *build* cars.

Jackie's front end looked crisp. The new supercharger looked about as burly and fantastic as things could get. The new hood waited for another person to help set it in place.

He might have stayed in the garage, but Tyler came out. "Hey, Uncle Dexx? Wanna play tag?"

Dexx wasn't nearly as angry anymore. To the point where he could pull up Paige's messages and read them. He still didn't feel like sending a reply. "That sounds like a challenge."

"Kate and Mandy have a new strategy cooked up."

"Lead the way. I've been *dying* for a tender human snack."

Tyler flipped the blanket-turned-cape over his arms and held them akimbo. He deepened his voice to a prepubescent superhero voice. "No. I will stop you."

"We'll see about that."

It was hard to remain mad when Tyler was around. He spun on his heel and darted through the house, yelling that Dexx was on his way.

Mandy and Kate smiled before running at Dexx at full speed, plowing into him for a hug. The little elf girl nearly toppled him over, which always surprised him. Kate was so much smaller than Mandy. After the two of them let him go, they went for the door.

Mandy wielded fire magick, and Kate was an elf that had adopted the family. Sort of.

Dexx kept the kids busy playing tag for more than an hour until Leslie called the kids in for bed with the yells for brushing hair and teeth and not making a mess while doing so.

After the kids disappeared into the house, Dexx wandered to the edge of the woods where Margo, the pack, and Nick lived. He avoided all of them, not because he was anti-social.

He just really missed Leah and the twins.

And Paige, even if he *was* still angry with her.

He pulled out his phone and responded with a poop emoji. He'd let her stew long enough, but she needed to know he still wasn't ready to *talk* with her just yet. He had emotions and rights to them.

He stood over Boot's grave. He'd been Margo and Clem's brother and a part of Dexx's pack, but he hadn't made it in the last battle.

Neither had Alma, who had a plot beside him.

How many others would join them if Paige fucked this up in D.C.? If she was distracted with the kids—

Okay. So, he *understood* why she'd wanted to take them with her. He did. He wasn't that much of an asshole.

But what if the graves joining these two were smaller ones? What would she be able to say for herself then?

Dexx knelt in between the two stones ordering his thoughts.

"Hey, Boot. I don't want to disturb you, so I'll be quick. You amazed me every day. I miss that."

He turned his head to the other stone and reached a hand to crumple leaves together. "Alma, you kept me grounded and challenged me in ways nobody else could. I wish you were here now because I need help. I have more than a little problem setting myself the challenges, and the one I have is more than I want to deal with."

He flopped on his back, looking up into the trees, green with life, standing as silent sentries over the gravesites.

He inhaled deeply and closed his eyes, letting the breath go slowly. "I got what I thought I wanted. Now I don't know. The big desk and responsibility."

His fingers found a small twig in the blanket of leaves,

and he snapped short pieces off until it was only one small piece among the rest. He picked another and repeated the process.

"I used to be responsible for myself. Just me. It was nice. Hunt a while, then move on. Now, I got an anchor. Kids. An almost wife who doesn't respect what I have to say. A life. Way more than I should have."

We have each other, cub. Hattie added in her deep soothing voice.

Hattie. Of course. His ever-present pain-in-the-ass conscience.

Dexx wouldn't ever admit it, but her voice in his head felt like petting a soft blanket. Cushy and comforting.

Sure. Just like an after school special, aren't you? "What are we doing, fat cat? I don't know if I can do this. Remember when it was just us?"

Hattie's ears perked forward. They'd never been just them. She'd come after Paige, but she was more than just the voice in his head that pissed him off at the wrong time.

You hunted the biggest of prey, and now you want rabbits again?

"You fat cat, what does that even mean?"

We are not doing what we do best. We have more than we can easily keep.

Dexx thinned his lips. *I thought you were the one that always wanted the top spot. You know, the alpha?*

We cannot be confined in that… place. To be alpha is to be with the pack.

"Not anymore, kitty cat. We kinda' did this to ourselves."

Others can. We are supposed to lead them, not push them.

"Same thing. Except for the perspective. What do *you* think, Alma? Do we stay in the boss chair and yell about black ink versus blue?"

She'd probably call him a name and tell him to face the

music or lie in the bed he made or some old-timey saying about being responsible.

Boot would just smile and carry on with whatever he'd been doing. He hadn't talked much, but he'd outworked *everyone*.

"I sure miss you guys." Dexx got up and walked back to the house.

Mandy stood outside, working her fire. A huge bird made of fire flapped around the back yard, breathing gouts with wisps of flame trailing behind. Her talent had grown. "Show me something *really* impressive, Man-Pan."

Mandy twisted around with the look Leslie got when she was going for an over the top creative punishment. She turned back to the bird of fire.

He sat on the grass and watched the show. Mandy passed the bird lower and lower, the heat from the fire scorching random leaves.

Jackie could wait another day. What could happen in a day?

3

Early the next morning, Dexx headed to Leslie's soap shop.

The variety of smells still assaulted his nose, but with time and instruction, he'd finally begun to filter the individual scents better. She'd made a new batch of lavender soaps with... lemongrass and... hmm, charcoal. Mmm. Tasty.

He picked up a bar that had cured—he knew *entirely* too much about soap now—in the "adult" section. The label said *Fuck It All*. It smelled like sandalwood and something else. Jasmine, perhaps? The bar felt strange like it was ready to wrap around him.

Huh. That was a nifty piece of spellwork. Witch soap. Honestly, he'd never go back. It was the best. "At the end of your rope?" Leslie Whiskey leaned against the end of the display rack. "It has a calming and rejuvenating spell in it. You lookin' for you or a special lady?" She wore a grin that might be playful, but with a bit of bite.

Dexx and his soon-to-be-sister-in-law loved to kid around. "My, you have a glow about you." Dexx placed the bar back on the shelf with the others.

Leslie only raised an eyebrow. "Maybe. I got something for you over in the bachelor section. It's a lotion I'm dying to get feedback on." Her smile became decidedly predatory.

Dexx bared his teeth. "I'll bet you do. Why don't you ask Tyler to test drive it?" Okay. Too far. Her teenaged son wasn't the right "test subject" for some of her rowdier mixes.

Leslie's smile stayed, but her eyes glowed a faint orange. Her scent went to dangerous.

He might be her alpha, but she was still mom. "Sorry. He's got a couple of years of innocence yet."

"Damn straight." Leslie pulled back to scout the door as it dinged. She threw the newcomer a smile and waved, telling her something benign before turning her attention back to Dexx. "Paige being gone got you *that* messed up?"

Dexx shrugged and scanned the other displays looking for something that might help. "I... I don't know. Things are..." Things were what? He'd felt strange ever since Mario had stopped by.

They were joined by a woman, looking nervous, and smelling terrified.

Dexx's brows wrinkled for a moment, but he schooled them to bland interest quickly.

Leslie turned pleasantly to the woman. "Can I help you find something specific?"

"I, uh—" The woman stammered and wrung her purse straps. "I think I need to talk to... the, uh..." She bobbed a nervous hand to Dexx.

"The what?" Dexx raised his brows, waiting for *what* he might be.

"The police guy. Aren't you the leader of the... uh, *new* department?"

"Oh." Well, *that* hit him in the gut. "I guess that's me. But you could just call. Everyone there is very nice and easily capable of helping your—"

Leslie's smile was like a dagger to his ego.

Right. "What did you need?" Dexx smiled. Usually, women were put at ease by that.

"I'm—" The woman inhaled deep and let it go slowly. "I need someone to investigate—"

Leslie raised a hand to Dexx and turned away. This was Red Star business.

"Okay, we can do that. What's your name?"

"Angela." She gripped her purse strap like it was the only thing keeping her standing.

"Angela. An investigation? We got a good team that can help. Is this a robbery, or mugging, or—" Dexx bit his lower lip. "— murder?" There was no diplomatic way to ask if a paranormal killed a mundane.

"N—no. It's not that. It's—"

This was old. She really needed to spill it. And soon. Dexx barely suppressed the urge to gesture her to hurry up.

"I see ghosts. I think."

Dexx's eyes flicked around the shop. "Ghosts. I—" They didn't do ghosts. They weren't in Red Star's charter. Demons, sure. Evil rusalkas? Got her covered. Is a witch stealing shifter powers? Had one in the bank, and he could handle that. But ghosts? They didn't do— "We don't have anyone for that, but if you come with me, I can hook you up."

Dexx led the way to the register, where Leslie had her notebook checking things off.

He stopped and waited for Angela to catch up. "This is your lady. She's the one for *really strange* appearances."

If looks could kill, Dexx's face might have melted.

"Angela here is seeing ghosts. We don't look for ghosts unless they're connected to a case we're working." Dexx turned to Angela. "But Leslie is our resident ghost expert. Her and her husband. Tell her what you saw, and she can help set things back to normal. Well, relatively speaking.."

Leslie calmed, and interest took over. As the Whiskey medium, ghosts were one of her talents, and she hadn't had a satisfying ghost hunt since they'd left Texas.

Leslie got the woman to tell her story and took notes in her inventory notebook.

Dexx backed away quietly. He couldn't hide the smile as he left the store with a finger wave. Ghosts. Cute little things.

Outside, the sun warmed the town, bathing the streets in a bright color. Soon it may be a little too hot.

Some people had left the town, thanks to the national-news-level battle, but a surprising amount had stayed. The population reduction was easily visible, and now the paranormal to mundane ratio hovered around one-to-one.

The population *had* dipped, but quite a few had businesses and had opted to stay. Not a big surprise, since most of them had their entire lives wrapped up in homes and storefronts. Moving wasn't easy when you had more than you could carry in your car.

No matter what happened now, though—with whatever was going on with the government or with demons and angels, or whatever—the Whiskeys were home, and they weren't leaving. They would find a way to survive, and if they were the last ones remaining in the whole area, they'd be just as happy.

Dexx would, anyway. As long as his damned kids and his damned not-wife were with him. He could drive the roads with no traffic and play. And nobody would be around to tell him to refrain from city breakage.

We should run. Hattie sounded hopeful as she sent him an image of them bolting up the road in cat form.

"Only if you found a way to put my clothes back on me when we switch back."

We are not like the others.

"Others? You mean Paige and Leslie and anyone else who's a witch and a shifter? Well, when you find a way to do that, then I'll let *you* do all the paperwork, and I'll take the naps in *your* head."

Hattie lay down in his head and went silent. She'd been cooped up a lot lately and only came out when he played with the kids. There just wasn't anything to chase in the office, and since Sven, things had been pretty quiet.

Well, on *his* streets. Maybe not out in the rest of the world.

His restlessness raised its head as if *it, too,* was a spirit. Being out in the world when there was this much chaos actually sounded a little... fun. The Red Star Station peeked around the abandoned furniture shop.

Dexx stepped in the station, looking forward to a nap. He hadn't had a good night's sleep since the twins had arrived, and with them gone, he *still* couldn't get one because *now* he was worrying. And because *he'd* ignored Paige's texts, she was not ignoring his.

He had a date with an office chair. Pretty comfortable, too. It better be, since he'd spent two hours in the office store trying them out. He wound up with one that had full padding and so many adjustments it resembled more of a couch than an executive chair.

The bullpen was empty when he walked through. He headed to the back, past the holding cells. "Hello? Anyone here?"

Nobody answered. Hm.

Maybe the nap would be earlier than he thought. Responsibility would still be there when he woke up.

A quick trip to the basement showed Ethel had somewhere more important to be as well. He was legit on his own. Oh well. The silence was golden.

Dexx made it back to his office and flopped down in his chair, trying to be more excited about the thought of a nap than he was. He walked it away from the desk enough to put his feet up, anyway.

He snuggled into his chair and found the calm relaxation of pre-amazingly glorious sleep when the phone rang. He attempted to ignore it and let it go to voicemail or something, but his eyes popped open.

Damn. It. His feet fell to the floor as he pivoted up to answer. "Red Star. This is Colt speaking."

The woman on the other end nearly panted into the phone, hysterical. "My baby's gone! I just know it's one of those wolf people that took him."

"Wolf people?" A pack member?

"Yes. One of those werewolves running around the city."

"Ma'am, I can assure you that there are *no werewolves* anywhere close to Oregon, let alone around your baby."

"They're all over the city. And one of them *took my baby!*" The woman ended with a scream into the phone.

"Just stay calm, ma'am, and we'll get you taken care of. Give me your name and address, and I'll come out myself to investigate."

"Joanna Glasser. Hurry…"

It didn't take long to drive to her place, but enough to think hard about getting a light to put on top. One person had stopped a little too long at the four-way. He wished he was as calm as he apparently appeared to be. He couldn't let go of his anger.

Paige had taken the kids into a dangerous situation against his wishes as though his thoughts didn't even matter.

Yeah, well, it mattered.

He parked Cab along the street in front of Joanna's house, trying to get a feeling for what he was getting himself into. It was a little place that had definitely seen better days, but it looked lived in.

Dexx scanned the area with Hattie's senses. Nothing looked out of place, and there were no demons, of course. He opened the door and took a deep breath. Nothing smelled out of the ordinary. Nothing had the scent of wrongness, and there were *definitely* no werewolves.

Hattie would have let him know about those things. Way too dangerous to just let them *be* werewolves.

All the way up the walk, he scanned for *anything* outside of normal. Nothing.

The house was mundane. The yard was mundane. The trees, the sidewalk, the few toys lying around the yard, all mundane. The grass could stand to be mowed, but there was nothing odd about that.

An old lady, obviously Joanna, met him at the door. The screen was a wood frame instead of thin pressed metal and glass. That was a bit weathered, too, with white paint flaking off.

The woman just looked at him through the screen, like maybe he had something to sell that wasn't entirely pleasant.

"I'm Dexx Colt with Red Star. We received a call from this address." There. *That* sounded professional. He smiled and unclipped his badge to show Joanna.

"Took you long enough to get here. That thing has my baby, and she could be dead for all I know."

"Can I come in?" Dexx put his badge back on his belt and stood back patiently.

The screen door swung open, and Joanna stepped aside for him to enter. She wasn't what he expected at all.

She was short, older, and severe-looking. She'd wrapped a yellow blanket over her head and around her shoulders. She wore a dark skirt that almost made it to her fat ankles, and her shoes were brown leather.

Dexx grimaced at the ultra-weird combination. *After* he looked away, of course. *If I was her kid, I'd run away too. And make it look like I was eaten by a werewolf so she wouldn't come after me.*

Hattie felt amused. Was she growing a sense of humor?

He glanced at the old pictures hanging in the hall. An old man posed with a little boy at a lake. They held fishing rods and a small fish.

There were a lot of pictures of the old man and the boy. Some had a woman, too. They *might* have been the lady in front of him. But they were old pictures, and the boy had grown up in some of them. The progression was easy to spot. The child wasn't really a child anymore.

"When was the last time you saw... did you say girl?" Something wasn't right here.

"Sure, right in here." She led the way to a table piled high with papers, magazines, and old dishes with crusty bits of leftovers in them.

The place was a hoarder's special. And the smell was... stale. Like even the crusted dishes had stopped smelling. He glanced at the side table next to the recliner chair. Dust. Not thick, but not cleaned, or used in a month easy.

"Ma'am, have you considered your girl might just be hiding?"

Hold on a second. A little person touched absolutely everything, even when they weren't supposed to.

Dexx's spidey sense went off for real this time. He went for the gun he usually had on his belt. His fingers grabbed nothing. He'd forgotten to bring it.

"Good senses, boy. But too late." The woman's voice was low and gravely.

Oh, shit. Demon.

Dexx spun around, bringing Hattie up, but there was something in the way, something that kept her back.

The world became dizzy, washed out. He felt Hattie drop in his mind as the floor came up to meet his face. It might have hurt, but the world fuzzed away.

Fuck.

4

Dexx drifted in and out of consciousness. One thing was very clear, though.

He'd been captured.

His current tormentor was a mage in a dark, leather outfit that hid everything but his eyes. He called up a ball of white light. "What are the weaknesses of her wards?"

Dexx fought against the ropes holding him in place, strung up from a beam above him. "Trade secret. Go make your own!"

The white light hit him like an electric current. Each time it hit him, Hattie was knocked out. It was like she was completely disconnected from him.

He hadn't been terrified in a really long time, but this? This was one of them.

Hours and hours, it went on like this. The mage was

looking for information on Paige and on how to get around her wards. She'd done well in getting them up because these guys? They seemed pretty scared of them.

As the hours slipped into days, he was greeted by another person, a demon wearing the body of a doctor. "Hello, *Dexx*." He said the name like it tasted bad.

"Demon," Dexx grunted from the hard concrete floor. With Hattie out of commission, his healing was extremely slow. He was bruised over a large portion of his body.

"You can call me Dr. Petra. I'll be digging into your memories to find the information I— *we* need."

What? How could Dexx defend against that?

A muted growl sounded in the back of his head, and he felt Hattie digging around in there.

"As it happens," Dr. Petra said, gesturing to people behind Dexx to help him into a chair. "What you'll be experiencing as days or weeks or—if you resist enough—months or years, will be mere hours and days to the outside world. No one will even know how to find you."

That... did a real number on his optimism.

The demon dug at his memories, but they slipped away just as Petra got to each one. They felt locked away under heavy doors. He had no way to get through.

Petra was getting miffed. "Dexx," he said carefully, towering over him as he was tied to a gurney. "Tell me what your children are. They were chosen, were they not?"

"Children?" Dexx didn't remember any—His head split open like someone was applying to jaws of life to his skull.

"Yes," Petra said calmly. "Your twins. Paige is parading them around D.C. as if they were baby dolls. I *heard* a rumor that you weren't happy about that."

Anger rushed to the forefront, but no memories accompanied them. Images battered at each other, vying for the top spot, but Dexx couldn't differentiate between them enough to be able to even see anything.

"Angels are interested in them. Demons are interested in them."

With each word, more anger reared inside Dexx even though he had no idea what Petra was even talking about.

"Even the shifters are scared." Petra leaned forward. "Of your children. So, what are they?"

Dexx had no idea what the man was talking about, but the rage was turning everything red.

Petra finally leaned back and pulled something out of a pocket in his fist. "Excellent," he said to someone Dexx couldn't see. "Let's try again."

When Dexx came to again, a man he recognized sat beside in him. He smiled when Dexx stirred. "Hey, mate," he said in a slight English accent. "Don't get up."

Dexx didn't know what was going on, but he *did* know this man *wasn't* his partner.

The man looked up to someone Dexx couldn't see. "What should I say?"

"Pretend he's your partner and has been for years," Petra said. "Whatever you come up with, his mind *will* build around.

"I don't know. He's never done anything to me. This seems…" The man trailed off and shook his head. "It's cruel."

"He won't give us the information we need, so we're going to get it another way." Mario Kester walked into view and crossed his arms.

The man shook his head.

"Paige Whiskey needs to be taken down. If you don't want this assignment ab-Rhys, I can get someone else."

"I— I'll do it."

Something stirred inside Dexx. Anger. Longing. Love. "I'm not telling you shit," Dexx growled.

"Oh, I'm aware." Petra came into view, looking smug. "But you *will* give me the information I need to bring her down."

Dexx pulled at the bindings that held him to the table.

"Agent ab-Rhys," Petra said slowly. "Just talk to him. Build a relationship. I'll do the rest."

Dexx wasn't going to allow *anyone* to build a relationship with him if it meant betraying his love. Shit. He couldn't even remember her name.

Her name was safe.

He didn't know where that thought came from, but it made him feel a little better.

And angrier at the same time. What the *actual* fuck!

He released a strangled roar that was half man, half beast, and tore at the bindings. They popped, and he leapt off the table.

He was immediately surrounded by lancing, white magick that sheathed him in nerve-stabbing pain before the world went black.

Muffled noises interrupted Dexx's sleep.

He almost understood the words, but he *did* understand the tone. Urgency.

The voices faded away. He sat straight up in bed, his heart hammering. He needed to… *be* somewhere. But why? He couldn't remember. He was blind. No, not quite. Blurry white covered everything. White didn't mean dead, did it?

Things became clearer. Well, sort of.

The room *was* white. Clinically white. What was he doing here? Equipment littered every open space.

A heart rate monitor beeped in a faster rhythm, and a tall stand dripped fluid from an IV bag that led to his arm. Well, crap. What was he doing in a hospital?

Oh yes. Louisiana. He and… someone else was fighting demons?

Images flickered through his head. A basement. A warehouse. A fight. With guns. A shit-ton of guns. Hair. Dark hair. Yes, that stayed. Dark hair but no face with it.

A flatscreen mounted to the wall had the news on. A ticker ran along the bottom with headlines. Some woman was making headlines with a baby on her hip.

Boring.

He turned to his other side, and the pain hit. Nerves lit the inside of his head. If he had paper and a pen, and if it didn't hurt so bad, he could map his entire nervous system using the pain.

As it subsided, he felt something else. Loss. Like something important was missing.

It was safe, though. He didn't know what was missing or why, but he *knew* whatever it was safe.

Laying back in the bed, which was way too hard, he flexed fingers.

Lightning shot up his arm.

The sheet hurt. *Fuck*, how did the *sheet* hurt?

How in the nine hells had he arrived here? Louisiana. Had to be Louisiana, but what had happened?

He blinked, and hand to God, he could hear them close. Little thunderclaps in his head.

Slowly, he took stock. What *didn't* hurt? Fingers. Hurt. Toes? Nope, those hurt too. Legs, arms, middle, back, shoulders, head… all hurt. How about his… shit, that hurt too.

No surprise since *blinking* hurt.

He attempted a deep breath. Little knives cut into his chest. Fuck it. He kept inhaling, filling his lungs as much as he could. He held the air, letting the pain soak in, then let the breath go slow and long.

Hmm. Much better. Breathing came easier, but the sheet was still heavy.

His fingers began tingling with tiny spikes, like after a leg or arm had gone to sleep.

He *hated* that.

The ticker on the TV listed the votes on the paranormal registration act. What the hell was that about? Paranormals?

So maybe he'd been out for a while. He hadn't heard anything about a registration.

Time to try sitting up again. He tried, a sharp beep sounded, kind of like a fire alarm.

His hearing didn't hurt. Scratch that off the list. One positive thing might lead to more, like vision and *everything*.

He sat further up, ignoring the pain streaking from his toes to the tips of his hair.

A nurse hustled in the room. *Three* nurses.

The first one stopped long enough to put a latex glove on and put fingertips to his chest. Fire exploded across him.

"Ow, fuck!"

The nurse's hand jumped off his skin. "Lay back, Mr. Colt." She let her hand hover over him but didn't touch. Intense heat rolled from her hand.

He lay back, a wary eye on the hand-of-ultimate-pain. "Where the hells am I? And what the hell happened?"

The nurse was attractive with a younger face, and her hair pulled back into a ponytail. Her blue scrubs looked attractive on her, too. "Take it easy, Mr. Colt. You're in the complex infirmary."

Dexx twisted a lip. "What? The *complex* infirmary?" What the blazing hell of all the other hells did that mean? "Is this a trick? I have to go. I think I left a roast in the oven." Or something. He shouldn't be there. He knew *that*. But *where* was he supposed to be? "Sorry to be a bother."

All three nurses exchanged glances. "Campus infirmary,

then. Everything is taken care of through your employment, Mr. Colt. Are you feeling all right?"

Employment? When'd he been *hired* to travel across the states to… To do what again? Dexx flattened his lips. "Do I fucking look all right to you? I'm in a fucking bed I can't pay for. And how do you know my name?"

"Your name comes up with your employee I.D. Everyone's does." The nurse looked over her shoulder to one of the other nurses. "Get Dr. Petra. Hurry."

A blonde head whipped around and left in a blur.

"What do you remember, Mr. Colt?" The dark-haired nurse smiled.

Dexx lay still in the bed, appreciating the view. Her smile really lit up the woman's face. It reminded him… of happiness. Yeah. Things still hurt, but a sense of loss surged in his chest. What was he missing? He shook his head carefully. "Louisiana?" That felt right and wrong at the same time.

"Louisiana." The nurse repeated.

That was strange. She'd said it like she was memorizing. "I don't know. A gunfight or something. Like I fell."

"I don't have your charts in front of me, but that's consistent with the bruising."

"Bruising?"

"Bless your little heart. You're about as colorful as a rainbow."

Colors blasted through Dexx's mind. A smile. Poofy hair. Extreme optimism. The image almost had sounds with it. Why did he think of water with that face? And who was she?

"So I fell?"

The nurse nodded.

"Who are you? Where am I?"

"I'm your nurse, silly." The nurse's smile softened, but her eyes hardened. "And you're in the campus infirmary."

"Which tells me exactly nothing." The feeling of wrongness bloomed in his chest. That fought with the pains and the feeling of yearning.

He'd figure this whole mess out later. "My clothes, please. I'm leaving." He'd have to figure out how to *move* with every nerve in his body on fire, but…he'd figure *that* out later, too.

"Not yet, agent Colt." Another voice came in from the hall. This one was male and confident. The doctor entered the room and looked nothing like his voice.

Stooped shoulders and milky grey eyes were the man's best features. The rest… not as much.

"Yeah, I think so." Dexx twitched an arm. His limbs weren't working properly yet.

"I must insist. I admire your willingness to get back to work, but we just got you back. I don't think Kester and Hopkirk want to lose their best seeker just yet."

"Look." Seeker? What was this? Harry Potter? Also, who were the people she'd just rattled off? "Thanks for the patch-up, but I've gotta get gone." That was the only thing that *did* make sense. Panic rose in him in a very…manly way. "My clothes *now*, please."

The doctor reached down to the bottom of Dexx's feet and gently pushed with his pen.

Dexx jerked from the electric shock of full-body *pain*. "Holy fuck, doc. What'd you do that for?"

"You wouldn't be able to walk out of here if you could even dress yourself. These are common symptoms for what you've been through. Just, please, lie back and heal some."

The sound of running feet in the hall caused some anxiety. That sounded like SWAT coming up the hall. Tactical equipment and clothes.

How had he known *that*?

The door shoved open, and a man pushed into Dexx's other side. The man was young. It couldn't be more than twenty-one or two.

"Damn, Dexx." He had a strong British accent. His face didn't match his words, though. "They said you were awake. I came down as quick as I could." He looked happy to see Dexx, but his words were strained.

When had special forces let limeys in?

An echo of a memory skittered through his brain.

Limey bastich.

Was that *this* guy?

Weirdness defined this whole situation, but having SWAT show up and worry over his well-being was the cake-topper. However, Dexx couldn't deny the sense of relief that swarmed him on seeing the man's face. "*How* do you know me?"

"You sure got the shit kicked out of ya. It was touch and go until we got you back." The man smiled again.

Strained. Didn't match the happy look on his face. Not completely. Something was going on here. "So how do you know me?"

"I'm your partner? You know, you go first, and I cover you?"

That sounded...possible? "No bells. Sorry, kid."

The man nodded slowly. "Okay, so let's start at the beginning. Alwyn. Alwyn ab-Rhys."

That rang a bell and brought some warmth and trust. "Alwyn? I know the name. But... things are a bit fuzzy."

The smile warmed to something more genuine, and he stuck his hand out. "Good to have you back, mate."

Dexx eyed Alwyn's hand. Just thinking about taking it hurt. "Raincheck. I'm a little black and blue right now. Partners? Not a good one if I ended up here."

Alwyn and Doctor Petra exchanged looks. Petra nodded once.

Alwyn hesitated. "We were cleaning out a nest. They had thralls, and we took a beating. You saved a dozen of the team, but you… You took a pretty good hit."

"I don't remember any of it. In Louisiana?"

Alwyn looked up at the doc again. "Don't bugger yourself up to any more. Now that you're awake, we'll have time to talk all about it."

No. The sense of *urgency* hadn't subsided with his conversation with his *partner*. If anything, it was getting worse. "I already rested. Time to *not rest*. I'm not dying in a hospital bed."

"No." Dr. Petra commanded. "You're going to lie there and recover."

Dexx's eyes went heavy. So heavy, he couldn't keep them open. Two tiny thunderclaps sounded in his head just before black covered him again.

Dreams hit him then, but nothing that made any sense. A woman. A dark red car and a cat.

Or was it a tiger? Bigger than that. Huge.

His eyes popped open as the images slipped away with his confusion. He picked his head up.

No monitors. The IV drip still dripped fluid, and the TV still had the news channel on. Someone woman was on the news with babies. Must have been a slow news day.

He moved slightly and didn't hurt like gas had been poured over him and lit.

That was a move in the right direction. He lifted a hand from under the sheet. A deep bruise covered his hand and even fingers right up to the tips in a sickly purple.

Spots on his other arm were fading to a greenish-yellow, but the majority was still black and purple.

Whatever had hit him had done a really, *really* good job.

The kid from earlier sat in a chair along with the window, leaning on a fist.

Alwyn, right?

Partners? They could be. But Dexx'd always worked alone before.

No. He'd partnered up with someone else, someone he felt *emotionally attached* to, and they'd taken on some really big bad guys. Someone with dark hair. But who, though? When? Wasn't there someone else in Louisiana with him? Maybe that was it. Alwyn had dark hair. Were they… *partners?*

Dexx let his head fall back to the pillow. *That* didn't feel right, so, no. Partners on the job, maybe. In life? No.

He felt tons better. How long had he been out *this* time? The news ran that ticker along the bottom about rallies and rioting spreading across the states in opposition to the paranormals.

When had *that* come out?

The feeling of loss, a yearning for something, came back as strong as ever. Something was missing. *Someone* was missing. Who?

He damn sure well wouldn't figure it out lying in bed.

Dexx sat up and groaned involuntarily.

Alwyn's head jerked up, and bleary red eyes looked at him. "You look like shit, partner."

"Still better than you." Dexx lifted his other arm, working the muscles. They were weak.

"Not on your best day." He smiled a lot easier than he had the last time.

"You going to tell me what *really* happened? I don't believe Doc Zhivago at all."

Alwyn's shrug said no, but his dark eyes hinted at a yes. "There are details, but yeah, pretty much just that."

"Hmm. Where are we?" He *still* hadn't got a straight answer.

"Back at the house. The hospital as you call it."

"The infirmary."

"Exactly."

Why was everyone struggling with what to call this place? "Are we still on Earth?"

"Yeah." Alwyn looked genuinely confused. "Why?"

"Because you still haven't told me where on the *planet* we are."

"Ah, yes. That. We're in the main Department of Delicate Operations, western office. As far as where on the map we are, we're in a secret location in Montana."

"Secret." Interesting in an X-Files kinda way. "And I agreed to this?"

"For five years, now, yup. I'm your third partner. They tend to die, and somehow you live. *I've* been alive for three whole years as your partner. We make a pretty good team."

That was doubtful. The best team in Dexx's book was … His mind wandered, trying to find the right answer, but it alluded him. Dexx and a gun. Yeah, that was it. Maybe two.

And a *ma'a'shed*. The new word bubbled up from somewhere and stuck. No idea what it was, except a word.

Huh. When was he going to get his head back? "Can I get up now? This bed is killing me. How long have I been in it?"

"Two weeks." Alwyn got up and dropped the side rails, offering his hand.

Dexx ignored the hand and twisted to swing his legs out from the sheets to stand. A few pins and needles, but nothing traumatic.

"Oh, hey, I don't need to see Big Jim and the twins." Alwyn turned away.

"Then hand me a robe. I got somethin' you haven't seen before?" Dexx looked down and almost expected to not find anything. But he was still intact. Bruised like everything else. There was something attached to his leg.

Fuck. A catheter. "Bathroom." He pulled the bag at the end of the line from a hook on the bed.

Alwyn pointed to a door.

Something tugged at his arm at two steps. The damned IV drip and tower thingy. He grabbed the pole and pulled it along too.

Well, at least the bottoms of his feet only stung a little. "Get me a robe. Please." Why didn't he have a damned paper gown? He closed the bathroom door behind him and removed the tube from his—yeah. Shit. That thing was way in there. While he was at it, he pulled the IV drip out too.

He opened the door, and Alwyn held out a white robe. Dexx took it and slung it on.

The earlier severe pain had receded to a dull ache every-where. "Come on, let's go for a walk." He needed to... *break something.*

Yeah, no. That wasn't what he needed to do. He *was* feeling some excess energy for sure. But walking would be fine.

"Sure thing." Alwyn smiled, reminding Dexx of a puppy for a moment. "Where're we headed?"

"Fuck, I don't know." *The wards?* Where'd that voice come from? "I don't even remember you. Not much anyway. Let's just walk and...talk." And figure out how to put all the voices in his head in *order.*

"Then lead away. I'm only around for moral support anyway."

Good to know.

They traipsed up and down the halls, gaining a few looks from nurses on their rounds. "How many people are in this place?"

"The infirmary?" Alwyn asked.

"Sure, let's start there."

"There are about twenty patients right now," Alwyn said, wincing through the thought. "Mostly broken bones, and a few who are sick. None are in as bad of shape as you are, though. Except one. He was on the same mission as us. He's still down. The doc doesn't think he'll make it."

"That's too bad." Dexx actually didn't care. They passed a door with a strange icon that resembled a biohazard sign but with wavy lines on it. But the circle slashed through with a red line saying not to enter was one he knew. "What's down there?"

"Super-restricted. More than our pay grade."

Challenge accepted. Secrets didn't stay secret for long around Dexx Colt. *That* was one thing he *knew*.

5

The campus turned out to be way bigger than Dexx'd thought. The hospital wasn't large compared to most hospitals, but the rest was insane.

The view from his window over the campus looked like a city, sort of. Plenty of trees and short scrub covered the mountains directly past the furthest buildings. It sure *looked* like Montana.

A few hours later, he recovered enough to walk without a babysitter, and they released him from the hospital wing.

The campus just got bigger from there. The place they called "the house" looked just like the house from *X-men*, set in the center of surrounding structures. Well, maybe not exactly like it, but if there was any house that did, this one fit the bill.

The weather sure felt like Montana, colder and crisping up nicely.

Little snippets of memory bubbled up that didn't belong. They faded almost as fast as they appeared, causing the strangest *de ja vu* ever. The DoDO house was familiar, but the feel didn't jive.

For the next five days, he tried to figure out what was going on, but nothing he came up with made any sense. They'd had him in nonstop classes inside the biggest building he'd seen yet, so he hadn't had a lot of time to investigate. But nothing was ringing any bells for him, and that seemed strange.

Especially since he couldn't shake this sense that he'd left the stove on or his car running or something.

And this burning anger that was almost twisted with… guilt? That didn't even make sense. How had he lost five years worth of his memories, and when would he remember why he was even there in the first place?

How had he gotten there? Why had he signed up? And what were they hiding behind the guarded doors?

"Dexx, would you like to share with the rest of us?" Director Kinsley asked with her head tilted up in that strange way she had.

"Share what?" He hadn't been listening to her drivel about best demon takedown techniques. She'd described a few good ways to get killed.

"Whatever it is that has you ignoring my class." She dropped her casting stance to an aggressively casual one.

Kinsley was a witch. Everyone in DoDO was a witch or elemental. Most weren't very powerful, but they were all witches. Except him. Very interesting.

She wasn't a tall woman, but her face could cut steel. She might have been pretty once, but dollars to doughnuts her girl parts had turned to dust almost a hundred years ago. She never smiled either. The popular vote was that she was hiding sharpened teeth.

Did she *really* want his opinion? "You want to get people killed, and you got these kids soaking it up like water on sand. I like to breathe. So, you go on with your thing, and I'll go on ignoring you."

"We've talked about this, Dexx Colt." Her face came down from haughty to piercingly angry in two-point seven milliseconds.

"We have? This is my first—" He air quoted. "—*class* back, and I have a feeling I may have actually listened."

The rest of the teams turned to look at Dexx.

Kinsley crossed her arms, and her eyes turned dark.

Alwyn actually sat back with a grin. This had the feel of having happened before. But where? The entire campus didn't feel right.

Kinsley's eyes went a little darker. "But this is *not* your first class. *Pay attention.*"

"What can you tell me about the accident that put me in the hospital?"

Kinsley's mouth twitched. No doubt trying to keep the knife teeth concealed. "We're still working out the details, but it seems like there was a loose cannon out there. One Dexx Colt. He went off half-cocked and let the demons know our locations and intentions."

"That's not the impression I got. I remember being told quite clearly, I saved a bunch of team members by myself, right before being pushed down a well."

"You did not go down a well." Kinsley's eyes flicked to Alwyn.

Her temper sure was short that day.

Dexx sat forward. He imitated her dark-eyed glare. "Split hairs with the difference. I don't think one has a softer stop at the end. My fingertips and the bottom of my feet were bruised. Don't get that from a simple fall. And I don't remember any of it. So, until you give me solid proof *I* did something wrong, I'm going to tell you that *you're* wrong. Or, we can go back to ignoring each other?"

Five days had given him plenty to think over, and these lame-ass classes really weren't one of them.

Kinsley huffed a few more breaths, then dropped her arms and pressed fingertips to Dexx's desk. "Fine. Then *you* teach. What would *you* do when you find two demons, one a common and the other a Type Two, and you have a team of six?"

"Well, I don't think I'd shove all my guys in the front door screaming 'clear' and casting bindings. Two guys—" He held up two fingers. "—go in. Don't announce your presence like a newb. The rest guards the entrances and sets a defense, hoping they don't just apparate."

Several of the teams laughed under their breath. *They* didn't want to incur Kinsley's wrath.

"Dematerialize. Not apparate." Kinsley's eyes drew down. "Keep going."

"After that, ask one out to dinner nice and gentle. The others can wait until we come back for dessert." The laughs weren't so masked this time.

Dexx started to laugh himself, but a vague memory passed in front of him. *We could handle one for sure, maybe two. More than that, we run from.* The voice was a female, but the memory was in his head. How was that even a thing?

The class went quiet. All eyes were focused on him.

Kinsley's eyes were tiny little laser beams boring into his head. "Is that all?"

"No. Seriously, though. To stay alive, if there's more than one, you stay out. Unless you have the power to send them back, one is more than enough to kill *all* your members. Even a shifter…" The memory slipped away before it really had a chance to take root.

"Shifters are just as bad as demons, Dexx. We've covered that in detail."

"Yeah, I remember." His words trailed off. He remembered the argument. He remembered many of them muddy and indistinct. Shifters were as bad as demons. Or fae. The fairies and elves were completely foreign to humans. But… why didn't that *feel* right? "I was only saying that shifters have a hard time with demons unless they can catch them off guard."

"In what world would we ever team up with them?"

"I don't know. It can't *all* be us against them, can it?" Somehow that felt a little more *right* than DoDO's teaching.

"It *is* us against them. *Only* us against them. That's how we're going to keep the bloodlines pure."

Kinsley had a real pureblood versus mudblood mentality. "Kind of puttin' them all in one box, aren't you? That's like saying Brooks over there—" He thumbed to another part of the classroom. "—is as good as ab-Rhys. And we all know Brooks is one brain cell away from monkey." Where had *that* come from?

Who cared what monsters were out there? None of them were good or people, but…

No. He *did* know. Most paranormals only wanted to get by in the world. Just like Paige.

What? Who in the nine hells was *that?* The name faded away as fast as it had arrived. He tried to bring it back, but it evaded him.

Dexx had his mouth open to say more, but he clicked his mouth shut. After another moment of staring, he cocked a grin. "My apologies. I was just playing devil's advocate. Continue. Send the team in shooting and yelling and dying. Then what?"

Kinsley stood over Dexx, fuming for a few seconds.

Dexx shrugged and turned his hands over on the table. He was ready to listen.

Kinsley turned and stalked to the front of the class. She slipped a micro-recorder in her pocket. She slashed out a diagram and continued teaching.

Dexx let her talk about the recommended procedure of engaging the enemy. Since that was the surest way to die, he let her speak at length, while he chewed on memories that bubbled up to the surface.

The memories were all fleeting, and he couldn't re-recall them after they flashed. What had happened to him? Something was wrong in his head.

But he was fine, right? Because... yeah. He was fine.

Right?

A knock came from the doorway at the back of the class turned them all around. Mario Kester stood there in his tactical vest. Warding charms lined the Velcro. His athame sat in a sheath in front of his holstered handgun.

"Alpha team. Get dressed. We have a class two para."

Class two para. A non- shifting paranormal that killed to feed. Did they need Alpha Team for *that*?

Alwyn tapped Dexx on the arm with excitement clear on his face. "That's us, mate. Shotgun." He stood and settled his emergency bag on a shoulder and quick-walked out.

Dexx frowned as he stood. Was *he* on Alpha Team?

Another fuzzed and muffled memory surged through him with force. *We could be alpha.*

The rest of the class pushed passed him through the door.

Mario stood just outside, waiting. When the last disappeared down the hall, he stepped in, his thumbs hooked in extra loops on his vest. "You ready for this?"

"Why wouldn't I be?" Dexx hadn't moved. Maybe he wasn't?

"You look a little scared." Mario smiled that smug smirk. "You need more time to recover your nerve?"

No. Dexx wasn't running from a fight. That's not who he was. "Show me the baddie. You guys would all be dead without me." He hefted his bag on his shoulder.

Mario's smile slipped a little, but he only stood aside for Dexx to leave first.

Dexx met the rest of Alpha Team in the portal room. Every one of them was already vested and checking camera feeds and equipment.

"Remember, do not use force," Mario said with his slight English accent. "Well, at least until we get our shields up. Then? Any force is allowed."

His first mission since his hospitalization. Was that the reason he was hesitating? Something tugged at him, but not nerves—something he couldn't name.

He grabbed his vest. Red tabs marked him as a rookie or injured so everyone could spend extra attention on him while on the mission. He raised an eyebrow at Mario and fingered the vest. "Really?"

"You know the rules, Colt. The first mission back gets the red. Put it on and get out there. Or you can stay here."

No, he didn't know, but Dexx hooked his arm through the vest, calling him some pretty colorful names.

The portal arced open. A wavering hole in the air showed buildings with leaf-bare trees. Someplace cold, then.

The team stepped through single file, each pulling out an athame or limbering their fingers before they disappeared from sight.

Dexx didn't have an athame. He wasn't a witch. But he had plenty of bullets for the six guns attached to him. Special bullets worked well on a demon, but most regular ones only worked on paras.

He pulled his silver and iron knife from the back pocket of

the vest. The policy said to be armed going through the portal, but not what weapon.

He stepped through the portal, and the hole vanished.

He slipped the knife in the vest along his side and cut his monitoring feed. They were a bit too intrusive when it came to analysis.

A voice squawked over the earpiece to recall Dexx, but he ignored them.

The buildings were small-town in size, some two stories tall. Some of them anyway. The others had three, but nothing over four stories except the bank, and that had five—First Bank of Portland.

A regional bank, or Portland's *first* bank?

Dexx caught up on the chatter. They'd stopped trying to get him to return.

"...should be a small waterway fifty-seven meters to the south, southwest. The subject is known to frequent a two-hundred-meter length at the path leading down from the rear of the building. Shields being installed. Do not use force."

Dexx slapped a hand on the team, moving out first.

While they waited for the shields to go up, he used signs to tell them to circle around the far edge of the area. Another team he sent out wide to come back on the flank and keep the target in. The third team he kept on this side of the area to do the same. Flush everything back this way.

He tapped Alwyn and motioned for him to stay close.

The city was quiet. No traffic, no pedestrians. That by itself was enough for extreme caution. If their target had killed everything in the area, they might need reinforcements, especially if they were stupid enough to tip it off.

The list of possible water creatures ran through his head. He wouldn't need a gun unless Brooks rushed in and asked it to coffee or tea or whatever.

Dexx smiled. Brooks would fuck it up anyway. He'd sent him to the end to flush the water para back to them.

How did he know that? Were his memories coming back?

Dexx crept low through the underbrush to the small stream. He signed Alwyn to stay on this site and be ready.

Stretching his senses out, Dexx listened and watched, or he tried to, but things became... overwhelming. Colors and depth sharpened. Sounds he shouldn't be sensing came at him.

He fell over with so much information streaming into his brain. Holy fuck, that had never happened before. Brief flashes of comic book heroes ran through his head. How many had gained superpowers after an accident?

He might have enjoyed that, but there was simply too much without warning.

Crashing sounds of water and leaves snapping underfoot assaulted his ears. The smell that burned in his nose would be Alwyn.

How in all the hells would he know Alwyn by smell?

Alwyn turned Dexx over.

Oh shit. The man *glowed*. Fear, more than anything, helped Dexx push the man away from him. "I'm fine," he croaked. "Get back."

Alwyn didn't move.

"Get the fuck back," Dexx hissed, "or I'll shoot you in the face." He might not even be able to pull a gun from the holster, let alone shoot where he aimed.

"No force," the voice cracked in his ear. "That means you, too, Colt."

Alwyn stepped back. Damn, he was loud. How would anyone be surprised?

Dexx blinked back tears, trying to calm the sensory over-load. He took a breath and let go slowly. He took in another.

Sounds no longer crashed in his head. Smells stopped attacking his nose. The light didn't stab as hard as it had.

Just in time, too, because two figures ran through the water. Not Alpha Team. Two women in earth-toned clothes were glowing similarly as Alwyn and were easily outdistancing the seekers.

Alwyn stood up and began a spell. His hands glowed brighter. He'd never seen *that* before. The glowing, not the movements. Never the… glowing.

The two women continued to run along the banks, one a blonde and the other with an afro bobbing with her movements. She passed her hand over the water, and the *stream*… got up… with tendrils that lashed out at Alpha Team.

"You are a go for force," the voice said over the earpiece.

Men were struck, flying through the air as if hit with a watery fist. They landed hard and didn't rise. Two more tendrils lifted, and one slammed Alwyn in the gut.

Air forced out from his lungs, and the glow in his hands sputtered out.

The other water tendril rose to get Dexx, and he sidestepped the lash of water. He leapt over the water, slashing with his knife. The leg-thick tendril dropped like water tossed from a bucket to the ground with a splash.

He had to hand it to the women. They were moving with the speed of a scalded cat. He put on a burst of speed. Gaining on the smaller woman with the afro, he jumped and managed to snag a heel.

She went down in a heap, and the living water splashed down, soaking the ground.

Without thinking, he jumped on the woman's back, wrenched one hand to the middle of her back, and ground her face to the dirt with his arm.

He looked up just in time to see blonde hair disappear from sight through the trees. The glow around her kept her in his sight longer. Finally, there were enough trees to disperse even that, and the woman was gone.

Dexx returned his attention back to Afro Girl he held firmly in the dirt.

He almost giggled. He didn't need to be a *witch*. He was a fucking *superhero*. SuperColt.

She bucked under him and nearly got him in the nuts.

The moment of personal back-patting passed.

The woman under him was breathing hard. "We weren't hurting anyone. We were…"

"Shut up. You're probably planning your next kill. Not that there's much left out here, right? Your killing days are done."

The woman stopped struggling. "Dexx? Dexx, is that you? Oh, I'm so gl—"

She cut off as Dexx yanked her over onto her back.

Her dark eyes were relieved and confused at the same time. "Dexx, please…"

He didn't give her time to talk, confused himself. If he'd been working with her, he didn't want her blowing her cover, but why would he be working with the enemy? That didn't make sense.

No. This was a ploy. A monster's best defense is to confuse people by saying what they wanted to hear. She had to have a bit of mind reading ability. She might be familiar, a little, but they'd never met before.

She stirred again, coming to.

He brought his hand back and punched her in the side of the head.

She went out like a light.

6

Dexx stood up from the unconscious woman, something about her tickling the back of his head like an irritating itch. Exactly what kind of para was she? Water for sure, but she'd gone down way too easy. Even a class two para should have been a harder target.

She'd known his name. And not *just* that, but she'd known *him*.

Unlikely. It had to be low-level mind reading. He wouldn't work with the enemy. Would he?

Maybe he didn't remember for a reason. Maybe he'd done this to himself because—

That was a rabbit hole of conspiracies he didn't need to go down.

Dexx twisted around to see what everyone else was doing.

Alpha Team. They were all sleeping like babies. He scanned the woods again for more paras but didn't see any.

"Report in," the earpiece voice squawked. "Someone report in."

His short-lived super sight had faded anyway, and he

couldn't bring it back. He should keep that little secret to himself. Like, clam tight.

He pulled standard-issue handcuffs and ratcheted them on the woman's wrists. "Tagged. The team's down."

She might have a world-class headache when she woke up, but she *would* wake up.

"Assessment. Are they hurt?"

Dexx sighed. "Sleeping like lazy kids, more like." With the target taken care of, he walked over to Alwyn and shook him.

No response.

Okay. Time to have a little fun. He played the bongos on the man's face. "Good morning, Mister Basset. This is your six o'clock wake up call. Wakey, wakey."

After a few more moments of slapping, Alwyn's eyes shot open, and he screamed. Like they did in terror movies. He flailed around, kicking and swinging fists without coordination.

Dexx caught both fists and leaned over Alwyn's face. "Hey."

Alwyn stopped flailing and looked around.

Dexx let him go. "Calm down. I got her."

Alwyn sat up. "What happened? I had nightmares. Things ate me. While I watched. I *felt it all.*"

"That's good?" Dexx squatted next to the woman. She was pretty, with a big afro. Her mouth looked like it was about to smile, even though she was unconscious.

Something tugged at him, like a brotherly feeling? He didn't know. It didn't make sense.

She wore a brown jacket with dark pants and shoes not really designed for forest hiking. How in the hell had she been able to outrun the team? Adrenalin, most likely. That was strange for a class two.

While Alwyn recovered, Dexx checked her pockets. She

had no wallet or phone or any I.D. "Go wake the others from their nap. Don't be gentle with Brooks. He probably fucked this all up, to begin with." Dexx bent down to the woman again, trying to see if there was anything he recognized on her.

She'd called him by name. Did she look familiar? Maybe? He didn't think he'd ever met her before, especially enough to talk to him like she was happy to see him.

Why *had* she looked *relieved* to see him?

His earpiece swung out in front of him. Crap.

He shoved it back into his ear but almost pulled it out again as Mario's voice blared in his eardrum. "… and somebody kick Colt. That idiot has this all bollocksed up. All we need now is for the news feeds to pick us up."

"Uh, you're welcome. I just saved the team *and* got the para."

"You were supposed to *kill* the para. And you disabled your feed. That is *not* allowed, Mr. Colt."

Dexx stood. "That para I bagged is an American citizen, for your information, and Americans get to go to court. Unless it's a demon, they stand trial. Besides, she'll be more useful alive, so we can ask questions."

Mario's breath sounded loud in Dexx's ears. "Get that para up and bring her here. There might be *some* information we can get from her. Maybe a line on more paras in the area."

"Now you're thinking like a boss. Interrogation." How had he decided to work with DoDO? They killed too often.

"Get the bloody hell back here now, Colt."

Wow, Mario sounded pissed.

Screams almost exactly like Alwyn's rang through the trees. Damn, this lady must have the *awful dream* superpower.

Dexx had two of the team carry the unconscious woman by her arms back through the portal.

Hopkirk, Mario, and Kinsley—how did Dexx know those

names again? He didn't remember anything else with them—were all waiting for Dexx when they arrived in the portal room.

"Explain yourself, Colt." Mario puffed up like a banty rooster.

"Explain what?"

"The target was supposed to be dead. That's standard protocol."

Was it, though? "Killing demons, sure. It makes sense. They don't really die, they get sent back to their plane, and it's pretty hard for them to come back." He tipped his head to the side. "Unless some idiot summons them. But people? You don't just kill *people*. That's considered *murder*, which, if I'm not mistaken, is *illegal* on this side of the pond." He pushed through the three of them and hung his vest on the rack. Next mission, they would *all* have the red except him. Ha.

Mario didn't have a witty reply to that.

Dexx made his way to the chow hall and dished himself up a load of mashed potatoes and meat. His entire team should be down at medical for a check-up.

Not even three bites in, he dropped his fork to the plate.

His vision darkened with a stabbing pain in his head. Slowly rising from his multiple plates—he *knew* there was only one, but he *saw* three? Five? More? He staggered toward his room.

One step after another.

His brain felt like it was trying to squeeze its way out of his nose.

He used the wall to stay upright.

Down the hall, turn right, down another hall, and another right. He had to think very hard on the directions.

He *could* go to medical. He *should* go to medical, but he was *not* going to wear the red. Not a chance in…

He barely stopped the heave.

Calm down. Concentrate on the floor and the walls.

Keep the end of the hall in central vision.

Amazingly, he made it to his room. The lights were already off, and he didn't bother turning them on. The light hurt too.

He let the door shut and used the wall to sink to the floor. He stretched out and let the coolness soak into his back.

The headache pierced at his brain, and spots formed in front of his eyes. The darkness helped, but not enough. His stomach settled, sort of, and the light didn't stab so hard at his eyes.

Fuck. He'd forgotten about this part of gaining super-powers in the comics. Sometimes they had side effects. Then he wouldn't be able to use them, or not all at the same time, at least.

He lay on his floor, warming the tiled concrete.

Fuck, maybe he *should* have gone to medical. Fuck them.

Eventually, he fell asleep.

The dreams didn't make anything any better. He was chased. By an animal. A hunter. A *big* predator.

He ran through night-darkened trees fleeing from the thing while his head pounded.

There was no way to see what chased him unless he wanted to be eaten, and that just was *not* an option.

Growls of anger followed on his heels, but amazingly he kept ahead of the beast. Two strides, maybe three. The thing's hot breath puffed on either side of his head. Maybe less than three strides, but if he kept running, it couldn't catch him.

Dexx's eyes shot open to a pounding on his door. "Dexx," Alwyn shouted on the other side. "Hey, dumbass. Are you in there?"

The handle wiggled against the lock.

The floor was cold, and his joints had solidified into concrete. "Yeah, I'm up." He yelled at the door. "Just a second."

Just rising was a huge effort. Damn, he was old. Or the floor was exceptionally hard. He sat up in the dark, stifling the groan.

Did Alwyn think that working the handle against the lock would suddenly open? Maybe he did. The boy could be pretty dim at times.

Dexx rose and flipped on the light as he opened his door, blinking against the bright stabbiness.

Fucking lights.

Mario had a key ready to be inserted into the lock.

"Hey, guys, what's up?"

Alwyn tried to step inside.

Mario had him blocked out. He must have had something in his eye, with the weird face he made at Dexx. "Get down to the infirmary. Doc wants to run a physical on you."

"Didn't he do enough already?" Petra had Dexx run and jump and a bunch of things he only did when chased, just a couple days before. Wasn't his idea of fun in any event.

"Your first mission back, and there were some anomalies."

"Really?" Dexx tried to hide the pain, which had receded. Or maybe it'd just moved to his joints. He wasn't sure. "Was one of them saving the team's collective ass again? No, that sounds about normal." Was it, though? "All of y'all. I don't need another chance to do sit-ups and pull-ups for that guy. He looks at me strangely. Like... sexually. I don't roll that way."

"Get down to medical, *now*." Mario's face grew darker by the word.

Perhaps he'd gone too far, but really, he'd had enough of the poking and prodding. And the nightmares put him in a bad mood. "Whatever. I'm heading to medical." He pushed by Mario. "Close the door behind you."

After he turned the corner at the end of the hall, Alwyn caught up to him. "Be careful, Dexx. I heard Mario talking with Hopkirk. They said you wobbled out of the mess like you'd gone on a boozer."

Oh, crap. Had someone *seen* that? "Well, I didn't. I was a little tired and went for a nap."

"That was six hours ago. You sure you're all right, mate?"

"Fit as a fiddle." *Something* was wrong. "You wanna go a couple of rounds? Knock your dick in the dirt. Got a Benjie that says I can." That was a huge bluff because Dexx was *pretty* sure he wouldn't be able to do much of anything in a fight.

Alwyn twisted a smile. "Not what I meant. In your head. You keep running on the ragged edge, and they'll toss you out. Don't mess with the doc."

Dexx went to medical like a good boy.

Petra stood next to his swiveling stool with his clipboard and pen. He directed Dexx to start the physical activities.

He started with some free weights, moved on to breathing deeply into a plastic bucket to measure capacity, then on to jumping jacks, then back to the breathing thing, and so on.

In between every exercise, the shriveled old doctor passed an athame up and down in front of Dexx, muttering words he didn't recognize.

Each time he did, a piercing pain hit him right behind the eyes.

"Damn, doc. Stop. That hurts."

"The proper delving spell has some pain normally associated with lower than average intelligence," Dr. Petra said in a weirdly familiar voice. "It can't be helped. Even those with low intelligence only have mild discomfort. You must be exceptionally low on the scale."

The doctor *felt* wrong. Just being a doctor, wasn't it. Something else didn't jive. Dexx almost had a PTSD reaction from the guy—his voice, his *smell*—as if he'd been tortured by this man for days, weeks.

Cub, a female voice said inside his head. *You were—*

Petra waved the athame in front of Dexx again. The pain hit his head, and the voice stopped.

This was getting weird.

Dexx showed teeth and followed Petra to the next torture. The treadmill.

Cub! Wake up!

Dizziness attacked Dexx along with the female voice, and he fell off.

Petra helped him up, and the dizziness passed quickly. The feeling of something being torn away from him, and now missing, returned.

The mission replayed through his head. The attack by the class two as they'd patrolled the border of the para town, on a strictly low-key scouting mission. The para had *attacked* Dexx as if singling him out. Alwyn had taken it down, somehow getting the upper ha—

He'd been passed out—

No. He'd heard Dexx shout out and had come in for the assist. Without Alwyn, Dexx might be dead. Brooks had been there to assist.

Something… wasn't right.

He had the notion that he lost something more than his balance during the check-up.

Petra spelled a bottle of pills and handed them to Dexx. "You're good enough for missions." And motioned for Dexx to leave.

A clean bill of health was all that mattered. The enemy had to be dealt with. Search and kill. No questions were asked. And paras *were* the enemy. They lived above and beyond the rules.

He tossed a bottle of pills in his hand. It made him think of a mental institution, like when the doctor wanted to keep the inmates pliable.

He *did* feel better after a fashion, though. More focused, ready to take down more paras, ready to kill them like Alwyn—

We don't kill people. That's considered murder, which, if I'm not mistaken, is illegal on this side of the pond.

He didn't remember saying those words, and he sure didn't feel them. Paras needed to die so the world could return to normal.

Time for a date with the sheets.

He went to bed again, and the nightmares kept their distance.

In the morning, Dexx felt better. No para could keep him down for long. Of course, details were fuzzy, like how had Alwyn and Brooks saved the team *and* bagged the para? A class *two* para.

Maybe he should give Brooks a little more credit in the future. Or not. Brooks probably got a lucky spell off.

Mario handed out assignments during chow. Alpha Team was going to the same locale as the para from the day before. The place had to be a hot spot. Alwyn was sporting a slight beard. When had the man had a chance to grow that? It'd only been a few hours since he'd seen the man.

Dexx rolled his shoulders, intent on fulfilling his mission. Search and kill. He pulled his vest on, no red this time. Petra *did* say he was cleared for missions.

The portal opened, and the team stepped into the street, not far from the day before. A chilled breeze blew through the trees with a distant whistle.

Dexx plugged his earpiece in and waited for the chatter to die down. "Alpha leader online."

An echo passed through his memory. *We could be alpha.* He pushed it down.

He shook his head, clearing it. "Targets?"

"A Class One demon and a human familiar," Mario said in his ear. "The familiar is a blonde fighter. Both are considered extremely dangerous. Do *not* engage alone. You read, alpha leader? We're not going to have a repeat of last time."

"Five by five, boss."

"Shields in place," another voice said. "Clear for necessary force."

"Where are they?" Dexx asked.

"Intel has them—"

Spells barraged in from a rooftop, punctuated the scream of one of the team, probably Brooks.

The teams scattered for cover.

Alwyn had his athame out and was spelling for all he was worth, shooting shield wards in between fireballs.

Three of the team were already down

The rest, plus Dexx, were still standing, and all except Dexx were casting defensive spells against... well, it had to be a demon.

Without warning, a blonde blur leapt from behind a police cruiser. The woman had fast feet and faster hands. Sheer instinct kept Dexx upright.

She clipped him in the ribs and thighs a few times. Many more and he'd be down for the count.

As a foot came at him, he spun away and caught the foot, yanking hard. The woman hit the pavement, and a flashing fist took the fight out of her. She slept peacefully.

He pulled a spelled binding charm from a pouch and placed it at the woman's neck. That should keep her down for a minute. No time to feel overconfident. The other para, probably the demon, was casting spells so fast the three team members still standing couldn't do anything except defend themselves.

Dexx ran down the street at full speed, slipping around the back of a building. He stopped to get a look at the place the demon was hiding. Great. Roof. Of course.

He sped to the rear of the building and found a ladder to the top.

Double damn. The ladder looked about four or five feet outside of anything he could reach, but he had to try. Half the team was down, and the other half was fighting for their lives.

He ran for the ladder and jumped.

Holy *shit*.

He'd *actually* made the jump and hung from a hand. Swinging the other up, he caught hold and pulled himself up. The ladder wasn't even an obstacle.

When he reached the top, sure enough, there was the second para slinging spells at the team below.

The demon wavered with a heat signature.

Okay, so *that* was cool and new. Supersight? Was he getting a superpower? Should he tell the team?

Probably not.

Though something struck Dexx as odd. Demons didn't fight for fallen friends. Ever. Mostly because demons didn't make friends.

Whatever it was, though, it *was* a para, which meant it was the enemy and had to be killed. With the team keeping the demon busy, Dexx quickly crept up behind the para on silent feet. He reached for his knife.

And pulled out spelled cuffs.

Right. Those should work on this guy. With a snap-jab to the kidney, the demon dropped to a knee.

Dexx grabbed a wrist, ratcheting the cuff on one hand.

The man roared in agony, then after a knee to the chest, the demon doubled over, and Dexx pulled the other hand in and fastened the cuff.

"All too easy." Dexx raised his fist to put his prisoner to sleep. He got a look at the man's eyes. Brilliant blue with a horizontal pupil, like a goat or a horse. Freaky.

Dexx pounded the guy in the face, and another one went to la-la land.

He heaved the man over his shoulder and went to the ladder.

More fucking coolness, he was stronger than he remembered. Not enough to lift a bus or anything, but enough to carry the weight of himself and the demon–thingy down to the ground without much trouble. Oh yeah, Dexx *was* a fucking superhero.

After securing Alpha Team, Dexx carried the demon-in-the-meat-suit over his shoulder to the portal, and two of the Alpha Team drug the woman.

Mario waited on the other side of the portal, looking pissed.

"What?" Dexx had to ask. "You wanted him. We got him."

"You *kill* demons. You don't bring them back here."

Dexx *knew* that. He had no idea *why* he'd pulled out the cuffs instead. "You got bad intel. I have no idea *what* he is, but he's not a demon." Dexx dropped the para to the ground and thumbed open an eyelid. The bright blue eye was slightly rolled up into the para's head, but it was enough. "*Not* a demon. Not entirely human either, but I'm not going to take part in killing for fun. Class Three for sure. Pretty easy take-down, though." Which was weird. "And I'm *not* killing for fun."

Mario Kester turned on his heel. "Lock them up with the other one. Colt, follow me."

7

Dexx followed Mario through the campus and into the mansion. Dark wood paneling made the whole place feel old-world and extravagant.

He must have done something extra annoying. What had he done this time?

Wall niches lined the hall to the stairs that led up to the director's office. Trinkets sat in every one of them, and a few held more than one. A full suit of armor stood in an alcove at the end of the hall, like the stone gargoyle guarding Dumbledore's office.

The whole DoDO house was filled with magick, but not in a Disney park kind of way.

One of the niches held a small stone disk next to a dagger with an overly ornate handle. It looked like a stone at least, but why have something so plain mixed in with all the other pieces that lined the hall?

Oddly, of the entire corridor, the only thing that even looked interesting to Dexx was that little skipping stone. The rock *called* in a way that made his hand twitch as he passed.

The strangest part was the feeling that it was *his*. As much as any of his guns. Or his poster of Bo Derek he had as a youngster.

Mario didn't look back as he led the way up to the boss's office. He just trundled on in his short-man sway, his pale blond hair catching the light from a few sources as they passed.

Dexx's hand twitched.

Up the stairs, they went and waited at the door. Weird, since normally Mario barged in any door, or least knocked once and let himself in.

Who could be in there?

Sound crashed against his ears, accompanied by a familiar growl inside his head. He turned back to the stairs, his hand clamped to his ear. He hadn't yet come to terms with his super strength, and now he had super hearing too? He should have more accidents more often.

Dexx crammed his eyes closed, willing the sounds to subside. Years of reading comic books came to the rescue. He needed to breathe and calm down to maintain his cover.

Dexx inhaled deeply to calm himself but hid it by pretending to wait impatiently as he dropped his hand.

"You *will* follow my orders," a voice he recognized as Hopkirk—How did he know her?— said on the other side of the door.

So that's what his super hearing was trying to pick up. Nice. Could his superpowers come with x-ray vision because that would be cool?

Mario turned a questioning look to him, but Dexx only lifted his eyebrows to answer. He flipped a thumb to the door with a half-grin.

Look at Dexx being all Clark Kent.

Inside, Brooks replied with angst in his raised voice. "... You can't just pass me over. That should be mine. He's a tosser and doesn't fit in with the lot of us. He's impure. You only want him because he's the—"

A sharp smack echoed loud enough to be heard without the super hearing, cutting him off. Hopkirk must have slapped her desk. Maybe she broke her hand.

"You have your orders. I expect you to act like an officer of this organization, not like a spoiled child."

"Right." Brooks just shut down. "May I have permission to leave?"

"You may."

Dexx concentrated hard on returning his hearing to the human level. And just like turning down an old stereo, his hearing returned to normal.

Whatever had happened in his accident, there must have been chemicals involved. Super *anything* didn't just happen with a fall. He'd have to worry about that later.

The door opened, and Brooks stepped out, pausing when he saw Mario and Dexx. His eyes narrowed, and he smelled furious. Rage bubbled through him, all spikey with adrenaline.

Shit, how did Dexx know that?

Brooks quivered, killing hatred in his eyes. Then he rushed to the stairs. "Fuck you, Colt."

Brooks said it so low Dexx almost missed it.

"Screw you too, pal," he whispered at Brook's retreating back.

"Mario, bring him in." Hopkirk didn't sound very happy.

Not much of a change from her regular demeanor, she was always kind of an uptight twat. Okay. Was that his memories coming back? He stepped into the room, trying to see if there was anything familiar that might bring back additional memories.

"Shut the door."

Right.

Hopkirk barely let the door click shut before she started in. "What in the hell did you think you were doing? You ignored a direct kill order. We're not running a daycare for paras here. You've been the thorn in my side ever since we decided to bring you into our organization."

"Kill order? When did I ignore a kill order?" He hadn't, had he?

"That demon. You were told no less than *seven* times to kill the demon on that rooftop. And your equipment was working fine today. You forgot to disable it, or you just plain ignored control. *Again*."

He normally disconnected the vitals recorder, but the earpiece was essential to comms. "I never *heard* a kill order. From the first volley, there was dead silence." Dexx was as surprised as Hopkirk at the total sincerity in his tone.

"That's not possible. It's been tested and found in working order."

"Good thing I captured it because that's not a demon. So that means the woman isn't a human familiar or a servant. They're paras for sure, but neither of them is a demon."

"You forgot possession. Either one could be possessed."

She had Dexx there. They *could* be possessed. "So would they react to holy water? The woman didn't react at all to the binding spells being thrown at her." Flashes of a different scene than he remembered hit him momentarily, but they disappeared as quickly as they arrived. "The guy could have just popped out. If that was a demon, we'd all be dead. He had the drop on us, and demons don't wait to see how well you'll do."

Hopkirk rose from her chair. "And you know this just by looking at him?" Her voice dropped dangerously low. "You take risks and defy orders and do whatever the hell you please and expect us to do whatever you tell your team."

"Am I being fired?" Dexx would rather have kept that in,

but it just fell out. He *needed* this job. He didn't do anything else worthwhile, and the only real skill he had was hunting demons.

"Do you remember a few months back? You applied for a position in the European Office?"

No, he didn't. Then, a fuzzy recollection sort of came back. But it was more like a dream, almost from a third-person perspective. Everyone had filled one out during a classroom session. He'd checked the box for an overseas assignment, and he'd checked the director's post. Probably as a joke? Had to be. "Yeah, I guess."

"An assistant to the Director of Training post has become available, and they want someone from this post. I still can't believe they asked for *you*."

"Me?" Something twisted his heart. Hard. He *had* to stay. Montana was as far as he wanted to go. "No. Pass. I like it right here in the states. Besides, who else is going to save the *whole* team's ass if I leave? Without me, you have a bunch of poseurs. And it seems like you need a Jiminy Cricket out there too. He was killing people just because they're different from you? How Crusades of you. I'm better off not going anywhere."

She rolled her eyes. "Too late. I've sent the confirmation, and *you* are headed to the London office. Get packed and clean your dorm. You leave tomorrow."

Well, fuck her very much. Dexx turned and left without permission.

Fuck.

He stalked down the stairs very similar to the way Brooks had, not quite sure why he was this angry. But he *was*. He was *pissed* without reason. He gave a good pull on the post thingy at the bottom of the stairs with a satisfying crack and into the hall leading back to the dorms. The London post was a *good* job. It was treasured and valued, and... he vaguely remembered actually wanting it. So, what was holding him back now? Did this anger churning in him have anything to do with his missing memories?

The niches streamed by and, without thought, his hand lanced out and grabbed the stone. He crammed it into his pocket.

Fuck 'em.

Dexx slammed the door open to his room.

Leaving.

He didn't clearly remember the application, all fuzzy and narrow like a dream. He would never *seriously* consider a spot across the pond, mostly because he *hated* to fly.

Besides, there was something *here*. Something was gone… missing. The hole hadn't left, but it rolled like a tide. Sometimes sharp and others a dull ache. But when he had no idea what it was, looking would be difficult. But it sure as fuck wouldn't be in Britain.

He left his room and his packed bags but kept the door open. There was nothing… personal in this room, even in his bag. He could replace everything.

Except for that stone in his pocket.

His stomach rumbled. He needed to eat. But more than that, he had this insane *need* to escape, to get out of there, to run.

Floor tiles passed under his feet as he headed to the cafeteria. The floor was hospital white. White surrounded the entire dorm with a sterile punch in the face. Even his room started out in that basic glaring color.

He burst into the large cafeteria to find Brooks sitting alone, stuffing his face.

Whatever was going on here, he was willing to bet Brooks knew something. "Don't eat your emotions, that's the road to the 'betus." As in diabetes.

Brooks glared back, standing slowly as he started a spell.

Well, that wasn't going to get any of his questions answered. Dexx turned on his heel, taking the soon-to-be fight out of the off-limits cafeteria. He wasn't super fond of Brooks, but he didn't want the guy kicked out. Also, Dexx *needed* this job.

He started back to his room and the wider corridors, pulling out the little stone in his pocket. Now, why would he want it so bad he'd steal it? Little black lines rimmed the edge. He palmed it as he opened his one-window room.

A hand slapped down on his shoulder.

He stopped in the doorway and stared at Brooks and his hand. "I don't know what's going on here, but you do, don't you?"

Brooks didn't answer.

"You know something."

Brooks's right cheek twitched.

"Tell me. I'll put in a good word for you."

"They're listening." He flicked his fingers as if getting rid of sticky hair and walked away. "Just stay in your room 'til you're collected. None of us want to see your festering face."

Festering. That was a bit harsh.

But also, what did Brooks mean by "they're listening?"

The smallish one-bed dorm was as stark as the day he'd walked in.

He hadn't hung any posters up either. He'd seen other dorms plastered posters of women, soccer teams, and prissy cars, but not him. Hunters with ideas of a good long life were childish and optimistic. Hunters just couldn't form long-lasting attachments.

Nausea struck him hard, and the world swam like he was looking through water flowing over the glass.

He sat hard on his bed, hit by a string of images rushing through his head. Memories all jumbled up, with no frame of reference.

He stood on a balcony, fighting meat suits possessed by demons, finally falling.

Wet snow, and the inside of an abandoned barn.

Standing in the middle of a police station, strangely shaped people attacking him and…

He was driving south through scrublands yanking the wheel to the edge of the road, with fur growing from his arms.

He was ripping the head from a demon-possessed man with his teeth.

He was stabbing a tall blond man in the shoulder. That man was a witch.

Being destroyed as a beam of pure power touched him. Protecting a random woman… from *something*.

Dexx jerked awake to a knock on his door.

At least the lights were still on.

The door opened, and Dr. Petra walked in, hands in his scrubs' pockets and a stethoscope around his neck. He wore a small smile. "Good evening, Dexx. I heard there are congratulations in order."

"Really, what did you hear?" Dexx scrambled to *keep* these memories, envisioning boxes and cramming them inside in any order, hiding them away before they were… stolen. What if… That didn't make any sense. Why would his employer steal his memories? He had to figure out how to get out of… leaving DoDO? Leaving the states?

Leaving the states for sure. The pull to stay was *hard*.

"I heard you're taking the post in the London office. Is this not so?"

"Nope. I'm staying here." Somehow. "Don't know who'd give you the idea I was leaving." Petra gave him the willies. For some reason, he just seemed wrong.

And all the memory collection efforts seemed frenzied as Petra stepped closer.

"I have the orders right here." He lifted a clipboard with papers and a pen clipped to the top.

Had he had that when he'd come in?

Petra made an exaggerated tick on the sheet. "Just a simple check-up before I give you permission to go." He reached in his pocket and pulled an orange pill bottle out, taking another step closer.

"You need to take one a day until the bottle runs out."

Didn't he already have a bottle? No. That had been... another time? His memories were all out of whack since... since when? Since the accident? But that had only been a couple of days ago. This felt like it'd been going on for weeks. Months.

"What are they?" Dexx leaned back to buy some room and crossed his arms. Didn't he have more from the last time he—

His arms itched, and the hairs at the nape of his neck rose.

Demon.

Dexx moved to punch the doctor with his super strength, but his arms were too heavy.

Petra glowed for a moment. Then the entire room blacked out.

With another blink, everything was back to normal.

Who was this guy? He was wrong. He was a...

The thought slipped away. For a second, the room... wobbled, and split into two, fuzzing at the edges.

Dr. Petra reached out a steadying arm. "You seem unstable. Do sit." He helped Dexx to the bed.

Dexx's arms itched along with his tattoos. He rubbed them like they were cold.

"Those are interesting. Do they have a story?"

Yeah, they did. He just... didn't remember what. He looked around his brain as if looking for something, but it was so empty. Like Santa's workshop after Christmas had been canceled. What was going on? "Why would they have a story?"

"Most people have a story for tattoos—one for each. A face might be a lost sister. A skull for defeating death or cancer. Do yours have special significance?" His hand hovered over one of them but didn't touch.

Dexx's words slurred as he spoke. "I…" He *knew*. That tattoo, in particular, had a *purpose*. In huntin— "I liked the pattern." The room spun hard and then slowed to a jiggle.

"That's not a pattern I've ever seen. Is that South Pacific?"

The room shifted again. This time it blurred so bad Dexx couldn't see anything but the general white of the room. "It's… I have no idea. They just sort of showed up."

"Good. Now, how about that promotion?"

"Promotion?" What was the good doctor talking about?

"The London office? You are to be the deputy director of training. You would like that, wouldn't you?" The doc's face swam in his vision. His smile… was too big. There were too many teeth in his mouth.

"I…" Dexx wanted the position?

Something clicked.

Yes. He *had* to have that job. He'd worked for it for so long. Promotion? Yes, of course. He'd worked so hard for it. He'd *thought* they'd give him the assistant position first, and he vaguely remembered hearing those words, but…the memory faded and was replaced with static. "Yeah. I want the job. Yes, that's what I want."

"If I was to say *Shedim Patesh* to you, what would you say?"

"I'd say thank you?" What the hell was that? A bar over there? "I don't know."

Petra's small grin became a wide smile. "Just word association. You passed. Remember, you're to take one of those pills a day until the bottle is gone. After that, you should be just fine. Permanently cured."

The world sharpened slowly until the fuzz faded. "From what?"

"Your ailment. Remember?"

He didn't.

Dr. Petra smiled. "Have a good flight, Dexx. I'll see you again. Soon" He placed a hand on the door.

Dexx felt energized. Like he'd been voted prom king, "Not if I see you first." He smiled at his joke. "I'm fine. Go, do your rounds. Go give Brooks some suppositories through the mouth."

"Remember the pills." Petra closed the door gently behind him, chuckling softly.

London. Whew, that would the best place *ever* to work. A grin split Dexx's face. He'd worked so *hard* for the London assignment. *Everything* he'd done, every decision he'd made, every assignment he'd taken had led to this. How many times had he grilled Alwyn about England? Perhaps a zillion. It could be more, but now he'd have a chance to go there himself. Not a *chance* but a *certainty*.

Oh shit, he had to pack. He didn't have posters or pictures hung up, so that made things easier. Hunters didn't have the luxury of forming long-term attachments, but maybe that would be different across the pond. Maybe he'd be a rebel and just *hang* one up.

Excitement welled up in his chest. He pushed clothes and guns in his duffel but set a funny stone on the counter of his wash sink.

A sharp stab in the middle of that excitement gave him pause. Was that excitement or anxiety? Was he missing something?

No, he'd worked for this assignment for a long time. Yes.

He finished the packing in about two minutes flat. Now what?

Holy shit, he couldn't leave now. He rushed out to find Mario Kester.

Mario was in his office, his door open. Probably for the first time in memory.

Dexx knocked gently on the doorframe. "Boss? Got a sec?"

Mario's pen stopped moving as his startling bright blue eyes shot up in curiosity as if unsure what he was going to get. "What's on your mind, Colt?"

"The promotion. Can I also take Alwyn? I know it's a big ask."

Mario looked up and scratched his chin. "Ab-Rhys? I'll have to run it by Kinsley, but I don't see a problem with that. Get packed. You leave tomorrow."

"Understood. Thanks. You're a great leader."

Mario's brow crinkled in confusion as his lips smiled with his nod. "You're... great to have on the team. You'll be... sorely missed."

Dexx turned away from the door and missed a step.

"Great leader" gonged through his head. Where had he heard that before? The excitement for London definitely turned a paler shade.

There was something missing, something he needed. He'd lost something, and he had to get it back.

No. He'd be in Britain tomorrow. That hollow feeling *had* to be for Britain. What else could it be?

8

———————

Dexx headed back down the hall to his room.

Tomorrow, he'd leave for his dream spot on a smallish island.

Dr. Who, Outlander, and that cooking show. *"It's underbaked."*

Not to mention all the royals to rub shoulders with. Not that he really wanted or needed to see any of them. Not really.

Okay. Maybe a little.

This was going to be *amazing.*

It should be a good time, though, with all the old-world baddies running through the country. Original vampires. Werewolves. His little hunter brain was having a great time.

He couldn't shake the feeling that something was missing, though. Like he'd forgotten something important, but what? He didn't have a car to store or a girlfriend—

His heart twinged with loss.

Or loneliness. Yeah. It was a little hard never being able to settle down and have a girlfriend, but one day, maybe he would. And have kids—

His heart hurt so bad there. He stopped for a second.

Man, he must really want kids. Well, he *was* getting a little old.

He surely didn't have a lot of friends here, okay, so *no* friends here, but they were all prissy Brits, and they weren't his idea of friend stock anyway.

Except for Alwyn. Somehow, he seemed pretty cool.

With his things packed, he was ready to go.

That feeling like he'd forgotten to turn off the stove came back. Great leader. Now, why had *that* rung a bell? There seemed to be mounting puzzles in the DoDO house.

Time to do the thing he hated most. Homework.

The doc had unwittingly given him an assignment. Not that his visit was memorable, but that word association game was pretty stupid.

The U.S. DoDO campus had an *amazing* library. Not that he wanted to spend any more time around books than he had to, but sometimes the best place to look information up was inside a book. The net was cool for normal stuff, but it wasn't reliable for what he needed.

The library wasn't like the mansion, made to feel old. A brighter reddish-brown carpet stretched under tall book-shelves. At least this wasn't as somber as the X-men house.

He went past the regular books and computers to the special research section set aside in a darkened room. An attendant stood guard at the door, eyeing the few people sitting in front of computers. "Good evening, Mr. Colt."

The guard was a woman with hawkish eyes ready to deliver a beatdown. He'd be especially nice to the lady. "Hello, uh, hello..." Dexx had never seen her before. She must be new.

"Mary. You never remember me. I've been assigned to your teams no less than four times. I thought you might start to remember me after your accident?"

Four times? "Mary. Right. Thought I might check a book or two out."

"You can't take any of the volumes out. Especially since you're leaving."

Wow, news traveled fast around here. "I meant I just wanted to look some stuff up."

"You aren't a witch."

"That makes a difference?

"It does if you're trying to cast, yes."

"Well, I'm not trying to cast since I'm not a witch. I just want to look some stuff up. Has nothing to do with the casting. At least I don't think so. And I only wanted to research a few things, not actually check the book out." He scooped a hand toward the door.

"Tell me what you want. I might be able to help." She smiled—a chilling smile like fingers down a chalkboard.

Warning flags went up in his head. Nobody ever wanted to help him. Sure, his smile attracted all things women, but this place didn't really scream "helpful." "Nah, I got it. I hope. If I need something, I'll call. Cool?"

"Sure." She didn't sound disappointed. She sounded pissed.

With a polite nod, he walked around her and into the darkened room. Some of the volumes were really old and a little reactive to light.

Great leader. That was too vague, but there was something that wasn't. What had Dr. Petra said? *Shed Pasta*, something or other?

Picking up a demon lore book at random, he flipped to S.

He poked his head around the corner to see what Mary was up to and almost jumped. She was right there, hands behind her back, looking at the volume he held.

"Sheesh! Don't sneak up on a guy like that. I almost screamed like a girl."

She was not amused.

Was there a reason he didn't remember her being assigned to his team *four* times? "There's a little thing I like to call personal space. I feel a lot better if I can reach out and *not* touch a person."

She took a step back. Not a big step.

Dexx took a large step back. "Help you with something?"

"I'm watching the books." No humor.

She thought she was supposed to literally *watch* the books? "Is there someplace I can read… alone?"

Mary motioned to a table. Dark cherrywood polished to a red glow in the low lights.

"Thanks. I'm just gonna go… over there."

She stood so close he had to hold his arm along his chest to point to the table in question. He squeezed by and pulled a chair out.

Mary stood by the shelf he'd pulled the book from. She really took her job seriously. Or she might have been told to keep him company.

His stomach fell as he realized that was the most likely scenario. Did he need to be *watched*?

Dexx propped the book upright on the table, hiding from the scary woman.

He flipped through the pages under S. He stopped when he found *Shedim Patesh*. The word burned in his mind like a neon sign.

He read quickly, then read again. All the book said was that demons had a name for a demon hunter of extraordinary power in the days when they'd freely roamed the planet.

Shedim Patesh had been a fearsome warrior and had been greatly feared in the demon ranks. Why should he associate a word with that? Was Dr. Petra testing his knowledge of long-dead demon hunters?

Possible, but pretty slim. The entry was disturbingly short on information. Only a name and a rough time period.

Shit.

Dexx shut the book and took it back to the waiting Mary. He slid it back into place, patted the spine gently, and carefully scooched by her and left the library. He was tempted to dig through other books and see if there was more information, but... damn. That little girl gave him the heebie-jeebies. Good thing he was outbound the next day.

Assigned to his team four times? Whatever.

He went back to his room and flopped on the bed. Things were packed. He was ready. Time seemed to *drag*.

He had the strangest feeling he was being watched. He twisted his head, searching.

His duffel sat next to the door, but not where he'd left it.

No. It *was* where he'd left it on his way to the library. His mind was playing tricks on him for some damned reason. Probably had something to do with the time wards—

Wait. Time wards? How did he know about that?

He vaguely remembered Dr. Petra telling him he wasn't losing any time as he'd healed, that time moved differently in his room, in the healing wards, in the...basement.

Right. That made sense. A bunch of mages would, of course, have access to time magick, and why wouldn't they use it to keep their best fighters in the game longer? It made complete sense.

His duffle didn't look *exactly* as he'd left it, though. It looked...messed with.

He got up and opened his bag. He had never been a super organized packer, but he'd never leave his gun, *any* of his guns near the outer edge of his duffel. Those were always rolled in shirts or pants. And right on top, sat his little last-last, last chance gun. Just a little one, he kept hidden for a two-shot escape.

If that had been just thrown back in, what else might have been tampered with?

He completely unpacked the bag and folded everything, taking care to repack the guns wrapped in a soft cloth, like jeans or something.

He didn't know *who* had packed his duffle, but it most certainly hadn't been him.

After that, he began a search around the room in cracks and crevices. Not looking for anything specific, but things that shouldn't be there.

He didn't find anything with his eyes, but then he took a deep breath, in through his nose. Something wasn't quite right with his sniffer. There was a *smell*, one that didn't belong. Faint at first, but as he pulled more air in, he deciphered meaning from the scent. Images filtered through with the meaning.

He had super smell? Maybe developed from the accident? No way, he had super smell!

Wait. He *knew* he had super smell because... he'd learned that before.

A few more memories stumbled back and then zombied around in his head just as lost as he was.

What had happened in that accident? It had really messed some stuff up in his mind.

Dexx shook his head and found another smell. This one was more powerful. He separated the individual smells because... he could do that. Oh, yes, now *that* was cool.

Humans. And something else.

There had been three people in here recently. But wait. There was more. He could tell it was two men and a woman. The woman hadn't showered.

Okay. That was kinda fucked up.

How long ago had he gotten the super smell, and how many times had he "rediscovered" it? And why couldn't he have gotten x-ray vision or something? Lots of secrets could be ferreted out with just smell, like Sherlock Holmes or drug-sniffing dogs. But he wasn't a dog. He was a demon hunter extraordinaire.

Shit! *That* was the smell. It wasn't an unwashed woman. It was a demon.

There was a demon in DoDO.

The wards should have kept them out. Or did they know how to do that?

Dexx sat on the bed and put his chin on his fists.

Kicked into a corner under his sink, a little round skipping stone had made friends with the dust bunnies.

He paused as the feeling of being watched increased. People had been in here and had searched through his stuff. A *demon* had gone through his tighty-whities. Most hunters were cautious by nature, and Dexx had learned to be more cautious than the next guy.

Was he being spied on right now?

He laid down on his bed, pretending to just be ready for the morning.

Oh. He bet this was Brooks trying to get to him before he left because Brooks had wanted this gig and had been passed up. Dexx didn't remember *how* he knew that. Only that he did.

But what was Dexx supposed to do about the demon?

He *should* get up and tell someone.

But his legs weren't moving, and something in him told him to stay down.

So he did. Why? He didn't know, but if his instincts said to remain in place, that's what he'd do.

What did it all add up to? He was being spied on. That much seemed likely. The accident *might* be a reason to watch him a little closer, but there was a high probability of a demon in the house, and something inside him was telling him not to do anything about that? What was *that* about? And the way the librarian had acted?

Dr. Petra had given him pills, like a lot of them. Why had he been so adamant that Dexx take them without telling him what they were for?

Dexx sat back up. Could there really be a demon in the employ of the organization hunting and killing demons and other paras?

That was a brilliant ploy. Infiltrate the enemy and attack from within. What better way to sabotage the whole place?

But that led to the question of why pick on Dexx? Why not Mario, or better yet, why not Hopkirk?

Too much thinking. There was no way DoDO would slip like that. Dexx reached under his sink and picked up the stone. He needed to stretch his legs.

The best he could do was walk up and down the halls. After two trips back and forth, he heard a whoop back down the corridor.

Alwyn streaked through the hall, shaking a piece of paper. "Hey! Got orders. I'm headed back with *you*."

Dexx backed up from the outthrust hand. "Congratulations. Now, if you'd like to get out of my bubble… We talked about this."

"No. we didn't."

"Oh." He swore they had. "Well, we're talking about it now. Your breath stinks."

"Shut up, fat man."

The world lurched, split in two, and wobbled. Not fat *man, fat cat.* An image of huge clawed paws hit a tall man with stark white wings. An angel?

"You okay, man?"

Dexx had a hand to his head, trying to put the double

vision back to normal. His vision blurred, then snapped back into a perfectly solid single vision.

"I was told to watch you." Alwyn frowned, his dark eyes worried. "Doc said you might be physically fine, but, uh, your head took a pounding. That might not heal for a long time." He glanced behind him and took a step closer, lowering his voice. "You take your pills like you're supposed to?"

"Yeah, just ate three."

"Well, do that." His look was two parts relieved and one part something else that looked like guilt. "If I'm going to trust anything you say, you *can't* be mental. You read me?"

"Five by five, boss."

"What *does* that mean?" Alwyn dropped his orders to his side, curiously studying Dexx. "Another American pop culture reference?"

"Google it." How many times had he tried to explain things to this guy?

"Why? I've got you right here."

"Then continue to wonder." Dexx couldn't help but feel a bit relieved that Alwyn was indeed coming with him. "You ready— packed and all that jazz?"

"Not yet, mate. Even got a few trinkets to take home too."

"Is any of it legal?"

Alwyn shrugged with a cocky grin. "Probably not. Don't tell anyone."

"Mum's the word." Dexx tapped Alwyn on the shoulder. "Go get your stuff together. You know if we're going by portal or more... mundane methods?"

"Mundane for sure. The further away from the portal, the more power and the longer they need to recharge."

Made sense, but if that was the case, he'd have to re-think how he'd packed his guns. Hmm. "Ah. Okay."

"Too right. I'll just jog on, then."

"Later." Dexx turned and kept his walk going. Why didn't he know anything about the portal and the power it took? Too many *fucking* questions. Why was he even leaving?

Because he wanted to, that's why.

But… *did* he?

9
<hr>

Dexx practiced his super smell, walking through the areas of the house he could reach while mulling over questions. No answers developed, but he had fun anyway.

He crossed the campus, where he haunted the detention center until he was shooed away. Actually, he had to be *escorted* away. He'd smelled something familiar, like…*friendly,* and he'd become curious.

Activity in the detention facility had ramped up. What were they doing that they didn't want to be known? And what exactly was in there?

The sixty-million-dollar question.

Along with his super smell, he'd developed super paranoia. Being a hunter sort of gave him that anyway, but the gnawing in his gut was more than simple curiosity.

Something in that building called to him. Not someone yelling, "Hey, Dexx," of course. That would be silly. Super silly.

The pair of heavily warded and armed guards who occasionally walked through the doors weren't for just for precaution. Something was definitely sensitive.

Gold? Possibly, but that could be in a vault and be just as safe.

A monster? Interesting, but why keep it a secret? Because usually, guards at doors like that hid highly suspect activities.

Dexx's smile at their retreating backs was more a baring of teeth. London might be exciting, but the secrets here were shaping up to be just as fun in the you-have-a-secret-I'm-going-to-expose sort of way. He walked away from the detention center for the third time—this time without an escort.

He took a deep breath just outside the campus gates. Mountains hovered close in the protected valley, creating either the protection or constriction feel.

He found a likely tree that might shield him from prying eyes.

There weren't any eyes to find immediately, but that didn't mean there were none out in the night.

He leaned against the tree, acting casual. What was casual? Could he be too casual? Maybe act like he needed to smoke or take a leak. Nothing to see here, just floatin' some teeth. Gotta take care of it.

Heavy cloud cover and the absence of outdoor lighting made the night as dark like a box. Soon, his eyes adjusted, and he strained to see.

As though he'd switched a light on, a faint red blinking light popped on and off in a nearby tree. Several trees had them, actually.

Cameras. Those *spying bastards*. How much did they trust *any* of their people? Sure, the camera didn't necessarily spy on people coming outside for fresh air, but it sure vindicated his growing paranoia. And proved the axiom.

Assholes. There wasn't a supporting word strong enough for the level of assholery that reached.

Relax, just relax. Time for them later.

Dexx pulled in a deep breath of his super smell.

Nobody had been around for a while. At least, he didn't smell people. He really should have come outside more. The trees and mountains were quite nice in the dark.

Dexx took off his jacket and hung it over the lens of the closest camera to dig in his pocket. Inside was a small… rock? It had a rough feel and was small round, and just like a regular stone. As he ran a finger across the flat, heat seemed to radiate from it.

Lines began to glow in the rock, lengthening to form, well, words. Maybe.

They looked like letters, but not any letters he could recognize. Sharp and angular, one looked like a P or a stick drawing of a pole with a triangular flag at the top. Others were… more complicated, and he had no idea what those might resemble. Stick figure scribbles, maybe.

What he knew, though, was the rock was *his*. Stupid, but there was a feeling of belonging. As much as holding his Baby Eagle, or his H&K. *That* was his, and it was just a rock. A rock with glowing letters like "the one ring."

And it had been displayed in a house dedicated to the paranormal beside some pretty impressive other stuff.

Okay. It obviously wasn't *just* a rock.

The sigils, or letters or whatever the lines were glowed and felt warm to his hand. The more he studied the lines, the more he thought he should know what they meant. Finally, he had to admit he had no idea what they were. He put it back in his pocket.

He pulled the jacket from the camera.

What the hell was that stone?

Where had it *come* from was a pretty easy answer—stolen from the wall niche.

But where had DoDO stolen it from, and why was it so

important to put it in the wall niche? So many questions assaulted him. He couldn't form one before another crashed in.

Spying bastards.

He turned around to go back inside.

His stomach cramped, and he went to his knees. He curled in at the extreme pain.

Images assaulted him next. He'd seen those before. A woman with nearly black hair and the most beautiful dark eyes. He saw a girl with blonde hair. She made him think of zombies for no discernible reason—three other children, young, like toddlers or babies.

Superimposed over it all was a dark form. Glowing green eyes accused him. Accused him and searched at the same time.

Why did he *want* those eyes to find him?

Red shapes floated over the ground. They circled and boomed. Dexx tucked his head in and braced himself against the pain.

Sound crashed in his ears, and his eyes felt about ready to explode while his stomach tried to pull the rest into a tiny black hole.

What the hell was going on? The pain increased as the shapes floated in. He was fucking going to die.

The cramps tightened to a crescendo of pain, and the noise blurred his vision. He screamed out in agony. It could have been a groan. His ears couldn't tell.

As suddenly as it started, the pain stopped. Nothing. No visions, smells, sounds. Dexx looked up, blinking tears from his eyes.

"You okay, dude?" A DoDO dressed in a tactical vest and body armor with a rifle crouched over him. "I'm sending for medical."

Dude? That wasn't… right.

He had to come up with something quick, or he'd be hip deep in… well, shit. "Yeah. I ate too much cheese and came out to smell the fresh air. Should've been on the shitter, though."

"You came out here to shit your pants in the dark?"

"Yeah." Okay. So, as far as fibs went, this one was beyond lame. "It's comforting." Stop. Geezus. "Kind of."

"Whatever. You need to be inside for curfew. We marked you as an intruder."

That was interesting. "Sure. The worst of it seems to be over. Try it out. It'll change your life." Dexx stood and wobbled toward the door, half-covering his eyes.

Nine hells, what was happening to him?

What if he was becoming a werewolf?

Hate that wasn't his own at "moon *shifters*" hit him by surprise.

Werewolves weren't real, and why would he think of them as a "moon shifter?"

Not a werewolf? Something else, then. The anger subsided.

Shifter?

Ha! Him. A shifter? No. He wouldn't have been allowed into DoDO if he was a shifter.

But…super smell. The supervision. The super hearing. It did kinda make sense.

Well, shit. He might be certifiable at this point, and all that was needed was voices to pop into his head.

He took a deep breath and let it out slowly. The accident just made him extra paranoid.

The promotion. London was waiting. Nervous energy pulsed at him with the urge to go. London had been—*was still* his goal.

He'd do his job, but he wasn't telling a soul about his super senses. That would be *his* secret.

He opened the door to his room.

Alwyn was waiting for him, leaning against the small alcove with the sink and mirror.

What was he doing there? "Get lost?"

"Nah, mate." Alwyn looked nervous. "I have something I want to say."

"Wouldn't you like someplace more private?"

Alwyn narrowed his eyes and passed a look around the room. "More private than this?"

Super smell fed Dexx a sharp scent. Wariness on the edge of action. "Or here is fine." Alwyn might not know about the cameras.

"I never thanked you for saving my life. The... ah, the first time."

"*That?* No problem, kid." He actually couldn't remember *ever* saving the kid's life. "Just what teams do for each other. You pulled my fat out a few times too."

No, he hadn't. Nobody had saved Dexx from *any* demon or para. He had too much experience hunting alone.

"The *first* time. When we first met." Alwyn emphasized the word like it was something important. "Thanks, mate." Alwyn's smell changed to something quivering, like the worry that he wouldn't be believed.

"You're welcome." What was Alwyn really trying to tell him? But Dexx couldn't question him further. Not here. Not with all the cameras watching. "If I didn't save you, I wouldn't have any friends at all."

He didn't understand how or why Alwyn was a friend if he had no memories of their times together, but...

"Well, because of you, I get to go home. DoDO tries to keep us away from familiar places, so we don't do anything stupid because we're attached to the place." Alwyn raised his eyebrows and gave one nod.

Like he was trying to say something but in a super-secret code kind of way. "Ah. Okay."

Alwyn stood and crossed the small room, and extended his hand.

Dexx looked at it for a second, then took it.

For a kid, Alwyn had a good grip. He looked Dexx in the eye like he was trying to make sure Dexx got the gravity of his thanks. Then, he released Dexx's hand and turned for the door. "We're going home soon. Thanks for that."

"Anytime, kid." The exchange confused Dexx more than a little.

Dexx had just sat down on the bed when a knock sounded at the door.

He sing-songed his answer. "Who ees it?"

The door opened, and his first impulse was to attack.

Dr. Petra stepped in. "Came to see you off."

Dexx sprang off his bed, not fully understanding why he had this reaction. Or, at least, he tried to.

Petra raised his hand, and Dexx froze in place. The doctor smiled impatiently. "I see you are still fighting the spell. How are you feeling, *Shedim*? Maybe I should bring you back up and run some tests. You're very resilient, and I really do not like that. Are you taking the pills I gave you?"

Dexx's super smell went into overdrive.

The voice in his head growled but cut off suddenly.

"I have the pills in my jacket." Dexx hooked a thumb at his jacket, his voice absent of emotion. "Got my first dose in at chow." Dexx showed teeth with the lie. It could pass for a smile.

"Good. I will check on you. We can't afford to lose you."

Dexx tried to jump, but his body just wouldn't respond.

"The house has spent a considerable amount of time and effort on you. I mean to have you. Right in front of me."

That sounded a little dirty. "Of course, you do. Everyone

does." He would have snapped a scathing mock salute, but his arms refused to obey.

Petra's eyes flashed.

The stone in Dexx's pocket flared with heat. He sat frozen hard on the bed and stared at Petra without emotion.

"Shedim onnus togai."

Waves of dizziness passed over Dexx. He swayed on his bed. What in the hell was going on?

The stone felt like a lit matchstick against his skin, but he couldn't move his hands. Couldn't move *anything*. He just sat there like a stone idiot looking at the doctor.

The words sounded… familiar, though. He'd heard that speech before, but the memory wouldn't come.

"Shedim. Toh arus tu agast ni jereholm onnus togai." Petra closed in on Dexx. The waves of dizziness intensified as the doctor repeated himself. "Forget who you were."

The thing had the feel of a spell and not a nice one. No way Dexx would forget *this*.

Kill the dark one, a voice growled inside him. Fury built in his stomach and radiated through his chest and limbs. *We must kill it.*

Dexx couldn't agree more, but he couldn't move. Not even a little.

The voice in his head growled.

Petra fuzzed at the edges, and a strange demon inside took shape for an instant, and then Petra was back.

The fire against his leg cooled, and Petra smiled. Not any smile but a greedy, evil smile that scared Dexx more than a little. If Petra wanted to smother him with a pillow, there'd be no way Dexx could defend himself.

What in the nine hells was happening?

"Shedim. Rores ann aast borund ann aast torha noess." This time, Dexx understood what he'd said. *Come find me far away.*

The dizziness passed and Dexx fell back on his bed. Weak,

more than a little confused. What the hell did that mean? "Come find me far away." Like he wouldn't track that bastard of a demon whatever it took?

Wait. Hold up. He'd just uncovered the demon.

But the demon was DoDO's doctor. How could he trust that DoDO didn't *know* about that?

He'd have to find another way to deal with it. Later.

Dexx felt at the spot that should be a deep burn, didn't hurt any more than the memory.

Well, fuck. And there was no way he was going to take any of those pills. They were headed for the toilet. As soon as he could sit up.

10

Trailed snow covered the ground from Dexx's hill to the next. A tree on the far side spread leafless branches in a wide dome.

The sky above held angry clouds threatening more snow. Beyond the tree on the next rise and snow-covered hills, he could see nothing—all the way to the horizon.

People appeared out of nowhere, surrounding him. All them naked, standing in the snow, lifting feet and blowing warm air into hands.

At a signal he couldn't see or hear, they ran at top speed down the hill to the next.

Dexx's feet felt the biting cold on his bare feet as he ran through the snow, but he ran after the rest, trying to keep up. They outpaced him easily and disappeared over the rise beyond the tree.

Panting, Dexx reached the tree. The bark was a smooth grey, and the trunk was huge. Branches as thick as his leg parted from the trunk low enough, he could climb and lookout.

Where the snow had frozen his feet and the air pebbled on his skin, the tree offered warmth and welcome.

He touched the bark, ready to climb into the branches and soak up the heat. It wanted him to carry on. How did he know that?

Well, this was his dream so he could know anything.

The earth began to rumble. The snow melted into cold rain and trembled with the earth beneath him.

He took a tentative step toward the sound that sounded over the rise, drawn beyond the tree. In one step, the rain warmed. The grass beneath the snow felt soft, inviting.

Another step and a warm spring day greeted him. The sun still hung behind the dark clouds, but it might as well be a bright shiny day.

Another step and the trembling earth sharpened, intensified.

A quiet rumble came from the next rise over.

One last step.

A fire erupted in his belly, spreading through his limbs and fading through his fingertips.

He lurched forward at the urge to be with the others. He fell to his hands and knees, but the fall was shorter than it should have been. He was somehow taller on his hands than on his feet.

The rumble grew, and from over the next rise came wolves. A pack of hundreds and hundreds. The hills swam beneath their running paws. He stood, moving toward them, but he walked on all fours. The movement felt unnatural, then faded away after a few moments.

He bunched up and leapt forward, towering over even the largest of the wolves.

The biggest of them was a great black wolf with golden eyes.

They passed Dexx, going the other way, splitting just

enough to rush by without slamming into his more massive body.

Dexx turned and looked in the direction they ran.

On the horizon, jagged black cliffs smoked a red glow at their base.

Dexx stepped forward and roared. A deep bass carried across the hills and the running wolves. They answered, howling as they ran.

I'm coming, cub. Keep fighting.

The voice was deep and rich. Also, somehow female. She felt ancient, powerful.

He ran forward, catching the wolves passed them without effort and caught the lead wolf. He bolted forward with another roar.

They closed on the cliffs that were now miles high with surprising speed. A red glow of heat from the earth melted rock into glowing magma.

With one more leap, Dexx ducked his head and crashed into the solid wall...

Dexx jumped awake from the dream.

He scrubbed his head where he should have been bloody. He still felt the memory of smashing the rock wall.

Cool air touched his face.

Somehow, he'd fallen asleep right where he'd flopped on his bed.

A shrill tone rang through the room and the hall outside.

Shit.

DoDO had a late-night mission. Alpha Team. And he had to show up. Or did he? He was on his way out in the morning.

Damn it all to hell. He rose and opened the door to the too-bright hallway. Alwyn passed as he walked out.

"Think they really want us?" Alwyn's smile was hesitant.

Maybe he thought they could get out of the mission. Anyone could die on a mission. Several had.

"DoDO. Of *course*, they want us. We're not gone yet." He was on edge from the dream and had some excess energy to burn through. "Wonder what the big deal is." Dexx scrubbed his fingers through his hair again, wiping away the dream. Wasn't there something else he needed to remember? Something recent?

Alwyn fell into step with Dexx. "Must have found a sensitive nest somewhere."

"Better be a demon. I don't like hunting paras."

Alwyn shrugged. "They're just as bad."

"At least they're people. People *aren't* demons. No matter how bad they might be."

Alpha Team filed into the ready room. It was almost like a classroom, but with better chairs.

A surveillance picture of a man walking across a street was projected on the wall. He looked Mediterranean with a large hooked nose and curly hair to his shoulders. An attractive guy, he looked like a successful businessman, or like he came from money. He also looked familiar, somehow.

"Wonder what he did to piss off the brass," Dexx mumbled as he sat next to Alwyn in their usual spot.

Mario stood at the front of the room, already dressed in his body armor and vest. "This our target. He's a major power player in the para community. They listen to him, and if he says something, it's the law. So, we take him down and effectively cut the head off the snake."

Dexx crossed his arms and scooted into a reclined position. "So, we take this guy down, and then what? Spend the next five years trying to find the scattered paras?" He wiggled into his comfortable spot and laced his fingers behind his head.

"Something big is on the horizon," Mario said softly. "We need to stop the threat he poses to us."

"Us?" Who exactly was "us" when Dexx knew a demon was on the payroll. And the more he thought about it, the more he realized brass had to know. They weren't dumb. "Not the people, but for *us*? He looks like he does well for himself. Can't be that bad if he's just doing business."

Mario frowned and folded his arms over his vested chest. "He takes from the paras under him. He's a criminal racketeer and is running a strong-arm protection scheme."

Dexx studied the picture of the man. He didn't *look* like the kind of guy running a protection racket, but then again, a lot of the witches around didn't look like witches.

How did he even know that? "So, where is he?" Dexx tipped his head to the side, trying to figure out why this guy looked so damned familiar.

"West coast. In an affluent city. That's all you need to know."

"Defenses?"

Mario looked down his nose at Dexx. "You all right with taking this para down?"

The rest of the team twisted in their seats to watch.

Dexx often questioned the directors, and the fallout was usually memorable. However, he couldn't *remember* actually having done any of that, so how did he know that was even true? Dexx didn't know, but he needed to understand what kind of order they were on. Capture or kill? "He's a para. And if he's as big a criminal as you say, he's *got* to have a few more paras walking around for defenses. An elemental or maybe a shifter or something. Soooo... did you find any defenses?"

Mario thinned his lips. "Take out any opposition you find. Is that clear?"

"Take them out. Would that be for dinner or a movie? It's

important to know how much money to bring. Dinner first? I hate movies on an empty stomach."

"You will remove any threat to your objective with deadly force. Is *that* clear enough?" Mario's pale face turned red with fury.

Dexx narrowed his eyes. That's what he was waiting for. Slimy bastards were spying on their own. Slimy bastards had demons posing as… the thought faded. Slimy bastards. It felt as though something *really important* had just slipped from his mind. "Clear as a summer sky."

"Then move out and get that objective."

"Sure." Dexx stood. "Alpha Team suit up. Let's go hunt some paras."

Alwyn walked with Dexx to the ready room and the portal generator. "One of these days, you'll yarble at the wrong tree, then all the shit's gonna hit the fan."

The man was probably right. "Well, after today, he won't need to worry about us. Get your vest."

Mario stood at the rack with a vest he held out for Dexx.

"What's this for?" Dexx flicked one of the narrow blue strips along with the vest.

"New team leader vest. So, in the event of limited sight and confusion, you can be easily identified."

Dexx stood there for a few seconds. Marking the officer was more like it. Or was there something else going on?

He snatched the vest and walked to the portal circle with the rest of the team, dragging the vest along the floor.

"No disabling it, Colt," Mario called. "It's for your protection."

There was something *definitely* up with it then. "Yep. Got it." He slung it over his shoulder.

"Remember, Dexx," Mario said, his soft voice striking him like an arrow through the muted noise of his team getting ready. "You promised you'd be professional for the time you were with us."

Dexx's vision split in two. Shadowy images crossed in his mind. People—a woman and smaller people. Children? A bird, but much bigger than a bird could be. Why did that make him think of a lion?

His vision snapped back together. The feeling of loss solidified. Something *was* missing, but whatever it was would *not* be found here.

He remembered one thing clearly. He wasn't taking any more of those damned pills.

"Let's get the show on the road." He pulled his arms in the vest and plugged in his earpiece. He carefully did *not* plug in his vest.

The room wavered, and then they stood in the country. Dexx let his eyes adjust to the dark, but amazingly, he didn't need to. He saw perfectly fine, even though the night was still full of shadow.

A large house sat across a large lawn, more like an estate in some movie set in England. The place felt familiar.

Dexx tapped Alwyn in the shoulder, held a finger over his lips, and motioned for his vest. Silently, they swapped vests. The vitals would be screwed up back at the house, but at least he didn't have the blue on.

Dexx plugged in and motioned for the team to spread out and proceed with caution.

They crept to the house without seeing anyone. No guards, no sentries.

This was a para criminal? That didn't seem to make any sense. Criminals always carried a retinue of thugs for protection. That's just how they operated.

Dexx pulled air slowly in through his nose. Scents came in. Familiar, stirring up emotions in his head that were unattached to memories.

The smells of the rest of the teams were the most foreign. In fact, those were the clearest smells around. Was this really a para's house? It smelled… clean.

Dexx took a position behind a corner of the house and waited for the others to catch up. Alwyn took up a silent position right on his flank, watching his back.

He saw other team members come forward. With two fingers held tight together, he motioned forward, then balled his hand into a fist, twisted his wrist, and sharply pulled back. Move in fast and hard.

The team moved to the front, and Dexx took Alwyn to the back.

A scent caught his attention. It was something he didn't know and was intimately familiar at the same time.

Shit. He motioned Alwyn to stop and hold his position. Palm out, he then turned down with a finger pointed at the ground.

Dexx held up tight against the stone side of the mansion.

Something in him knew this place, but he'd never been here before.

He slipped around the corner, knowing the layout he'd find. The back was as empty as the front.

Nobody in sight. His eyesight shifted to heat vision, and he saw the world overlaid with a reddish color.

He needed to figure out how to control this, but not at the moment. Later. When he got to London.

He scanned the grounds along the rear of the estate and saw nothing out of the ordinary, none of his guys.

A small flowerbed had freshly turned soil. He knelt down and grabbed a handful of it, and scrubbed his bodycam. Hopefully, the footage wouldn't be of any use.

By now, his guys should have breached the inside.

Faint pops of gunfire grew louder with each second.

He found the back door and waited.

Sounds of crashes and things breaking came from the inside.

Faintly, he saw his team tear up the house with bullets.

He was actually *seeing* through the house, ghostly as the images were. He was looking *through* the *walls*.

So he *did* have x-ray vision. Neat?

A person inside fought against his guys. His team fell like trees. The guy fought like no other. He had skill, but Dexx and DoDO had numbers.

A few managed to shepherd the para through the house, chasing him closer to Dexx.

Suddenly a window overhead exploded out with the para falling to the ground.

Dexx pounced on him before he had a chance to get up. He twisted one of the para's arms hard in the middle of his back. He went to yank on the man, to bring him to his feet and bring him in.

The kill order. This wasn't a bag and tag.

Staring at the back of this man's head, though, something pulled on him harder and tighter than anything DoDO had. He *couldn't* kill this man. Shit. And right before he was headed to London. Damn it. "Listen close," he whispered in the man's ear. "Are you a criminal?"

The man stiffened, turning his head around to look at Dexx with eyes that flared.

Something inside Dexx answered back.

"What are you doing?" the man asked in a soft, Greek accent.

Dexx had no fucking clue. "You're being targeted, and the best place for you is *not* here. Run and get someplace safe. Get me?"

The man nodded. "Are you in trouble?"

Dexx gave the man a confused look. "You are. Now, go."

He released the man and yelled over his shoulder, "Cover the front! He's headed your way— Alwyn!"

The man ran *fast* to the back.

He became a shadow and disappeared even from Dexx's super sight in less than a second. *That* would be a good superpower.

Alwyn burst around the corner.

Dexx pulled up short, faking being out of breath. "Did you see him?"

Alwyn shook his head. "What happened?"

"He jumped out the window. I tried to pin him down. Fucker twisted and threw me off. Fuck. He got away."

Three of the team showed up around the corner.

"Whose job was it to set the shields?" Dexx looked at the team.

Those who were standing. He was missing almost half of his team.

They all shook their heads.

Relief swept through Dexx, though he didn't know why. Was he *glad* his team had failed? "Are they dead?"

Heads shook.

"Pick 'em up. Let's go home."

Another failure for DoDO. Another win for Dexx.

Slimy bastards.

11

Dexx propped his chin on his hand as the plane closed in on the runway.

Alwyn had been talking nonstop for about an hour before they sighted land. He'd started with the bigger things like Stonehenge and Hadrian's Wall, then had moved on to history, and then when he'd run out of that, he'd moved on to his own youth.

As the plane descended, Alwyn finally ran out of steam. "Hey, you listening?"

Maybe he hadn't run out of steam. Maybe Dexx had grown super selective hearing. Was that a thing? "Yeah. You dripped spelled water, and when it dried, it turned into paint. Clever."

"I told you about that a while ago." Alwyn sounded as excited as when they boarded the plane. Alwyn had managed some sleep. He said the jet lag was going to run hell on them for a while, and he had wanted to minimize that.

Dexx managed exactly zero minutes of sleep. Flying wasn't fun.

He *did* manage some time examining his *object*. The stone

with the strange markings. He still didn't know how it "belonged to him," but it was *his*.

The tan disc was flat and round, and while not smooth, it wasn't rough. It'd make a helluva skipping stone. What was it, and why did it make him think it was older than the words written along the side? The symbols weren't New Times Roman, for sure.

Still, in his *hours* of not sleeping, he'd worked the several inconsistencies of the past few days through his head. He had fleeting memories, super smell, intermittent super sight, and a rock that glowed with letters like the *one ring*. A doctor had been… A fuzzy memory that didn't quite make sense floated to the top. He didn't quite remember, but he did know the doc was a bad man for sure, and with all those things, he'd come up with no solid reasons why any of it should be happening now.

Except everything had happened *after* his accident. If he could get the particulars on *that*, the other mysteries should be a little easier to explain.

The plane touched down and bounced once hard.

Dexx *hated* to fly. Give him a good car any day.

Car? He hadn't owned a car in years. He actually couldn't *remember* his last car. He could drive, of course, but what car had been his last? Or his *first* car? Maybe it had been a truck?

The plane's air brakes popped up, tugging on the passengers. Howling filled the cabin as air rushed over the extended flaps.

Sure, maybe his first car had been a truck. He had vague thoughts of an old beat-up orange truck.

Tuck's old truck.

The skin on his back prickled. There was something there. Even as he tried to pull the memory, the thought evaporated.

The forward pull ceased, and the plane slowed to a

manageable speed. Passengers moved around, pulling at bags that had been stuffed under their seats.

The flight was full, and they had seats close to the rear of the plane. They were going to be there for a while.

Sure enough, everyone took their own sweet time disembarking, all the while Alwyn kept up a stream of childhood antics.

"So were you and Harry in the same house?" Dexx didn't even look away from the window. Baggage handlers emptied the hold scooting to and from sight.

"What? Harry who— oh ha, ha. You know that's a story, right?"

"So are we. But we don't get to live as long."

Alwyn frowned in frustration at Dexx. "Something wrong? You've been pulling the wanker the whole flight. I thought you'd be happy to be here."

"I am, I guess." He wasn't, but if this was what he'd been working so hard for, why not? "There's just something... *off*. I can't put my finger on it."

Alwyn looked at the other passengers.

The line dwindled, and their turn finally came.

Dexx pulled his travel bag from the overhead compartment, and they made their way to the terminal and customs.

Customs was a bore with the long lines and slow attendants. They tried to intimidate Dexx with stares when he had nothing to declare. He held his tongue, though. What he really wanted to declare was they were all a bunch of idiots.

The trip had frayed his temper badly.

It wasn't until that moment, though, when he realized he had this annoying feeling gripping his gut like he was in the wrong place. He needed to go back home.

Not to DoDO.

So, with his missing memories and his other super

senses, maybe this gut thing was his mind's way of reminding him what he needed to do.

After they cleared customs, they were found by a woman dressed in all black. Her glasses immediately screamed DoDO, but everyone else might have taken her for a limo driver.

Dexx dared not use his super smell here, since he might get a snout full of unwashed humans. And things humans did in open spaces.

"Come with me if you please." The woman turned and led them away without checking if they followed.

Dexx passed a look to Alwyn made the sign for "enemy ahead."

Alwyn turned his laugh into a cough, but the woman didn't respond.

She had a hot woman assassin look with the suit, her hair pulled back into a stylish bun that curved along her head, her sunglasses obscuring her eyes.

A super ugly ride waited outside the terminal. A brand new Mercedes SUV with square lines and no personality. Nothing but the best for DoDO.

And of course, the steering wheel was on the wrong side.

Dexx hopped in on the passenger side. It turned out that it wasn't the passenger side.

Their escort lady guide didn't appreciate it.

"Wrong side, Yank."

Her scent said she stepped in dog shit, with her bare foot.

Whatever the model Mercedes was, it rode well though the ever-narrowing streets of London.

"You got a name?" Dexx held his hand out.

The woman— no, she couldn't be more than around twenty-five, if that— glanced at his hand, then concentrated on the road.

"We taking you away from some important plans?" Dexx

appreciated a cold shoulder like the next guy—yeah, no. No guy *ever* appreciated a cold shoulder. "A hot date, or a visit with the Queen?"

"No. Do you?" She kept her eyes on the road, veering through traffic.

The driving might have scared him, but she wasn't the only one driving bat-shit crazy. Well, when in Rome.

"Cassandra Mills. You're Dexx Colt and Alwyn ab-Rhys."

"So not a kidnapper. Good to know. How long to get to the house?"

"We go to a safe house first. Then we take a portal to the campus."

"Right. And that takes about how long?" Dexx crossed his arms before he throttled the woman. Cassandra.

"We should be there in about an hour."

"Is there a place we can get something to eat? Maybe hit the head?"

She finally turned her head to him. Her nose scrunched up. Kinda' cute, actually. "Hit what?"

"Go. To. The. Loo. You've got those around here, right?"

"We have loos, yes." She didn't sound nice. But her accent rocked. "Why didn't you do that when you had the chance at the airport?"

"You kind of scooped us up, and I didn't have the urge. Now I do. And airplane food sucks. So, if we're going to be out, why not keep our bellies off our backbones and our teeth from floatin'."

"You Americans are so crass." Cassandra's face twisted with distaste.

"Somebody's gotta keep the stereotype going. How about you, Alwyn? Care to hit an old favorite?"

Alwyn's smile widened. Yes, yes, he would. "Dexx is the new deputy director. We'll be taking his orders soon enough, so why not?"

Cassandra stared out the window, her mouth pinched. She looked pissed. Super pissed

For a moment, Dexx remembered a different position he'd been offered. But that wasn't right. He was the boss. He shook himself.

Cassandra glowered. "Sure. Who could be more powerful than the new deputy director of training?"

Did she just insult him? He could play that game. Wait, with a brand new position, came great responsibility. "Thanks. I'll be sure to remind everyone you said that."

Alwyn smirked, but his scent said he thought Dexx was going too far.

Okay, fine. He'll rein it in a bit.

They pulled up in front of a pub. The sign hanging out front said they'd stopped at *The Queens Head*.

Uh, weird. "So, they don't like the Queen?"

"It's only a name here." Alwyn shrugged. "We don't really suffer from the hurt feelings Americans do."

"Not me. I just thought Queenie might not like her head as the draw. So, let's go see the Queen's Head." Dexx opened his door on the wrong side and stepped out.

The smells hit him immediately. The airport had stunk like unwashed masses and jet fuel. This place had a much different scent, like unwashed masses and beer.

Dexx followed his super smell into the pub to the unfamiliar food. Oh, yes. There was definitely something to eat.

He paused just inside the door and scanned the room. A long bar at the back had bottles of liquor he didn't recognize, lit by golden yellow lights hidden in the ceiling. The tables had three and sometimes four chairs each. At the far end, a small sign read "gents" with an arrow pointing further back.

"I'll be right back." He shot Alwyn a look and went for the sign.

The bathroom wasn't much different than any he'd seen in America. He unzipped and leaned an arm against the wall.

Nothing in the world like a good piss. The world righted itself.

Dexx zipped and turned around and froze.

A woman leaned against the wall next to the door. She was more than pretty, with a slim build and dark hair hanging over her shoulder. Her eyes were almost black and playful, but her smile was all predator.

Sharp spikes of her scent rolled to his nose. "I'm not sure how this works in your country, but in mine, you wait your turn. In the correctly labeled bathroom."

"Oh, I think I'm in the right room." She stood from the wall and walked toward Dexx. She swayed most seductively. She looked right, but she didn't smell right.

The tattoos on his arms weren't tingling, but that didn't mean much. Only that if she was a demon, she wasn't currently trying to possess him.

He pushed his belt back in place.

Whatever the wrongness was about her smell, spiked.

"I just landed in the country." What were her weaknesses? "I don't want any problems." Dexx held his hands up in front of him.

All his tools were still in his baggage, and stick-in-the-mud-Cassy was probably snogging Alwyn.

"So you're the American they've all been talking about."

What? Who'd been talking about him? "I doubt anyone's been talking about me. I'm just on vacation and needed to use the facilities." Dexx backed up until he hit the wall.

"Oh, you can *lie*. I almost believed you." Her smile widened, but the predator didn't change. She got *way* inside his personal bubble. She put her hands on his shoulders and pressed herself against him.

Okay, so he'd heard Brits had different ideas of impropriety, but this was the *men's* room. Plus, that smell was all wrong. Was she a para? Most likely, but she hadn't done anything to him yet, and the last thing he needed was an international incident.

"Too close." Dexx moved to push her away— gently.

She grabbed his wrist and moved his hand over parts… that he shouldn't be touching.

She growled, throaty, and low. "Or not close enough. Let's make your first day memorable." Her hands slipped up Dexx's sides and to his shoulders. She began to pull on him as she raised on her toes, coming closer to his mouth.

Dexx caught a glimpse of white tips growing from too plump lips.

Vampire. He shoved with everything he had.

She flew backward into the far wall.

"You're good, hunter. They lose a lot that way. But we have the upper hand here. You think you're big and strong. Well, I'm strong too." She lost her seductive smile and the sexy walk. Her fangs protruded from her lips.

"Gross. You're really not all that." Dexx slipped to the corner, limiting the vampire's access to him. "You leave now, and we'll meet at another time. Call this an introduction."

"And if I don't?" She stood with a hand on her cocked hip, like this was any old bathroom introduction.

"I'm working on that, but I don't think you'll like it."

The woman laughed. Genuine with real amusement. "I don't think so, hunter. You've got a price on you, and I intend to collect."

Dexx almost dropped his hands. A price on his head? So soon? Her smell put his defenses back up. "A price on me. Do you even *know* who I am?"

"I know you, hunter. You're the American, Colt. I want the bounty."

"C'mon, really? Let me get over the jet lag, and I'll send

you a personal invite. I promise, it'll be a fair fight." It would be, too. Mostly. "All I want to do is spend my first day here, not dead."

She laughed again. "You have a sense of humor. They said you had wit. I don't think I can let you live. He said you were too powerful to let you catch your breath. So—"

In a blur of motion, she attacked so fast Dexx blinked and didn't see her move.

But something in him did. He opened his eyes, and he had her throat gripped in his hand. He slammed her down to the black and white tiled floor.

He felt the grunt, but her breath was stuck behind the hands he had clamped around her neck.

She beat at his arms, trying to free herself. She hit hard, but he stayed there, gripping for all he was worth.

He searched his memory for what killed vampires. They were technically dead already, but they had bodily functions. Somewhere in his mind, he knew that coffee made them shit. Interesting, funny even, but not helpful.

She relaxed under him and dropped her hands, her eyes staring and glassy.

Dead. Scratch one vamp.

Dexx almost let go, but another memory kept him there. They had the gift of illusion. What if she was only playing?

He twisted his shoulders and pressed harder with one hand and brought the other up and pounded a fist into the side of her face as hard as he could manage. The vision of the girl faded away and was replaced by a man.

Aw, really? Talk about the sickest, most— ew.

Okay. So, at the very least, the vamp was knocked out. It wouldn't have a pulse to check.

Dexx grabbed a wrist and hauled the thing over onto his belly. He pulled the vamp's arms behind him and locked them together.

Now for the hard part. How to get the vamp standing to get it into custody? He didn't have a stake or even tools to kill the thing. Should he call Alwyn?

The decision was taken from him as the door flung open, Alwyn and Cassy barging in.

Well, that'd taken long enough. "*Now* I know why you need me here. 'Cuz you guys *suck*."

12

Dexx stood, pulling the vamp up with him. "Call it in. We need this one for questioning and a team to sweep for more."

The vampire started to struggle, pulling at Dexx.

Cassandra stepped forward with surprising speed and pulled a silver spike from her vest and stabbed the vampire in the heart.

He dropped dead.

"What the *fuck*'re you doing? I *told* you to get a team in here, and *this* one should have been questioned."

"Procedure is to kill on contact. I did my job." She wiped her dagger on the dead vamp and slipped it back into her vest.

"What you did was bollocks up the *one* lead we had." Dexx dropped the corpse. "Things are changing in the house. Right now." Maybe. He didn't know what kind of power he had. But it sounded good.

"You haven't assumed the position yet, so my last order stands." Cassandra held her head up, looking down her nose at Dexx.

Oh, that pissed Dexx off. "Okay, sister, you can assume the position. You're going to be my special project." Dexx glared at the DoDO agent, reining back his desire to punch her in the face. "We have to vacate before somebody sees us all in here and wonders what sort of sick shit we're up to."

"We aren't backward like some places. I'll call a cleanup team. It'll be here in a few minutes." Cassandra oozed smugness.

Dexx looked over at Alwyn, who shrugged. "I had no idea."

"Then get a cleaning crew here. You need me sworn in before you request one?" Dexx put as much duh-what-are-you-waiting-for-you-stupid-ass into his words as he could. That lady was going to be a major pain in his ass… unless he could ship her to Siberia or Kazakhstan, whichever came up first.

She pulled her phone from her pocket. "We have a wet cleanup at my location."

"Send a necromancer, too," Dexx added flippantly.

Cassandra turned wide eyes at him. "What? You can't be *serious. A necromancer?*"

Dexx's eyebrows rose. "I wasn't before you killed a lead, but if you have one, it wouldn't hurt."

"Those are too dangerous to be a part of the organization." The look on her face asked him if he was crazy. "We have none."

Maybe he was, but he had a feeling like he'd used one before. "Okay, then it seems as like maybe you should have seen the humor. You killed a lead. How else were you going to get information from him?"

A portal opened, and six witches ran in. They began casting as soon as they understood the situation. They burned the vampire to ash and burned the ash until it disappeared into the vents. They washed the blood from the floor to the drain.

The cracked wall they left alone. They couldn't Harry Potter that back the way it had been before.

The cleanup team was pretty effective, and in just a few minutes, most wouldn't recognize that there'd been a brawl in the loo.

Dexx tapped Alwyn on the shoulder. "Come on. We're taking the short cut home." He twitched his head to the portal.

"I'm not sure we should—"

"Be my guest and ride back with Stony Mcstone-face. I'm tired, and I want some sleep."

Alwyn closed his mouth and bit his lip. A grin replaced the serious thought, and he nodded. "After you, Boss Colt."

"Damn straight." Dexx walked to the open portal.

Cassandra stopped micromanaging the cleanup team and barely caught them before they walked through. "You can't use the portal."

"Why not?" Dexx raised a brow at her.

"That is for official use. You aren't to use it that way. You are to go to the safe house, then use the portal from there. Policy."

"Oh, my apologies to your policy. We'll wait here."

She nodded and turned to give more orders.

He waited for her to take two steps and pushed Alwyn through the hole in the air. Dexx followed a step behind.

The portal chamber looked *exactly* like the one in the states. The thick golden circle set in a white marble floor was the same, as were the rows of computers with technicians monitoring the teams in the field.

Apparently, there were two other teams out at the same time as the cleaning crew at the *Queen's Head.*

The director on duty dropped his jaw as Dexx joined Alwyn.

The room went silent.

"Uh, hi." Dexx raised a hand.

"You aren't supposed to be here." A tall black-haired man said with an accent. That might be Russian or something. Dexx'd always been terrible with accents. Maybe the guy would say more, and he could nail it down.

Dexx put on his best smile. "Surprise inspection. New deputy director of training, Dexx Colt. Take me to my rooms, please."

The man just stood there, his eyes flicking in several directions at once. "You—," He touched a finger to his earpiece, and the look of surprise faded to one of concentration. He finally looked up. "Yes, of course." He pointed to Alwyn. "You vait in the next room." Then, he pointed to Dexx. "You vait here. Someone vill be here momentarily to collect you."

Russian for sure. He sounded *exactly* like the kid on *Star Trek*.

Alwyn waited for Dexx to nod before he went to the ready room.

"You guys didn't expect me?" Dexx wanted to be a bit smug about it, but something in his gut told him to actually pay attention to what was going on in the room because someone needed this information. Who, though? He couldn't quite wrap his head around that answer. The room went back into buzzed motion like a kicked anthill.

There was a lot of information on the screens. This branch was reviewing several operations simultaneously—all paranormal. But none of them raised any flags. He noted the equipment and personnel the best he could, hoping that would be enough for whoever he was taking these mental notes for. Dexx didn't have to wait long for a tall man in a business suit complete with tie showed up. Totally Kingsman style. "Dexx Colt." He had a no-nonsense British way of speaking.

Dexx liked the fact that he had these guys off guard. He didn't *want* the prepared song and dance. He wanted the impromptu one.

"You were expected later." Mr. BBC continued disapprovingly. "We don't like surprises. That could get someone hurt or worse."

Dexx pulled in a breath to retort but held back. Some little old man voice in his head told him he'd fought hard for his job, and now he had it.

Damn. Was this growing up. Or was this something else?

He held his breath for a moment, then deflated, unable to resist. "I'm sorry. I've been in the air for too long. Besides, I need to see what you guys are made of." The strange part was he really *was* sorry.

Where had *that* come from? He'd never felt any remorse for *any* job before. If they didn't like him, they could go screw themselves.

"My office. Now." The man turned and left the room. He didn't look back to see if Dexx had followed, just like Cassandra.

Dexx narrowed his eyes as he followed, taking a few more notes of what was going on inside the room before he left. There was a reason he'd been hired for this position, and it wasn't because he had a proven track record of following directions.

He clenched a fist and followed the Kingsman to his office but not before another long hallway crammed with wall niches and artifacts. They passed doorways to rooms filled with people—classes on paras. Holy crap, *all* those classes were full. A few turned around as Dexx passed open doors, but most never even twitched. Those would be the first dead in a fight. No situational awareness.

Dexx followed the Kingsman up the stairs. Why didn't he know the man's name? Sure, most of this was new, but shouldn't he know his new boss's name at the very least?

The familiarity of the house in America, and this one ended at the top of the stairs. The balcony ended with an office, but more stairs went higher.

Dread swallowed every other emotion running through him, but why?

One more set of stairs and another balcony hallway, and they entered the office. The Kingsman took the seat behind the desk and steepled his fingers.

"First, I suppose I should introduce myself. My name is Sayyid Maxwell. Sir, to you, and I am your boss's boss. If you came here to embarrass him, you're off to a good start."

So, they were going to be the easy-to-embarrass sort. Awesome.

"If you didn't come here to embarrass him and it's just you, then excellent. I will return you to the backward village you came from, and you can end your time with us. Which is it?"

Dexx took in a big, deep breath and expelled it. "First off, if I'd known you'd be this easy to piss off, I wouldn't have taken the position."

But a voice inside his head reminded him he'd *fought* for this position even though he had no recollection of it.

Sir, as he preferred being called, raised an eyebrow.

"Secondly, I needed to see what I was walking into. Sure, I got the position, but what was your response. First, you overkill on paras. Got it. Then you don't even raise the alarm when someone invades your headquarters. Really?" Dexx made a tsking sound. "And *then* you keep the leader of the invading force in your headquarter brain trust. Poor form."

Sir narrowed his eyes.

"However, with all that said, I… apologize. Sir." But did he? Really?

Sir Maxwell blinked. "I didn't expect humility. From everything I heard, you're unpleasant, rough, self-centered, and crass."

Dexx shrugged. "I'm all that." He winced with a shrug, remembering having a similar conversation with another older gentleman who was an amazing teacher. But what had his name been? The only thing he could recall as a mustache.

Sir Maxwell rolled his chin as he turned his unfocused gaze to the room.

Dexx gave the man some time and rubbed his hands along his pants. His thumb bumped the stone in his pocket. Warmth spread from it. Warmth like… the memory wasn't there.

"Well, Mr. Colt, I'm inclined to give you another chance. We can call this a warning, and chalk it up to first day jitters. Maybe arrogance."

That rubbed Dexx the wrong way, but he put a cork in it and sat back, a grin splitting his face. "Aside from the fact that some of your protocols need to be updated, this place is *really* cool." And mildly terrifying in a way he couldn't explain. "The one in the states is impressive, but this—" Dexx waved his hand around. "This is something else."

"Glad you like it."

That wasn't exactly what Dexx had said.

Sir Maxwell stood. "If there is nothing you would like to discuss, *I* have nothing further. I can escort you to your office, then bid you a good day."

Dexx stood as Sir Maxwell—really? He was going to have to call him that *forever*? No. Sayyid. The man's name was Sayyid.— buttoned his jacket. "Oh, I have plenty to discuss, but I'll compile my notes as I sleep and give you the rundown

—or my boss the rundown since you're 'my boss's boss,'" he said with his best poshly British accent. No need to waste his BBC marathon watching experience. "But I'm smashed from the ride." Dexx applauded himself for some well-played slang.

Sayyid—ah, fuck. Dexx couldn't do it. Sir Sayyid narrowed his eyes in a very unimpressed manner and stared for a moment. "You are on a very thin edge, deputy director."

Dexx snorted. "I'm here for a reason." Though, what that was, Dexx wasn't entirely sure.

"Indeed, you are."

Well, that certainly sounded like someone knew something Dexx didn't. He followed his boss's boss from the room and backed down the stairs.

Sir Sayyid wound around the campus and through another building before stopping at a set of double doors. The sign overhead said that read *Training Ward*.

Somebody must have been playing a joke because the "training ward" was massive. There were more classrooms, but there were also gymnasiums, workout gyms, and other halls that were unmistakably living quarters.

The people they passed stared. He'd smiled at the first few in friendly greeting, but then the numbers escalated, and before they reached a door with the name Director Harris on it, a crowd had gathered.

Among them was a pretty Asian woman who leaned against the doorframe. Her eyes widened for an instant, but she recovered quickly. Her scent said otherwise. She cycled between shock and worry. Then it went cold, laced with not hatred, but something that said she didn't like him. Or trust him. Or both.

The spiky scent almost had Dexx rubbing his nose. Super smell could be a curse at times.

Did she know him? Had they… spent the night together and he'd left before saying goodbye?

No, her scent said she'd been the one to leave.

Sir Sayyid knocked politely and opened the door. He led Dexx to a man at a desk covered with reports in haphazard stacks, cups full of pens, and a dual-monitor computer. He tapped at his computer with a pen stuck sideways in his teeth.

Director Harris looked up from the computer and pulled the pen out. "Director." He sounded surprised, as his eyes flicked over Dexx. "I wasn't expectin'…" His British accent was sharper than Sir Sayyid's. Less, cultured maybe.

Sir Sayyid casually lifted his hand toward Dexx. "Mr. Harris, this is Dexx Colt. He arrived a bit earlier than expected. I trust you have the situation well in hand?"

"Yes. I believe I can take it from 'ere."

"Good day, then. Mr. Colt." Sir Sayyid bowed his head slightly in a very British, very respectable manner that was almost equivalent to a silent flip of the bird. "Consequences are… severe here."

"Mmm." That was all Dexx had, really. He wasn't certain what kind of rights he had in this country. He felt a little like John Wayne. All cowboys in a group of prom queens. He gave a high-noon sigh, his hand where his gun should be. "I came here for a reason. I'm ready for the responsibilities." That triggered a flash of light in his mind like a nuke going off. Visions exploded in his head, but he kept himself upright and hoped he could keep them long enough to catalog and stash away for later.

Sir Sayyid nodded once and left the room, closing the door behind him.

Something took the wild array of memories and organized them in the back recesses of his head, giving him a moment of quietness in his mind. He knew one thing for certain. He was in the wrong place. A calm settled over him. But he'd find a way back to… her. Who? He didn't know. But…someone. Important.

"Well, as you can see, there's a lot of paperwork here." Director Harris motioned to his desk. That's your job."

No. It wasn't. "I don't do paperwork." That sort of fell out before he could help himself.

Harris gave him a harried head shake. "That's *all* you'll be doing, deputy." A phone rang at Harris's desk. After a second or two of digging, he found it. The thing had a cord with simple push buttons that lit up. "Yes?" Harris lost focus as he saw outside his office. "Sure. He's here now. We'll be right there." He set the receiver back on the ancient hooks.

"Wow." Dexx put a sideways grin on. "The eighties called, and they want their phone back."

"Stow it, deputy. Get dressed. We have a call." Harris snagged his coat from the back of his chair and slid open a drawer. He pulled a long thin stick out, then slipped it in his jacket.

"What was that?" Dexx drew his brows together in amusement. "A wand?"

"Yes, it is."

"Like Harry Potter?"

"No. This has *actual* magick. Pick your three. You'll be responsible for them out there."

"Right *now*? I just got off a plane." Dexx could use a week-long nap right then.

"Yes, now, Deputy. *This* is your job."

Dexx followed him. "A second ago, you said my job was paperwork. What is it?"

Harris rolled his eyes at the door. "Get your three and get to the portal room."

Something wasn't right here. "Fresh off the boat, no

sleep, don't know any of *your* recruits. What's going on here?"

Harris shrugged, doubt etching a worry-line in his brow. "If you can't do this, we'll ship you back."

A twisting sensation tied Dexx's inside into knots. He *couldn't* lose this new spot. The stone in his pocket surged warmth through him, and the sensation went away. What in the nine hells was going on?

Harris swept past him and left the room.

Dexx took a deep breath and followed. He knew no one here, so how was he supposed to *pick* anyone? "You, you, and you." Dexx pointed to three random people still swarming the hallway. "Get dressed. We have things to kill."

Something wasn't right here, and he was going to do what he could to keep these three alive.

13

The portal room buzzed just like the house in Montana, but this one felt different. The feeling of *doing* something was sharper, more *experienced*.

Smells passed through Dexx's nose. Confidence definitely had the high spot, but threads of nervousness wound through the crowd.

He finally motioned for his three random team members. Two men and a woman. Not bad. Two women would have been better.

Wait. Why? Not for naughty reasons, but because he just *knew* they were capable.

But *how* when he'd never worked with women before? Not really, anyway.

"What're we after, anyone know?" Dexx asked the team already suited.

They weren't burly men, but they looked universally snooty. Alpha Team. "Vampires. Got a real problem with them here."

Not surprisingly, the man had a British accent. After all, most of DoDO were Brits.

The man looked at Dexx with a raised chin. "You got any experience, Yank?"

Dexx waggled his head back and forth. "Some. Demons are my specialty." But he was burdened with new recruits. "These are just a poke in the ribs with a stick, and they go down."

The man snorted. "Yeah, sounds about right."

The rest of his buddies laughed.

The first one huffed again.

That guy's scent went beyond confidence into arrogance. Dexx could deal with that. Those guys would go down first. Arrogance led to eulogies, and sometimes that was good, but not always.

"Excellent." Dexx mimed a stab with an imaginary stick. Like he would *actually* use that move.

The team snorted in laughter.

One of his randomly picked team members sidled up close. "You mean what you said? You been up against a demon?"

"Yup. They're my thing." Enough with sizing up the first team, what about his own? Had he just killed three random people? "You got a name?"

"Fred Harrison." He swallowed hard, and his eyes shifted around the room.

Why in the hell were they sending out kids like this on missions? Was it that bad? Or that easy? "You scared, Fred?" Maybe he should have sized the crowd up a bit more.

"He's not really the... field type." The pretty Asian woman from earlier finished adjusting her vest. Not so easy with a top-end like hers.

Dexx was experienced with taking "the not-the-field" type, though. Wait. Really? He was? "Be cool, Fred. Stay close to me." He turned to the woman. "How about you? What's your name?"

The smell surged again. Worry, mixed with a not hate, but not friendship, either. "Quinn. Quinn Winters."

Tingles ran through the base of Dexx's neck and spread up through his skull like one of those plasma balls. Images flickered through his mind. A nice house, a hallway, a bathroom, and blood. A lot of blood.

Before he could process the images, the third member of his team nearly pushed Quinn out of his way and held out his hand. "Leonard Lester. I heard we were getting new deputy, but it's been sort of hush, hush, you know like they didn't want to say anything because it might not happen or something." The man was young. Too young. He *might* be eighteen if he was even seventeen. He sported red hair and had a strong resemblance to Ron Weasely.

"I'm not all the way in the door yet, kid." Dexx put on a smile he hoped might make his team relax a little.

The teams separated themselves. They ran things a little differently here on the island. There were five other teams going along with Dexx and Harris, not just one on a cowboy mission.

Dexx looked around the semi-familiar room.

Circled runes were carved into metal doorways and walls. Why would they need those, and what did they mean?

Dexx slipped his vest on and his earpiece in. Background comms buzzed in his ear. Other members were being told to adjust pieces of equipment, or glitches in one vest or another, and the general chatter of a large operation like this one. The chatter cut off suddenly.

"Listen up." Director Harris raised his arm for attention.

Conversations died down.

"My team and I have the lead and operational authority over the other teams. Dexx, since you're new here, yours is a reserve team. You flank the targets and take the rear guard. We'll call if we need you."

Harris's team snickered at Dexx and his team.

Fred looked relieved, and Leonard hadn't stopped twitching, but Quinn Winters had a scowl on her face. She wasn't happy to be in the back.

Dexx could use a nap. Like really.

Alwyn was probably elbow deep in sawing logs. Too bad. He could have really been helpful.

Oh. They were waiting for him. "Got it. We flank, take the rear. We wait."

There was another round of derisive looks from Harris's boys. They snapped to at a look from him.

"The rest of you know the procedure. Form up on me. Sweep and clear. We wait in a large-room clear. Move on 'go.' Got it?"

The team leaders all nodded as one.

The teams were so much better on this side of the pond. They actually had *training*. Or at least they acted like it. Dexx felt a little out of his league. He was only good as a cowboy.

Harris nodded to the techs working the portal equipment.

A wavering hole split the room. Runes lit up, and the hole steadied, the wavering becoming a sharp view into another location.

"Okay, guys," Dexx said to his team—mostly to the two newbs. "If you find yourself in a bad situation, calm your shit, point at the enemy, and shoot. Freaking out, out there won't help anyone."

Fred gave him a wide-eyed nod.

Leonard raised a cocky eyebrow.

Quinn Winters just frowned at him as if puzzled.

"If someone tries to kill you," he said, watching for their turn, "when you try to kill them right back." He didn't remember *where* he'd heard those words, but he did somehow recall that he'd used them before.

Quinn huffed a chuckle.

The teams went through at a run, magical equipment, and magic-laced bullets ready for action.

A tech held his arm out, stopping Dexx and his team. He made them wait for nearly a minute, with Fred getting more and more nervous as their wait dragged on, before releasing them.

Dexx led his team through at a quick-walk, his head on the swivel. Never rush into a new place. Rushing got people killed. So did staying stationary.

The room was dark. Well, vamps liked it dark, didn't they?

No, somehow that didn't feel right. Vampires didn't need the dark. They needed blood, but the sun didn't vaporize them like the movies always liked to portray.

Dexx held his hand out to his team. "Stay. Stay low."

Chatter from the other teams came through his earpiece loud and clear. The sweep was well underway, with no kills as of yet. Dexx leaned to Fred. "Are the raids always this easy?"

"I, um… I think so."

Quinn shook her head. "This is too easy. They should have found something."

That's what he was thinking. They'd gone in with five teams—and a fresh one—for nothing? But again, why had Dexx and a team of newbs gets brought in? Didn't make sense. Dexx made sure his mic wasn't hot. "Set up. Be alert, guys. This smells bad."

"Cut the chatter, Colt," a voice said over his earpiece. "Save the waves for the rest of us."

Quinn's eyes widened, with a flare of fear. She recovered quickly and set to watching everywhere at once.

Of course. So he couldn't disable the mics. Interesting.

Dexx made motions to the team. *Quinn, take point. Leonard, watch her six, Fred, with me. Weapons hot.*

Quinn darted out a strange, bladed weapon in her hand that looked like a half-moon blade with a handle on the straight side

Leonard stayed three steps behind. If nothing else, they moved quietly for military, not para-hunters.

They went further into the house, and the light fell even further. Then the light went completely black as blackout curtains pulled over windows.

"Lights," Dexx whispered into the dark.

"Negative, Omega team," One of the techs from command sent back. "Stay in flank position."

"Contact," Harris said over the earpiece. "Alpha team moving in."

No gunfire, but that didn't mean anything. Spells often didn't make noise.

"Are you serious?" Dexx's whisper threatened to climb to yelling. "We can't see shit down here."

"Negative, Omega team," command said. "*Stay put*. Alpha Team has contact. Catch any that come from behind the sweep teams."

Oh fuck. Contact, and they couldn't see shit. Dexx squeezed his eyes shut and pushed his anger down. When he opened them again, he could *see*—everything in sharp relief. Like a *really* good black and white TV, but his team had a sort of glow around them, like heatwaves in the desert.

Dexx made motions for Leonard to get off Quinn's tail and cover the next door.

Leonard didn't move from his spot, but his eyes bulged with his effort to see.

Dexx made motions more exaggerated with big motions to his DoDO team.

They simply ignored him.

"Hey," Dexx whispered sharply.

His three looked at him. Sort of. Their eyes were wide, but they looked past him and off to the side.

Dexx saw them just fine. What in the nine hells?

Only Quinn seemed to know where he stood and waved.

"Dexx, we can't see as good as you." Quinn put a hand to her collar and said softer, "You should know that."

How the hell would *he* know that? Except he *did* sort of. But how did *she*?

"Cut the chatter on your *team*, Dexx." Director Harris sounded less than pleased.

Even as Dexx tried to put the pieces of the new puzzle together, his super smell let him know they weren't alone.

Cold, stale inhuman smells wafted from behind them. Dexx spun and stepped around Fred.

A man and woman walked in complete calm. They didn't glow at all, not like the rest of his team. But they were dead silent—no noise from their clothes or shoes.

The woman wore a smile, but it sure wasn't friendly. Not even a little.

Fred whimpered as he looked around in the dark, clearly blind.

Dexx stood to confront the two. "Who are you?"

Fred and Leonard squawked and waved their wands toward Dexx, obviously unable to see the new paras in the room.

Quinn pulled in a breath and held it like she was waiting for something.

The man dropped his smile when he saw Dexx looking at them, obviously able to see quite well.

Okay. The enemy. Nice to know.

"Shit. It's him." The pair turned and ran out the door.

That sparked all kinds of movement.

Gunshots split the silence.

Fred, already scared, barreled into Dexx with a moan of terror. They went to the floor in a jumble.

From somewhere, a wordless tune began to rise. He felt oddly pulled to the sound. The melody was haunting and... just... so... beautiful. He could just fall into the sound forever. He would do anything for... it... to... go... on.

No, he couldn't. He wouldn't give over. He pulled away from the song.

Fred lay on the ground, not moving. Leonard, amazingly was also down, with the same stupid expression.

Quinn was backed up against the wall, scared but just fine.

Bullets and the sound of crashing walls from spells tore through the house, or building or whatever this hells begotten place this was.

Something or somebody must have broken an outside wall or window because light filled the room.

Dexx flung up an arm to shut out the suddenly stabbing light.

He pulled his arm down as his eyes adjusted oddly quickly.

The sound of the music stopped as Quinn fell to the floor.

The walls shattered as rushing figures burst through. They didn't have the warm glow his team did.

His earpiece went mad with the shouts of the other teams under attack.

He couldn't worry about them right now. He had more important things to address.

Five, six, eight, a *bunch* of paras rushed him.

No, not just paras. Vampires.

Dexx stood to face them. He had his gun out in an instant, firing.

One thing vampires were not was slow. They moved as fast as he could aim.

Dexx emptied one magazine in the time it took to pull the trigger fifteen times. He dropped the mag and slipped in the next just as the first vampire slammed him into the wall.

Dexx pulled the trigger three times, and he felt the slugs slam into the para's chest.

It fell away and didn't move. He twitched a few times, but that didn't count.

The rest of the vamps didn't even break stride. They were coming for Dexx.

Then, the world just kind of... stopped.

The vamps fell to the ground sort of frozen in place, and the following silence was almost as loud as the shooting.

Holy shit, the shooting had stopped too.

Dexx swung his pistol in wide arcs waiting for... something to happen. But the quiet wasn't broken by anything more than shadows.

Dexx looked around in the silence.

His earpiece had gone quiet too. "Base, is this you?."

No answer. Comms were dead.

Dexx patted his vest to the power supply in his vest to the recorder. One of the vamps must have destroyed the radio. Well shit. The first day on the job and his entire team wiped out.

The only one left alive again.

Fuck.

He crouched to take Fred's pulse. He might still be alive. He'd fallen over when that strange song had started. Dexx's eyebrows rose as far as they would go when he felt a pulse. Strong and steady.

He rolled Fred over, looking for blood.

He'd been sprayed when Dexx had killed the vamp, but Fred didn't seem to be leaking any. He'd fainted or something.

The rest of the team was the same way.

Dexx looked around the strangest nest clearing ever. What in the nine hells was *this?*

In the sudden silence, he heard footsteps. They made a steady clicking sound. Not hurried, not cautious. Like someone walking to announce themselves.

Dexx snapped his pistol up to the doorway.

A shadow moved through the dark and resolved into a man with a tailor-cut suit. He moved and looked like a very rich businessman type, with greying at the temples and dark piercing eyes.

"Stop." Dexx sighted his gun at the man's head. Anyone who walked in here unconcerned was a clear threat.

The man didn't even break stride, walking through the mass of stilled vampires.

Then his scent reached Dexx. "Hands where I can see 'em, *demon.*"

The man casually put his hands in the air. "I'm unarmed, but you *are* right." His voice was pure confidence. He was used to being obeyed at all times.

How the hell did some people *do* that?

"I *am* a demon, and I mean you no harm, Dexx Colt."

Shit, things just got worse. When a demon knew a person's name, that person didn't survive long.

Dexx didn't wait. He pulled the trigger. Repeatedly.

The demon never twitched, and none of the bullets came close. No surprise. If demons weren't caught off guard, the chances of killing one slimmed considerably.

"Please. I'm not here to fight. I'm here to help." The demon emphasized his words with his arms.

Classic demon ploy. Demonology one-oh-one. Assume everything they say to be a lie.

"You can help by fucking off. I know you, demon." His best hope was to stall long enough for help to arrive. He was one guy against one demon. He *might* stand a chance. When the house realized everyone on his team was down—

Wait. They weren't down. They were frozen. So, would the home office be frozen, too?

"I've been watching you for a long time. You may thank me later for helping already." He flicked his eyes to the vampires, frozen in attack positions scattered around the room.

"What did you do?"

"A simple spell to prevent them from interfering with our discussion."

"This was a trap." And the reason he'd been called to come out. But how had the demon—there was no reason to ask why. He was a demon, and with this kind of magical ability, he was…pretty up there in power.

"Probably. These aren't mine."

Dexx flicked his head to the dead vamp. "You here for the bounty?"

"I don't know about any bounty, but this one clearly did not know who he attacked. No, don't worry about him. I'll handle them. *You could* handle them easily as well, but you aren't at your full strength."

Fucking demons. They'd lie if it was easier, to tell the truth.

The demon shuffled a foot forward.

Dexx twitched his pistol. Damnit, none of the rounds were demon loads. The raid had been set up for vampires. The bastard really *had* planned this.

"If you allow, I can help you." The demon took in a deep breath and tipped his head to the side. "You aren't you, Dexx. This goes deep. I'm on your side."

Huh? "That's not how demons work. You're on *your* side and let the rest of the rabble serve you."

"Correct." The demon's shrug said *normally*. "For the

most part. You have good instincts, but not all of us think of *rabble* that way."

"*Still lying.*" Dexx clenched his jaw, trying to figure out what in the hell was going on here. This should have been over a long time ago. What the hell was that demon waiting for?

"We spoke before. You listened, then. Please try again. Trust me. If you allow, I can remove the block. It *will* hurt, but I can remove it. Enough to *help*, anyway."

Dexx pressed his gun toward the demon. It only made him *feel* better, though. "You stay back. I'll fill you full of holes."

The demon smiled. "How exactly does that work? *Full* of *holes*." He put a finger to his chin and looked away as if he really considered how that made sense. He put his hand down and looked at Dexx intently. "If I wanted you or anyone else here dead, you couldn't stop me. Your gun isn't, as they say, loaded for bear. In fact, none of you here can hurt me if I'm prepared. I'm here on good faith, *Shedim*. I'm looking for your help, not a fight."

The thing *actually* looked sincere.

But there was that word again.

"Why do you call me that?" Dexx backed up a step.

"It is who you are, but." The demon clamped his lips shut, closing his eyes for a moment, before sighing. "If you cannot, believe me, I will go in peace. And maybe the next time we meet, you will listen to a little more. After all, trust is not built in a day, and my kind have done little to gain it. There is one demon I know you trust."

Who the hell was that?

"I want to be the second."

Maybe there was a reason Dexx had lost his memories. "What demon? I don't trust any of you. Never have."

"You do, though. My name is Furiel. And I want your protection. As a show of good faith, I offer some aid to you."

Oh, this couldn't be good.

"I know some about what happened, and I can reverse a little. I won't lie, the process will be painful, but in the end, you will thank me."

Dexx shook his head. "I will owe you nothing."

"Then do not think of this as a debt favor. I will take this *rabble* with me. They'll think twice before trying to collect on that bounty." Furiel raised two fingers and flicked them. Then, he disappeared. Along with the vampires. Except for the dead one still at Dexx's feet.

"What the hell just happened?"

14

———————

Director Harris stood over Dexx, fists planted hard to the wood of his messy desk. "You turned off your comms *again*. The American branch said you did that as a matter of course." He pushed off the desk and circled back to his chair.

Dexx didn't really want to play. "No. I didn't. Comms went dead in the middle of the sweep. Most likely, when everything froze."

"There wasn't a freeze in time. No one *lost* time. Nobody else had a failure, and then *your* comms came back online. Explain *that*."

"Well, I was standing. And like I said. I got rushed, killed one, and then..." He knew he needed to tell them about his conversation with the demon, but he stopped himself. "Time seemed to stand still for a bit, and then it came back on, and all the vamps disappeared. That's it."

No one understood what had happened, and there were no theories still. According to the other agents, Dexx's comms had gone off-line, and then the vampires they had been chasing had blinked out of existence. That's what their equipment had recorded as well. The single vampire that had been killed in the entire nest had been Dexx's kill. No injuries and no deaths on their side.

Dexx felt better since the encounter somehow, though. Okay, so not *better,* but he felt better about his decision to come to England.

He still felt like something was missing, and that feeling had ratcheted up a bit. Something *was* missing, but he couldn't point at it. He felt like it was *right there,* and if he thought hard enough, he'd remember what that thing was.

"I don't know what to tell you." Mostly because they didn't believe his story anyway.

Harris flopped down into his seat. "You come here, bollucksing up every rule we have, and you smirk? I ought to send you home today."

"That *is* an option." And one Dexx was okay with now. "But also ask yourself why I was called in there in the first place. Just go into town. Mandated to take three newbs whom I'd never met into the field. Where'd that decision flow down from? No one with a brain, obviously. Or maybe someone with an agenda."

Harris's expression went sharp as he thought about that.

"And if it was an agenda, what was it?"

Harris shook his head and met Dexx's gaze without an answer.

Dexx slapped his palms on the arms of the chair and pushed up. "I'm tired, and I'm going to bed. I haven't slept in oh, a whole *bunch* of hours. I'm taking a nap until I'm ready to get up. Then I'm going to eat some of the fabulous cuisine of this island. But not haggis. I'm not doing haggis. I learned that one in *Highlander.*"

Harris pressed two fingers to his forehead. When he spoke, his voice was quiet and so forced he may as well have shouted. "Get the fuck out of my office. After you rest, I want you back here so you can start training."

Dexx turned and headed to the door with a *very* satisfying grin. Oh yes, he felt a shit-ton better. "Hey, boss, you want your door closed?" He hung on the doorway, smirking back at Director Harris.

"Get out!" Harris roared at Dexx's retreating head.

Dexx reached in and pulled the door shut. Yeah, the man probably needed time to cool off.

So, if the new place was mostly the same as the house in Montana, his old room would have been down the corridor second from where he stood right now. If he could find a guidance counselor or something, then he could just have them print off the map. Of course, that was high school, and this was... well, it wasn't high school.

He turned down the corridor that should have led to individual sleeping quarters.

On his next turn, however, he hadn't made it to the dorms.

This was more like a museum. Or a trophy room.

The room held things just like a museum might, some in large dioramas, and others on pedestals in glass cases. These things were just like the trinkets in the states, but there were hundreds, maybe thousands, if the room was big enough.

Dexx whistled softly through his teeth. He spoke in his best library voice. "Now, *this* is interesting." He hadn't seen any signs to stay out, but he may have used up all his luck for the day. He slipped further into the room and away from the door.

DoDO probably had this room under constant surveillance too, but just looking couldn't hurt that bad.

Swords dominated a large section all to themselves. Some were corroded and pitted. Others shone brightly in the slightly dimmed light. Almost too brightly. Were those magical in nature?

Dexx sniffed the air. Dry, cold, treated. The room had a sanitary smell with no organics. The unnaturalness bit at his nose like the beginnings of illness.

If the room hadn't been full of cool shit, he'd have left. But the displays overpowered the artificial air.

The next section had knives instead of swords. Those had a more practical application in a *civilized society*. Easier to conceal, but only up close and personal. They worked on paras pretty well.

The knife section eventually led to an area that seemed to be trinkets. One looked like a golden disc with an offset red gem. Could that be Egyptian? The intricate carving held Dexx's attention for a minute, but he moved on.

Most everything in each display case looked to be from the same time period or from the same area. Or whatever. They looked like they belonged to a set.

As Dexx passed through the collection, the pieces began to look... less refined. Detail became rough and primitive.

One of the objects was a shallow bowl made of a tan stone. Maybe. The stone had a large crack, nearly broken in two, and the crack was blackened along the edges like it was charred from the fire. Markings surrounded the rim.

That thing looked familiar. His fingers brushed against the stone in his pocket. Dollars to doughnuts, the two would line up perfectly except the crack.

Dexx tapped the glass lightly with a knuckle.

The thud told him everything he needed to know. The glass was too thick to smash or pick up without trouble.

Moving along, the novelty of the exhibit wore off. He moved faster through the room, glancing quickly at each before moving to the next. He almost left after he reached the end of the aisle, but he turned around and froze.

Something caught his eye, a small figurine.

Like the stone in his pocket, the stone figurine made his hands twitch.

The little carving almost unrecognizable was *his*. How? He didn't know, and he didn't really care.

Dexx bent down to inspect it closer.

The stone looked more like a child had mushed the form from clay, but a few of the details jumped out. Small bulges resembled a cat. Small specks of green almost colored the grey stone into an overall dark green color, but not quite. Of course, the stone could have been formed in a riverbed with water flowing over it for, say, a million years, but the familiarity and ownership didn't fade.

The rock was *his*.

How could that thing be his? It had to be made in the Stone Age or something.

Dexx almost pressed his nose against the glass. "What the hell are you?"

"It's something from a time long past."

Dexx snapped up and turned so fast his back twinged in pain.

A bowed little man with a white cape and cap resting heavily on a cane stood swinging looks between the stone and Dexx. The small smile and round little body made him look more than a bit grandfatherly.

"You scared the shiii—" Dexx trailed off before he completely embarrassed himself.

White cape. White beanie with no practical purpose. Cane.

"Um, sorry." He was obviously someone high up. Maybe? Probably *not* the janitor.

The old man chuckled in a soft, easy way. "Be at ease, my child." His soft accent was… Italian. Or German. Was that a soft French accent in there too?

"You're not running around here in body armor and tactical magick gear."

The old man chuckled again. "Too true. But if I might make the observation, you are not either."

Dexx bobbed his head. "Just got off the clock. Headed toward my bunk and got lost. So, what is this place?"

"This is a depository. Dangerous, unique, and important things find their way here."

Dexx wrinkled his nose. "Why?" Outside of the swords, most everything there was just a collection of interesting— the word slipped away— stuff. "So, this is stuff made by paras?"

"Some. Others are things we don't understand, and more are dangerous items we've been able to secure from the paras."

"Huh. Okay. Swords, sure. Knives, maybe. Gold carvings? That sure fits the bill for interesting, but a lot of this shi— stuff is rock. Why keep that?"

"Because there's always something hidden beneath the surface, isn't there, Mr. Colt?"

Well, fuck. The old man knew his name. "Sorry." He held out his hand. "Dexx Colt. And you are?"

The old man looked sad for a moment as he considered Dexx's hand, then waved him off. "Cardinal Bussemi. You may address me as cardinal, or Immanence, or Vicar Bussemi, if you prefer."

The stone in Dexx's pocket spread waves of warmth through him. Strange. Add one more question to the immense pile. The warmth faded as soon as the cardinal put his hand back to the cane.

Was that a warning? "Do I have to kiss your hand or something?"

"Nothing so formal, unless you're planning to enter the diocese?"

"No. I was headed to my bunk, then get some chow after a long nap. Jetlag."

Cardinal Bussemi chuckled the soft laugh again. "No, my son. Are you called to follow God as a member of the church leadership?"

Dexx felt like he'd answered that question already. "Still nope. That sounds like a lot of paperwork, and I don't do that."

"You are a very interesting man, Mr. Colt. I hope to have more words with you in the future." He smiled an odd toothy grin.

He looked familiar—something recent and very long ago.

"Oh, sorry if I kept you from… your appointed rounds." That sounded pretty formal, appointed rounds. Right?

"You're no trouble, but I *do* have to say that this area is not restricted exactly, but it is not for the casual pedestrian."

"Oh, I wouldn't say I'm casual—" Dexx nodded and shook his head at the same time. "No, I'm totally casual."

"Then peace be on you, son, today, and your days going forward."

Dexx nodded. "You too, padre." He caught the cardinal in the beginnings of a frown before he spun on his heel and left the rooms of all the neat stuff. The *curios.*

As the room receded behind him, he slipped his hand into his pocket. He could *feel* the shapes on the rock. Little runes maybe. They looked *exactly* like the picto-word things on that tiny bowl-rock all blackened and cracked almost in half.

After getting lost a few more times and expressing some supreme self-control, Dexx found his room. A single bed tucked against a wall with a small counter. A mirror above a sink made up a bit less than half the room. His duffel sat on the floor by his bed.

Not spacious by any means, but better than the cramped cell in the states.

Maybe this really *was* the dream slot. Working up to director. Dexx allowed himself a minute to daydream.

Then the time daydream was over. Now that he'd stopped moving, exhaustion rolled over him.

He flopped down on his bed. Waves of strangeness washed over him. Sleep pulled him under.

Dexx sat up in his bed. He'd been asleep with the light on. He dug his phone out of his pocket and checked the time.

Only five minutes had passed since his head had hit the pillow.

Well fuck. He stood and went to the sink to splash some water on his face.

He looked in the mirror to pull a towel from the rack and paused, the water still dripping.

Something glowed in the mirror. Two bright, green specks behind the glass came closer, becoming defined. They looked like... eyes? He couldn't see well enough. He brought his face closer to the mirror, attempting to see the bright dots.

The mirror exploded outward, showering Dexx with shards and impossibly large teeth, and a snarling mouth crashed through.

A woman leapt out of nowhere, her hands extending into twin fists of darkness. She shielded him from the blast and reached out with one of those inky hands and yanked at the eyes, shoving them into her chest where they disappeared.

Wind tore through the room as she turned to him, her dark brown hair flying around her face. Her lips moved, but he couldn't hear her. The black hands receded back to her body, pieces of mirror dancing in the air, caught up in her maelstrom.

Her face screwed up in concentration as she balled her hands into fists at her sides and yelled, "Come back to me, Dexx!" in a tone that echoed with aching familiarity.

Then she shattered into a silver mist that shook him.

Dexx jerked up in his darkened bedroom. The automatic light had shut off. For just an instant, he saw his room in relief as if he had on night vision goggles.

It had been a dream. Just a dream. He fell back and went back to sleep. But the nightmares of being hunted returned and repeated.

But the haunting woman whose face twisted his heart didn't return to him.

15

J ust three days into the new job, and Dexx had managed to go through some of the training modules for general para hunting. Snooze-fest. Seriously. It was just going through a bunch of modules on a computer and watching Harris do a ton of paperwork while glaring.

In short, they sucked. Sucked so bad, in fact, that how any of the teams *ever* survived an encounter was a miracle all by itself. Maybe having the cardinal praying for them every day had a positive effect. Maybe the guy had some magick or something. Like, he could have been a wizard. Right?

However, the meeting with the cardinal did open his eyes to a few things. The church's fingers stirred a lot of DoDO pots.

No engagements here, restrictions on other things over there, and just general over-management of the process. Walking a request all the way up the line instead of the field team making decisions. Well, Dexx would have to change that. Like yesterday. He'd never had anyone enforce that level of bureaucratic red tape on him before. Not even Pa—

The name blipped right out of his head, along with an overwhelming feeling of loss.

Harris's eyes popped out when Dexx asked for a Sharpie. A fat one with a wide tip. His face went red, and that vein throbbed when Dexx marked out huge sections of the hard-copy manuals. They were all on the computer too, so his devastation of the sucky parts wasn't *actually* gone, but *this* was going to be Dexx's bible.

Chow was unbelievably slow in coming, and when the time came, Dexx dragged himself to the cafeteria, looking for anything to distract him.

Alwyn had found places, more or less, making the two seats claimed by the pair of them. No assigned seating, but somehow everyone separated themselves to do just that.

"Thanks, bud." Dexx set his tray down and flopped into the seat across from Alwyn. I'm pretty much starving after doing all that paperwork shit." A vague conversation flitted through his memories to quiet to actually recall.

Alwyn laughed. "Coloring in the manual isn't paperwork."

…adding color…

Okay. This was starting to get strange. Were his memories coming back? Had Furiel managed to do something? Was that the "help" he'd offered?

"A toddler could do that."

Dexx gave him a crooked smile at the joke, but that struck him a little strange. For just a second, he had the thought that he should have one—a toddler.

Not that he should *make* one, but that he *already had one.*

He shoveled a large bite of something that looked like potatoes into his mouth. Wouldn't that be something he'd remember?

Too much strange shit had been going on the last week, even before his plane ride to the *Great British Isle*. Dreams were too vivid, even if he couldn't remember some of the better ones. The nightmares? Well, *those* tended to be epic.

The most common was the thing hunting him. No matter where his dreams took him, the thing always showed up, crashing through a wall or mirror, or anything that broke. But who was the woman who occasionally showed? And why did he have this lingering ache inside him when he recalled her?

Dexx's neck hairs tingled. Since the nightmares had started, he had the feeling of someone watching him. All the time. Maybe a few someones.

Dexx scanned the room as innocently as possible. Someone *was* watching—him and Alwyn.

Quinn Winters held a tray in her hands, staring right at Dexx. When she got caught staring, she headed toward their table. "Mind if I join you?" Her smile was the uninviting sort like if he refused, he might not survive lunch.

"It's a free country." Dexx tipped his head toward an empty seat. Then he leaned to Alwyn. "It *is* a free country, right?"

Alwyn laughed through a mouthful of food. "Yeah, it's as free as yours. Maybe a bit more."

Dexx exaggerated a nod to Quinn. "Yes. It's a free country. You may sit down if you want."

Quinn sat down next to Alwyn, playing with her food and humming under her breath.

Alwyn shoveled his food in his mouth and smiled stupidly at Dexx, bits of the mash on his lips. He managed to swallow and looked down at his empty plate. "I think I want more."

What was wrong with him? He looked drunk. "Wow, did you even taste any?"

Alwyn stood up with his tray and left.

"He sure seems to like the food." Quinn daintily took her first bite.

"Yeah. He kinda does. He talked about the food here the

entire flight over nonstop." He jabbed a finger toward her. "Winters, right? On my team on the first day."

"I am." She smiled again, a *very* inviting smile. "Though, you *could* call me Quinn."

He already had inside his head, but he couldn't quite grasp if this was more of a military operation or civilian.

"What brings you here to England?"

Dexx shrugged. "Plane. They couldn't use the transporter."

She laughed softly. "You don't really seem the *team* type. Why are you here?"

If *that* didn't sound like an interrogation-like question, he'd never heard one. "They needed a deputy director for training. I said, yes."

"That's it? No ties to another organization, no—" Quinn twirled her fork in the air searching for her next word "—search for anyone. Maybe missing?"

Dexx scooted on the seat, leaning toward her. "Are *you* looking for someone?" He lowered his voice, looking around the chow hall. "Someone who might be hiding here?"

She shook her head slowly, studying him carefully. "No." She paused before she spoke. "Do you have the feeling you know me?"

Yes, but he wasn't quite sure what was going on inside his head. "Does that one work often?" Dexx folded his arms on the table.

"I don't need pick up lines. Will you answer, please?" She wasn't really asking.

"You're not overly familiar to me. Maybe a little on that first day... but we just met a few days ago. You seem competent, and I'm looking forward to having you on my team to really assess your skills." DoDO would have to do a better job picking their spies. Quinn used a hammer instead of a knife. Not very good with the sneaky interrogation thing.

Still, he couldn't be sure whether she'd tried to pick him up or not. She definitely had certain assets going for her. Maybe they *could* find a...

Dexx looked up, and Quinn was gone. So were most of the people who had been there when she sat down.

Nine hells. Now he had to worry about *blackouts* and *lost time?* Ever since his accident, things had been spiraling out of control. His new abilities weren't worth all of this.

Okay. Maybe a little.

Dexx took his tray back to the trash and tapped the rest of the food in the bin, setting it on the dirty pile. He sighed.

His path back to his office, the little cell with a window in the door, took him right by the artifact room.

The curios— great word, that— kept calling him back. Not *all* of them. Just the one, really. Maybe two.

Several times since he'd first found the museum, there'd been guards at the door.

Cardinal Bussemi had said it wasn't out of bounds, but it wasn't *in bounds* either. So, let the games begin.

Dexx inhaled deeply, tasting the air for people. There happened to be a *lot* of scents, and most of them were heavy with food. Either he was going to the dorms or on a mission even though things had been uncommonly quiet after his first day.

Dexx entered like he had an invitation. No stopping, no looking to see if anyone watched. Those would be dead give-aways that he shouldn't be there.

Once inside, he passed the rows and rows of other objects, closing in on the single piece that interested him.

He almost missed the scent just before he saw the man. The cardinal was here too, and he was looking at the figure of the cat-thing.

Shit. Double shit.

A good reason for no guards on the doors. The guard was *inside* the room.

Dexx slowed but didn't stop. He'd have to spin this in his favor. "Cardinal. I'd hoped I wouldn't have to shoo you out of here again." He put a sideways grin on his face and clasped his hands behind him. Best to seem less threatening. The cardinal was a tiny man, after all.

"Young Mr. Colt. We *do* seem to find one another in the oddest place." Bussemi had a grandfatherly smile of his own. He deep red robes swished around him as he leaned on his cane with both hands. "It's not often that anyone speaks to me without… reverence."

"Like hero-worship?" The cardinal's scent lacked a few of the markers Dexx generally associated with people. He *could* be extra clean, but that didn't fit. More like he'd hidden a few. But how? Not even demons could hide from his nose.

Wait. How did he *know* that?

Bussemi's smile turned a little sad. "Something like that, yes. I find you to be—" His smile slipped a fraction and returned easily. "—a breath of fresh air. Come. Talk with me." He waved a frail hand to Dexx, motioning him forward.

A breath of fresh air, huh? "I'll probably have to work on that. Most people see me as a trial. Penance for horrible deeds."

Bussemi chuckled. "Quite so, young man. I've received a number of complaints. But you're too important to let go."

That wasn't ominous. Nope, not at *all*. Dexx's brows climbed almost to his hairline, but Bussemi turned back to the figurine.

"Tell me, what do you see when you look at this piece, here?" He lifted his frail hand to the glass case.

The stone in his pocket radiated a calming warmth. And something else. The room around him wavered slightly like heat waves rising from a hot blacktop road. If only Dexx understood what that meant.

"I'm not really sure what you're looking for. I couldn't tell you what any of this is, outside of being old. I think."

The cardinal chuckled again, and Dexx felt pressure on him. Like a drafty room during a hard wind.

Shit. The old man was up to something and looking for a specific answer. How in the *hell* was he supposed to know what the man wanted?

The pressure increased, calling Dexx to answer. The stone didn't stop him from the compulsion, but it *did* let him answer in his own way. "I see me..." In *his own* way. So, like a smartass. "Shaking hands with Dumbledore. I've won the House Cup."

Bussemi's eyes sharpened on Dexx for a moment. "Is that a game you youngsters play, House Cup?"

"No, it's from a movie— never mind. I don't understand what you want, cardinal." Dexx really didn't, but if he could just get a read on the old man, he could fake it. Probably.

"You know of Heaven and Hell, don't you?" Bussemi leaned on his cane with both hands again.

"Yeah." Dexx wasn't a complete idiot.

"The eternal souls of man and woman have a destination after this mortal coil is thrown off. One is a place of eternal joy. Of exploration and pursuits far beyond the imaginings of any living person. The other is a place of torment. Pain and suffering. Fear and negativity. The chosen, and those who answer the call, go to Heaven. The rest... don't."

So, a boring history that everyone knew. Dexx fought off a yawn.

"But there are a few who don't follow this path. They are stuck on the earthly realm to *repeat* this life. Over and over again. Certain things bind them to the terra and never let go."

Okay. That was *marginally* interesting. "And you're saying that's a soul stone? Like the Avengers movies?" Dexx wrinkled his upper lip.

"Exactly that. They had to get the idea from somewhere. They have no original ideas. Even you should know that."

"Oh. Yeah, after they remade *Ghostbusters*, it's just a remake of the same old shit." Dexx knew the cardinal was hinting at something deeper, but Dexx was getting frustrated with this conversation. So far, it wasn't super illuminating.

The cardinal crushed his lips together in an old man moment of interruption but went on. "Indeed. Through forces we don't understand, these few individuals—" He bit off that word like it was an insult. "—have sidestepped the natural order and have cheated their fate. Men shouldn't sidestep their destiny. I won't let them."

Power trip much? Dexx blinked several times.

The rock in his pocket sent a sharp wave of heat into him. A warning? He changed his impulse response.

"How many have done this?" Dexx looked up from the rock to the red-robed man.

"That's not the ordinary question people ask after they hear what one of these does."

They were just stones that kept a soul there. Why wouldn't that be a normal question? "Well, since you think this is a soul stone, I'd think it'd be important to know how many recycled people I'm dealing with, don't you?" And if they were dangerous, though he didn't *think* they would be. The cardinal made it sound like the worst thing they'd done was to fall out of the herd mentality. Dexx couldn't blame them for that. He wasn't much of a pack animal as it was.

"Perhaps." The cardinal speared him with a look. Not a friendly one. "These stones are *kadu*. They are vessels for a resting soul and release them at intervals to be reborn into the world."

Oh, spooky. No. Not even a little. "And how many are there?"

"Very few," the cardinal finally answered.

"Why?" Why were they needed for rebirth when there were entire religions centered around that belief? Why did this cardinal believe they were bad? Because he clearly did. And why was he so focused on this one?

"These are not well-understood, but the threat they pose to the world is very real." The cardinal's voice quavered. Fear?

No. Dexx finally caught a scent. Anger. Layers of pure hatred. Interesting. Maybe it was just the soul attached to this one *kadu*. So, then the question was, who did this one belong to? "Then break it. Crush it and be done with it."

The grandfatherly smile came back. "You're a bright boy, I'm sure. How do you crush something that diamonds can't scratch? Few have the power to touch them."

"Woah. That's *hard*."

"That it is. They *are,* however, vulnerable for a very short period of time, when the soul is released and when it is taken back into the *kadu*."

Creepy. "How do you know when that is?" A sick feeling crept through Dexx's belly.

"The easiest way is to find its owner and kill them. When the soul re-enters the *kadu*, smash it with magick." The cardinal's gaze went to the broken bowl, scorched along the crack.

Dexx's insides quivered. A few pieces fell into place. "And how do you find an owner?"

"We don't." The cardinal's voice was heavy with threat. "They usually find the *kadu*. It *calls* to them."

Oh, shit. One plus one. Carry the one. Fuck. Dexx'd been drawn to this one. Well... crap.

"But this one right here is even more special."

"Really." Dexx crossed his arms, feeling *very* uncomfortable. "Why?"

"Because this one was found in a nest of demons. It's powerful. Very powerful. The legend is that it was the first-ever to be made. This one who hunted the demons. Maybe even frightened them."

That sounded a little too like a *Buffy* reference. "Why would demons have it?" Dexx fought the urge to reach out and touch the glass. He wanted the figurine in his hands, but by collecting it, by claiming it, he'd be signing his death warrant. What in the *hell* did this *mean*?

"They could have been guarding it for a master."

Hunter turned master? Probably not. They might have been watching it.

Bussemi's eyes went wild for a moment like he wanted to clutch the figurine too.

Thoughts of Gollum raced through Dexx's head, but the cardinal wasn't some twisted hobbit. He was a man of the cloth. Right. Did that mean anything? J.R.R. Tolkien had to have been influenced by something to write the story of the walking hobbit. *My precious,* echoed between his ears just looking at Bussemi. "A master what?"

"A very powerful para. If we could destroy the *kadu,* we would have. This one is very dangerous. Dangerous to humans and anything else it comes close to."

And if this thing called to Dexx, that meant Bussemi was talking about him being the very powerful para.

Dexx smelled the lies. Like an overpowering perfume on a hooker. "*We're* close to it. Aren't we in danger or something?" Demons holding something like that didn't have to be servants. They could be waiting like DoDO to destroy it themselves when the hunter returned.

What had Dexx been called? *Shedim* something or other? Demon Hunter? Fuck. Fuckfuckfuckfuck.

"Nonsense. The thing *itself* doesn't have power, but it holds the power of the para inside and waits for the para to be called to walk the earth again."

"Is there a soul in there now? Maybe someone could—"

Bussemi jerked his head up, cutting him off. "This vessel is empty. We could not kill the para before it escaped. We did not have it then, but we know now." The cardinal rubbed the top of his hand on the cane with the other. "Oh, yes, we do now."

"Empty is good, right?" Yeah, except that could mean that *Dexx* with the soul that should have been in that *kadu*. Maybe that was the "accident?" Some hidden para abilities awakening?

And if that was the case, then Dexx was in some serious shit-tastic trouble sitting in the middle of DoDO like it was fucking nothing.

"I would like to extend you an invitation—" Bussemi's calm exterior settled over his face like a mask "—to meet me in here every other day to discuss these vessels and what we might do about the paras who use them to sow fear and death."

Dexx's talisman in his pocket sent warmth and warnings surging through him, even as he felt a spell settle over him, and a compulsion to agree. Dexx rubbed at his chin, hiding the sudden onslaught of conflicting effects. "I'm only a deputy of training. Are you *sure* I'm the guy you want to bounce ideas with?"

"You are the *only* one I can talk to about this." Bussemi's light gaze turned dark. "You have the gift I've been looking for."

Oh, fuck...a...duck. He opened his mouth to tell Bussemi to go to hell, but he couldn't finish.

The spell tightened around him.

The stone burned hotter, vaporizing it like glowing metal

in water.

He felt, or maybe closer to, *saw* the spell's intention. To make him feel better about making time to talk with the cardinal.

Okay. He could fake that if he completely *ignored* how he knew that. Dexx let a grin slip into place. "Yeah. Sure." Exactly what "gift" was Busemmi looking for? Dexx picked up with his false excitement. "Yeah, that'd be excellent. Then we can get to the bottom of what these things are and who this person might be. I bet we could find out a lot. Yeah." Dexx drew out his final word, whimsically. Like he already saw the future and how much fun he was bound to have.

"Then I shall see you in two days." The cardinal gave Dexx his grandfatherly smile that smelled more like the fox guarding the henhouse, and tottered off, leaving Dexx to stare at the small figurine.

He half lifted his hand to the glass but stopped short. The urge to leave snuck up and hit him hard. His spidey sense went crazy. He had to leave, like now.

Outside in the corridor, the feeling tapered off, but another one was ready to fill in. Loss. Something so very close and very distant.

Dexx spun on his heel, away from his office, heading back for his dorm.

Two DoDO's walking in front of him split apart down separate halls like they'd reversed polarity, at the next intersecting hallway.

That was weird.

As he rounded a corner to his room, he met Quinn just as she held up her hand to knock on his door. She snapped her hand down when she saw Dexx.

What now? "How're things?"

She didn't say anything at first. "How do you like karaoke?"

1 6

―――――――――

The problem with hangovers is a tendency to forget how the night before had gone.

Dexx crushed his eyelids together from the stabbing sunlight. His head banged gongs and pounded in time to chaos. Or maybe his heartbeat.

And the noise. The noise, noise, noisenoisenoise. He almost grinned for the mind-recording of the Grinch, but his headed pounded too hard. For *anyone*.

The stink of too many people too close wrinkled his nose.

The sound of soft footsteps rang in his hears as gravel poured from an excavator bucket.

A round, hard thing poked him in the ribs. Hard.

He tried to move, groan, anything, but he didn't have control over his body. Except for his eyes, and those were starting to see spots behind his eyelids.

The poke came again, harder, and this time several more pokes followed.

"Hey, you can't sleep here. I'll run you in for indecent exposure." The thick British accent belonged to a man.

He smelled thick coffee and something else. He'd doused

164

himself in some cover smell to hide the other smell, but all that did was make two overpowering odors.

Another poke and this one made the last three pokes seem like gentle prods.

Dexx flinched hard enough to sit up.

That was a mistake. His head *just* about fell off his shoulders.

"What the hell—" He almost finished his *scathing* retort, but the pain cut him off.

Alwyn was going to die.

Then, what he heard and smelled… and felt through his eyelids clicked.

He wasn't *in* his dorm. He wasn't *at* the house. And he wasn't *in* his clothes.

"Fuck."

The man was a cop. A bobby? He wore a bright yellow vest over cop gear— bobby gear?— whatever, and a billy club in his hand poised for another poke.

"Stop with the stick." There were a lot of *other* things he probably should have said, like maybe ask for clothes or where he was, but the stick seemed most threatening at the moment.

"Next time you get buggered up, take some mates with you to make sure you get back to the flat in the right order."

Dexx picked a few words out of the gathered crowd, but nothing strung together. His head still pounded too hard for much sense to be made of anything they said. Their cell phones were clear as a bell, though. He would soon be an internet sensation.

"I—" He was going to say he would, but then things started to come back. He'd never made it to the pub with Quinn. Or *any* drinking place. She'd taken him to a tattoo parlor. Got a tattoo across his— he looked down at his chest. Brand new ink in the shapes he'd seen on the rock was in black and gold from one shoulder to the other across his chest.

Then he'd blacked out—sort of.

"I have to go." Dexx smiled apologetically up at the bobby.

The cop shook his head. "Changed my mind. You'll have to come with me." He pulled the radio mic close to his mouth and clicked the transmit key.

Dexx didn't even wait. He bounced up and ran fast. He ran like that para back in the states had. A blur so fast, Bigfoot was a sharp picture in comparison.

While running was great, even as his head began to settle, he had *no* idea where he was. England, sure, but he needed a little more info to get back to the house. Last time he'd checked, England was like a state. Rather big.

He skidded to a halt in front of a retail clothing store. He ripped the door open so fast the window threatened to shatter.

So many weird things were happening too close together. The accident, the paras, the promotion, the cardinal, the new ink, just... *all* of it.

Cub.

Dexx fell to his knees beside a pants rack in the shop.

His head *had* started to feel almost normal during his sprint, but it rang sharply with the voice.

A deep and rich female voice. Like the most confident and capable woman he'd ever heard. Not sultry, or young, or... *fuck!*

He was going crazy, and he wasn't even in his own country. Maybe they had better health care over here. At least, that's what all the liberals said.

Feet padded through the shop. Probably to investigate all the commotion.

Dexx slipped into the center of a circular rack and

squatted on the lower brace. He should be properly concealed. Hell, if thousands of kids can hide from moms all over the world in these, he should be able to—

A face poked through clothes, a youngish girl with straight blonde bangs smiled at him. "Naked is good. The problem is where to keep yer money."

Dexx coughed and smiled at the same time. He pulled his brows up. "Oops?"

The door opened again. This time the bell dinged to announce a customer. The face pulled from the rack.

"Good day, officer. Can I help ye with something?"

"Right. I'm looking for a naked man."

"We don't do that here. But there's a pub just down the way—"

Dexx clenched his jaws together.

"No, not like that. He was in the park sleeping naked as a jaybird."

"You weren't hoping to ring him up, were ye? We *could* set ye up in something he might find attractive on ye, but he still might not swing that way."

The man went into full bluster. "I'm following a man I caught sleeping under a tree. Going to take him in for questioning. That sort of thing is not to be tolerated. Free country an' all, but the kids. Shouldn't see that. Bad example and all."

"Oh." The woman drew the word out as she'd finally realized the cop wasn't looking for a man-lover. "Well, I think if he's running, yer falling behind. He's nae here."

"Right. Thank you." The cop's feet turned around and headed out. The doorbell rang, and the door shut behind him.

The girl's face reappeared in Dexx's space. "Get a little tipsy last night?"

"Not even close. I got a tattoo."

Her smile turned into a thoughtful frown. "Never heard that one before."

"Look, can I—" Dexx lifted his eyes to the clothes around him.

"Aye, but I'm gonna to get a good look at ye first." Her eyes took him in hungrily. "Don't get too many Yanks in here, and ye look positively delicious. Come out." The face disappeared, then a hand appeared and beckoned to Dexx.

He drew in a deep breath and released it slow. Dammit, all to nine hells. He *wasn't* that shy, but he wasn't made for public display either.

The hand beckoned again.

Dexx stepped off the rack and took her hand. On the other side, Dexx stood in front of *two* women. They looked like they could be a mirror. They were young and pretty with fabulously round hips covered by pleated skirts.

"What do ye think, sister?" the girl who found Dexx asked the other woman.

Obviously, a sibling.

"Don't know. Have him turn 'round." The other woman had slightly longer hair, and the tips were frosted a light blue.

Dexx stood in front of the pair with his hands covering his junk. They might be a little more easygoing about nudity in this country, but... "Can you just point me to the back door? I'll be fine after that."

"Not so fast, strange-man-who-came-into-our-shop-naked-running-from-the-bobbies," the second sister said. "Lift yer arms and give us a spin. Ye Yanks are a bit prudish, and we want a good look. Never seen one quite like ye before."

Dexx paused in the middle of lifting his hands, then put them back in front of his giblets. "One like me?"

The two sisters spoke to themselves, ignoring Dexx. "Quite pretty, don't ye think?"

The first one motioned for Dexx to lift his arms and turn. "Yes, but the colors. Like he's repressed or something. That's not a boy. That's female."

What were they talking about? "Hey, totally a boy. I'm showing you." Dexx looked over his shoulder as he slow-spun.

"But the pairing," the Blue Tips said. "It's… ancient. What's yer name, strange man?"

He stepped sideways to the women. "Dexx. Dexx Colt. Can I have some clothes now?"

"I am Bruna," the first one said. "And this is m' twin, Doxy. But yer name isn't that. Turn front. We want to see somethin'."

"You already got a show. Can I have some clothes or a door? And yeah. *Dexx Colt* live and in person. And chilled."

"Stand front," Bruna said, with a finger lightly across her upper lip.

Their eyes widened considerably as Dexx faced them.

He blew out a breath. "Satisfied? Clothes?"

Bruna took two steps forward and placed a hand gently on the back of his shoulder and the other flat on his chest. She closed her eyes and mumbled in a different language.

Doxy raised her arms out to roughly shoulder height, palms up, and mumbled along with her sister.

The sisters were crazy. Or were they?

Images overlapped the inside of the store—faint shadowy things in green hues. Nothing had substantial weight, but the shadows moved. He remembered those things. Well, sort of. The memories played in his head along with the shadows he saw, but he really couldn't recall any of it.

Last night with Quinn came back sharply, though. She'd asked if he liked karaoke and didn't wait for a response. She'd just turned him by the shoulders and pushed.

They'd walked from the house and into the streets of

London and had hailed a cab. Or Uber. That all happened too fast.

Then Quinn told the driver where to go.

They wound up at a hole-in-the-wall place, but completely devoid of karaoke. That was fine since Dexx didn't sing.

It was really a tattoo shop. He'd blindly followed Quinn as she hummed a tune.

Once inside, she'd pulled a drawing out for the guy and said Dexx wanted it.

He wasn't opposed to ink since he already had them crawling up his arms to repel demon possession.

Something about the tats had drawn him to the chair. To wait.

The wait didn't take long. Because he'd blacked out... kind of. The night had turned into a blur of its own, and everything after the first couple minutes of ink just wasn't there.

"Strange man, Dexx. Do ye know who ye are?" Bruna trailed her finger down his chest to rest just above his navel.

"Pretty sure I *told* you who I am." Dexx tried to pull away from the women, but he couldn't even twitch.

"Ye told us yer name. But ye don't know who ye *are.*" Doxy Blue Tips swayed with her hands still raised.

"Then, who am I?" Rules for engaging crazy women who could root men in place were simple. Cooperate. Comply. Maybe live to talk about it later.

"Yer not yoo. And you're more than yoo. Yer older than time, and younger than man. You have a beast locked inside ye. Yer the beast."

"Well, that certainly cleared things up. Can I go now?" Clothes could wait. Putting the crazies behind him jumped to the top spot.

"The magick is too powerful. We can see ye, but we can't free ye."

"You're paras, aren't you? Mages?" Dexx squeaked the last question as Bruna's hand went a bit lower.

"Mages, no. We're witches." Bruna looked into Dexx's eyes and smiled. It was the same one she wore when she'd found him, but it seemed a little... less humored.

"Careful, sister. He's taken." Doxy *sounded* worried, but in moments, she was molesting Dexx just like her sister was, running her hands over his chest and back. They never quite reached any sensitive bits, though.

Dexx'd never *been* in a situation like this. Dreamed of it? Yeah, sure. Had he been here? Uh, no. He was more than a bit uncomfortable. "Wait. What? Taken by what, who?"

"We canna say," Doxy said with a sad sigh. "But we can certainly give ye the aid ye need. Don't worry, though, payment won't be made by ye."

Fuck. All these two did was talk in riddles. "Can I go now?" Preferably with clothes.

"Not yet." Bruna reached behind him and pulled out a pair of underwear. Women's *silk* underwear. Memories teased at his brain as they swung from her finger. "Put these on first. And we'll get the rest for ye.

"Pretty sure a blanket would work just as well." Why would they seem familiar? Also, what guy wore women's silk undies?

"Put them on." Doxy used the mom voice—no room for argument.

"Damnit." Dexx took the silkies and put one leg through then the other. He snapped the band as they worked into place. "Happy? Now what?"

The sisters flew into motion as they pulled items from racks and tested sizes by placing shirts against him.

An eternity later—okay, so maybe a couple of minutes later—Dexx had all the clothes he needed to be presentable in public. And silk panties.

So maybe they cupped the boys a little more gently than his normal stuff.

"I'll come back and pay—"

"We already told ye that the cost will not be paid by ye," Bruna said firmly. "But remember this. Not all ye see is what ye think. Not all ye think is what is real. Not all ye think as real is what ye see."

"Got it." No. He *didn't* get it. "Pretzels taste like roofs, and blue is really forty-two."

"I told ye he wasn't a normal Yank." Bruna's crooked smile lit her eyes with humor.

"So ye did." Doxy gave her twin a wry grin. "Remember ye said ye'd help us." She pushed Dexx toward the door.

"No, I said I'd come back and pay." Dexx craned his head around to talk to the pushing girls.

"We'll see ye again. Remember."

That struck a bell. The next thing Dexx recalled was walking into the house.

Catcalls followed him to his room. What the hell was all that about? Because he didn't come back last night? And how had he made it to the house? He didn't even remember walking there or hailing a cab. Nothing.

Alwyn waited for Dexx in his room.

Was *everyone* going to walk in on him? Maybe not that, but couldn't a man find privacy *anywhere*?

"Next time," Alwyn said a bit primly, "take me with you if you're going to get so pissing drunk you forget to come back in the clothes you left in."

Dexx really looked at the clothes the witches had given him. Layered shirts, the top one a belly shirt with pink accents and letters, and the undershirt full length and an ugly brown. His pants were red corduroy, but his shoes were a very nice pair of leather dress shoes.

Uh. "I suppose." Dexx shrugged. "Why are you here? I need a nap."

"Can't. Director Harris sent me here almost twenty minutes ago. Another five, and you'd have gone on the deserter list. Come on, let's get back to work."

Dexx crushed his teeth together. "Fine. Wait outside so I can get dressed. These pants are tight."

"Sorry. Disrobe and dress in front of me. Orders."

What kind of fucked up orders were those? "I didn't dress myself. Two crazy chicks did."

Alwyn's smile widened.

Dexx smelled the fury before he reached for the doorknob.

Harris and Sir Saayid were silent, but if their stone faces were any clue, he was headed home. Cardinal Bussemi stood apart from the two, but he seemed mildly pleased.

Another person stood in the back of the office, but Dexx had trouble computing her presence.

Angela Hopkirk, his old boss. Her arms were folded in front of her, and her expression—well, it wasn't ever pleasant, but she had an especially un-nice frown on her face.

Alwyn stopped by the open door and turned around. He closed the door with a small click.

Harris exploded toward Dexx. "You stupid American bastard. You go out and get blitzed at the first chance you can and make a mockery of this organization."

Dexx took a step backward, surprised at first, but then anger bubbled up, and he fought against tearing the man's throat out with his teeth. "Slow down, hoss." Dexx held a hand up between them. "What?"

"You insignificant mealy-mouthed moron. Do you know how hard it's going to be to get that *off* the net?"

"Still not following, chief."

"Mr. Colt." Sir Sayyid stepped forward, pulling Harris back with a pull on his shoulder. "I told you I was watching, and that the next time you stepped out of line, you'd be on the first plane home."

Not exactly, but his meaning had been exactly that.

Dexx felt pressure on him. One like back in the states when the creepy doctor had told him to forget. He hadn't forgotten that, and he wasn't going to forget this. His new tattoo began to heat on his skin. And where had his stone gone? He'd had it last night.

He felt something trickle into him. Not blast him like the rest of the pressure suggested it should, but there was definitely something changing his attitude. "Hey look, I'm sorry about last night, but it—" Dexx forgot what he was going to say. Last night became a blur. Or not so much a blur as fuzzy around the edges.

He'd gone out... with someone. They'd done stuff. Drinking? Maybe. There'd definitely been a place. Then, blackness. That's all he had after the... the... place anyway. So drinking was as good an excuse as—

"There is a flight back to the states in one hour." Sir Sayyid held a ticket out to Dexx. "Be on it."

"I can only express my deepest regrets." Hopkirk spoke for the first time. "But I believe I told you he wasn't ready for *anything* more than the meanest of tasks. Sometimes, he does well as a team leader, but anything else and disaster strikes. When we get back, I have a particularly unpleasant task for him."

Dexx felt the altering in his head. The feeling seeped in and warred with everything he was. Anger boiled and then subsided. Rose and then fell. The pendulum swung from ready to do whatever they said to fuck this whole place.

There were... others who needed him.

The loss of his... something flared. Something was out there, calling to him. Frustration was too light a word to describe things flashing back and forth through his head.

The tattoo intensified the burn against his skin.

Then, as suddenly as it all began, the feeling subsided. His skin cooled.

Cardinal Bussemi stepped forward with his hands raised. "If we could all just calm down, I think we can let our wayward son speak in his defense. After all, we didn't bring him all the way over here to be sent back so soon. Is there anything you wanted to say on your behalf?"

Dexx reeled. *That* wasn't expected. The big boss coming to his defense? The big boss that had shit piled to his eyebrows?

"Well, like I said," Dexx said, taking this opportunity to... figure out if he even wanted to fight to stay. "I went out, and then the night got blurry. I really don't know what happened." And that was starting to piss him off. Was he going senile? When would he be able to remember...anything?

Coolness along his new tattoo became ice cold. He raised his hand to cover the icy skin but forced the hand down.

Something went off in his head. *Do not let them know.*

The voice seemed to be his and not his.

But Alwyn had watched him dress. Surely he'd seen. Too many directions. His head went in too many directions to think straight. "Okay, what do you want?"

"I want you gone." Sir Sayyid had steel in his deep brown eyes.

"I don't care as long as you're not here," Harris said at the same time.

"You don't have a place in our organization." Hopkirk slashed a hand in front of her.

In that instant, Dexx felt whatever had been pushing at him slide home. He would do *anything* to stay. Distantly, he studied the newfound desire. He remembered everything clearly, but there was absolutely *nothing* he wouldn't do to stay with DoDO.

But he also had no *reason* to *want* that.

Cardinal Bussemi smiled at the glowers in the room. "I say let bygones be bygones. Let him repent. I will take care of him personally. I will train him right. Is that how you kids say it?"

The protests were unanimous. None of them wanted Bussemi to take a direct hand with Dexx.

Not even Dexx.

Sir Sayyid was first with actual words. "Your Immanence, you have way too much to concern yourself without taking care of an insect."

"Watch who you call an insect." Where was this desire to stay coming from? From him or from somewhere else?

Bussemi raised a hand, ending the discussion. "I understand your concerns. I am not so busy I can't take on a new student. He's a good man, and the first one of us who is without sin or mistake can cast the first stone." He looked at the others in the room.

None of them spoke, but none of them looked any less pissed either.

Bussemi looked up at Dexx with his grandfatherly smile that was starting to look more and more sinister each time Dexx saw it. "You *will* do whatever we require of you, won't you?"

Outside. Definitely outside. But why?

Because of the *kadu*. Did Bussemi know it belonged to… No. Because it didn't. Dexx was just drawn to dumb things.

"Well, yeah." He swallowed hard. "I don't know what happened last night, but it won't happen again." He really meant the words, but they felt wrong, like someone else had control of his mouth. At least he wasn't lying about the night. He was going to have to talk with… with whoever he went out with.

"Can we have the room for a moment?" Bussemi cast his gaze around the room to the other directors.

They looked ready to chew rocks, all of them, but they left. Alwyn poked his head in the door for a second, surprise written all over his face when the directors left first.

The door closed.

Bussemi turned to Dexx. "My son, you really have a fine line to walk here. There is not one person here as interesting as you in a long time. Not even director Sayyid. He may succeed me one day, and he isn't like you."

"What, you mean American?" Whatever Bussemi was talking about wasn't nationality.

Bussemi chuckled. "Heh, no. I mean in other ways. How well did you know your parents?"

Hey, personal. "What do they have to do with this?"

"I only ask because you have… issues with authority figures, and sometimes that has an effect on personalities."

Dexx didn't want to tell this guy anything, but at the same time, he was struggling to keep things to himself. "I guess I knew them about as well as any kid knows their parents." He answered truthfully, but that wasn't the question Bussemi was after. He wanted whatever was gone, missing from his mind. *That's* what Bussemi was probing for.

That much was clear as crystal.

"Then, that will have to do for now. Tomorrow, I want you to meet me by the stone. Don't worry about the time. I will be there. Go now. Repair your fractured relationship with your superiors. I fear they are most upset with me."

Bussemi had an unnatural obsession with Dexx. And with the rock in the curio room. Dexx was gonna have to play that one very carefully. He was connected to it. That much was becoming clearer. The reason for that?

He didn't want that answer in front of Bussemi.

Dexx turned and left the room before he even knew he'd decided to.

Alwyn caught up to him almost halfway down the hall. "So, what happened?"

"What happened where?"

"You know the room with *all* the big shots. What happened in there?"

Dexx had a hard time concentrating on something so mundane. "They said to get back to work. And that's what I intend on doing." He left Alwyn standing there, working his jaw.

Dexx stopped in front of his bunk and blew out his cheeks, a little upset with himself for being so abrupt with Alwyn like that. That man was really his only friend.

Whatever the tattoo was, it did the same the stone had, even if it wasn't as complete. Where was that thing? It was *his,* and he wanted it back.

That could wait. Sleep now. Maybe for a week. Perhaps all his new work friends would forget his walk of shame.

Damned women dressing him anyhow.

The next day, Dexx met Cardinal Bussemi in the curio room. And every day for the next two weeks before doing his regular job. The every other day schedule just didn't pan out. Not that doing paperwork and procedure was ever fun, but it sure beat the looks Bussemi gave him.

The new tattoo burned and froze at every one of their meetings. The cardinal wasn't just a cardinal.

He was a witch pretending not to be one and spelled Dexx every morning.

Or he tried to.

By the end of the second week, Dexx began to recognize weaves of spells. Each conversation with Bussemi ended with a headache. Not the kind that split from front to back or even the kind that blinded. No, these were worse. He could have mapped every one of his nerves. They swayed from side to side, searing pain all the down to the middle of his back.

The episodes were always worse right after leaving the cardinal but faded after an hour or so.

Dexx remembered in vivid detail how he'd been pushed to serve DoDO whole-heartedly and everything he was told. That pissed him off. Why the scam job? But even though he tried to rebel, the absolute desire to do whatever they required stuck.

The training regimen he was developing was almost complete. Sir Sayyid came down from wherever he was to check in on Dexx daily.

The best he got was grunts, so Dexx took that to mean that things were going well.

Harris actually got past being perpetually pissed and even gave a few compliments.

Through all of this, the dreams persisted.

He was always caught in a cage with a wild animal slashing and tearing at everything within reach. Dexx dodged and twisted from the teeth and claws, but usually sustained a light trampling. In the morning, he hurt from head to foot, where the pain lasted only as long as the shower.

Rarely, the woman would appear. Sometimes, she was only a fleeting vision like mist. Other times, she'd shield him. But she always looked at him with those dark eyes and silently demanded where he was.

He might have enjoyed his new job without the compulsion, changing the training styles to incorporate the different types of paras they would be dealing without in the real world.

Reports had started coming in that the mortality rate of their teams had significantly dropped.

Now, maybe one in eleven or twelve died on a mission instead of one in four.

Harris really warmed after that.

Thirteen days after waking up naked in a park, Dexx gripped the sides of his desk, gritting his teeth, waiting for his headache to subside. The particleboard snapped and cracked as he twisted his hand with the pain pulsing through his head and neck.

Bussemi had upped the voltage on the spell or ward or whatever.

The spell had been meant to soften him up to suggestions. So far, he'd been able to deflect, but that day had been powerful.

His tattoo beat in icy counterpoint to his head, alternately freezing and searing his chest.

He crushed his eyes against the pain and imagined a dark place, a soft place where he could sit under a tree and just stare at the horizon.

Being dark, there would be stars, so he made a few. The ground he thought had been soft wasn't soft enough. Grass thickened and cushioned him. The branches of the tree blocked out the sky, so the branches parted, leaving a magnificent view.

A fog rolled in. Sounds that had been sharp and high pitched dulled to a wooly distance.

Oh, yes. This was more like it. The constellations didn't look like the ones he remembered. Orion wasn't there, although one of the bright stars sitting midway in the sky could have been Betelguese. The Big Dipper wasn't anywhere. So, what had he imagined?

Dexx felt a presence. Something familiar, something he could trust.

You have come. Finally. Free us.

"What the fuck!" Dexx jumped to his feet. "What the *hells*?"

He must have taken the daydream right into full sleep, but he could remember *everything*. But, no, this *had* to be a dream.

What else could it be?

Whatever it was, the monster that had been in the cage had followed him to his made-up place.

"I can't even daydream without you trying to kill me." Dexx leaned against the tree he imagined. It felt so very real.

They have us caged. The cat's voice was female and oddly familiar in a comforting way. Why? How? *Both of us. You must fight and break us free. I cannot. You will have to find the way, or we may lose ourselves.* The fog almost formed a shape—a large shape, with glowing green spots where eyes could be.

What was going on? "I'm going crazy. Crazy as fuck, and it's all from the accident." Dexx spun around, looking for a way out. There wasn't any he could find. And for some reason, he couldn't wake up.

As he searched, the sky lightened, but the fog rolled in on itself to a small cloud at his side.

Cub.

Dexx lurched as the word hit. Full of compassion and command. Full of the weight of memory.

I can only talk when their cage is weak. And only if you meet me halfway. Please remove the cage from me. I am weak. Weaker than before. Come back to me and make us whole again.

"What? Exactly what am I supposed to do." Though, he had a feeling he wanted to do as she asked. He just didn't know how. Or why. "And why in the hell of all hells am I talking to myself in my daydream? Or to whatever the hell hallucination this is?"

Your marks. They are complete, but not enough. You must recover the shamyir to make them stronger and break the cage, break the binding. We are in danger, and you are at the heart of it.

The tree melted into the landscape, and the land turned a light shade of green with short grass. He stood on a cliff overlooking a vast plain with animals grazing.

Way off at the horizon, he saw mountains. Tall and covered with snow, but with a red tinge at the bottom, and wisps of black smoke rising.

No, not snow. The mountains were mile-high sheets of ice. Glaciers.

The thin clouds obscured the sun barely, but there just wasn't a lot of heat in the weak rays.

He knew this place. Not well, but he remembered this place from—

Thumps flowing up from his feet were Dexx's only warning.

You can't be here while they have their claws in you. A big shape thundered right at him.

The only thing he saw was... a house swinging right at him. Something speared into his gut and lifted him off the ground. The point of a longhorn from a massive animal poked through his front and tore through the skin in his back.

Blood spewed everywhere as his flight through the air carried him a long way over the cliff face.

Cub. The voice was commanding and comforting and ancient. The deep female voice carried... *him* with it.

Dexx fell back in his chair and landed flat on his back. He scrambled to his feet, tearing his shirt open and feeling for the gored hole. His hand came away wet with blood, but no real damage.

"What the?" Dexx looked around his office and familiar things.

The other world, the one he'd made up in his mind, was completely gone. And so was his headache. No trace, no lingering pain. That was a first. The headaches always held on for a while before they subsided.

The intercom beeped, and he flinched, not expecting it.

"Get dressed. We have a big one." Harris's voice clicked off.

The first mission since waking in the park naked.

Excellent news, but he no longer cared to serve DoDO blindly.

Dexx led his team through the portal, wondering why they were really there.

The all-call for the nest clearing gave him the chance to pick the first team he' formed in England. Quinn Winters, Fred Harrison, and Leonard Lester, except this time he also had Alwyn with him.

Dexx's confidence ratcheted up a bit. Of everyone in DoDO he knew, Alwyn seemed to be the least stupid. And maybe Quinn.

They appeared to have been dropped off in Russia or Latvia or Shitbakistan.

The walls of the buildings were grey. The cobblestones were grey. The *water* dripping from the nearly rotten eaves was grey.

How did paras *always* find the dreariest structures forgotten by civilizations and make them home?

Dexx passed a look through the silent city. It might have been abandoned. There wasn't anyone hanging out on the streets. So maybe? "Feels like a colder, wetter version of hell. The kind you go to when Hell doesn't want you."

"Cut it, Colt." Director Harris already had control of the streets and presumably the target location.

Dexx cut it, but he had to bite back a response.

He led his team through the door marked by a glowing sigil. One of his changes to the training. Marking a cleared doorway to cut down on unnecessary radio chatter.

Dexx stopped two steps inside, allowing the rest of the team to catch up and make their own assessment of the dark room.

Fred performed a complex motion with his fingers and a wand. A transparent blue bubble popped into existence.

"What's that?" Dexx reached out an experimental hand to the sphere.

"Wait. Stop–" Fred pushed out his hand to catch Dexx, but too late.

It passed through with a tingle.

Leonard alternated looks between Dexx's hand and face. "That... should have stopped you. You shouldn't be able to do that."

Quinn snapped her fingers in Leonard's face. "Hey. Never mind what *he's* doing. Focus on the paras." She grabbed Leonard's thin face and turned it outward.

"Drop it, all of you." Dexx shrugged his vest up higher. "We'll figure out what went wrong with your... thing later. Right now, let's be amazing."

Fred waved his stick again, and the ward thingy vanished.

Knowledge of those things just appeared in his head. They could stop demons if they were performed properly. They could also stop paras, but a powerful witch could negate the ward. Or pass through. An interesting question for when they weren't likely to die.

Dexx let his team move forward through the door, taking rear guard. They weren't super likely to be ambushed from behind, but the possibility kept them sharp.

Dexx moved through the spot where Fred had set his ward. Nothing.

He entered the next room and paused to sniff the air. Old warehouse office smell filled his nose like one from the sixties.

He spied rounded edges on the desks with thin metal skirting around the tops. A memory of falling to a desk like this one tugged at his memory. Louisiana?

The team moved forward.

They found nothing.

He heard nothing on the radio. And he smelled… confusing stuff. Layers of use, cleansing, and fear. Not human fear.

DoDO definitely had their own scents, but none of that felt like the fear he detected. It had less humanity, and more all bundled together. That made him think of shared existences.

Quinn came back from lead with Alwyn. She stepped beside him and looked up. "You good?"

"Yeah."

"Then get up there." She motioned forward. She slapped a hand to his shoulder as he passed.

The next door was in sight. Leonard and Fred flanked Alwyn and… Quinn.

Dexx spun around in time to see a big body flying straight at him. Big feet slammed into his chest, sending him flying back to the doorway. The flimsy wood shattered against Dexx's flight.

He laid on the ground, stunned as chaos broke around him. DoDo agents were casting spells as fast as their fingers and wands could complete them.

Shifters pounced on agents, some bloodied, others just down and unmoving. It looked like the attack of the Separatists on the Galactic Senate ships above Coruscant, a massive melee with no clear winning side.

Lightning crackled along the floor, leaving scorches and smoke slamming into a wolf body. The creature landed hard and stopped moving.

Two more DoDO agents stepped together, linking fingers in complex motions. They threw an arm out to their side, and light trailed their hands in an arc. Fire followed motes of light shooting out radially. Several more shifters fell to the ground.

The chaos slowly formed into order. The shifters fought, but they were losing.

His body wouldn't respond to his commands. Stand up. Fight. Stop the killing. He wanted the paras to just stop. His people were winning but at a huge cost. The numbers belonged to the paras, but the advantage was firmly DoDO's.

The door lay in splinters around him. He didn't feel damaged, just unable to get up.

Alwyn and Quinn backed up as a pair as the big para stalked through the door. A massive black deer thing with twisted horns pressed forward, head down, taking one step at a time.

Alwyn pulled out his athame and made a series of movements. His hands and athame glowed, and the air grew warm.

Dexx felt the heat of the air and the piercing by the stag. If Alwyn finished the casting, the stag would be dead. If he didn't, then Alwyn was a goner.

In that instant, Dexx had no idea who he wanted alive. Alwyn was a friend, someone he knew, but the twisted horned stag was... *his people.*

That was impossible. Paras were the enemy. Paras and demons.

Alwyn finished his cast. The blast that tore through the

stag scattered large chunks of the shifter back into the room. Amazingly bloodless.

More of the shifters fell, but those weren't as clean. Crimson coated the walls like a gory paint.

Horror hit Dexx hard in the gut, and he wanted to retch.

DoDO agents pressed forward, clearly taking the upper hand.

Dexx's hands twitched. His head was filled with cotton, and his vision shrank to pinpoints. Just before everything went dark, a form brushed his consciousness. The cat from his vision. It was the biggest damned cat of all time. The thing was the size of a car

He forced his hands still, his vision to clear and fill again. The fight lasted all of a few seconds, but the world stopped. The killing cast by an agent stopped in mid-flight, but the thing that held his attention was the eyes. Ancient glowing eyes that commanded.

Commanded him to be still and to act.

Why the hell couldn't he just take a position and go with it?

You must stop them.

This time, the voice didn't terrify him.

You must stop them.

He knew that, but how was he supposed to manage that? *Those shifters are why we're here.*

The vision cat shook her head. *Not the spirits. Stop the humans.*

He'd known what she'd meant. *Shifters are a menace, and so we have to clear the streets to be safe.* But even as he said the words—thought them—he didn't feel them.

You are not one of them. You are one of us.

One of us who? Was he about to get the answers he'd been seeking? *Look, I have a fight to get into, so if you'll excuse me, I have to go.*

Dexx pushed back against the tunnel vision and the involuntary muscle twitches. Not that the frozen solid world outside the tunnel vision had much movement.

His vision slowly grew as he pushed, and the world picked up speed until the sounds of fighting crashed against his ears.

Bodies from both sides were scattered everywhere. This had to stop. Like now. Paras were borderline criminals, but they didn't deserve the kind of massacre DoDO could lay down.

Were they that bad? His gut screamed that they weren't.

The fight quickly fell apart for the paras. In the few seconds, Dexx had fought for control of his body, DoDO had taken command of the fight, knocking down several of the paras with no more loss of agents. A few of the paras turned to run and were cut down before they could take more than a couple of steps.

Fair was fair, and with demons, fair was never fair, but to kill people when they ran didn't jive.

The final para left had held his own until too many of his fellows fell. He was bloody and slowing, but he shifted from a fox to a human, keeping just in front of killing casts.

Dexx pushed all he had into pressing his hand to the floor and rolling over.

The more he moved, the more control he gained. Blood pounded in his ears, and his vision cleared enough to see, but something sat inside his head looking out onto the world. Something that was him and not him.

With decreasing effort, he pushed himself up. The para had been backed into a corner and looked to be weighing his options.

Dexx placed himself in between the para and the agents. "Stop." He put all the command in his voice he had.

Amazingly, the para stopped.

Unfortunately, an agent whipped his athame around in an arc and cut the para in two.

"What the fuck?" Dexx spun on the agent jamming his arm under the agent's chin and slamming him against the wall. "What'd you do that for? He was giving up."

The agent gasped around the big arm pressed against his throat. "It was a para. It deserved what it got."

Dexx's vision greyed. He didn't see the bodies across the floor as people. They were rapidly cooling heat sources. The teams of DoDO agents in front of him weren't people. They were the enemy, still warm, and glowing with another light, something he couldn't explain.

Something pressed against his self-control. He pushed back, but the tide swelled into something unstoppable… kind of like the tide, but with less care of the shoreline. Control slipped from his grasp.

Then he was dreaming. DoDO agents fell in front of him. He clearly saw his hands spearing forward, grabbing whatever happened to be in reach. Arms, vests, throats. All were things to grab and crush.

He actually felt the things he did, killing his own people, and he didn't care. The beast who took over had cascaded her feelings through him.

Slowly, he became aware of something slowing him. Bindings. Bindings to prevent him from going forward, like heavy stones. He dragged those but only inched along with their pulling weight.

Leonard and Fred were in front of him, cowering like two lost children. He would be sorry for their deaths, but they'd lost so many. Too many.

No. These were a part of *his* team. He couldn't kill them. He pushed with his will to wrest his body back, but climbing a greased pole would have been easier. There just wasn't anything to hold on to.

One more step forward, and he would take their miserable little lives from them with spurting gouts of blood. They would pay for what the humans had done.

Something else was in his head, driving the new emotions that melded with his own.

But this was familiar. Somehow. He knew how to handle this.

Dexx stopped, unable to take the last step. Something—not him—impeded him. He turned, growling, actually growling at the source of the impediments.

Six DoDO agents had wands or hands in casting positions, pulling him back.

Fine. If he couldn't go forward, he'd go back.

The look of horror on their faces lasted only as long as it took him to close the distance. He ripped them apart in the blink of his eye. So maybe a dream-blink took longer than one when awake, but still.

Every room he passed into, the anger for the dead paras pushed him forward. Well, not him exactly. The anger was hers, but he shared it.

Dexx's point of view began to shrink again, turning into a very small TV with reception issues.

On his way out, he felt the brushing of a mind slide by his.

Dexx slipped away as the cat overtook him completely, leaving only a sliver of self-awareness.

There were vague impressions in an I'm-trapped-in-my-own-body-and-someone-else-is-using-it sort of way, and he imagined some of the things he did on the outside. Running on his hands and feet, using his shoulders to jump, and biting were among the stranger things.

The troublesome strangeness was another person's problems. Thoughts rose and faded before he could really unpack any of the sensations.

His mind blanked, and the carnage he watched himself cause disappeared from his thoughts.

The fight he'd been watching his body wage was gone, and now there were more immediate issues to consider. Like where the hell in his head he stood right now.

Complete blackness surrounded him, peaceful and calm. This was the black of sleep, not nighttime in a mineshaft.

The dark had the feel of a heavy soft blanket, but also very boring since he wasn't tired.

Dexx slapped his hands together.

The sound vanished before it echoed. "Huh. Guess my mind *is* kinda small." He chuckled at his joke, but without humor. "But now what? Can't get out. I can't watch TV. Can't… anything."

The darkness pulled back, and light illuminated him. His arms were bare, and when he looked further, the rest of him was too. "Aw, come on." No clothes for him. Again.

Dexx blew out his cheeks. At least there wasn't a crowd with cell phones hanging around.

"Since there's nothing else to do, let's at least figure out two things. What's going on, and why I'm talking to myself out loud."

He ran a hand through his hair and sat. Soft grass surprised him until he remembered he was trapped in his brain, not a jail.

"Am I possessed? No, maybe. My tats've always stopped possession before." He held his arms out and twisted them in the spotlight of his mind. His tattoos were intact and just as potent as ever. The possession debate would have to be tabled for later.

"If I'm not possessed, and this is my daydream, then who's the big girl?"

The voice he'd heard was definitely not from the type of women he normally went for. But she was familiar.

"And fucking fuck. Am I *actually* fighting my *own* people?" Maybe being trapped in here would be better than… *forever* in the outside solitary. The ground was warm and furry, the company was better than most, even if the scenery was sort of, well, limited. "But at least I won't have to worry about prison yard rape. I hope."

It was still a little weird that he was talking… to himself.

"If there was a tree or a little bit of a hill right here, I could lean on, that'd be great."

No chairs popped up, but a circle of light appeared in the distance. It grew larger, and for a moment, he thought his possession might be over. A chaotic image of a fight from a first-person point of view, like a television, stayed just long enough to be confusing, then disappeared.

He blinked several times, trying to recapture the image and make sense of what he'd seen.

Quinn and Alwyn had stood defiantly guarding a cowering Fred and Leonard, who had taken a knife cut to the arm. Or had his vest and black overshirt been shredded? At the very least, his arm was a bloody mess. There was more than blood on their faces.

Fear. Lots and lots of it.

Okay. No. He couldn't just *stay there*. He had to get out. That was his *team*.

The next vision came with pain. Right in his side. The kind of pain that came with like a month of aches and rehab. Mostly rehab with a large bill waiting at the end.

Alwyn and Quinn still stood protectively over the other two, but Alwyn was casting, then the pain came from behind him where he couldn't see.

There were more casters than he could manage. He would snap at one, but another stepped in to hound him as soon as his back was turned.

Cub.

Bolts of bright light hit, and the vision wobbled, like thunder or high winds, would shake a camera.

The snapshot faded quickly. Okay, it ended like a light had been turned off, but the pain stayed. Throbbing and pulsing, pounding against his side, his head, and under his jaw.

Several more flashes from outside flickered in succession. There wasn't much to see from them, just fluorescent ceiling lights passing over him, and a pair of body armored people hauling him along from under his arms. The dark claimed his mind again, and he was back in his spot with short grass under his feet.

Oh, crap. That was bad. That was really fucking bad.

Cub. The female voice was desperate.

Yeah. No shit.

The blackness pulled back, letting more light in, and he found he wasn't alone in his head, or wherever this was.

There at the edge of the blackness was a form—his cat. The body was too wide in the shoulders, too heavy for any cat he'd ever seen. A lion might have that sort of size in the shoulders if its mane were a hell of a lot bigger.

Dexx felt a pull and snapped back through the warm and comforting place to the outside.

Please don't be a prison yard rape in progress.

All too familiar pain cascaded down on him, and then he opened his eyes. It was mostly an automatic movement since his eyes felt too heavy to open on their own.

The first thing he noticed, after the pain, of course, was his naked body.

Fuck. What the hell was up with losing all his clothes?

The next thing was the ring of people standing around him. Cardinal Bussemi was flanked by Director Harris and Sir Sayyid Maxwell.

Shit. It'd be better if it *was* a prison yard rape.

Sir Sayyid's stare bored open hate at Dexx, but he spoke

to the cardinal. "I told you it was a mistake to bring him on as one of us."

"Not a mistake. Just a miscalculation. The result is the same." Bussemi reached in his robes and pulled out a golden circlet.

It looked heavy. Heavier than it should have been.

"The only difference is now he will cooperate *without* his consent."

The cardinal placed the ring around Dexx's neck, and fire raced through his veins. Dexx screamed until his breath gave out, then screamed again.

Unconscious wrapped him up, but the pain stayed. The pain lashed at Dexx's entire being.

19

Time passed, but that might have been in his head.

Fire, pain. More fire. More pain. When the eternal torment sort of leveled off and became manageable, he almost thought they'd removed the gold circle of whatever.

His new tattoos burned on his chest. Might have been freezing too, but the difference didn't make a difference.

Somebody kicked him in the ribs. Not hard. More like telling to wake up with a foot.

Didn't matter. Not really.

Experimentally, Dexx flexed his fingers. Yup. Prickles of iciness pushed out just like when his foot fell asleep when he sat wrong. Except for this time, it only *added* to ambient pain from the... thing.

The foot poked his ribs again. "Get up."

The voice wasn't familiar, but it sounded just like his when he'd taken a para prisoner. Hard, unyielding, but mostly indifferent. Wow, he'd been an ass of industrial proportions.

Dexx tried an arm, but it was a bit too uncomfortable.

The foot poked again, this time somewhat harder. "I said, get up. Yeh don' want my help carryin' yeh, para."

The voice was thick Irish. In different circumstances, Dexx would have offered to buy the man a beer.

Well fuck. Talking hurt. Breathing hurt. Being *unconscious* hurt. What the fuck did they expect him to do?

Get the fuck up, of course.

Become the pain. Make it yours.

The female's voice of the cat inside him? Was he *really* a para? He'd read books when he was younger, and in one, the main bad guy suffered a psychotic break in extreme circumstances and began to hear voices. Maybe he'd gone schizo.

Those were the wrong questions.

If he was a para—and it looked like he really was—then why had DoDO brought him in?

Maybe he'd snuck in. Maybe he'd gone to someone to erase his memories so he could get vital information—

Yeah. That sounded great and all *Mission Impossible,* but unlikely.

Okay. Then why had DoDO brought him in?

Cardinal Bussemi.

The *kadu.*

Dexx was fucked.

He gritted his teeth and pulled his arms in to roll over and get up.

"Gah." The first intelligent word he'd spoken for... however long they'd had him on the floor. He drew a deeper breath. "I'm up."

The DoDO agent stepped back as Dexx rose.

Like *he* was dangerous wearing that thing around his neck.

The heavy snap of a magnetic lock said he'd been taken to max security. Never been in one of those before.

The blur sharpened to a grey room, with a *very* narrow

bed of concrete at the back of the room. Either he'd fallen off the bed earlier, or they hadn't even bothered to get him there.

Something odd about the walls played in his mind.

The DoDO agent was strange too, and several moments passed as he tried to regain balance before he figured out what had looked so odd.

The spot where he'd been laying glowed and the DoDO did too. Not like a light, but *exactly* like a light. Dexx would be able to follow that guy through pitch dark.

"Lead on, asshole." Dexx shuffled a foot forward and stayed upright, but he sure did want to lay back down. Sure was easier to take the pain when gravity wasn't part of the equation.

His guard stood back against the open door to let him pass. He had a black stick like a billy club, but the end glowed red.

Elemental magick in a stick. Fan-fucking-tastic.

The man gestured with the club that Dexx should lead. In that direction.

"Dick with a stick. Pretty scared of me, aren't you? You should be." Sometimes empty blustering could put them off guard.

"Para in chains. Just where yeh belong." He tapped the back of Dexx's bare thigh with the stick.

The fire flared in his leg, threatening to topple him. He managed to stay up, after a few shuffling steps, and help from the wall.

"What's your name?" Dexx half turned as they made slow progress up the hall.

"Why, writin' a book?"

"No, making a list." And an assessment. How the fuck was he getting out of this one? "And you're on it."

"Jes move, para. Got no time fer yer blusterin'."

Well, *sometimes* blustering worked. Dexx moved up the hall, trying to stay just out of reach of the stick. At least the way out was simple. There weren't any joining corridors. But there was a corner up ahead. Maybe if he hurried around and caught the guard by surprise...

Movement signaled a guard standing there.

Shit. One plan down. Sooner or later, they would slip up, and guess who'd be there? This guy.

Yeah, if he could *move* faster.

"You won' be able to cast with the inhibitor on, para."

Cast? Wasn't he a shifter? That cat in his head was his shifter spirit. Right? "Dexx."

"What er yeh goin' on about?"

"My name is Dexx, not *para*." How many times had he had the same argument with paras? One, two hundred?

The man swished his club. "Move, *para*."

Dexx rounded the corner and came to a stop at the next door. Another heavy slam and the door swung open. Dexx realized he was still as naked as the day he woke up in the park. "How about we stop by *Kohls* and get something nice for me to wear?"

"How about yeh shut yer hole an' keep movin'? I'm supposed to bring yeh alive. Did nae mention broke."

"Come on, man. You really want me to go out in public dressed like this?"

"Yeh won' need clothes where yer headed."

Well, that was ominous. Visions of the firing squad and hot pincers made little cameos in his brain. Certainly, they could do that, but there wasn't anything to say they wanted him dead. Mr. Hard-ass had already said he was supposed to be alive.

The next door was a regular security door—the push bar kind in banks and... police stations. One place momentarily solidified in his thoughts.

This remembered place sat along a quiet street where he'd spent a lot of time. A place he knew as well as he knew his own. The thought wafted away as he pushed the door open, but it didn't disappear completely. He entered a new room, a faint feeling of just how many times memories had slipped by him in the past. Was he finally gaining ground?

This was an old room. He knew this place—the room of all the curios.

Oh, shit. The *kadu*. Bussemi was going to kill him and break the statue. But what if his wasn't the soul that belonged inside it?

In the back of his head, he knew it was.

They were just a few feet away from the case holding the statue that sang like a song to his soul. Yeah. It was his, he was pretty sure.

Fuck.

Cardinal Bussemi regarded the stone inside and ignored Dexx as the two came close.

"As yeh, ordered, your Immanence." Mr. Hard-ass bowed slightly and backed away.

"So much for being friends." Dexx tried to stand straight, but the fire in his body kept him a bit hunched. And he was breathing shallow.

"I wouldn't say that necessarily, young Colt." Bussemi's voice was quiet and slightly familial. "But the paradigm may have shifted to one more like a master and servant."

"Closer to slave. Or convicted in a witch hunt." Dexx snarled a lip at the cardinal.

"Odd phrasing. Are you a witch, Mr. Colt?"

No. He didn't have any powers at all. Unless super smell was a witch power. But something else traveled up from his memories. Shifter witches could shift and *keep* their clothes. Yeah. So… not a witch.

The old man didn't look even the tiniest bit moved. "You are thinking of escape."

Well, he probably should have been, but no. At the moment, he was too busy putting two and two together in order to reconnect all the pieces of his life.

"And then revenge."

Okay. Yeah. Dexx needed to get his shit together because that—yeah, that was definitely on the menu.

"I am safe from you. Safe from anything you could do. I… made sure of that a long time gone." He ended with a snarl on his face.

Dexx could have kept the witty exchange going all day if he wasn't shackled with a continuous gut-punch. "I'd like to get on with it, Cardinal Douchebag. I'm not dead, and not in the honeymoon suite. You want something. So, what is it?"

Bussemi smiled slightly. Not the grandfatherly nice smile, but more of the tight-lipped angry sort that preceded unpleasantness. "Very well. I was told you were not a gracious man this time. I can accommodate you."

"Gracious?" This time? How many "this times" had he suffered through? Dexx snapped straight and lunged toward the cardinal's neck, but before he got halfway, the fire intensified and shriveled him back over his cramping stomach.

Bussemi chuckled slightly.

"How about you take this off, and I'll be as gracious as you've never seen in all your life," Dexx groaned.

Bussemi pulled his lips back. "You have no idea what I've seen in my life. Empires rise and fall. People flit from life to death, currents swaying the masses to and fro. I have seen much, and I have seen graciousness. I have *been* gracious."

"I don't know what you're expecting with chains." Okay, so he wasn't actually *in* chains, but the metaphor fit.

"You're a para. Paras *belong* to me. You live at my mercy. You might wish to return some."

"Show me on the doll where the bad man touched you when you were an altar boy." Dexx really wished he had a way around this damned collar. "You're *really* fucked up."

Bussemi raised his chin. "You have a singular way with words, Colt."

Dexx sneered. "That's *Mr.* Colt to you."

"I hope you'll understand when I don't use an honorific to address you." Bussemi lazily raised his elderly hand toward Dexx and placed the other on his cane. "With the pleasantries concluded, how about we discuss why you still draw breath."

Yeah. About that.

Bussemi turned to the figurine in the glass case.

Dexx's eyes beat him to the stone. The pull on him had increased to crack-addiction levels. "I'm too pretty."

"I'm curious to find out how long it will take to find the end of your quips. If I killed you now, I could do what needs to be done, but there are other matters that need some attention. Some that require you alive." He smiled his grandfatherly smile, but the eyes were little black balls of hate.

Now he will cooperate without his consent.

Oh, shit. "Let's make a deal. You let me go right now, and I'll kill you last." That sounded good. Where'd that cat go? "It'll be quick, and you won't see it coming. Because when I get out of here, there's going to be a lot of blood." Just as soon as his dumb ass got out of this damned collar.

"My first task is to make that incessant tongue stop flapping with bravado and turn it to devotion. Devotion to me and be a servant of my army. A servant to me."

A sermon *now* would be torture. "Just get on with it. Why am I not dead yet?"

"An excellent question. What you are feeling now, aside from the inhibitor we have on you, is the pull of the *kadu*. More specifically, *your kadu*. It seems as though distance is one of the main ways to keep a bonded pair safe. I mentioned these were made by witches long ago, and this one here was special. It is. And the closer you get to your *kadu*, the more you want it. The more the pull for you to possess it. It'll be as a lover to you, and you to it. This much I know. These keep their knowledge tightly held." Bussemi tipped his head to the burned and cracked stone bowl.

For a villain, he did a lot of talking. Which would be good if Dexx was buying time, which…he wasn't. He was just… not dying. Yet.

"The *kadu* are rare, and finding one is momentous. But finding the soul alive in the world? Well now, that's a treat unto itself. And before you die, you will help us destroy every last one of those abominations."

Ah-ha-ha. "So, how am I supposed to help? Seems you know a hell of a lot more than I do. Already have all this locked down. What am I supposed to do, your royal pain in the ass-ness?"

"For now, nothing. You are the bait, and now you know of your soul keeper, your *kadu*. The draw to possess it should make you very pliable." Bussemi took his black eyes from Dexx and turned them to his guards. "Take him back to his cage. I want him to see his stone from his cell for an hour every day. See how soft he gets."

He waved them away as though ridding the room of trash.

Mr. Hard-ass waved his club toward the door for Dexx to move.

Dexx hesitated, sliding a look at the *kadu* rock figurine. It *did* pull at him. He wanted it. Crackheads must feel the same thing to have their next bump just out of arm's reach.

The dual problem of why Bussemi wanted him alive and how to get out of the house immediately kicked into gear as soon as the *kadu* left his sight.

After a while, Dexx heard some shuffling outside his door.

He rose to see the *kadu*. No glass, on its pedestal, just begging to be held.

All other thoughts sort of melted away, and he just wanted… it. The entire time the *kadu* sat outside his door, he stared at it.

Feelings and almost formed thoughts and memories roiled just below his consciousness. There was something there, something unexplainable.

After a while, two men took it away. They didn't even glance at him—just movers with nothing else to do but move furniture.

Dexx fell asleep, trying to work out the puzzle of how to get out of there with his treasure. Then the dreams started.

They were formless, masses of feelings, dread, and loss being the worst of them. He felt time pass slower than the slowest Christmas. The shadows of the dreams sharpened toward the end when they took a more violent cast.

Dexx dodged jagged bolts of shadow while they moaned unintelligibly.

One shadow, the biggest so far, seemed to be speaking. He *almost* understood the words, as though it were inviting or commanding.

He raised a hand to the darkness. Pinpricks of green luminescence came together and illuminated the outlines of a giant cat. His cat. The other half of his soul.

The heavy snap of the lock on his room shocked him awake. The door flung open and Alwyn stepped inside. "Get up. Your time has come."

Dexx peered through blurry eyes to Alwyn. Did he really just say some over the top corny shit?

"Get *up,* para. New orders. Execution in twenty." Alwyn had his entire set of body armor gear on, an athame tucked in his vest, and he carried his automatic rifle.

With the collar on, Dexx wouldn't be a match to the rifle. And it wouldn't be necessary in any case since he couldn't be whatever they thought he was. Of course, with the super senses and the overpowering need to have that rock, they might have a case.

Alwyn. If he had a choice of just one person in this whole place he'd be sure was an ally, it would have been him, But after the attack on the paras? Dexx knew he'd single-handedly killed a lot of DoDO agents. He couldn't expect Alwyn to just forget that.

Alwyn smelled nervous. Why would he be nervous with Dexx all crippled up?

Dexx struggled to his feet. The inhibitor or whatever this thing was on his neck kept his stomach in cramps, and his limbs stiff as logs.

"I'm not going to say it again. Get up." Alwyn gestured to the door with the gun.

"Helluva partner. How long did it take you to switch sides? I saved your life so many times."

"Move." Alwyn put the rifle to his shoulder and took aim at Dexx's head.

Dexx shuffled out the door a few steps in front of Alwyn.

Quinn had a paper in front of one of the guards for him to read.

The guard shook his head like he was trying to stay awake, and the other stared at the opposite wall.

Quinn stashed the orders in her vest pocket and turned to escort Dexx down the hall. At the corner, she pulled the paper out again to show the next set of guards.

Confusion rolled from the pair.

Alwyn was getting more nervous.

So, either they didn't know what was going on, or they had conflicting orders.

What was going on?

Alwyn stood Dexx up roughly. "Stand up, para. At least show a little *backbone.*"

"Take this thing off, and I will." Dexx turned his head enough to look at Alwyn sideways. Something was going, and Dexx wasn't entirely sure it was what his partner *said.*

Alwyn pulled him up further, and when Dexx reached a fully upright stance, he felt a little click. Not his back cracking but from the inhibitor. A little strength returned. Enough to stand up straight, anyway.

He narrowed his eyes at Alwyn.

He just widened his eyes minutely and shoved.

Quinn took an arm, and Alwyn took the other.

"When we reach the outer door—" Quinn looked straight ahead, mouth barely moving, "—you're on your own. Run. We can't go with you. Got it?"

"No," Dexx growled as things clicked into place. They were breaking him out. "I don't get it." Dexx looked over his shoulder to the guards frozen in place. "What did you do to them?"

"A little spell." Quinn grunted with effort. "They'll be fine in about two minutes. That means you have about thirty seconds to get to the sunlight."

"Sunlight?"

The two agents hauled Dexx along faster.

"What the hells is going on?"

"Dexx, it's you." Quinn shook her head, holding his wrist tighter. "You have to find Hattie."

"Who?" Dexx stopped, but the two hauled him on.

They reached the last door and the curio room. The lights were off except for a few for minimal lighting.

Dexx stopped and pulled from their grip.

"We've had you for a little over a month. Well, in the outside world. It's been over that for you." Alwyn spoke from his other side in a tight voice. "I thought I hated you, but you've *actually* saved my life. And I owe you."

"And you don't hate me?" The shadow dreams had been bad, but *this* was a nightmare. He *had* to be dreaming of the escape. And very, very soon, he'd wake up in his cell again.

"I *owe* you. They'll kill you when they're done. And whatever else you might be, you've pulled my marbles from the fire, and that has weight where I'm from."

Honor from a Brit. A DoDO Brit.

Quinn glanced sidelong at Alwyn.

There was more going on than Alwyn was copping to.

Quinn looked him full in the face. "Find *Hattie*. She's in there." She poked a finger against Dexx's forehead. "Let her loose."

"Who's Hattie, Winters?"

"It used to be Quinn. You used to call me Quinn. And you

gave me the fairest shot anyone ever had. And you treated me with dignity. Remember that."

Okay. A few more things were starting to add up. The *reason* she'd asked the questions she had when they'd first met. But...she'd been trying to *covertly* find out if he remembered her. Was she hiding here? "Why don't we all leave together? Then you can help me figure this all out 'cause I'm confused as shit. When did it used to be Quinn? Shot at what?"

She shook her head. "I'll be doing the most good here. I can hide in plain sight." She smiled mischievously. "Ten seconds."

Dexx looked to the room. The whole thing glowed on the inside. Not bright, but detectable in the low light.

The floor thumped. Soft, but like a bomb had gone off somewhere. Now, what the fuck?

The warning light above the door began to flash with a siren buzzer. Intruder alert.

"Shit," Quinn said. "Zero seconds. Get your ass out of here, Dexx."

The sounds of running boots set his feet in motion. Boots that would be connected to rifles, spells, elementals, and a whole host of unwanted attention.

First things first. Dexx bolted. He needed to evade an entire building of DoDO agents, get clothes, his *kadu,* and get free. Sure, no problem. He should wave his arms and sing real loud so he'd have a challenge.

Or not.

Dexx dove under one of the long stands of corroded swords.

The stand was freestanding and open below, but they were also hollow underneath, so if he could jam himself in between the legs, he'd have a pretty good spot to hide for a while.

Just like hide and seek when he played with... the memory slipped away. But a kid. And one he liked. A lot. Like a big brother. No. No, like a father.

Shit. Did he have *kids?*

Dexx tore the golden inhibitor from his neck and almost threw it away, but he thought better of it. It'd make noise, and if he got out, it could come in handy. Maybe.

There, under the display case, his fingers found a ledge. His fingers grasped the tiny edge, and he pulled. Then he pulled one leg up, then the other.

His body rose up out of sight, so anyone who looked would have to be under the display to find him.

He shouldn't be able to do that, but whatever was going on, he had a *lot* more strength than he normally did. Good thing too, or he'd be hamburger.

The running stopped. Thin tendrils of anticipation tickled his nose. Every agent in here had an itchy trigger finger.

"There's nobody here," said a voice trying to be quiet. "How'd he get by us?"

"Jenkins, go cover the door." A set of boots quickened away.

Shit. One escape was out of the question.

"I'll get the other one." Boots shuffled slowly away toward the other door.

Double shit. He was stuck in there. Stuck, and he had no idea how long he'd be able to hold on under the display.

Well, fuck. He had to fight or stay hidden in the DoDO house forever like that one guy in that one movie. Boy, it had been a good one where the... what the hell movie was that? The one where—

Boom.

A distant explosion brought him back to DoDO.

What the hell had that been? Could have been anything,

but nothing to help him escape. He needed a weapon, or a big ass shield or—

A *kadu.*

Hadn't Cardinal Asshole said it kept a person invulnerable? No, the *kadu* themselves were indestructible. The person behind them was able to live and die and be reborn over and over.

A voice in his head from long ago and far away echoed, "You're magick born, Dexx." The voice was old and craggy. Not the same voice he'd heard in his dreams. This one made him think of cookies and constant pestering. Good, solid, old-time advice. And fierce love.

He *almost* had the memory. It slipped away, leaving that incessant feeling of loss. But it was *close.*

No time to poke at those things. He *had* to get away from here. But first, he needed that little rock.

Dexx lowered a bare leg to the floor.

If there was anyone nearby, they hadn't seen him.

He dropped his hand down and silently brought everything else out.

Dexx pulled in a deep breath through his nose, seeing what his super smell could sense.

Every scent in the room came to him, and a picture formed. He was closer to the long hallway to the cells, and the door had an agent blocking it. The *other* door had a person at it too.

Okay, so if he kept real quiet, he might be able to get to his *kadu.* He couldn't get it out of his head. It *belonged* to him, and he needed it back.

He looked around for it, but it wasn't in its case.

Shit. Where was it?

That idea was shot to shit, which wasn't good. That asshole could use it against him.

New plan. Don't die. That red-robed bastard should die of old age, and then he could come get it.

Except that he'd "lived longer than anyone else" or some shit. Fuck. Really, that was more of an end result than a plan, but the rest should fill itself in before the end of the century.

The DoDO agent standing at the door tried to watch both ways at once. His nervous stance named him. Fred had been assigned to watch the room with all the important toys.

Well, knowing Fred, he'd watch everything and see nothing. Good news for Dexx. Technically, he should be able to go up to Fred and ask for help, but… Dexx'd tried to kill the man the last time he'd seen him.

Yeah. He needed answers. If he was indeed a para, and a shifter, then…

He had a lot of answers to uncover.

Timing was everything, and if Dexx played his hand right, Fred would be down before he knew a thing. But not dead. Just down.

Dexx jumped just as Fred turned. The man had enough time to widen his eyes, and then a sharp blow to the head put Fred to sleep. Dexx kept Fred facing away, but it wouldn't last long. The sudden change in Fred's vitals would send up red flags.

Lowering him gently to the floor, Dexx swiveled his head to see if the noise had alerted anyone. His super smell didn't carry scents of fear, so he quickly stripped Fred of his pants.

The nervous man was shorter and fifty pounds lighter, but bulging out of pants was better than no pants at all.

Dexx squeezed into the too-small pants as best as he could and painfully finished the button. "Dexx the muffin top," he murmured as he took Fred's rifle.

The weapon was just a mundane thing, not charged with elemental magick. Oh well, he'd get as far as he had with just the regular kind anyway.

The sounds of explosions came closer.

One thing explosions were good for was confusion. And right now, confusion was his favorite ally.

He met two DoDO's running down the hall in full flight. They were scared, wide-eyed, and glancing back over their shoulders every other step.

Dexx calmly held up his rifle sideways and let the two clotheslines themselves. They hit the floor like a sack of potatoes, down for the count.

One of them was more Dexx's size, but he didn't have time for the pants that actually fit, so he slipped off the armored vest instead and snapped the vitals line.

Let Control think the man was dead. They'd have a lot more than just this guy to box up based on the noise level coming from the cafeteria, and the action was here, so tracking one lone agent wasn't as likely.

Dexx trotted to the corner and peered around the edge. Whatever he thought might be happening wasn't what he saw.

A thing stood coiled onto the floor with about a dozen tentacle things that could have been roots and root-like limbs. Agent after DoDO agent fell before the snapping whips.

Sometimes a person fell in more than one piece.

The thing's snake-like head brushed against the ceiling, bringing down tiles and filling the air with dust, further obstructing the view. It had about twelve club-like arms that shot out like headless snakes.

Dexx stepped out from behind the wall, completely dumbfounded. "Holy shit." He remembered his jaw and closed it with a click.

Nobody ever, in the history of all time, had taken out an entire room of DoDO's like that *thing* had just done.

The last DoDO agent fell over. The body twitched once

and then lay still. She could have been dead, or just dazed for the movement. It was hard to tell.

Then the killer tree? Weird snake-thing... shivered. The limbs pulled back, and arms and legs formed. In moments, a smartly dressed woman stepped over bodies as though she did this every day.

Dexx snapped up the rifle in her direction. "Stop there."

She stopped, narrowing her blue eyes like he was dim. She opened her mouth to say something, then changed her mind, quirked her lips, sighed tightly, and said with a slight eyeroll as if she was going to kick herself later for having said it, "Come with me if you want to live, you wank."

"I'm not going anywhere with you, lady... thing." He'd make it out of this place all on his own, thank you very much.

"We don't have time for this, Dexx. The others are distracting the larger garrison, but we need to move *now*. They can't hold on forever."

"I don't know who you are, but that's the most fucked up para shift I've ever seen."

"Dexx," the woman growled his name. "Get your ass *moving*. We don't have time for you to turn into a pussy right now."

Ouch. That hurt. "How about this. I go my way. You go your way. I won't shoot you, I promise." He'd even keep it. She was one scary para.

The woman shook her head. "Okay. Well... Paige."

Dexx rocked on his heels, completely numb.

Paige.

The name rang his bell harder than anything else had done since his accident.

A vision formed for an instant. The woman terrifyingly beautiful and powerful beyond all measuring. Lightning flashed from her hands, and the earth trembled in her footsteps. Power crackled around her like a Tesla coil set on eleven.

The woman of his dreams.

He blinked once and had time just enough to see a fist the size of his thigh coming at his head.

Fuzzy. That's how Dexx felt. His brain was fuzzy. His fingers were fuzzy, toes, hair, all of it. Even his *teeth* felt fuzzy, and that was gross. Well, that could be from inadequate brushing over the past few days. But the rest?

He opened his too heavy eyelids to a scene from too many dystopian movies.

A high-ceilinged warehouse with some windows intact, and the very same coloring of grey that *all* abandoned buildings had.

Sunlight poured through the offset roof joins.

He trailed his sight down to the chair across from the most uncomfortable couch in the universe to a man in variations of the grey theme, eating cereal. At least the milk was bright white.

Great. He'd found the mysterious Abandoned Building Squatters Club.

Dexx tried out his fuzzy vocal cords. "Grraah."

"'Sup." The man just watched Dexx as he spooned the

flakes to his mouth. He smiled with his bulging mouth and crunched.

"Anyone get the number of that truck?" Dexx let his head fall back to the hard couch and wished his pants were a little looser.

"Truck?" The man repeated Dexx through the mouthful.

"Yeah. The one that ran over me. Looked like a woman in a business suit dressed as a whomping willow."

"Ah, yes. She is a most amazing woman." The man's accent clearly labeled him a Frenchman.

"Yeah. Whatever." Dexx struggled to rise from the couch. It wasn't much more difficult than pushing a house over. When he finally reached a sitting position, his heart began to play a driving Metallica tune in his head. The one with all the double-bass.

Then his head snapped up, his eyes in a frenzy to find the threat.

"Where am I? What happened with DoDO?"

"These things, you will have to ask another. It is not mine to tell." The man took his bowl and left Dexx cradling his pounding head in his hands.

A few moments later, he heard movement coming closer. The chair across from him creaked. The woman from the cafeteria sat down, elbows on knees, waiting for him to look up.

Which Dexx did, but with difficulty. "Please don't hit me again."

"You can take more," she said with a refined British accent. "About as much as I could manage and a bit more, I'm sure. You're hard for a Yank."

"Feels like a herd of elephants tap-danced with Danny Kay on my head." Dexx loved the tap dancer, but not in his head.

"I also had to make sure you couldn't interfere with the extraction." She gave him a hard look with her cold blue eyes. "He said you had a stubborn streak that would make rocks stand and applaud."

"Not me, I'm the picture of cooperation." At least his wit had made it through the concussion intact. But had he really been saved? Or was this just another frying pan?

"We couldn't risk any more of our people than we did. Our orders were to bring you alive, but asleep might work better. I hadn't realized what he'd meant until you came into the room. You're a bit dim, aren't you?"

Dim? Why'd she have to cut so low? "He who?" So, this was only a lackey. Only evil organizations like Dr. Evil sent representatives to talk to people. And corporate ass hats.

"The big boss." She settled into her chair with a cool smile that lit her eyes with ire as if she read his interpretation of her position. "He sends his regards, but he has business to attend to. He can't be here all the time. Has an entire resistance to run."

Dexx didn't know what questions to ask now.

The woman scooted forward on the chair. "I don't know about *you*. This plan is yarky."

He didn't know what that word meant, but he could guess. Maybe he'd made the wrong assumption? "Okay, so who are you? And what resistance?" He had several guesses, though, and one topped the list.

"The Department of Delicate Operations. They are worse than Mussolini, Stalin, and Mao all rolled into one."

Hmm. Not what he'd thought. He'd seen the headlines on the news, though he hadn't paid a lot of attention to it. There was a big para resistance going on at home. "Forgot Hitler."

"Overdone. Besides, it's helping me gauge your mental facilities. You're recovering nicely."

"Cool." But it felt like he was pulling information out of an obstinate toddler. Wait. How did he know that? "Do. You. Have. A. Name?"

"Yes." She smiled smugly and raised a challenging eyebrow. "Call me Medusa."

"Fuck. Call *me* a cab. I can't believe I fell in with a comic book group of wannabe's." But seriously, if he was sitting with… no. It couldn't be the real Medusa. None of the agents had turned to stone. But how many other legends had gotten it wrong? "I have to leave before you get me killed. Thanks for the—" Dexx mimed a punch. "— but I think I should be going now."

"You will stay." Medusa stood, her eyes going from confident to pissed in zero seconds flat.

Her smell quavered from anger to uncertainty.

"Why?" Dexx turned to the woman. He was tired. He needed a nap, but not on the torture sofa.

"Because, luv." One of the sisters. Bruna, or maybe Doxy from the shop that dressed him ridiculously and sent him back to DoDO stood with her hands clasped tightly in front of her. "We wanted another good look atcha."

What was up with Dexx's dumb luck?

"Go ahead. Give us a spin. You're a proper man. All strappin' an' bulgy in all the right places." She looked down to the too-tight pants he still wore.

Dexx groaned. The sisters were a pain in the ass in the worst way, but Dexx felt a bond of trust. One like… the name and the face were intangible, but *right there* out of reach.

He heaved a sigh. "Alright, *Medusa*. What's your game?"

"DoDO has been systematically wiping out all the paras in Western Europe since World War II, and we're losing. Until a few years ago, when the boss came, we were all but wiped out. Now we have a real chance to hold on. Maybe even win."

"You won't. There isn't a win condition for you. They have resources you can't imagine. Tech you've never seen. They've got backing from the government and the church.

You don't stand a chance. Not even a slim one." Dexx held his fingers tightly pressed together. "Zero."

"We *have* to fight." Medusa stood like a tight bow ready to release. "Aren't we people too? Why do *they* get to live comfortably, and we have to scrape by or better yet, die?"

Dexx had very similar thoughts. They were people too, just as long as they weren't possessed.

Wait. He was a part of them. Gah. "What do you think *I* can do for you? If your big boss gave you such an advantage, why do you need me?"

"Because you've been inside." Medusa tipped her head to the side. "You know how they work, their soft spots. They can't be so powerful that they can't be brought back under control. Well, maybe not control, but even footing with them. A fighting chance. We don't really expect to replace them, but if we could match them, then things would be different."

"And if wishes had wings, we'd all have pants that fit." Dexx unsnapped the top button on his tight pants.

Medusa looked down with a small smirk on her face. "Well, as to those, we can fix that. Bruna can take you back and get that remedied."

Dexx groaned. Who *knew* how they would dress him this time? Red stripes with gold accents, no doubt. "Just go easy on me. Please."

"Don't rush your bum, good man." Bruna, or maybe Doxy, smiled wide and held her hand out for Dexx to take. "We've got the goods for ya."

He let her take his hand with a great deal of reluctance. Actually, he had to force his hand out for the sister to take. More visions of eye wrenching combinations reeled through his brain.

Bruna had endless cheer as she led him through the concrete and steel hallways, sometimes passing open doors, closed doors, and missing doors. Some had people inside.

Others did not. But they were *all* a pathetic bunch. Their eyes were haunted by things they'd seen or experienced.

Dammit all to nine hells. These people need more than the Big Boss and me if they're going to win.

Lead them, a female voice said inside his head.

Dexx jerked his hand away from Bruna's grasp. Had she spoken into his mind?

"Oh, luv. You're in too deep now. You need clothes that fit you. Not that I mind lookin' at what ya have on, mind ye."

"Did you just…"

"You still aren't you, but at least we can dress you proper. Come on, luv." Bruna reached out and tugged on him again.

He followed, but with growing apprehension. "Which one are you?"

"The pretty one." She shot a grin at him. "Bruna. Remember that."

By the time they found a room with clothing—actual clothing, not just second-hand rejects—Dexx's headache had receded to a light tingle.

"Doxy," Bruna rang out with barely concealed joy. "We have a customer. Repeat clientele."

"Oh, really?" Doxy's head popped around the end of a cart of jackets. She stood straight and locked her eyes on Dexx. "My, my. Aren't ye a sight to behold? I can't get over how yummy ye are." She rushed forward as Bruna came around to the front of Dexx, and they stood together in the same pose, chin propped in a hand, and the other crossed along their front.

It might have been comical, but with Bruna and Doxy staring like that, he just got the feeling that something horrific was going to happen.

"I think…" Doxy began.

"With the coloring of his skin…" Bruna added.

The two of them shot into motion, talking in clothing

gibberish, and probably a different language while snapping stuff from the carts. They slipped things out and slipped them back in, apparently unable to pass the desired look.

In all too short a time, they closed in on Dexx with armfuls of clothes.

Dexx didn't have time to react as Doxy yanked his pants down. He shouldn't have been surprised, but the shock of losing his pants had a visceral effect from all the way back in middle school.

"Boxers or briefs, luv?"

They both stopped moving and stared at Dexx.

"What?"

"When ye tuck your bits away, do ya prefer boxers or briefs to tickle the yams?" Doxy looked significantly at Dexx's package.

His hands unconsciously covered his boy parts.

Bruna smiled at her sister. "Told ya, he liked the silkies."

"Boxers will be fine." Dexx answered quickly as the women turned in place to look for "silkies."

Bruna's smile faded. "Ah, well. Sometimes it's nice to feel pretty." Then she added in a stage whisper, "Let me know when you want some, and I'll fix ye straight away."

Doxy swung fabric at him. "These should work. Ye have a lovely set, and these would be happy to adorn ye."

Dark blue boxers sailed through the air. Dexx caught them and slipped on the undies as fast as he could. Once Big Jim and the twins were decently covered, the rest of the process was surprisingly fast and efficient.

They conjured a mirror from somewhere, and he looked at what the sisters had done.

Well, they might *actually* know clothing after all. What looked back was very nice. Not Double-oh-Seven, not Kingsmen, but something very close to both. Fine fabric, all of a really nice cut.

"How did you do that?" Dexx swiveled back and forth, enjoying the look. He'd *never* been a suit and tie guy, but this might change his mind.

"Got a gift." Doxy turned around coyly. "Now as for payment—"

"You're charging me for this?" It was a dumb question, but how in the hell was he going to *pay*?

"As for *payment*—" Doxy twisted back and forth, her skirts swishing, "— ye have to take us out on a date. One at a time, mind." She waggled a finger at him. "We aren't *that* kind of sisters. And *I*, for one, want *all* of yer attention on *my* date."

Bruna's smile said the same thing.

Dexx grumbled. "I don't have money."

"Don't worry, luv. We'll pay, ye be the trophy."

Damnit. Extortion was alive and well in England. The smiles both of the sisters wore was sort of infectious. Okay, so it was more than that. They were downright uplifting. But how many men got this kind of offer? "Okay. deal." Dexx smiled back. A real honest to goodness smile.

Bruna and Doxy rushed forward, throwing their arms around him collectively and then separately several times.

Upper-end lady parts squished against him each time they went in for another hug.

There were worse things to happen than having the two happiest people alive squishing themselves against a person.

By the time the hugs slowed, Medusa had shown up and waited patiently for Dexx to extricate himself. Once he got to the door, Doxy had disappeared, and Bruna joined them, all smiles and overly-friendly hugs gone.

"So, what's this place all about?" Dexx waved his hand in all the random directions.

Medusa gestured with her hand as she continued down. "We're the paras nobody wants, and everyone fears. Vampires, shifters, elementals, witches, other things."

Dexx stopped when she said "vampires." "I don't do vamps. No demons either. One is gross, and the other can't be trusted. Most paras are just people, but those…" Dexx let the words trail away.

"Vampires are our very best source of information—" Medusa took a deep breath. "—and they really aren't as bad as they're made out to be. In fact, they seem to be more human than most mundanes are when they find out about paras. Just look at what's going on in your home."

He should probably actually pay attention to the news. "Then, this is just one big smorgasbord of a para grab bag?" That came out wrong, but… vamps. But also, when would DoDO hit?

Bruna sighed, her arms folded at her waist. "We're the ones DoDO passes over for selection. If we don't meet their criteria, we're thrown to the side and are either ignored or killed out of fear."

Chosen? "Vampires make more vampires by intentional means."

"Shifters are made that way too. One bite from an alpha and poof—" She spread her fingers in front of her. "—another shifter."

The familiar tug of something he should know pulled at a memory. Cold snow, a ruckus in a small police station, the pain of… It wasn't quite there, but it wasn't disappearing either. Were shifters *made*? "Well, it takes an alpha, right? Not everyone can spread the gene around."

"A matter of genetics, then?" Bruna's sly smile and sidelong look made Dexx pull back.

Medusa bared her teeth. "More a matter of magick. Vampires are born too. It *does* have to be two vampires to make a child, but they're not always made from a bite."

"So, what are you then?" The memory of what she did in the cafeteria was… vivid.

"I'm a mythos. Part gorgon and part… something else." Medusa looked to the floor, not quite in shame.

"What's the something else?" She had something to hide.

"I'm technically a lillim."

"I don't understand, what's a—" Dexx cut off as a high portion of the ceiling exploded inward.

Darkly clad figures in body armor swarmed in like a flood of ants.

"Run!" Bruna grabbed Dexx's arm and pulled him with surprising strength and speed.

Paras ran forward and fought individual DoDO agents. People on both sides fell like dolls.

Something inside pushed Dexx forward. Anger rose. He had to act, or he might burst. The paras weren't his targets, though. The was agents were. He knew that with a deep certainty.

Before Bruna dragged him another step, he lashed out at the nearest black-clad agent, with a punch to the throat.

The man who had been crackling with a spell crumbled.

More. More of them needed to fall. *All* of them needed to die. Dexx took another step forward.

Bruna barred his way. "We have to run. Come on, Dexx. They'll be fine. Just hurry. Come with us."

Dexx turned to go with them, but he stopped, a strange sensation sweeping over him. An irresistible urge more powerful than anything he'd ever known overwhelmed him.

Bussemi, dressed in his red robes, stepped from a circle of the armored DoDO's, holding his *kadu* high in the air.

2 2

Dexx took two steps before he realized what he was doing. He stopped only when he met an invisible wall.

Somebody screamed something at him, but he heard it from far away.

The *kadu*. He had to get to the *kadu*.

"Dexx, please." Bruna stepped in front of him, waving her hands in front of his eyes.

The contact was broken. He refocused on her.

"We have to leave." She pushed on his chest, while someone else pulled on his arm.

Finally, sound and thought crashed back in. The sounds of fighting were everywhere. Paras and DoDO agents fell.

Cardinal Bussemi remained calmly holding the *kadu* in the air, taunting Dexx with it.

"That's my—" Dexx raised his other hand out to the small stone.

"Not now." Medusa growled as she passed in front of Dexx and the sisters. She transformed into the beast-thing and whipped her tentacle limbs at the invaders.

"Shit!" Dexx turned and ran, the witch sisters guiding him along.

They moved fast for curvaceous girls.

And they knew every twist and turn, where to pause, where to rush. Until they didn't.

Down deep in the complex, DoDO set off a bomb or magical attack and brought the entire hallway exploding inward.

Dexx grabbed both sisters by the waist just in time to keep them from being buried alive.

Dust and debris choked the air, sending plumes straight at them.

They coughed at the suddenly unclean air. "Anyone know if that's asbestos we're breathing?"

Bruna and Doxy faced each other and clasped hands together. The tunnel glowed a soft blue, lit up from the witches.

Bruna spoke in a voice that wasn't her usual tone.

The voice was powerful and confident, as though she'd gone from giddy fifteen-year-old girl to thirty in a heartbeat. "The tunnel is too far gone to use. The way back is patrolled. Survivors are fleeing. Medusa is hurt but alive. More are dead."

The glow faded, and the sisters turned to Dexx in the dark. It really was dark now.

"What do we do?" Doxy wrung her hands in her skirts.

"I, uh…" He always had a way with the right words at the right time.

Wait. He *saw* them in the *dark*. He could use that.

"What's the plan," One of them asked again, worry but not panic clear in her voice.

Good question. "I promised you a date. In order for you to collect, we have to get out of here. So that's what we're going to do. Got me?"

"Of course, pretty man. I intend to collect.

Dexx drew in a deep breath. A bit difficult with the air still so full of abandoned building material, but there *was* a faint odor of not-as-deadly-dust in the breath.

"There's a way out. Come on. It's probably back this way." Dexx motioned with his arm, but the two stayed put. "Are you coming?"

"We can't see anything. There's no light." The two shook their heads like one was a mirror.

Dexx stepped back and grabbed a hand. He tugged, but the hand stayed right there.

"Bruna gets a hand too." Doxy stroked his hand.

Twins. Can't give something without the other getting jealous.

Dexx grabbed a hand from Bruna. "Are you both satisfied now?"

They nodded in simultaneous agreement.

"Okay. I'll lead you through, but if I let go, you have to let go too. I may need to fight, and I doubt you work well as a club."

The girls snickered, but they moved.

Dexx followed the faint trace of clear air back up the hall-way. Slowly at first, but as he led them away from the collapse, the trail strengthened. The surest path out was right through the DoDO raid, but since they came looking for Dexx, that way wasn't a viable option.

Empty rooms and forgotten corridors were the words of the day. A few windows had to be broken as quietly as possi-ble, but each time he dropped a hand, it was picked back up as soon as they were through to the next room.

Even after the darkness turned to gloomy light and finally a brighter gloomy light, Bruna and Doxy petted their portion of Dexx like he was the cutest kitten ever.

They managed to stay away from anything black and

armored. Not that they didn't see any. They just managed to avoid all contact with anything DoDO. The super smell, combined good old fashioned sneakiness, kept them safe. As safe as could be under the circumstances.

Doxy bit back little squeals every time they saw an agent, but they were unseen in their escape-in-progress.

He heard teams talking to each other or into their mic's to Control. Apparently, they hadn't had the time to learn or implement the protocols he'd tried to teach them. Good. Let them rot.

Once they hit the outside, and with a reasonable amount of surety they weren't being followed, Dexx dropped their hands a final time.

They crushed him in a hug.

He found himself returning it.

"You did that on purpose. A little sneak peek at the date."

They looked at each other with a devilish grin.

"Lasses never tell."

They were too bubbly by half and a bit annoying, but if he had to take someone out to a bar, those two might be the most fun. And they were just too… vulnerable. Just like… Leah. He didn't remember much more than the name. A small person holding him *just* like the sisters had. They were clinging because they had to borrow some of his confidence, some of his strength.

Things were coming back. Slowly. Very slowly.

Dexx pulled away from the sisters and kissed each on the top of her head. "You did well in there. You've graduated to master sneaks. Now it's your turn. Where are we headed?"

They stood outside more dreary buildings, but not far away were a few that looked like they did actual business.

Bruna and Doxy looked at each other, totally leaving Dexx out. "There's only one place left—"

"—only for emergencies—"

"—which this may qualify as—"

The two rattled away so fast, he almost couldn't keep up. They didn't talk in complete thoughts, just as if they shared a brain.

"—he may not like this—"

"—but we have a present—"

"—but he's not ready—"

"—There isn't a choice—"

"—not anymore—"

Dexx knife-edged his hand between the two. "Hey. Number one, slow down. You're giving me a headache. One for the each of ya. Number two, who is this guy you want to see?"

Bruna spoke first. "The big boss. We have strict instructions *not* to let you meet him until you're ready."

If it meant answers, he was ready. "Why would I not be ready?"

Bruna cupped his cheek. "Ye sure are pretty. But ye have a few flaws that go all the way down." She shrugged and stepped back. "Yer not ready to meet him. But right now, we don' have a choice."

"Please be open when ye meet." Doxy ran her hand down his arm. "Can ye promise?"

Were they pleading with him to *like* their boss? Was he a vampire? "Wait. Is your boss... God?"

The laughed so fast, so suddenly that he almost left them there, laughing guts out.

"No, ye pretty, pretty man." Doxy quieted to a chuckle. "He's *not*... that. But you *will* have to see us, *really* see us before you can meet him. Everyone in the resistance knows this. So, don't go thinkin' you can trick someone into settin' up a date."

He realized she was talking about him being one of them. He shook his head. A part of him *knew* they were right, but...

maybe he wasn't ready to see the big boss just yet. "Can't we just go back to your place? Your shop?"

"What, that ol' thing?" Doxy thought about that for a moment. "I guess we could. But it's a long way off."

That could only be the truth. The shop was in the middle of a bustling city, colorful and full of life. This place appeared to have been dead for more than a century. Maybe not that long, but certainly since the eighties.

"How long? Is the boss closer?" Because he did want to get to a protected place. But where would that be?

"Oh, the boss is closer to be sure, but I like yer thinkin'. We'll hide out in the shop. We could play dress-up too." Bruna eyed him up and down and waggled her eyebrows.

Maybe the shop wasn't such a good plan.

The twins grabbed a hand and pulled Dexx along in their wake.

Definitely not a good plan.

Dexx was saved from silkies and bad wardrobe malfunctions only two blocks away. A bleeding Medusa stepped out from an alcove of a doorway.

Her suit had been torn, the sleeve only tatters.

Bruna and Doxy rushed to her. The babble that followed was way too fast for anyone except them to follow.

Dexx did catch a few snippets, asking how she'd gotten out, where they should go, who else made it out, what a horrible mess she'd made of her suit. Fairly standard stuff.

Medusa waited for the flurry of questions to subside. Then she broke away from the twins to address Dexx. "Come with me. We have a place ready."

Bruna turned to Doxy, clearly confused. "We do?"

"We do," Medusa said properly British. Now, if you'd like to get there, let's go. If not, we could wait for a friendly DoDO team to pick us up."

They shook their heads and murmured, "No, please. Lead on," set Medusa off down the street.

The walk took less time than strictly necessary to feel really safe from DoDO.

"We're not very far from the old hole." Dexx peered around the not-as-dreary building. This one could have been abandoned only *ten* years ago.

"We don't have a lot of choices out here." Bruna's tone was unnaturally clipped. "So yes, this is a little too close for comfort, but right now, we don't have a choice."

Medusa moved with a limp she was trying to hide.

"You look like hell." Dexx still wasn't sure he cared, but he had a hard time *not* caring. "Are you sure you're okay?" She'd had earned a bit of respect from him, though.

"I'm going to live." She spoke mechanically while she peered around corners, assuring herself nobody waited in ambush.

Okay, tough girl. He vaguely recalled another woman who was tough. She pushed herself too hard and refused to acknowledge when she couldn't take anymore. But who? He was glad the memories were coming back, but he needed them to hurry up. "Yeah, but for how long? You must have really taken a beating back there. Here, let me take point. Just point me in the right direction."

"I'm looking for teams of DoDO agents."

"Yeah, I know." So was he. Part of him wanted to return to them and make sure they were okay. The other part of him wanted to tear their entire organization up. "I'll make sure there's nobody there. Just trust me."

"I—"

Dexx pushed ahead of her and let his nose lead the way.

He could smell the un-showered, the fear, the determination ahead of him.

They snuck to a large abandoned warehouse. The thing

looked like it had produced airplanes in the forties. Everything had an art deco feel with rounded edges and thick steel girders and foundations.

They found a half-boarded door and wedged it open enough for them all to enter one at a time.

The door led to an outside corridor along the length of the building, like the longest arctic entry of all time. Then the hall ended, and the main open area of the hangar, production facility loomed just outside.

Faint voices carried whispers of sound too faint to make out.

Dexx turned to wait for Medusa.

She must have been hurt worse than she let on. Bruna and Doxy had her propped between them.

Dexx was glad she'd let him take point. "What kind of reception are we going to get if we go out there?"

The open area was huge. The warehouse *must* have been an airplane hangar with the wide, open trusses and windows high on the sides.

The group of people of this make-shift tent city gave off a mix of emotions Dexx could smell from way off. Way, way off.

"Let me go first." Medusa stumbled forward, both sisters under an arm to keep her upright. She called out before she got to the corner. "We're safe. I brought the alpha with me."

Who the fuck was the alpha? "Who?"

Bruna and Doxy carried Medusa to the crowd.

Dexx followed a short distance behind.

The homeless paras parted for Medusa and the witches but closed in after they passed.

One of the crowd turned around. The first person Dexx had met— could it only have been that morning? "Dis? Dis is de guy we're supposed to be so worried over? Looking all fine and dressed for a dance, eh?"

"What, are you twelve?" Dexx didn't know exactly how to handle this situation. He was pretty sure Medusa had introduced *him* as the alpha. "A dance, really? I don't know who you think you are, but I'm not here for—"

Dexx cut off as a blinding light erupted on the other side of the crowd. Dexx held his hand up against the light, just like everyone else.

Great. What could possibly be hunting for them now?

Several people turned and ran, considerably thinning the people between him and the light. He began to blink tears away, refusing to run from any more dangers.

The light faded, leaving a considerable portion of his vision occluded with the afterimage of a… person?

"Dexx?" a rough, female voice asked. But this one was American. She sounded strange after so much time away from normal accents. "Dexx, is that you?" Whoever she was, she walked quickly, bordering on a trot toward him.

She smelled relieved, though. And very happy. That was a relief, but who the hell was this woman?

"I thought you were dead. We all did." The sounds came closer, and then somebody plowed into him, hugging him. The hug was brief, a perfunctory thing, then the arms let go. "So, this is where you've been?"

"Uh, yeah, I guess."

"Careful, girl." Bruna cut in. "Ye can wait in line. Pushy American twigs."

Dexx's sight had cleared up considerably, and just the center of his sight had a dot of fading purple and green.

The new woman was dressed in a cheap business suit, the kind that people wore when they didn't wear casual to work. She had dark hair pulled back in a loose ponytail and a slight frame. But the woman knew how to wear a gun.

Her scent became clearer once he worked through the

relief. Trees. A thousand different kinds, forest floors, and leaves. She smelled like a complete forest just by herself.

"I didn't think it would work." She narrowed her dark gaze up at him, then took in their environment. "I mean, I knew she said she could. And she *is* who she is, but I still had doubts."

"Who are you?" And who was *she*?

Disappointment filled the woman's face. She looked over her shoulder to another person, just rising from her knees like she had run a marathon. "She said you—" She bit off a curse and turned back to him, a little pissed. "Michelle. Michelle Gomez."

Oh. Well, her tone certainly said they knew each other.

"Molly said *you* took Rainbow, Tarik, and Frey. And now you're *here* in the middle of a refugee camp with a really great suit on and no idea who you are? What the fuck is going on here?"

Dexx put his hands up to protest. He had no idea who those people were at all.

"And your *kids*. Not even *one* call to check in, to tell them you were safe. *Alive* or *anything*."

His *kids?* He opened his mouth to say something, anything, but the woman steamrollered right over him.

"—been just me and Ethel, trying to figure out what the hell happened and where the fuck you've been, and if Roxxie hadn't shown up and told me you *were* alive—I mean, what the fuck, man?"

"Kids?" Dexx pulled his brows down in a severe frown. "You're going to have to back up quite a ways. I don't have kids."

"Paige would pull your beating heart out and show it to you if she heard you say that."

Paige.

The word hit him like a punch to the gut. The vision of

the woman with dark hair and lightning cascading from her came to him.

The new woman— Michelle—reached a hand to steady him. "Are you okay? Roxxie, what's wrong with him?"

The other woman looked up from her hands and knees, her blonde hair cascading down her shoulder to sweep the floor. She looked like hell. "He's broken, Shell. That's what I was trying to tell you."

"Well…" Michelle flared her nose, her lips flat. "Fuck."

Dexx shifted from foot to foot, trying to counter the sway. He might have discovered a new dance move.

Michelle pulled her hand away when he stopped overcorrecting and shook his head.

"There's a powerful spell around him." The blonde-haired woman finally made it to her feet and came up to him, a faint golden glow emanating from her hand. "I can see it. But it's strange. I haven't seen this sort of work in thousands of years." She was beautiful. Not the sort of beautiful that Maybelline made, but the sort that made other people more so by being closer to her. Her dark blonde hair framed her face perfectly, and even her concern looked beautiful on her.

"Wait a minute." Dexx backed up.

The rest of the crowd backed up too.

Huh. Interesting. "What sort of para are you?"

"Para?" The blonde took another step toward him, but a small one. "That's not how you talk. You've been the target of a powerful spell, and perhaps worse. Let me see if I can help you."

"No, you won't. What kind of para besides a demon can blink in and out of existence?" But a golden glow. Demons didn't have that. "That's not a normal thing."

The only other thing that came close was the portal DoDO used to get places. *That* could be considered on the edge of normal, but not a person. Demons did that, and she smelled clean. Clean and pure. *Nothing* smelled like that.

"Please, Dexx. Let me see if I can help." The woman took another small step.

"Not on your life. And what's this about kids?"

The blonde turned and looked back at Michelle.

She studied him like he was a broken puzzle. "What's the last thing you remember?"

"You two showing up in a blaze of light. Then blah, blah, kids." And a name. Paige. His brain lit up even when he thought it.

She smiled, but it was a sad smile. "A little further back, please. I see the strings. They've changed you. What's the last thing you remember? Before Working for DoDO."

Before the accident? An abandoned warehouse. Demons were possessing a whole herd of innocents. Blazing gunfire and falling. "Nice try, but identity theft is on the rise, and the best defense is to not give out personal information." But maybe there was more to the accident. That would explain Bussemi's actions. He'd been *hunting* Dexx. The thought twisted his gut.

"That much is you, at least." Michelle crossed her arms. "She's trying to help you, asshole."

"I don't care if she's the last best hope for humanity." Except he did. He just wanted some damned basic common ground. "I still don't know who *you* are, and the people I *do* know are hurt. *They* have priority."

"That much is you, too. Fine. I'll help as much as I can,

then we talk. Got it?" Michelle pointed her sharp finger at him.

"I will do what I can. I'm not what I once was." The blonde knelt next to Medusa.

Medusa pulled away as if she was about to be burned. "Angel," she spat.

"Roxxie," Michelle warned.

The angel shook her off. "My peers would not touch one, such as you. But I have… *evolved*. I owe Dexx. More than I can ever repay. His actions went a long way to make me who I am. They *all* did." She placed her hand gently along Medusa's face, and light poured from the wounds on her arms and other places.

A strange look came over Roxxie's face, like concentration, or hiding pain. "I have done what I can. The rest will be up to you. There are things I cannot heal. I am sorry. I *am* sorry." Her voice trailed off into a whisper.

Medusa frowned and turned her head away.

Roxxie pulled her hand back but stayed kneeling, her head bowed and her hair covering over her face.

Michelle turned out to have a talent for organization and first aid. Soon, she had groups of people lined out from broken and bleeding all the way down to scratches and out of breath from frightened running.

After a few minutes, she set the crowd of paras to begin to look after themselves. "We need to talk. You and me and Roxxie." Michelle pulled the sleeves of her jacket down. "In Private. Is there a place we can do that?"

"Got me,—" Dexx shrugged and looked around the empty hangar, "—I just got here myself." Dexx glanced around the wide-open warehouse. Besides the small hallway they'd entered from, they would have to cross the space to have privacy.

"Oh, that will do nicely." Roxxie stood slowly, pushing

her hands against her knees to stand. "We shouldn't waste any time."

Bruna placed herself between Dexx and Michelle, Doxy, by her side. "Ye aren't takin' him anywhere. How do we know we can even trust Ye? We can't read ye. For all we know, yer agents sent by DoDO to gain our confidence or kill our Dexx. We won't allow that. No, we won't."

"That's all Dexx, too." Michelle shook her head with a look of disbelief. "Got the local girls under your spell. How do you do that?"

But he didn't have *her*. "I gotta a perty smile."

Michelle's dark eyes flared. "That's *one* of the things we need to discuss in *private*."

Doxy deflated a little. Whatever was going on, Michelle knew more about him than they did. "You gonna tell me what's going on?" Medusa waved him on from her impromptu bed of rags, her arm laying across her eyes. "Go. Do what you will. I was sure you wouldn't work out anyway." Resignation wafted from her.

Frustration burbled out of Dexx. "No. You don't get to tell me what I'm going to do. *I* tell me what to do. I just need information."

"It's time." Roxxie had a sort of command about her.

Dexx blew out his cheeks. "Fine. But I want Bruna and Doxy to go with me."

"I said private," Michelle said darkly, flicking a concerned gaze to the two women.

"They're the only people I know and actually trust here."

Michelle looked up to the high ceiling for patience and then spun on her heel and led them away from the other paras.

He followed and fell into step with Roxxie matching her slow stride.

Roxxie's smile lifted Dexx's spirits much higher. "Hey, Dexx. I see you in there."

Was he? He hoped so. This being in the dark thing was getting really old.

Michelle waited at the door to an office while the four caught up.

Bruna and Doxy said nothing, but their expressions said they knew what was going on.

Once they entered the room, Michelle started before the door was shut. "I want to know what the hell is—"

Dexx stopped her with a raised hand. "I think you should start first." He looked at Bruna and Doxy.

"We shouldn't." They said in unison.

"Uh, yeah. Otherwise, I'm not even gonna know what we're talking about."

Michelle frowned. "What do *you* think happened?"

He shrugged. "Only what I was told. There was some kind of accident. Been healing from that."

We've had you for a little over a month. Well, in the outside world. It's been more than that for you.

"So, fill in all the little gaps. Things have been all sorts of fucked up in my head lately, and everyone knows it but me."

Quinn Winters had said to find Hattie. Was Hattie a girlfriend? Wife? For sure, someone important.

"That's a lot of gaps, Dexx." Michelle rubbed her eyebrow in frustration.

Bruna bit down on her lips.

Doxy shrugged. "We got a tip that you'd be coming over the ocean, and the boss said he wanted your help, and to help you in any way we could."

"Why me?" This could only get better. "Why's everyone out to get me?"

"We have no idea why *they* want you," Bruna said.

"I do," Michelle said grimly. "Or at least I can guess. Paige is waging war on DoDO back home, and it's getting pretty hot. She just took down nearly an entire unit all on her own." Michelle rolled her eyes, crossing her arms over her chest. "Nearly. They want to weaken her by keeping you away."

He opened his mouth to ask just who Paige was.

Bruna interrupted. "Maybe that's one reason. But you're also one of the most powerful alphas in the world."

Shit. Which question should he ask first? "What's an alpha?" He felt like he'd heard the term but just didn't remember what it meant.

Michelle took a step forward, unfolding her arms. "You're a shifter, dipshit. And your spirit is powerful. *You* are powerful."

"I hunt those." Pieces were finally starting to really fit with what the cardinal said, though.

"You're a *shifter*, not a *para*," Michelle spat. "That's DoDO spewing out. But you're not just a shifter. You're an alpha, and you have a pack. A very, very powerful one. It scares DoDO, and they want you and your pack out of the game." Michelle snarled slightly. "And if that wasn't enough, your *wife* is a powerful witch. Paige Whiskey?"

Gongs exploded in his head again. He swallowed hard, trying to overcome the immense feeling of crappiness growing inside him. He *did* have a family.

"But wait," she continued with anger-filled mockery. "There's more. You're my boss and the head of the magickal police department. Red Star."

This made sense but didn't jive with the memories he *did* have. "That's... *insane*. Before five years ago, I worked *alone*. Then, I was approached by some weirdo in body armor and tactical gear. Mario Kester. I joined DoDO to help end the demon invasion. Paras were thrown in somewhere along the way." But were they? He'd been *ordered* to kill them, and he hadn't.

That'd been what had broken their spells on him, actually. Probably. The fact that they kept telling him to kill paras— paranormals—and he hadn't. They'd been trying to *break* him.

Those…. mother fucking assholes.

Michelle must have seen something she approved of in his expression because hers softened. "Speaking of, you captured *our* people and imprisoned them. Rainbow, Tarik, Frey. I escaped your notice somehow. I don't know if I should be insulted."

With the names came faces. Sort of. He vaguely recalled memories of taking them down, but they were weird, almost as if there was a double exposure, and they didn't make sense.

"We met two years ago." Roxxie quietly intruded. "In Louisiana. You and Paige were over your head in demons the first time you went head to head against Sven Seven-Tails. You lost. You were in the hospital and almost died."

"Fuck." Had DoDO manipulated his memories? Five years' worth? Fit their M.O., and it wasn't beyond them to resort to underhanded means. The ends justified the means.

"Do you still have Hattie?" Roxxie stared up at him with too-blue eyes. They were deep pools of… infinity.

"Are you really an angel?"

Roxxie nodded.

Bruna took a step back, eyeing Roxxie like she was a serpent.

Doxy just looked at Dexx, watching him.

Dexx looked over at Bruna, confused. Crazy woman. "Can't you just smite these people?" But why hadn't he asked that question before?

"Heaven's power in this plane is weakened. I am one of seven pillars that keep the dimension from tearing away forever. My kind cannot enter as they used to. The demons cannot enter as easily either, so at least there is symmetry, but my powers were never as great as Michael's, or even Xael's. It took a great deal just to bring Michelle here then to heal the lilim."

Bruna lifted her head. "The Host is gone?"

Doxy mirrored her twin. "We felt something shift, but we didn't know."

Roxxie lifted a pale eyebrow and nodded.

Great. Awesome. "So that's it? I'm a *shifter* and the head guy for a police department and the lead guy for a pack and a husband to a crazy powerful witch? And DoDO kidnapped me to get me out of the way?"

Michelle nodded, her lips flat. "You have four children, too. And Jackie. Can't forget about that stupid thing."

"Crap." So, he *did* have kids. "Is one of them..." Did he *want* to say the name out loud? "Leah?"

"Yeah." Michelle stuck her head out, elongating her neck. "She's a necromancer."

That's—oh. So, they'd been able to manipulate a lot of his memories, but they'd been trying to find a way to punch through this whole time.

Michelle stepped forward, head low trying to see into his face. "Are you telling me you didn't know? Really didn't know?"

"No. I— not really. I know I've been off for a few weeks, but I thought it was part of the accident."

Michelle shook her head. "Tell me about the accident."

He wasn't sure it was even an accident anymore. If they'd stripped his memories, he might have awakened that bruised thanks to torture. "That's what they told me. We were in a nest, and I fell from a balcony or something. Who's Jackie?" Of the string of names, Jackie felt like home.

"Your stupid car. Your juvenile, gas-guzzling tribute to

your swelled ego of a car." Michelle pressed her lips together in that way women had.

"I have a car? Is it a Corvette? Wait, I bet it's a Chevelle. Mustangs are cool. Maybe it's a Torino, or a 'Cuda." He really didn't mean to ramble, but he was buying time.

"You need to stop deflecting." Roxxie stood next to Michelle. "I can see you in there, but I can't see *her*. Is she there with you? You haven't let her go, have you?"

They had to be talking about the other name everyone mentioned but refused to define. "Hattie."

Roxxie nodded. "She's your shifter spirit."

"A cat?"

She nodded again. "A saber-tooth cat."

That would explain why the dream cat was the size of a car. That must be the reason he kept waking up naked.

Roxxie stepped close enough to Dexx to place her hand on Dexx's head. His tattoos under his shirt warmed pleasantly as Roxxie touched him. "I cannot break the wards on you. With a little recovery I could, but that would leave you blank. These are the work of someone very powerful. I haven't seen this sort of thing for a *very* long time as counted by your years."

"What, like the sixties?"

"As in the sixties after humanity first walked the Earth, yes."

"Oh." That was... kinda ancient.

A knock at the door stopped the conversation cold. It swung open, and Medusa stood there, jacket still torn, and she held her arm gingerly across her stomach, but she stood tall. "We got some intel, and we have to move quickly. DoDO was injured, and we have a chance to strike before they can collect themselves."

With what forces? *They* were beat to shit. Who would send them intel?

"I agree. Yes, you must." Roxxie passed a look at Dexx. "I can't go with you, but I can help a little." She reached behind Dexx's neck, and for a brief two-count, her hand glowing.

A warm tingle spread through him as she took her hand away.

"What did you do?

"I removed their tracking ward."

No wonder the base had been attacked. That meant this one could be too. "Bastards." His hand went to the place where Roxxie had touched him and probed his neck. He didn't feel anything back there. "Shit, they know where we are. We've gotta get these—"

"They don't know." Roxxie smiled tiredly. "I've been shielding you since I found you. My power isn't what it was, but I can still do things."

"So, what are you going to do?" Dexx rubbed the spot, imagining he felt something.

"Lead them astray, of course. They can't track you now." Roxxie rested her hand on the hilt of a silver dagger.

"Thanks." Time for humility. "We'd probably be stuck back in DoDO's prison soon if you two hadn't shown up."

Medusa studied Roxxie for a moment, then turned her attention to Dexx. "We need to hit them hard."

"If you hurry, I can duplicate their portal signal to get you deep into the compound. The echo will fade soon." Roxxie gently pushed on Dexx to move him to the door.

"You can do that?" Dexx looked back over his shoulder.

"I can *this* time." Roxxie didn't sound very confident.

24

"You will have a very limited time to get in to do what you need to do." Roxxie stood tall, but she looked tired.

Medusa gathered the people in rows four deep.

Roxxie passed her gaze around the group ending with Dexx. "After this, I cannot help. I'm already at my limit, so when I send you in, it will be up to you to get out."

Dexx stood in the very front next to Michelle. He had to admit it felt natural to head into battle beside her.

One *kadu* and Bussemi could go fuck himself forever.

But wait. He also had team members inside DoDO, people *he'd* put there. He needed to locate them as well.

"Just have to ask. What kind of paras—paranormals—do we have here?" Dexx tipped his head to Medusa.

"Mostly vampires. One water elemental and myself. Plus, whatever your girlfriend is." She motioned with her head to Michelle.

"She's not my girlfriend." Apparently, he had a wife.

Paige.

Just repeating her name brought back a rumbling sense of himself. "What about Bruna and Doxy? Aren't they coming?"

Medusa stared him in the eye. "No."

Okay, then.

Dexx rolled his head, cracking his neck. "I have kids, huh?" The missing part of him?

"Yes." Michelle kept her eyes forward while Roxxie gathered a ball of light in her hands and coaxed it larger.

"She can pull my heart out?"

"And keep you alive for minutes as you contemplate your eternal fuck up. And then her daughter will raise you from the dead and seriously fuck you up."

Okay, then. He married the scary witch of the—

The portal cascaded over the rag-tag group of paras.

—west.

There was exactly one half a second of complete silence, then they scattered.

Dexx grabbed Michelle. "Come with me." He barely heard himself in the sudden noise, but she inclined her head and motioned for him to lead.

Roxxie had put them right in the portal chamber, so destroying it would be cake. Any teams in the field would now be stranded.

Two techs at the monitors went down before they had a chance to react. Three more went down as they grabbed for weapons or alarms.

Vampires were fast when they wanted to be.

With no way to bring their agents back, the paranormals might have a chance to do some real damage.

"Don't—" Dexx was about to tell them not to bite anyone, but if anyone deserved to be their own worst enemies, those bastards did.

Forget it. He needed to take Michelle and get his shit.

Once again, his super smell came to the rescue, noticing

the DoDO agents before they saw *him*. Several times, he stopped Michelle in order to catch the agents off guard.

Dexx took two strides beyond the curio room.

Michelle bounced off his back. "Damn you. Watch what you're doing."

"Oops. This is the one we want." He paused for a moment before he went in, letting his nose lead.

The rows of ancient and not as ancient weapons were silent as always. But they looked different with the knowledge that he was a para. Had these been used against his kind, or had they been taken from them like his *kadu*?

Dexx led them deeper into the room to the magical objects *definitely taken* from paras. If the *kadu* could be used against *him,* then surely these could be used against others. "Here. We have to take all of these." He motioned to the twenty or so rocks with the strange lines covering them.

"How? What are they?"

"Just do it. Put them in your coat." Dexx pried at the glass, but it resisted his fingers. "Hell. I don't have anything to break the glass."

"Men." Michelle rolled her eyes. "Move out of the way." She pulled her arm back as though she was going to punch the glass, but when she speared forward, her hand... changed.

She just went T- One Thousand on the glass and her hand, fingers, wood— jammed inside and swelled. Glass popped and left the *kadu* open to the air and Dexx's grabbing fingers.

However, his *kadu* was nowhere to be seen. Hells.

At first, he planned to just slip the stones in his coat pockets, but there were more than he thought, and they were a bit heavier than they looked. He took off his coat and made a basket from it.

After Michelle broke the last glass, she stripped her coat off and did the same.

Dexx threw the bundle over his back like a dead-sexy-Santa Claus and made for the exit.

He turned into the hallway and stopped dead.

Quinn Winters stood there in her under-gear like she was headed back to her bunk, with wide eyes staring behind him. At Michelle.

Her instant fear stank like sharp needles in his head.

"You," Michelle whispered in surprise.

"You," Quinn repeated, but not whispering. "What are you doing here?"

"What are *you* doing here? Were you working for them the entire time?"

"No." Her blue eyes sent Michelle a warning to stop asking questions.

Dexx had to agree. A battle wasn't the time for a cup of catch-up.

"I helped you escape once. Go on. Don't come back. If they catch you again, they won't let you go." She looked at Michelle. "Run." The word came out as a singing note.

Michelle ran. Down the corridor back toward the portal room.

"You too. But you'll have to hit me this time."

"No." He didn't understand what was going on, but she felt like an unfinished thread. "Come with us."

"I said run. You either hit me hard enough to knock me out, or I hit the alarm. Those are your choices."

"Why? Five words or less."

She shrugged slightly. "Taking it down from the inside."

And it was her choice. "You need me."

"I'll call."

Dexx hooked a fist to the side of her head. Winters fell to the floor, limp. Hopefully, he didn't hit her too hard.

He caught Michelle almost back at the portal room. He didn't know where his team or his *kadu* were. He needed to find those, but how?

"We're out of time," Medusa shouted. "Get out. We've done what we could."

But they hadn't. At least, Dexx hadn't.

The surviving paranormals gathered in the portal room.

"What the hell are you doing here? We can't leave this way. You heard Roxxie." Dexx wanted to punch the confused looks right in the face.

Medusa glared. "Then, where?"

"This way." He growled as he turned away. He could lead them to the exterior and maybe find a way to locate what *he* needed.

From the massive piles of destruction—dead piles and broken equipment—it looked like the paranormals had come in with a single plan of destruction but very little else.

Medusa kept up with no effort, even though she looked as laden with pilfered things as Dexx and Michelle.

He hit the doors to the compound at a dead run. There'd been very few agents remaining inside. That meant they were waiting for them outside. "Be prepared for magick fire," he yelled.

But he didn't stop. By his count, there wouldn't be a lot of them.

Magick bolts struck all around them, but after a few moments, shields popped into existence, deflecting the vast majority either back at their sources or into harmless places.

Like buildings.

Big holes appeared in those.

The sun was high in the London sky, the surrounding buildings unable to block it.

At the iron-wrought gate, Michelle pushed her jacket of *kadu* at Dexx and worked the same magick as she had on the display cases. Her wooden arm spread the metal as easily as it had shattered the glass. In seconds, they were free and running for their lives on the streets of London.

Medusa took the lead, and soon they were far away from DoDO headquarters and closing in on the warehouses of greyness.

The paranormals walked through the front door before anyone sent a scout forward to see if their hiding spot had been tampered with or discovered while they were gone, and the celebration commenced as soon as the first paranormal walked inside.

That seemed a bit premature. Dexx turned on his super smell and scouted.

No extra looming DoDO teams around, so they were safe.

Dexx went for the one place that had even a hint of privacy. The office at the far end of the hangar warehouse thingy.

Michelle followed him and shut the door behind her, blocking everyone else out.

"You have some explaining to do." She set her coat down and crossed her arms, an angry girlfriend-who-just-saw-you-kiss-another-girl expression on her face.

"Can't help you. You know more than I do about me, remember?"

"I'm talking about Quinn Winters. What was she doing there, and what did *she tell* you?"

Dexx didn't know what exactly was going on. "She's trying to take it down from the inside."

"I don't trust her. Paige would be furious, and you should be too. And you still didn't say what she's up to. How did she just miraculously just show up and start helping you?"

"*That* I can help a little with. I don't think it was planned. She was scared the first time she saw me, and after that, we just sort of hung out together. She helped me out of the cell.

And the last thing Alwyn said was is that they'd had me for about a month. Or something like that."

Michelle dropped her hands, concern overcoming the anger. "Alwyn? Wasn't the little shit you arrested in that demon trap?"

He didn't remember that instance, but... "Actually, I remember a lot of times saving his life. A few years' worth." And he recalled a strange conversation where Alwyn had thanked him for the "real" time Dexx'd saved his life. Had Alwyn been trying to tell him *then* that some memories were planted?

If that was the case, then could he *trust* Alwyn?

His gut said yes.

His brain said hell no.

"Damnit, Dexx. They really scrambled your brains." Michelle fell against the window wall and blew a strand of hair that fell in her face. "Yes. One of the first times we met up with them, they sent a bunch of their little toadies in to clear a nest. A demon had a trap all ready for them, but they still managed to kill one. Anyway, you pulled one of them out before the rest got killed. I'm pretty sure that was the kid."

Why would *that* memory be taken? "Makes sense. He was *really* sincere when he thanked me."

"What's your first rule about demons?" Michelle's face was completely open.

"The same rule as when a woman asks a question out of the blue and catches me off guard. 'Don't trust it.'"

"Well, DoDO's the demon. Don't trust anything they say or do as good for anyone but them. And that includes Quinn Winters and that Alwyn kid."

"Ab-Rhys. The kid's name is Alwyn ab-Rhys. And he's the closest thing I've had to a real friend in there for years. A month. Whatever. I remember a few years with him."

"Case closed. Don't trust a fucking *one* of them. Got it?"

"Sure." Hopefully, they could move on to more important things. He opened his coat to look at the *kadus*. They were all small stones, different shapes, but all of them had those funny lines etched on the surface.

"What are these?" Michelle sounded tired and not a little disappointed.

"*Kadu*. Didn't you know?"

"No. What do they do?" The disappointment turned sharp.

Maybe there was some good that'd come from being kidnapped. "Well, each of these represents a soul. If it's yours, your soul lives forever."

"Great. You've found the secret to Horcruxes. Harry Potter is safe."

"No, if you remember, a Horcrux makes your *body* live forever. These scoop up your soul and keeps it until it gets spit back out again."

"Why would anyone do that?"

"Beats the hell out of me. But if I had to guess, it's because it keeps something of your old self in your next life. Don't ask how because I'm drawing a blank there."

"Fine. What does this have to do with you?"

"Rule number seven. If it's something they want, it's something I don't want them to have. And weren't you listening? Each one of these is a soul and are virtually indestructible except when the soul is just dead or just born. They can't have that kind of power, don't you think?"

Michelle threw up her hands. "I'm going to rest. Don't bother me unless the place is burning down. Understand?"

"Rest? You mean sleep?"

Michelle didn't respond to him. She merely walked to the corner and rooted. Not stood still in a spot, but grew roots and limbs and became a tree. She *Grooted* right there in the corner of the office.

She was a cute tree, though. Smooth, slender limbs with hints of femininity.

"Nice ash." Dexx turned away his focus on the *kadus*. So, this was about the *only* thing he'd managed to take from DoDO. Okay. And he and the other paranormals had been able to kill a lot of them.

But if he was as important as Michelle seemed to think, if DoDO had taken him to weaken his wicked-witch-of-the-west wife, then shouldn't he be doing *more* with his time behind enemy lines?

The *kadu* called his attention. He set all of them out in neat rows. Twenty-six.

Two were missing. The little bowl with the crack halfway down and his little statue. Was Bussemi hiding those?

If they could be used against Dexx? Yeah. Probably. The cardinal hadn't seemed dumb.

The door creaked open. Medusa stepped in with the first smile he'd seen on her face. "I just wanted to say thanks for the—" Her eyes went to the tree that Michelle had become. "Dryad." She almost whispered, her face going slack. Her smell went cold with what almost felt like jealousy until she looked away.

"I am Groot," Dexx said to lighten the suddenly heavy mood. Was she allergic to dryads?

Medusa pulled in a deep breath. "You really came through for us. I mean, thank you. We were told you were— *are* a great alpha. I admit I didn't believe it. Not just by looking at you, but I was wrong, and I apologize." She held out her hand to Dexx.

He took it and returned as much of the grip as he could, but it was a little like sticking his hand in a vice.

"So, in addition to looting some *very* valuable stuff, we have a dryad, an alpha, and some rocks. Not a bad haul, considering. And I have something else for you." She smiled again. "A gift."

He wasn't sure he'd appreciate what she had to offer judging by her tone.

"Come on."

25

e followed her out of the office.

Outside, most of the paras had dispersed to do whatever they did in abandoned warehouses.

That didn't stop a certain amount of anticipation, however. What possibly could have brought the faint scent of nervousness from Medusa?

His patience was wearing a little thin. "Okay. What are we doing?"

Medusa looked not quite scared, but something more than concerned.

Something big, then.

"It's time."

"That sounds more than a lunch date." He had a feeling he knew what she was talking about. "Time for what?"

"I'm taking you to see the boss." She turned and led away from the office, heading for the center of the main open space.

"I thought I had to *see who I was* and stuff." And wasn't he? He was fighting the whole para thing a lot less.

"I considered what you did on the raid. I think we may

have a real chance at taking a big piece out of DoDO, and I would rather strike while the iron is hot."

That was...cool, but as far as actions went, he hadn't *done* a whole hell of a lot on the raid. Roxxie'd been the one to get them in. "Got a good taste of what I can do for you, eh? Well, that was me off the cuff. There's a lot more where that came from. I can tell you that."

"You *don't* see us as you should. You *are,* however, quite helpful in the field."

Again, he hadn't *done* anything.

"And only in the context of knowing how DoDO works."

Dexx stopped, unsure of how to ask his burning question. "Um, just to be clear- you *won't* rip open your shirt for a little alien guy to tell me to start the reactor, right?"

The angry scent hit the same time her words did. "Are you taking a piss at me? Is it just you, or are the Americans breeding to make the whole country berks?" She waited as though the questions weren't rhetorical.

They really got swearing to a whole new level. Berks? She didn't appreciate humor, and she didn't speak pop fiction. "Sorry. Just trying to lighten things up a little. I'm nervous. There's a lot riding on me, and I don't like it."

Medusa quirked her lips as if understanding, then turned around and continued to walk on. She mumbled to herself, but Dexx heard every word as though she grabbed his ear and pulled it to her face and screamed. "Stupid American cowboy piece of bellended bint bait."

Wow, he hadn't heard a string like that since he accidentally broke Alma's—

The world spun, shaking up his senses. He clearly *heard* the lights spinning him to a salty taste. Memories and voices and visions and smells and emotions attacked him. *"You're magick-borne."* That came through clearly.

Eventually, the mix of senses separated themselves to sight, sound, touch. Taste.

He'd bitten his tongue somewhere along the way. Blood dribbled off his lip. The spinning warehouse slowed to a stop.

"Fuck." That was new.

"Are you alright?"

The voice was almost familiar, but mostly distortion through the tunnel vision. Things became familiar, and the conversation replayed through his mind. A clear name rang though his head along with some foggy memories that didn't… quite settle.

That was a step in the right direction. Right?

"Huh?"

"I said, are you all right?"

The voice *was* familiar. Medusa. Heh, that was a funny name.

"Sure. Sometimes I fall down just to get a closer look at the floor. Of course, I'm not all right. I bit my tongue."

Medusa actually looked concerned *for* Dexx, and not *because* of him.

"Yeah. I'm okay, now, I think. I think whatever they did to me is starting to unravel. Big boss. Let's get this over with."

Medusa studied him for a few seconds.

Was she re-evaluating her decision to take him to see the big boss? "Let's go before I change my mind. I'm pretty busy."

Medusa put her face back on and made her decision. Again. "This should be close enough. Stand here and don't move outside the circle."

Dexx worked his wounded tongue against his teeth. He had a feeling this wasn't going to feel great. "What circle?"

The space had the *least* amount of random shit on the floor.

"This one." Medusa held up a piece of chalk and bent low

to the floor to draw a circle around them. Then she made little squiggles and odd lines. The lines had a familiar look to them.

While he watched, the pain in his tongue stopped then healed over.

Then sensation just about made him miss what Medusa had drawn on the floor.

Not quite a pentagram, but not just a star inside the circle she'd started with. The odd little marks began to glow, and then... squiggle. They moved like little shivery maggots before blackness engulfed him.

Dexx tensed. Traps were easiest to set off in the dark, and this was certainly— not dark. The room appeared around them like a light switch.

Warmth. Low lighting. The stink of something not quite right. Something inside Dexx roared to get out and tear down the walls, the ceiling, the entire place.

They were in a room. Something crossed between a doctor's office from the seventies and the set of *Archie Bunker*. Overstuffed threadbare sofa seats took up the middle of the room. A lit lamp sat by the armchair pressing out dirty yellow light. A garish red carpet lined the floor all the way to the wood-paneled walls with the patina of the cigar smoke and gear oil that lingered.

Magazines lay scattered on the old-time coffee table from somewhere in the sixties. The magazines were newer. The Corvette on the cover of one magazine was the new mid-engine design. Another had a dark cherry car, but the front looked like—

"Don't be a wanker when you see him. We worked hard to get you out, and *he* did most of the heavy lifting." Medusa paused with her hand on the much newer lever handle on the door.

"Wouldn't dream of it. But I have some advice for the office decorator."

"Cut it." Medusa didn't raise her voice, but she slashed his train of thought pretty well. She pressed on the handle and swung the door open.

Dexx pulled at the gun he didn't have as a familiar instinct crashed over his nerves. His frantic search found no weapons to use, so he launched himself at the man in the room.

Dexx froze in mid-leap, a toe still barely touching the carpet.

"Don't make a fuss." The demon in a familiar meat suit smiled, showing a lot of teeth. "I'll have the maid clean the room."

Dexx pressed against the bonds holding him in place. This had to be some weird, cruel joke.

Medusa walked past him. "I asked. I did."

If she was working for a demon, then…what other lies had he been served? Was there anything he could trust?

"Please forgive me, Mr. Colt," Furiel said with a sigh. "That was a feeble attempt at humor. I know you are quite familiar with it, though."

The force holding Dexx released enough to let him speak. "Let me go. I'll show you a joke that'll keep me laughing for years to come." Heat infused Dexx. He pushed at the barrier and felt little spiderwebs of fatigue flake away.

"I apologize for the attempt. Let me begin again." He folded his hands in front of him. "I don't know if you remember me. My name is Furiel. I *am* a demon. And I want your help."

Dexx remembered. He just still didn't believe it. "I don't help demons."

But some, I do.

He didn't know where that thought had come from, but at least it sounded like his own damned voice.

"Dexx, you said you'd behave." Medusa stood close to him, her eyes filled with emotion. Could it really be a concern?

"That was before you served me up to a demon." More cracks in the barrier let him flex a little more.

"I'm *helping* my kind." She glanced around. "And yours. That's why you weren't supposed to meet him yet. You're still consumed by the spell they put on you."

Did *DoDO* give him the instinctive need to kill demons? It didn't feel quite right.

"What do you remember of Sven Seven-Tails?"

"I remember—" Nothing. He knew the name. Roxxie had said it. "Does he have anything to do with this?"

"How about a show of good faith? I know you're about to break through my barrier spell. Soon anyway, but I'll release you. I only ask that you restrain yourself long enough to let me explain. As an extra measure of good faith, I have a gift."

What was up with all these "gifts?" The urge to go after this demon was pretty strong, though.

"Relax, and I will release you."

Dexx relaxed for an instant, ready to go back on the offensive. The demon's spell set him on the ground but didn't kill him.

"First, this." The demon reached in his suit jacket and produced a knife. The black handle came out of an ornate sheath of bronze and leather. With two fingers holding the knifepoint, the demon gently laid the knife on a small pedestal right behind him. He stepped away, keeping his hands out and plainly visible.

"What's that?" Against Dexx's will, he stepped toward the knife. The handle was pure black, pulling light into it, while the ornate sheath's swirls and lines covered the two-edged split blade.

Dexx reached for the knife, then stopped. "What is it?" He stepped back. After all, the demon had barely touched it.

"Do you not recognize it? That is like the one you took from Genael. You might remember him more as Mike Jones."

Dexx's brain began whirling, and his heart sped up. Mike Jones and Genael. "That sounds made up. You might just as well said John Doe." Except Dexx knew there was something there.

"All words are made up. But sadly, no, he was not made up. Genael was a fallen angel that you as good as killed."

"As good as? How did I 'as good as—'" Dexx air quoted. "—kill an angel?"

"You beat him almost to death. But the punishment of an angel falls to an angel. Not a mortal. Michael himself came down and threw him into the pit to suffer forever."

"And *I* did this." It'd started as a question, but ended as a statement as the answer hit his gut.

"You and a few others, yes." The demon took another step away from the knife. "That is a *ma'a'shed,* a demon knife. And I will give it to you for a few moments of your time."

His hands itched to take it.

"I'm not your enemy. I do not wish to *be* your enemy."

Dexx turned to the demon, giving him his full attention.

The demon bowed. "There are certain assumptions made because I'm a demon. One is that I'm bloodthirsty and power-hungry. I crave no more than most humans."

That wasn't saying a whole hell of a lot. "So why do you want me?"

"Because I believe you can help with my... situation. A few of us saw what you did, and we would like that for ourselves."

"What did *I* do?" What all had DoDO hidden from him?

"You stood by a demon. Helped when you didn't have to. Called him a friend. I am aware you are still uncomfortable with me. Take the knife and go for now. Take care. Those are dangerous on the largest scale. And take this. It's yours, I believe. I recovered it and kept it safe until it could be returned to you."

The demon reached in his jacket again, this time pulling out a small round stone with strange characters on the outside rim.

"You had this?" Dexx held his hand out, relief washing over him.

"Only until I could return it. You dropped it when you... let's say the *shamiyir* was the least of the excitement at the time. Please think about my request. I will have Medusa take you back, and she can contact me when you want to talk again."

"Who says I want—" The room vanished, and the warehouse flashed back.

The black-handled knife the demon set on the plinth fell to the floor with an odd ringing note.

"Would you like to go back to the office?" Medusa bent over and retrieved the knife.

Dexx stared at his rock. "Okay. What did I do to make a demon seek my help?" Waves of heat washed over him. Not uncomfortable heat, just a warming sensation like he'd been colder than he thought. "What does it want?"

"*He.* That demon is a *he,* not an *it,* and his name is *Furiel.* He's helped us from the beginning, and he's given you things that he's never—" Medusa stopped and pulled in a deep breath. She let it out slow and long. "What I mean to say is that Furiel is on our side. He helped you and gave you a demon blade. A *ma'a'shed.* Do you know how hard those are to come by?"

"I'm not sure, but I think this is my *second*?" Rule four of demons. If you have a gift from a demon, run.

"And you still think he's the evil one in all this. You probably think those tossers from DoDO are the good guys."

"No." He definitely didn't. But paras—yeah. He was still calling them that. They weren't above the law either. "I'm pretty sure everyone is a bad guy except me." Dexx swiveled his head as Michelle, and the angel appeared from the office. "And those two. Have a nice rest?"

Roxxie smiled. "I did. Thank you for asking. Did you have a nice conversation with the demon?"

"How did you—"

"I'm not at my full strength, but there's still a lot I know. What did you discuss? I wasn't able to hear."

Dexx looked at his stone with the engraving or whatever those lines were. "He gave me a rock and a knife." Dexx turned his hands out so they could easily see them. "Said he wanted my help. Who the fuck am I?"

26

"That's a particularly good question, Dexx. And about time you asked, too." Roxxie smiled. A too familiar smile. She looked at Michelle. "You can fill him in. I need more rest."

She stepped forward so fast he didn't have time to respond. She hugged him quickly and turned around to disappear in a flare of light.

"Why does she need more rest? She looks pretty powerful to me."

Michelle gave him a dry expression. "She's only one of seven keeping an entire dimension from falling away from this plane. You already know this."

There'd been a lot thrown at him. "You tell me I'm a para. I have abilities I don't remember. None of it." Except he had abilities, and things were starting to fall into place. Dexx held out his rock. "And then there's this. I have no idea what it *actually* is or does, except I know it's mine. I feel it. Like my shoe or something."

"That's very interesting. Can I see that for a minute?" She held out her hand to take it.

Dexx made no move to give it over. "No."

Michelle pursed her lips and dipped her head in close to study the rock while he held it.

"I don't even know you. You come at me like you did, and all you say is 'hey you know me, I know you, and now we're all good friends.' Why don't we cover some ground first? And speaking of friends, why is that angel playing nice with a demon?"

Michelle straightened and cocked a hip. "You know, your stupid *man brain* gets you into more trouble than we can handle at times. You have a *demon* for a *friend*. You almost *died* for him. Tarik. You remember Tarik?"

"No." But he did when she said his name. He recalled the strangest set of eyes he'd ever seen, blue with a horizontal slit, like a horse or a goat. Dexx's balance went crazy for a moment.

Memories came with vertigo.

"You okay?" Michelle steadied him with a hand. "You did that before."

He was fucking sick of this. "My memories are starting to come back, I think. Did he, uh, have blue eyes?"

"Yup." Michelle tipped her head to the side and studied him. "Paige."

Dexx wobbled on his feet as the world rocked. It wasn't just memories, though. It was like double-exposure events, visions stacked on top of one another.

"Jackie."

The warehouse spun. Hard. Another hand rested on his shoulder.

Medusa.

Michelle smiled tightly. "I think that's something. Maybe we shouldn't go too far into your past until we can get you past the dizzies."

Dexx agreed, just glad he hadn't eaten in a while. "Are you always like this? Pushy and stuff?"

"Nope. I leave that to Pa— I leave that for the other people in your life. You're actually a pretty good pushover. Do what you're told usually."

Dexx shook a fist at her in a motion that felt familiar. "To the moon."

"You're still you at the core, though. That's a good sign. What's that?" She pointed to the knife.

"The demon—" Dexx pulled in a breath and released it quickly. "I mean, Furiel gave it to me."

He slipped his rock in his pocket and popped the knife from the sheath a few inches. The split black blade had two ragged silver edges.

"He gave your knife back to you?"

Dexx snapped his head away from the knife. "This was mine? He said it was another one."

Michelle gave him a deep shrug with a fish-mouth. "Could be. It looks like the other one you had except for the pretty holder, and the edges were blood red."

The demon— Furiel hadn't lied? That didn't mean he trusted the thing any *more*. "What do you know about it?"

"Not much more than you told me. Well, everyone who would listen really, but it's sharper than anything that can be made on Earth. Stronger too. And you do this thing, and it grows into a sword. Roxxie had one, but the angel version."

A knife that grew into a sword. "What do I do for that? Call *Thundercats* and stop when it gets long enough?"

"Sure, if that what does it. Only you and the demons know how."

"Me?"

"Spoilers, Dexx. I'm worried if I tell you too much, you might actually faint. But we need to talk to Roxxie when she's done recharging. Until then—" She held her hands up a little. "Can we look around?"

"Sure. Medusa, can you introduce us to our new digs?"

Turned out, the place wasn't so much a backup slummier building as it was a planned retreat. The stairs that led down were rusted piles of deathtraps to the untrained eye, but they led to an underground system of dorms, workshops, and equipment, much like DoDO had.

Michelle gawked at the rooms.

Dexx stood back a little. Clearly, the *resistance* hadn't told him everything. "What the fuck, Medusa? You had all this, and you *still* stayed at the other place to get killed?"

"We had to make you see what we were up against." Her look was unapologetic. "The fight is real. And you're still, being manipulated."

By everyone? "Yeah. Looks like *that* was you."

"We had to be sure. You wouldn't walk up to a stranger and ask to see their pucker arse, would you?"

"Sounds like something he'd do," Michelle put in helpfully. "But he wouldn't put it so nicely."

Medusa smiled. "I like this one."

Michelle returned it.

"What's the deal here?" Dexx asked, curious to know if they had the means to locate his old team and his *kadu,* which was probably being held by Bussemi. "What are we looking at?"

Michelle bent forward to inspect a few of the technician's screens.

Medusa waved her arm over a section of computers. "The command center. We have more than one so that if one goes down, another can be started. We're trying to hack DoDO constantly, and a few times, we were close, but they changed their protocols. We'll have them someday."

Dexx could understand the covert ops. DoDO seemed...

pretty bad. But if they couldn't get in, he couldn't find what he was looking for. "Would it help if you were already in there to hack their shit?"

"Optimal, really." Medusa winced. "That's actually what Furiel was trying to ask you earlier when you freaked out on him."

"Well, I have an idea. But before I go into that, *why* didn't you just do *this*—" He gestured at the tech, "—before? I mean, you had it, so why use me as bait in that other rat hole, then go in for a smash and grab? Help me understand here."

"We were instructed to use that as our base until you were out. The raid happened out of convenience. We had the opportunity, and we took it. Wouldn't you do the same thing?"

Fuck. He just might. He might have less opportunity. "Fine. So, what's the play now?"

"We were hoping that maybe *you* could tell *us*. You're the best source of information we have."

Sure. And he was also the biggest, juiciest piece of bait they could have ordered. "When did you plan on telling me?"

"We're still a long way off from that. More plans, contingencies, traps. We have a lot to do first."

"You're the biggest bunch of contradictions I've ever seen."

Michelle stood up from the screens. "Except, you, Dexx. You're the biggest. And you're starting to sound like a broken record. Look, I knew you were stubborn, but seriously? You need to grow a little. There are things we need to do."

She was right about needing to do things. Dexx growled a little. "Where's Bruna and Doxy? I think I'm done down here for a while."

"You said you had an idea?" Medusa cocked her head to the side.

"I need some time to think."

The two witches appeared after a minute and escorted him and Michelle back to the broken-down office on the ground floor of the warehouse.

"What are we doing back here?" Michelle looked properly disgusted with the place now that she knew there were better accommodations elsewhere.

"I like it here. So many good memories." Dexx motioned to Bruna and Doxy. "I *know* you know something about me. Spill it."

The two women did their brain-share again and turned back to Dexx. "We can help ye sort of. But not in the way ye think we can. See, we're—"

Roxxie appeared in a bright flash. She looked more haggard than when she'd left. Which only meant she looked as beautiful as a mortal woman could. "You shouldn't be tampering with your memories yet. I discovered the ward on him was put there by a demon. Maybe more, I couldn't find that out."

"Did you rest at *all?*" Michelle's voice seemed more concerned with Roxxie than she'd been with Dexx.

"I couldn't. Is there a place to sit?" Roxxie blew out her cheeks a little.

Dexx rolled an old dusty office chair behind her as she sat, hand resting on her lap.

"Thanks." Her smile was pure and clean. Just like her scent.

Dexx hesitated. "You're welcome?" He scrubbed fingers through his hair. "So, what in the hell is wrong with getting my memories back?"

"The demon most likely couldn't possess you." Roxxie sagged in the chair. "I don't know for sure, but that's my guess. When I saw the conflict flare, I went to investigate. I found some answers, but not all I wanted. The important part is, the more you remember, the stronger these reactions will be. If you don't find a way to lift the ward, you *will* die from the conflicts as your memories fight their way to the surface."

"Why can't you do it? You're supposed to be all-powerful."

"That's one thing I love about you, Dexx. Your faith in me is complete." She smiled her pure smile again. "I can't do that anymore. Judging from the power and complexity of the ward, I don't think I could have done it before the sundering either."

"How did *you* get to be the one who holds the world together?"

"One of seven. I am the least of us." Roxxie shook her head, and she yawned. "But I was in the right place to do the most. The others were on missions of their own, and we were trapped between the veils. Our strength holds the dimensional planes in relative positions."

"You're telling me you're in two places at once?" This was actually interesting.

"Yes and no. I am here, and in the veil, the space between. The others are in our own plane and in the veil. They are not here. And coming here would break the connection. The same would happen if I went there."

"But you can? If you wanted to, I mean."

"Maybe. We just don't have enough information yet. Our orders are to stay where we are."

Orders from who? "Can you die?"

"Death is a possibility anywhere. But what I think you're asking is if this will kill me. I don't know. The conduits are almost all gone. Now we have to exert more power to cross. Some of us aren't powerful enough to do that on our own. I wouldn't be able to."

"You expect me to believe you're like the guardian angel

for the whole planet?" If she was, that could mean, well, he didn't know. If he had his memories, he might. But right now, it didn't seem so good.

"There are no absolutes." Roxxie smiled again.

"Okay, so that time, I didn't get an answer."

"You weren't supposed to." Michelle sighed. "That's a pretty way of saying she isn't going to say more. I tried to get more out of her when she came to get me to bring me here." She lifted her arms a little and dropped them back to her sides.

He let his head fall back with a frustrated breath. "Fuck DoDO." And their mind wipes.

"I understand but don't push things. You should find the demon who did this and have him reverse the spell."

"How do I do that? Give it a kiss? Dinner and a movie? How do I even *find* the prick?" There was a good place to start. The Montana campus. He knew there was definitely a demon there, *and* he was fairly certain he'd uncovered who it'd been because there were a lot of double images there.

Roxxie had her chin on her fist, thinking hard.

Dexx closed his eyes, battling his frustration. "Forget it. I don't like sittin' around with my thumb up my ass. We need to hit them. Hit them hard, for reals, and fuck the fuck outta them. Maybe get some real information. Find the… team." He gestured to Michelle. And get his *kadu*. "How about it, Roxxie?"

"I would need to rest for many of your days to recover from the effort I've expended. Can you wait until then?"

Damn, he expected a straight up *no*.

They might be able to wait, but maybe not. DoDO was hurt pretty bad with the raid—hopefully—but they'd recover soon and set up protections. "Sure. We can wait a few days."

"We'll go with you, too." Bruna nodded.

"I'm in. I don't have a choice." Michelle crossed her arms.

"Just let me know when we move out. I'm going to visit some trees."

How much did he know about dryads? Nothing. So, that meant that the dryad information was something he'd discovered in the past two years.

Roxxie nodded. "I'll come back when I've rested. Please don't do anything until I return. I wouldn't want you hurt."

Sure. Where was she when he got mixed up with DoDO?

"Good. So, date night. Right? Which one am I taking out tonight?" Dexx smiled at the blushing twins.

"Neither." Medusa stood in the doorway. "We have movement."

27

Dexx might have been surprised if anything shocked him anymore. Date night was postponed.

"Movement, huh?" That was never good in the movies. Movement meant that they were under imminent attack, and they had no idea who it was. There were fewer options here than the movies, but hey, real life was stranger than fiction.

"We don't know who they are." Medusa frowned like she was listening to someone. "Bruna, Doxy, what can you see?"

Bruna and Doxy faced each other and activated their Wonder Twin powers. "Refugees. Vampires. McAllister Clan. Friends, mostly." They spoke in unison, almost perfectly. The slight differences made their voice sound otherworldly and a bit creepy. They broke out of their trance as soon as they finished.

"Friends." Doxy smiled sheepishly, apology written all over her face. "They should be able ta help us. Hopefully, they're nae still mad about the thin'."

Medusa just turned on her heel and left.

"There's a story there?" Dexx nodded approval.

They left the office to meet the clan.

They already had vampires. A small force, but sizeable enough. They'd already taken DoDO head-on, but Dexx needed information. He needed to know where his *kadu* was, and he needed the location of his Red Star team. Even if he couldn't remember much about them, but he needed to see if he could trust this new clan enough to invite them along.

What he had tentatively planned was going to be a bit of a suicide mission anyway.

Medusa met the first of the vampires at the main entrance. "Jonas." She rested a fist on her cocked hip. "I don't believe I invited you. How did you find your way to our doorstep uninvited and uninformed?"

Jonas sneered slightly as though saying the site wasn't exactly a secret. "Spies are everywhere." Jonas had a French accent, but not thick. Probably made the ladies a little weak in the knees to listen to him talk. "We had to deal with a mite. That's why we're here. We were hit."

Them too? Okay. Why were there so *many* attacks on paranormal in quick succession? Dexx had *studied* their previous plans, and while not super awesome, they still didn't go on back-to-back hunts. Not like this. What was going on?

Something was going on, and they needed to know what that was. His rough idea of an information stab and grab was starting to take a bit more shape. They needed to take DoDO down, and the best way to do that... would be to destroy the things his teaching plans had sought to bolster.

He was hedging his bets that Harris and Sir Sayyid had completely ignored Dexx's hard work. So much the better.

Dexx stepped next to Medusa and imitated her pose.

"Bloody wanker." She whispered, but he still heard her as clear as he heard anything.

Super hearing. He needed to come to grips with the fact that he was a para—paranormal. That would only help him in the fight with DoDO. "Dexx Colt. Demon hunter extraordinaire. How many of you made it out?"

Jonas turned his head to the vampires brave enough to walk up to the door with him. "Thirty-four here, another fifteen… elsewhere."

So. He had a few out in flanking positions ready to surprise attack. Not a bad tactic.

"How about you bring them in? Do you want to get back at DoDO? I got a plan, but I need bodies."

Jonas narrowed his eyes, obviously skeptical. "You."

Medusa bared her teeth at Dexx. Definitely not a smile. "You might be more trouble than you're worth. You got a Yank of a plan. Am I right? Guns blazing, storm the front, and hope enough survive to get killed on the inside?"

She wasn't too far off the mark, and that hurt a little. "You want DoDO?" Dexx nodded significantly at Medusa. "Then we need these guys. Vampires have speed, and that's something we can use." He held up a finger. "But we could use a few more people too. Did you get more shifters? I can use about fifty Girls Scouts selling cookies on their front stoop." Dexx wrinkled his nose. "Or you chicken?"

Jonas flashed his elongated fangs. "I could tear you to pieces. Right now."

The memories of Dexx shredding the paranormals in the other warehouse hit him upside the head and reminded him to cool it. "Save the shredding for DoDO. Besides, I'm more than you can bite off. Pun intended." Vamps were gross. Remember, they could be useful. Sometimes.

Jonas twitched in place like he wanted to try Dexx anyway.

Dexx popped the cover on the *ma'a'shed,* ready to drop the sheath and carve on the vamp.

Jonas ran his tongue along his teeth and relaxed. Sort of. "Very well. What's your plan?"

Medusa threw up her hands. "Macho arse bull buggers."

Doxy and Bruna came up on both sides of Dexx.

Doxy spoke. "We're not sure this is a good idea. We see orange."

"Orange is a good color. My second or third favorite color. Maybe sixth, but still a good one. We got this. Besides, I'll be there to protect you. I got a couple of superpowers now, and a *real* good plan." He snapped the knife back into the scabbard. "Real good." It wasn't a plan. It was a goal. They needed information.

But as he talked it over with them, the actual plan grew. The vampire leader that had gone in with them previously joined. Soon, they had a raiding party, a goal, and a plan that would only get a few of them killed. Like… half. Maybe.

Medusa grudgingly changed her tune.

Michelle wasn't as easily swayed, but in the end, the limited recourses brought her around. They needed information.

Bruna and Doxy came around to the plan over the next few days. They flanked him constantly as though they were already in DoDO, casting spells and generally destroying toys.

They also chose when to be serious and giddy girls at the oddest times.

If he was alone, they were serious as a heart attack. No nonsense. If Medusa or Jonas were around, they became chatterboxes and… embarrassing. They fawned like no other, and after a thousand attempts to make them go away, they said he was their protection.

But against what exactly and why?

A good reason he always worked alone. Or had. A few more memory fragments surfaced, but the spell that'd been put on him was really well done. That was one more thing they needed to figure out. Another was who was the demon who had cast the spells on him in the first place so he could take them off.

This led to a few sighs, and finally, when Roxxie came back, they left like hurt puppies until he let them come back. Then they only *grinned* like giddy girls.

Four days of rest had Roxxie looking radiant and, well, angelic.

Their plan had them all gathered them behind an apartment complex undergoing a renovation near DoDO headquarters. The construction had been abandoned for the evening and provided excellent cover. Between that and the dark night, DoDO shouldn't be too on guard from this location. And they had an angel looking over their shoulder. Sort of.

"Okay." Dexx addressed the two groups gathered loosely around. "You know what to do. Jonas, don't stay too long." Over the past four days, Dexx had started to *like* the vampire a little, something that had surprised him more than a little. "You get their attention and keep it. Push only as hard as you have to and remain safe. You are only a diversion. When they push back, get out. That should buy us enough time to get what we want."

Roxxie's clean scent proceeded her.

Vampires spat in front of her.

She ignored them. She was probably the only angel to ever work with demons and vampires. "Is everyone ready?"

She looked much better to Dexx, but the difference wasn't just in the way she looked. She carried herself differently, and she was just... happy.

"Sure am." Dexx rubbed his hands together. No time to remind DoDO there were a couple of blind spots in their protection plan. "Now, you're sure you can cover them and get back here to blip us into the house, right?"

Roxxie's smile sure was contagious. "I'm as sure as you

are. Get ready, because I won't warn you before I take you in."

Shit. She knew. And she wasn't certain how far her own power would go. Time to toss the dice and see what pips turned up. "Come on, *Yahtzee*."

Medusa and Michelle turned to him. "What?" they asked together like the twins would have.

"Means we're about to win." He paused for a second, inhaling, then, "Go."

The vampires took off sprinting toward the DoDO campus, while Roxxie disappeared in a brief flash, hopefully covering their rush to the campus gates for more distraction.

Dexx had to hand it to the vamps. They could run *fast* when they wanted. They also had some ability with illusion that should be helpful with the raid.

"You guys ready?" He *had* to ask again.

Michelle stood half-transformed, her arms and legs covered in bark. Her fingers swayed lazily back and forth in long whips.

Medusa stared off toward the DoDO house.

Doxy and Bruna stood together, playing some sort of game, sometimes staring at each other sometimes at Dexx, but thankfully they were silent.

Dexx pulled in one more breath, and before he exhaled, the scene changed to the portal room inside DoDO.

"Go!" Dexx ran at the operators before they could react. Michelle and Medusa clipped more. The surprise attack took them all off guard.

The alarm never tripped.

Bruna and Doxy put their hands together. They began to glow. "Two on the other side of the door," they said together. "They don't know. Powerful. Take them quickly."

Right. Dexx motioned to Medusa. Her tentacles whipped around like writhing snakes.

She slammed the door open to the other room and slashed.

Dexx didn't see what happened, but the blood spray gave him a good clue.

"Let's go." He took a step to the door that led to the rest of the campus.

Michelle hovered over the screens. "Shit. Dexx, look at this." She had no trace of the tree along with her hands as she accessed one of the terminals.

Dexx bent down, looking at the monitor. On the screen, a picture rotated, displaying facts and figures.

"Are we moving on?" Medusa's voice wasn't hers. She sounded gravelly and, well, monstrous.

"Just a second. We may have something here." But what? Then something else flashed on the screen, and his blood ran thin. The gold collar. However, there was a room making them by the dozens. "That just like the thing they slapped on me." Dexx rubbed his neck. That thing hadn't been fun.

"It's the same thing they had in the states. They put one on Pai—" Michelle glanced up at him before returning her gaze to the screen. "—on people there."

"Why would they do that?"

"Control. They were testing a prototype in Alaska."

What did that have to do with anything? "How do you know that?" Something wasn't adding up.

"Right, just trust me, Dexx. This is what they were doing then, and they've had a year to perfect it. A few weeks ago, they put a very powerful shifter witch in one on national TV. This one looks more advanced. If this is right—" She pointed to some information on another screen. "—they've added compulsory motivators."

"A what?"

"Physical control. They can force the wearer to do things."

That's what Bussemi had said he'd do to Dexx. "Like rob banks and stuff?" What else could Bussemi do with Dexx?

"Like cast spells or other paranormal action. Kill people, cast wards, anything."

The alarm went up. No sirens were wailing, but a little light right next to the fire alarm panel began to flash. DoDO knew something was up.

"Bastards. Can you get that information on a thumb drive or something?" That would be something to hang them in court. If they could bring charges.

"Uh, twenty-first century. How about I send it to the cloud?" Michelle pressed her lips together but tapped the keys way faster than he could follow.

"Oh, wait," she said breathlessly with a ghost of a smile. "I found Frey and Tarik."

That was good news. "Wasn't there another one, though?"

"Rain—yeah." Michelle continued to search. "I can't—" She released a frustrated breath. They're not here. They're somewhere else."

"Then grab the information, and let's go. That's the plan. Let's stick to it."

After a few seconds that felt way too long, she hit the enter key and stood. "Let's go. Where's Medusa?"

Bruna pointed. "She left. You were really wrapped up in the computer."

"Dang it." Dexx hadn't wanted anyone to go off on their own. "Which way?"

They pointed down the hall.

"Destroy everything you can so they can't use it again."

Michelle grew vines at her fingertips and jammed them under the desk. A few more sapling shoots wriggled up through tiny cracks just before the screens went blank.

"Every bit destroyed all the way to the plug. Remote storage too. They lost a lot right here."

"Is that portal down? Don't know how it works, but if they use tech to work it, then let's make it go, too."

"Fuck yeah."

"Bruna," Dexx said, listening and sniffing the air. "Lead the way."

The twin witches led the way, hips swaying in time as they looked in rooms along the way.

Dexx sniffed the air. He could smell Medusa not far up, and she was surrounded by blood, but he couldn't hear the skirmish yet. "Hey. Let me slip ahead of you." He put a hand to Bruna's shoulder.

She gave him a look but let him by.

He led them past the high-security section, following the trail Medusa had left in her wake.

Guards that had been posted at doors were now dead, their heads separated from their bodies. The separation wasn't from a *sharp* tentacle, either.

Bruna and Doxy stepped lightly through the clean spots on the floor.

Dexx traipsed through the blood. He'd had practice. The next corridor had DoDO agents a head shorter there, too.

"Dexx." Michelle stopped at the doors to the secured section. "This way." She hooked a thumb down the corridor.

"Why? Medusa's that way," he said, pointing in the other direction.

"I have a feeling."

Well, so did he. He *had the feeling* his *kadu* was in the direction Medusa was headed. But feeling or no, he needed his *kadu*. He couldn't allow it to remain in Bussemi's control. "I smell old stuff down there. The more important things are up here. So's Medusa's back that we're supposed to have."

"I'm telling you, there's something down there."

It was possible he was so distracted by needing his *kadu* that he was overlooking something else. They had multiple objectives. Dexx turned to Bruna. "What do you say?"

The sisters turned to face each other. They pressed their hands together and pulled away immediately.

"There's nothing," Bruna said. "We don't know."

Dexx growled. "Damn. There *better* be something good down here. If you only discover a really interesting smell, I'm gonna be *pissed*."

Michelle darted down the hallway, coming to another set of doors with a small window to see on the other side. "No guards."

Was that a good sign or a bad sign?

Before Dexx could turn, Michelle jammed her sapling fingers into the lock. The door swung open.

"Useful, but things are *this* way." The smell hit him before he finished, though. The stench was powerful. Unwashed bodies, mixed with anger, fear, and perverse pleasure. And another little something he couldn't quite place. Okay, so there might be something down here too.

Crap. He followed Michelle in but flagged Doxy and Bruna to stay behind.

"Stop." Dexx put his hand on Michelle's shoulder. "Let me go first."

Michelle let him pass.

Oh. How was he supposed to know?

The doors led them through a short hall to, yup, more doors. The room had lab coats and rubber boots stacked in neat rows. A gurney parked next to the wall cut the pathway in half.

The next set of doors didn't have a lock on them, just hinges that allowed the door to swing both ways. Beyond those, Dexx heard the most soul-wrenching cries. She sounded like a woman, pleading with a guard not to hurt her more.

Dexx almost pushed his way through the door but stopped as the scent hit him. The cardinal.

And the pull of his *kadu*.

28

Dexx pushed them all back. "Nine hells."

"What?" Michelle didn't get her question out before the scream tore out of the tortured woman.

Michelle's eyes widened in horror, and she charged past Dexx into the next room.

"Fuck me." Dexx followed Michelle, who was already engaged in a magical battle with Cardinal Bussemi.

She did well, fighting against a senior citizen.

The man blasted elemental magick, and she batted it down or away, but for as old as the little guy was, he was quite spry.

Almost immediately, Dexx could see she wasn't the cardinal's equal. She'd caught him off guard, but he recovered quickly, and now she backed up a little at each of his strikes.

Michelle's tree limb hands glowed a faint blue, batting red lightning away. Her hands brightened the more labored her defense became.

The scene behind her looked about like the most fucked up description of an inquisition he'd ever seen. Except the equipment was up to date and shiny clean. Freaky clinical clean.

A woman laid stretched out on a stainless steel gurney with wide leather straps around her wrists and ankles. She watched Michelle battle it out with the cardinal, tears streaming down her face, her body convulsing with sobs.

She looked familiar. Like really familiar. Her afro hair had been matted from abuse and neglect, but parts stuck out at odd angles.

Suddenly, he remembered where he'd seen her before. She was the para he'd first bagged after the accident in Louisiana.

Right. Probably *not* an accident.

This meant she was a part of his team. Fuck. Well, all righty then. One of the goals of their invasion was reached.

A stray bolt of power crashed into the wall next to Dexx, leaving a smoking crater.

He spun and tackled Bruna who had come in right after him. Another smoking crater formed above them showering debris down, filling the air with smoke.

Dexx let go of parts he shouldn't be holding on to and stood, looking for the best way to help Michelle who was definitely on the defensive.

Bussemi glanced Dexx's way for the briefest of moments before turning back to the dryad with renewed vigor.

Senior citizen or not, Dexx had to end this. Michelle wouldn't last much longer. Sweat beaded her brow, and her hands were almost glowing white. Her back touched the far wall, and her feet began to slip out from under her.

"Run!" Dexx yelled as he stepped up to draw the cardinal's attention.

Bussemi only had a moment to react, and that was to widen his eyes at Dexx who had leapt through the air.

Dexx wrapped his arms around a solid metal pylon.

Pain ran all the way down to his toes as he hit the old man, but they both tumbled head over tea kettle into stainless steel devices.

They slammed into the wall, things from the table pelting them.

The cardinal sat up, fire in his eyes. Not real fire. That would have been silly, but if looks could kill, Dexx would have melted.

He took that moment to attack Bussemi with everything he had, reaching deep inside to pull on whatever had come out in the warehouse before. He'd been able to shred entire units—plural—of agents before.

He didn't even put a dent in Bussemi. Whatever was making him feel rock hard was still in play. Just *hitting* Bussemi was having a greater effect on Dexx than it was on the cardinal.

The man was impervious.

A fire extinguisher wobbled on its hook and fell on Bussemi's head. His eyes rolled up in his head and he slumped over.

Finally. Shit.

"Dexx. Are you well?" Bruna asked over the cries of the woman on the table.

Yeah. He was fine. Mostly. "Fuck me, that hurt. How's the woman?"

Michelle wobbled to her feet, holding her head. "He—he's *powerful*. He shouldn't have been— Rainbow! Are you okay?" Michelle pushed off the wall, grabbing things along her path, finally stopping at the table with the woman bound to it.

Rainbow blathered, snot coming out of her nose.

"We're here." Michelle fumbled at the leather straps with fingers that didn't move right.

The woman shook her head violently trying to speak through the sobs.

Dexx reached out to her.

She shied away as far as the straps would allow.

Dexx stepped back.

Her cries continued as she jerked at the straps. She squealed, turning her head to the fallen cardinal.

He groaned and twitched his hands, then rolled his head.

"Come on, we have to go." Dexx grabbed Michelle's shoulder.

She ripped away from him. "No. We came for Rainbow."

"He's waking up." Bruna raised her hands, backing up into her sister. "Please. We can't—"

Rainbow, screamed again, trading looks of pure terror between Dexx and the cardinal.

"We have to *go*." Dexx pulled at Michelle again.

She pulled away from him again, working the straps that wouldn't budge. "*You* run. I'm getting her out of here."

Frustration welled up from Dexx's depths.

His *kadu* calling insistently, Bruna wailing, Rainbow crying, and Michelle obviously upset, Bussemi groggy but recovering. They *had* to leave. "Are the straps spelled?"

Michelle's hands flared. "Must be. Bruna, help."

"Stop," Dexx commanded.

Michelle stood still.

Rainbow stopped crying, her eyes locked on Dexx, calm.

Bruna quit her whine.

Bussemi raked his hand across the floor, pushing to get up.

They were out of time. How could they get Rainbow out of there?

"We can't break the straps," Doxy whispered.

Shit. That only left one other option. "Let's go. We'll

come back." He met Rainbow's gaze. "Stay strong, I'm coming back." Why in the *hell* had he said *that*?

Rainbow nodded once but began crying again almost immediately, shuddering as she had before.

Dexx pushed Bruna and Doxy in front of him and pulled Michelle along behind him. She didn't resist.

That was a trick he'd have to remember.

Clattering of steel against a hard tile floor chased them out the door and down the hallway.

"Why did you *push* me? We don't leave our team behind." Michelle ripped her hand out of Dexx's as soon as they cleared the hallway.

Bruna and Doxy kept in front of them

"Push?" Dexx puffed as they ran. "I *pulled* you out."

"You *alpha* pushed me. You've *never* done that to me. Not once."

She was choosing *this* moment to go over that? "New and improved me." Okay. Well, they knew where one team member was, but Bussemi was much too strong. So, what did they need?

More fire extinguishers?

Okay. Real solutions. Trees weren't enough. His fists weren't enough. But Bruna had managed to temporarily knock the cardinal out with a fire extinguisher.

But what was going to break the locks on the damned straps holding Rainbow down?

And where the fuck was his *kadu?* He'd felt it there.

Which meant Bussemi was keeping it *on* him?

Great. Next plan: the next time they managed to bonk the red-robed man in the head hard enough to knock him out, they needed to do a body search.

Yeah. Great plan.

So fucking much for fucking recovering the fucking *kadu.*

Or his team. He hoped someone else was getting something else or this mission would be a bust.

They sped up down the hallway past the dead guards and instead of heading toward the exit, Bruna and Doxy turned back the way they'd come and to the control and portal room. That was still a dead end.

"Stop. Slow down." Dexx puffed out when they'd passed into the room. "We have to get out, not back in. We can't get out this way."

"Where is the angel?" Doxy cast wide eyes around.

"Not here. She said she couldn't help. We have to get out on our own." Damn, he sounded like a broken record. This must be what a mother felt like. "You know, like, through a door. You know? Like the last time?"

Bruna shook her head. "No. Goddess, no. What do we do?"

"Stop running the wrong way and move in the right one." It pissed him off that he was leaving Rainbow back there. His mind didn't know her.

His heart did and it *hurt*.

Michelle looked worse for the wear, though. She still wobbled when they stopped, dark rings growing under her eyes making her look old and feeble. She'd hit Bussemi a lot more than he had.

"Stop right there." A male voice came from the far end of the room. "Targets acquired, Portal and Monitoring."

Dexx flattened against the wall, pressing Bruna back with him.

Doxy ran, Michelle following.

Double damn, things were going to hell so fast. "Shh." He whispered even though he'd already been caught.

"He's casting." Bruna breathed into Dexx's ear. She still sounded out of breath.

Oddly enough, Dexx could *feel* the casting, just not the weaving of the spell. "Can you stop him?"

"I… don't— I don't know." Bruna twitched a hand and pulled it back.

"Well, can you try?" The shit was going to get deep in a minute. He attempted a step out but his feet wouldn't move from their spot.

Bruna shook her head. "I can't. He's too powerful." She sniffed back tears. "Not without Doxy."

"You didn't try. Do it." Dexx tried to command them like he had before when Michelle had said he'd "alpha pushed.".

Even if his attempt didn't work like he planned, Bruna still held up her hand, palm out. Her other hand squeezed Dexx's shoulder tightly and she buried her head into his back.

The air grew warmer. A sudden flash of light in the center of the room blew out the heat and the man at the end of the room fell over.

"Nicely done." Dexx moved a foot forward. Whatever spell the man'd been casting had gone with his consciousness. "Let's go. Doxy and Michelle are way ahead of us."

Bruna said nothing, but puffed after Dexx down the hall, following Michelle's scent. The air became disturbed only two turns away.

Medusa was whipping more of the agents around, killing most of them outright. The few who escaped were either bloody or unconscious. Some were being pulled away to safety away from the monster lady.

Dexx waded right in helping Medusa pounding at whatever she left.

Bruna fell back, staying away from the main fight, apparently having used up her magical reserve.

Medusa wasn't moving as fast as she had been earlier. Her

stamina must be way higher since her fight was way been longer than his.

Men and women fell as he slammed them with his fists or feet, whichever put them down faster.

Soon, there was silence. The agents who lived weren't conscious or had disappeared and looking to regroup and return with a better front.

At least that's what he tried to teach. Probably ignored that too.

Medusa's gravelly voice echoed in the common space. "You go. They fled down there." Her monster arm pointed down a hall.

"Well, then let's move." He'd already left one person behind. He wasn't leaving two. "They aren't going to just let us out."

"I'm not leaving." The huge monster lady lowered her body like she was taking root.

"Bullshit. We're *all* leaving, and then we're coming back for the others." Dexx craned his neck up to the Cthulhu head and tentacles. Hopefully her face was up there looking back at him.

"This is my—"

"If you say *destiny* or *fate* or some other lame shit, I'm going to *kick* you all the way out of here." And hope it didn't hurt as badly as attacking Bussemi's old man body had.

"You lack the strength. Not even with the *ma'a'shed.*"

What? Blast it all to nine hells, he'd forgot he had it at all. He pulled the knife out and brandished it. "We *all* go or we *all* stay."

"No." Bruna panted, her hands curled as her eyes roved the hall.

"Mostly, we all go. That includes you." He pointed to Medusa. "Get your tentacley ass moving because Bruna needs your help."

Bruna nodded vigorously.

Medusa's tentacle head nodded. Sort of.

"Okay. That way?" Dexx gestured with the knife.

"Yes."

"At least they're headed the right way." Though Dexx didn't remember this part *as well*. "If we hurry, the distraction will still keep a few busy." If they were lucky.

Bussemi was sliming around somewhere, too.

Dexx's dorm room was across the campus on the far side from where they stood. If he could get them circled around to the dorms he would. He liked his guns and he wanted them back.

"I'll lead." He took a moment to gather Bruna. "Remember, I said I'd protect you. I can do that, but you have to *help* do that. I need you to keep the other witches from casting."

Bruna looked away. "Orange. All of it."

"Can you do that?" Where had her spirit gone? "We have a date. You have a place picked out?"

Bruna nodded again. Less vigorously, uncertain.

"Good. Because we have these bastards, but we have to get out first. You up for it?" He'd drag her if he needed to, but that would take a *lot* of energy.

"Yes. I think so."

"*Yes, I know* so. You try it."

"Yes, I know so." Bruna's voice was flat and even as he'd ever heard it. No emotion at all.

Not good, but she had to believe it and they were out of time.

"See? All good." He started out, Bruna beside him, Medusa following with a little distance behind.

Bruna looked up, steel in her eyes. Something resolved in her brain.

"That's my girl. Stay close and we'll be out in no time. You'll see."

The way forward was clear.

Bruna picked up steam, her steps more grounded and confident with each stride.

"Nobody can stop us now."

Bruna looked up, her brow wrinkled. She pointed down the hall, solid and strong.

Sounds of fighting became more pronounced, but still far away. Down a different corridor.

Dexx followed his nose, trusting it to tell him what his eyes couldn't.

One last length of hallway and the front doors showed a brilliant brushed nickel portal of freedom.

Dexx stopped, studying the doors. There was nobody. No fighting, no guards, no paras, nothing. He waved Medusa up to him. "What do you think? I don't smell anything, and it looks clear. Trap?" The way out seemed too easy and too inviting all at once.

Medusa scowled. "I don't think the arses are capable of that. If they aren't here, it's because nobody can be spared."

Dexx nodded. "I think I have to agree. They don't do subtle. At least not subtle sneaky. Head out."

Medusa took the lead, making the doorway before Dexx got a good head of steam going. He followed at a trot.

Bruna slowed to a fast walk. He gained distance on her easily.

Michelle and Doxy appeared from a side hall.

Relief swelled through him, giving him another burst of energy to his legs.

Doxy's relieved smile made him feel a bit better about dragging them along. The sisters would be a good addition to his team. With a little work.

Dexx was still thirty feet from Michelle and Medusa when Doxy's smile went to horror. She Jerked back like someone yanked her by the hair.

What the hell? She wasn't being attacked.

The scent of fury and hatred sliced the air.

"Dexx Colt. Stop where you are." Cardinal Bussemi sounded pissed.

Dexx stopped and turned. "Go," he shouted to the women behind him.

Cardinal Bussemi had Bruna by a significant amount of hair in hist fist and a bright silver knife at her throat. "You leave now, and I kill her."

The look of terror in Bruna's eyes was absolute. Her hand alternately grabbed and released the hand gripping her hair. She had no idea what to do.

Dexx could talk him down. Maybe. "Calm down. Let's everyone take a few breaths."

Bussemi didn't show signs of being worked up outside of his voice. "I think you have an awkward sense of the situation, Colt. *I* have all the power. All the cards as you kids like to say." Bussemi flicked his knife toward them. "Stay where you are, young dryad. I have a use for you."

"First off, fuck that." Dexx wasn't giving that man the upper hand. "Second off, stand down, Michelle. We'll make it out of here. Just calm down." Dexx held one hand in front of him and the other tucked his knife into the sheath.

Smells crowded his nose, but almost all of it was fear. Bruna went way past all of that into ultra—terror that was almost matched by Doxy.

The mission was mostly a success. They'd gotten information on their team. He now knew where his *kadu* was. A lot of their equipment had been destroyed. All he had to do now was to get him and *his* team out of there alive. "Okay. What do you want?"

"Can you really be that stupid?" The grandfatherly façade slipped away completely. "The five of you. But you most of all, Colt. You escaped not once but twice, and I cannot abide that. You have a friend on the inside, and I want to know who that is."

"Inside of what?" He didn't— oh, wait. He did and he had to hide that.

"In *my* organization. Someone helped you before and I want them. And you. You have a particularly special spot. I didn't finish with your training."

Oh, no. He was *finished*. But there was one more piece of information Dexx needed; the name of the demon who'd tied up his brain. "Fine. We have two ways to deal with this. You try to take us, and we go down fighting."

Guards filled the hallway behind the cardinal, but Bussemi waved them behind him. "You." He pointed to a fully suited figure. Looked feminine.

She took Bruna from Bussemi, holding her hair like he had, and producing a wand at her throat.

Oh, great. There were more of them now. Awesome. "*Or, you let her go, and you can have me.*"

Wait. What? No. Where'd that come from?

"No!" Michelle started forward but Medusa wrapped her up with tentacles. Michelle struggled to get free, but couldn't break out.

"Come here." Bussemi crooked a gnarled finger a Dexx.

"That's it? Even trade? I go over, you let them go?"

"You have a command of how compromise works." Bussemi motioned to the agent holding Bruna.

The agent released her grip.

Bruna quietly sobbed as she shuffled slowly away from the woman.

Dexx walked slow, pulling his knife from his pocket along with the stone Furiel had given him. He held them behind his back to Michelle.

A tendril wrapped around his wrist and tightened. He

turned and gave her a look. "Take them and *go*." The sapling loosened and pulled the things from his hand.

Dexx walked toward Bussemi closing the gap on Bruna.

A guard rushed forward, grabbing Dexx's arm, and twisted, painfully high.

"Kill them." Bussemi smiled.

Bruna's guard stepped forward and blasted her in the back. Blood and gore burst through her, spraying the walls and floor.

She fell forward, no expression on her face.

29

Dexx had only a second to watch as Bruna fell forward, Doxy exploding in a perfect mimic of her sister, falling exactly the same as though she had been blasted too.

Dexx reacted before he had a chance to think on Bruna more. He jumped and twisted his arm straight.

He surprised his guard with a jab to the throat.

The man went down, clutching at his ruined neck.

The rest of the cardinal's guards rushed forward as Dexx engaged. "Run!" Dexx roared as the second person fell with a crushed windpipe.

Screw those guys. They deserved to die.

But the women *didn't* leave.

"Run!" Dexx repeated. This time, he put force behind his words.

Michelle turned and left, Medusa left slower, after she scooped up Doxy's body on their way out.

The next two agents stepped forward to intercept Dexx, but even as he swung, he slowed. First, as though jelly encased him, and then it solidified into lead. He stopped, ridiculously overbalanced, but held upright.

"You damned bastard," Dexx growled through his teeth, turning his full attention on Bussemi. "She wasn't a threat to you. I let you have me in good faith."

Bussemi looked almost bored, but his eyes belied his anger. "How could she be a threat to me? She died because you were her shield, and her shield failed. The first small repayment I intend to take from you."

"You wrinkly old motherfucker. I'm going to kill you." Dexx's vision began to grey at the edges.

The thing in his head pushed to come out. He'd let it if it helped him carve that old man out of existence.

"You may want to. However, you have a lot to answer for. Personally."

The doors to the outside snapped closed. Michelle and Medusa were gone. Bruna and Doxy were gone. *Really* gone.

Dead.

"Slimy bastard. I hate you."

"Not as much as I hate you."

"What the hel—" An image of a person squatting by a fire of small sticks just out from the cover of a cave began to form, then his other personality brushed his mind and shoved him in the back seat.

He sat so far away from seeing what his body did without his permission that he didn't even have a sense of movement.

The darkness kept him swaddled in… well, darkness. Not even his tree popped out of the dark to keep him company or to give him something to lean against.

After a while, the darkness faded and ground formed. He stood, waiting for the light to come out. It did, and the tree formed shortly after.

Hot breath warmed his neck just before he levitated off the ground. "Sonofa—"

He turned to see the biggest… tiger of all time. The thing easily stood taller than he at the shoulder.

He backpedaled, trying to escape the foot-long saber teeth. His feet tangled together just before his ass thumped on the ground, but he twisted around to scramble back to his feet to run. Fast.

His hands gripped the loose soil to push off, and a heavy foot crushed him back down.

Cub.

"Gha— shit!" He managed. He couldn't move, but he wasn't dead. Not yet.

The giant paw pinned him to the ground, but it moved against him. The rest of the body was moving. Hot breath washed over his neck again. Then the gentlest nuzzle from the tiger—cat.

How was his imagination so fucked up that he imagined this beast and let it play with its dinner?

Cub.

The word was in his mind, but he struggled too hard to process it. What was his subconscious trying to tell him?

Come to me, cub.

There was no way he'd be dinner for a monst—

Something strong slapped him across his face, waking him up. Fuck.

Dexx hung by the wrists in the torture chamber where he saw that— *damn.*

The woman—Rainbow—was on the gurney still. And she was awake and gagged. Tears rolled down her dirty face in an unending stream.

He'd really fucked up. Like the ultimate fuck up. Way beyond just the regular kind of fuck up, this was the worst of the worst, and his name was in big letters at the end of it. Dexx Colt, the fuck up.

Cardinal Bussemi held a stick with a gnarled bulb at the

end. "Wake up. I want you to see what you did to your own people. What you did *for* me."

"You killed her. You killed—" Another brutal whack with the stick stopped Dexx from going further. He spat blood from his mouth. A few teeth might have been knocked loose, but in a few moments, his teeth felt better. He didn't want Wolverine's healing. He wanted Hulk's *smash*.

If he had that, then he'd have the ability to crush Bussemi and get Rainbow out of there, and this wouldn't be such a bust.

"No, *you* killed her. Killed them *both*."

Bussemi's shoulders slumped, and that grandfatherly feel came back, only to be erased with the cold look on his face. "You were so confident you could just *walk* in here and *walk* out again. Your hubris killed them. *You*. Your crimes go back over the years, through *lifetimes*. Always the same, always the one to make it out, always skipping through the fallout of your actions."

What the hell was this guy going on about? "Could you be more specific? I'm having trouble following your bullshit."

Bussemi swung the club viciously at Dexx's chest. A rib popped. Shattered really.

Dexx couldn't moan or even make a sound. His chest tightened until there was no breathing. No air on the planet at all.

"I think the next thing I'm going to teach you is to keep your tongue civil. You will call me *master*, and the only words you speak are going to be in direct response to me. And you will begin and end everything you say with…*master*."

Full Metal Jacket popped into Dexx's head. They didn't have a chance against the mental conditioning. Even the fat guy was turned into a fighting machine doing exactly what he was told until he went over the edge.

Slowly, so slow that lights flashed in his vision, air came

back into his lungs as his rib healed itself. The pain lingered longer this time.

Dexx shook his head. Spittle and blood dripped to the floor.

"I did not hear your answer." Bussemi sneered a smile.

"Slimy—"

The club slammed into the inside of his thigh. His leg bone snapped. The scream that tore out of him lasted a long time.

"Do you like my *shay'bet'el*? Literally translated, it means rod of God. Or staff of God. But the important part to you is that the more I swing it, the harder it hits. I put it down, and it starts all over. You see, I *will* break you. One way or another."

Dexx looked at the woman on the table. He had to figure a way out of this. Somehow. But with the stick of God-whomping in the hands of an evil sadist, Dexx's chances were slim.

"Ah. You must be wondering who this woman is."

Oh, Dexx already knew. Well, the words. He didn't remember, but yeah. He *knew* who she was.

"She is one of your... *pack*. Your *animal pack*. Your disgusting pack. She is not the only one. We have more. The one thing I regret is that I have not been able to get them all. That witch wife of yours—" He bit out the words like they tasted like dirt. "Whatever powers she has, I will rend her powerless. Everything will change. Starting with you, and I will make you bring them all to me and watch as you kill them one by one until you are the last. Then I will take your power. And you will give it to me willingly."

"Mmmmmm—"

The little man in his red robes leaned forward, waiting for Dexx to finish.

"—onster."

The club broke his collar bone through his armpit.

Dexx cried through the pain. Searing heat rippled through him. The kind that wasn't real but made staying still impossible. The bones knitted slowly, nerves tracking the broken bits with exactness.

"Master. I'm of two minds about this, you know." Bussemi's voice lightened, his slight Italian lilt coming and going. "One part of me wants you to break quickly so we can get on with my business. Now yours, too. But the other part of me hopes you'll hang on for years. I've waited to be in front of you like this for a *long* time." He drew out the word, really illuminating the hate in his eyes.

Dexx spat blood to the floor. "Huh. Old and wrinkly as you are—"

Bussemi's swing crushed his pelvis, deforming Dexx's hip.

Dexx screamed until he passed out. When he came to again, the cardinal stood in front of him positively gleeful. "I thought I would be happy when I had you in the inhibitor."

The collar.

"This is more…cathartic."

Dexx clamped his teeth shut, his pelvis still healing, and put all his will into breathing through his nose. He shifted his gaze to the woman.

She shook as she watched the brutal beatdown. She cried as her fingers moved strangely. He recognized the motions. Those were his personal signs in his made-up sign language. 'Stay strong,' her fingers said.

She must have been trusted for him to teach her. That alone told him more about who she was than anything else. She was a para, but she was *trusted*.

'More.' She hooked a thumb beyond her to more people.

He saw two more wall—hangers. A man and a woman. Both were unconscious.

Bussemi turned to see what Dexx was staring at and beamed a wrinkled grin at him. "More to your tally. You took so much pleasure taking them. Remember?"

How had that happened? Dexx couldn't believe he was the type of guy who would just turn on his team no matter what the other team did to him.

"*I* spelled you as the good Doctor Petra. I modified your memories and made you hate your people. Imagine my surprise when you kept shrugging off the ward. No matter." Bussemi leaned close and spat, "That's what you get for choosing *them*."

His words hinted that he and Dexx shared a past. But more than that, the reality of what he'd done hit him harder than the God-Whomping-Stick could. It hit him in the soul.

He *was* the kind of guy who could turn on his own team. That knowledge and the sheer exhaustion from all the healing and the beating and the blood loss.

Bruna and Doxy had died. He didn't know how Doxy had died by the same bullet that had killed Bruna, but they'd been the first people he'd trusted since the acci—since Bussemi had captured him and erased his memories. He'd been the demon in the states. The weight of all their blood pulled him down.

He couldn't figure out a way out of there. He wouldn't be able to free his team—who he now recognized. He had all three of them right there, right where he wanted them. But could he *do* a damned thing about it?

What the fuck had he done to Mr. Red Robes?

He slumped against the chains as defeat wormed its way into his heart.

Bussemi swung again.

Dexx's knee buckled, bent the wrong way. Probably as much as he deserved.

Bussemi hit him in the jaw.

Dexx'd *hunted* his own team down, had turned them in to DoDO. His *wife* was out there, fighting the fight with his *kids,* and he was turning on her? On all of them?

"Why?" Dexx forced through his swollen mouth and healing jaw.

Bussemi rested the club on the floor and leaned on it like a cane. "Why. Now that *is* a story. You wouldn't remember this, of course because you succeeded in *our* efforts with the *kadu. I* had to settle for something less... elegant. Made a deal with a demon. Might have been the first time that had ever been done. Do you know what centuries of life does to a person? With what you forced me to? No, of course not. And why would you even care? You move through time living and dying, keeping the power, the skills, the memories that come again, but always with a rest in between. Living little slices of life at a time while keeping *everything.*"

Dexx's body knitted back together, his bones mending, but still far from pain-free. His knee popped back into place. What the hell was this guy talking about?

But as confusing as all this was, things were starting to make a little sense. Dexx stood gingerly, but he stood.

The cardinal wound around the others in the room. "You want to know if these are followers from another life? No. Pathetic examples from this one. A water elemental." Bussemi tapped each of them with the stick as he passed by.

A name drifted up from the pits of his memories. Rainbow.

"A djinn that isn't."

A box in his mind opened, and another name sprang to mind. Tarik.

"And a blood-diluted messenger of the ascended. What you might call an angel."

Greta was the name that flitted up. But she preferred the

name Frey because who wanted to go through life as a Greta? And she was a Valkyrie, not an angel.

Rainbow pulled against her restraints in clear pain, but the other two might as well have been dead.

Bussemi stopped in front of Dexx. "I was the stronger of us. Better. But you stumbled along and stole the secret of *my* solution. You destroyed the way of making it so I couldn't replicate it, but you kept something, didn't you?"

None of *those* memories swam to the top.

"You left me to find another way. A longer way. I had to *watch* as everything I loved disappeared, turned to dust. I lived as my ways became outdated, and I was forced to *change* while *you* lived and died and learned anew as you grew again —" The club struck him in the ribs. "—and again—" The club swung out and back in harder. "— and again—" He brought the *shay'bet'el* out and back-breaking more ribs, gaining power with each swing. "—and again."

Dexx lost consciousness.

When his head wobbled up again, the cardinal had the *shay'bet'el* planted on the floor and rested his hands on the top. "You have a way of escaping your punishment at the most inconvenient of times, little thorn. I was not done showing you how many times you got to come back. I do not have a full count. Nobody does, but I want to make certain you know how many times you got to be young again."

This asshole was pissed because he got to live forever? How many would trade their whole families for a chance like that?

Not a super choice, since living forever was as bad as he described, watching everything become a memory.

Maybe he could get Red-Robed Jerk-Bag to talk instead of beat. Dexx didn't know how much more healing he had left in him. "My name?"

"Ah, that. A good question. We started our first life as

primitive humans." Bussemi held the *shay'bet'el* up to strike but lowered it without breaking more bones.

Good. Good, good. Now, to get more of this story—Dexx just wanted to find a way out. Obviously, but he also knew he *needed* this information. It was important somehow.

He also knew that if this feud or whatever had been going on since the days of "primitive humans," it'd be real neat to find a way to end it now.

"You might have been called betrayer. Judas. Does it matter now? We reveled in the force we call magick. It saturated the air. It was *everywhere*."

Oh, thank the gods. It was going to be a long story. Dexx could heal through that.

And so could Tarik and Frey. Rainbow? He didn't remember her having super healing but was pretty sure a djinn and a Valkyrie did.

"Demons, angels, djinn, others, all around the world. Humans had access to magick just like they did, but we lacked the capacity to form complex intentions. Our magick was more instinctive. *You* took my idea. Stole it. Made a *kadu* and poured your life essence into it. You refused to show me the final step. You made the thing, bonded your soul to it and vanished. You took the *kadu*, hid it or died with it. You gave it to *demons* to keep it from me. You forced me to *this*." Bussemi held out his arms to his sides. "Old age forever, never to be young again. But maybe not." Bussemi's smile turned less grandfatherly.

Damn. Healing took a lot of time. Dexx felt hungrier than he'd ever felt before.

"I spent *millennia* hating you."

Too bad Dexx hadn't. He could use a little of that hate.

Cub, the cat voice cautioned in his mind before disappearing again.

Damn it.

"Hate is a motivator such as one as you have never seen. I have manipulated the world, watching it change, *causing* change, looking for the single person I hated most in this world. But it gave me time to think. To experiment. To lay a trap for you when I found you again."

Rainbow went through bouts of crying. She never stopped her signing Dexx, though. *Stay strong, stay strong, stay strong.*

He would as long as he could. But at some point, he was going to have to claim defeat. The pipe holding the chains binding him was strong. I couldn't feel a weakness as he moved.

How long had Rainbow been strapped to that table, and she's telling *him* to hang in there? Now *that* was one strong woman.

Dexx tugged against his chain. He *needed* to find a way out. Where was that damned saber-toothed strength when he needed it?

Hiding in his broken ribs? What about the broken jaw?

Or his broken mind?

Anger rose in him, giving him a bit more power. *Bussemi* had killed Bruna and, somehow, Doxy. *He'd* captured Rainbow, Tarik, and Frey. *He'd* beaten them to a pulp.

Stay strong.

Bussemi had captured Dexx and unleashed him against other paranormals in a one-man war. That prick thought he was going to take Dexx's body? No. Dexx might have fucked up—badly— by falling into the cardinal's trap, but he was going to find a way to fix this. Bruna and Doxy hadn't died in vain. Not yet.

But how the hell was he going to raise that damned cat and break out of here?

Bussemi tipped his head with a smile as if seeing the thoughts flash across Dexx's face. The *shay'bet'el* impacted several times breaking all sorts of bones. He didn't bother trying to act macho. He screamed in pain at the first whack and continued until he passed out. Again.

He regained consciousness slowly with his body on fire, much like when he'd awakened from the "accident." He hung from the chains with his knees just and inched off the floor.

He couldn't stand with bones broken but knitting back together slowly.

Bussemi leaned over to put his face in Dexx's. "I want *you* because you *owe* me for making me into this, forcing me to make a pact with a demon to live, living half a life. You have something that will help me. All that power you have inside you."

Okay. So, if Dexx was the "great demon hunter," or whatever, maybe Bussemi was the reason for that. It made a strange kind of sense. Maybe he was searching for the demon with Bussemi's contract? That, strangely, made a ton of sense.

Bussemi beat the broken bones to a mushy mess in his body. The next blackout didn't last nearly long enough. Cardinal Bussemi waited with old grandfatherly patience, his stick at the ready.

Eventually, this old guy would *have* to get tired. Right?

"You and I were *strong*."

Oh, god. He was *still* talking. Shit. Dexx was in too much pain to really *care* what the old man had to say anymore. He was *trying* to just dredge up the give-a-fuck to get out of there.

"So strong that we held the sort power that none would understand today." Bussemi's pale eyes stabbed Dexx painlessly. "But I was stronger." He shook his head. "I'm going to live forever in your skin, and then I will reclaim the power time has leached from me."

That explained why Dexx still lived. "No." He needed to buy healing time. *"Master."* Dexx put all his hate, all his determination, all his everything into pulling the chain from the wall.

That wasn't enough. He had to pour something else in. That damned cat wasn't showing up.

What else was there? He had nothing magickal about him. No matter what the cardinal said. Right?

Bussemi smiled and then shook his head. "Oh, Dexx. You are so perfectly predictable." He picked up his stick and began the beating. Agony beyond agony tore through him.

Something more than bones broke.

He would do anything to make the pain stop. *Anything.* Call him master, kill anyone, do *anything* if he would *just stop.*

Lights flashed in his head. The beginnings of death? He could hope so. Dexx fell unconscious, but the pain chased him through the blackout. Chased him and mounted in pain.

Run away. He had to run from the pain or to a solution *if* there was one to be found.

Two names came to mind from nowhere, or maybe somewhere.

Hattie.

Paige.

Cub.

Hattie. I need you.

In less time than it took to blink an eye, Dexx fell beyond unconscious. The torture lab where Bussemi held him was replaced with the deep darkness and the tree.

A virtual TV-like hole rent the air. Through it, he saw the cardinal become enraged and beat Dexx unmercifully with the *shay'bet'el,* breaking every major bone in his body. And all the minor ones too.

Motherfucker. He's going to kill me. But at least I can't feel it.

Cub, do you remember?

Dexx spun. The monster-cat-lion-tiger thing sat a few feet away from him, towering way bigger than one of those big horses on the beer commercials. The cat had a tan coat that looked soft, and saber teeth a foot long were more than a little scary. Green eyes peered at Dexx with ancient intelligence.

Hattie?

Do you not remember?

In the real world, Bussemi slowed the beating. The TV in the air wavered and disappeared.

Images flooded through his mind filling in holes.

He stood in a police station. *Nederlands, Colorado.* A shifter raged and as Dexx tried to fight him off, the shifter bit him, bringing the spirits. Well, one spirit.

Hattie.

I remember.

Another time he stood in front of a stack of stones naked and painted with colored clay. He went to a knee and the spirits again chose him.

Hattie.

He was born from a young girl, the spirit already with him.

Hattie.

The visions went on and on, showcasing many lives in many places. There was a warrior, an outsider, royalty, poor, young, old, and all things in between.

In every vision of every lifetime he was two things except in his current life. The first, he had Hattie and the shifter she made him. The second, he was also a witch. A magick user.

What? I've never had magick. Not even with... the name came easily. Paige. Her face did not. She was a blur covered with glowing bands of black-lined, teal magick in his mind. Those were restricted memories.

Hattie stood and dropped her chin to rub her face along his. *I could not tell you with Paige. I was unable.*

Hattie. She'd always told the truth straight. *Why? Because you were sworn to secrecy?*

No, cub. You would fight her war with what is lost.

Magick. *His* magick had been lost.

Dexx looked at the tattoos across his arms and chest. The tattoos that kept demons out. The newest he didn't even remember. *Is this why these work so well? Because of my magick?*

Yes. The protections will work for all, but you always have the part of you that is from that world.

Why was this magick cut off from me? It would be real neat to be able to shift and *not* lose his clothes like Leslie and... Paige.

With that name came so much *weight*. The weight of love and intense frustration. But the thing he really recalled was that Paige could shift without losing her clothes, even though he wished she could. She was one sexy momma.

He was overwhelmed with a tidal wave of longing for this amazing woman. She might be frustrating and a little condescending, but she completed him in a way he hadn't felt in centuries.

So, his magick was, what? Locked away for safe keeping? *If I'm magick-borne, why don't I have any now?*

Hattie looked over the bluff and surveyed the plains. Grassland deer munched on grass without concern. *I cannot say. Even with what I know about you and our past lives, I cannot look into that part of you.*

So I don't have superpowers. None at all. He blocked out any thought that came close to Bussemi.

Anything to stay away from him.

No. I have enjoyed watching you play out your dreams like a cub attacking prey already caught and killed, pretending to have made the kill.

Is this how it's going to be— me, not remembering who I am, and you making fun of me?

Hattie brought her head back around to Dexx, with her cat-smile. Amused.

You are the— Another memory from the very first life he'd had when the spirit of the great cat had bonded with him hit. They'd spoken, but without words. *You help me. I help you?* Not an exact language, but the intent had been clear.

Dexx'd had magick. The monster of a cat had had magick of her own. They'd both walked on the earth when many of the rules of magick hadn't been solidified. They'd formed a bond, the cat and the man. She'd given him abilities beyond his own magick and had received a magick not her own.

Dexx stared at the cat. *You had a name. Hat'ai. Wasn't it?*

Hattie stood and rubbed her face along Dexx's face again. *Yes. You have not called me by that name in a long time.*

Yeah, like from the first life we bonded. Dexx raised his arms and hugged his big-assed cat, a feeling of home settling over him.

She made a sound low in her throat. Maybe a growl? Her fur was soft and warm, and very comforting. She had a smell that wasn't a scent. But the feeling it conveyed was deep. He had found a piece of his soul.

Do you expect me to call you Hat'ai now?

Cub, you will call me whatever you want. You always have.

"Hattie it is. How long are we going to hang out here in the time before?"

Your body is near death. You will recover if you are not damaged more.

Sudden realization struck him. "That was *you* chasing me. Shit, you had me scared to fall asleep."

I was keeping you together in your dreams. They ripped you apart. You are still not whole, but now you can begin healing on your own. It will take a long time. And you have to have those rocks you spent all your time with.

"Fuck. I have to get the *kadu*?"

There were more the first time. In our first bond.

"I had more *kadu* the first time?" So those hadn't belonged to others? "There are *more*?"

Two, and then another one.

"You can't just say *three*?" He could have been annoyed, but with his memories restoring, he was willing to give a little.

You had two, and after, you made one more.

Perfect logic.

"Which one did I have? The one I gave to Michelle?" Walking through his past life memories was a lot like walking through deep puddles. Sort of. The memories around his current life were still like reading through mud.

That was the last you made. I do not know much about it. But I feel protection when you have it.

He vaguely recalled creating that stone with that very purpose. Was the exact intent, though? He didn't recall.

How had DoDO acquired the stone in the first place? An insignificant stone in the middle of all those other pieces of priceless magickal pieces? Two things came to mind. They'd set a trap, a far more elaborate plan than they'd needed, or the demon, Furiel. He'd given Dexx the— *shamiyr*— the stone of protection once.

Had he given it to him *twice?* Had Furiel been one of the demons Dexx had entrusted to protect his stones?

Bussemi had said they'd recovered the *kadu* from demons.

"I don't have all my memories back."

They caged your mind and set a trap over it. I can feel your memories, both old and new, but there is danger around them.

"Why didn't they do that to *all* my memories?"

Those were not there. Or they did not find them.

He had to free his mind. If he could tap into his magick, that might be the way out of this predicament. Break away from Bussemi, "How are they trapped? If I knew how, I might be able to find someone to break the wards."

That is more than I know. I am sorry, cub.

There had to be a workaround. He refused to believe they were going to fail here. "Well, we'll just have to get you trained up. How did *I* learn?"

Hattie just looked at him, her cat-smile gone.

"Fine. How do I get my memories, my *kadu*, and the other rock back—" Because Michelle only had one. "—and can I get my magick back so we can get out of here?"

Hattie remained silent as she thought.

"I know who *you* are. I know *I'm* a shifter, and a *mage, sorcerer, wizard,* or *witch*, but I can't know anything about my current life. How is that going to affect like, everything I do?"

I do not know how things will be when you wake.

Wake. Maybe he should just stay. Bussemi was on the other side, and, no. Just no.

He'd spend his time away from consciousness as much as possible.

But if he could just *take* this information with him to the waking world, that might be enough? He still didn't know how yet, but... "Then how do I get back here and visit? Not that I really want to, but just in case I need something."

Of course, cub. Just in case you need something. Hattie's smile came back. She didn't really move, but there was something that said *smile* about her. *Become calm and come to me. I do not know more than that. That is how you taught me, and that is all I ever knew.*"

Damn. Just go to her. Well, shit. He could work with that if he had to. Blast it all to hell, he *had* to. "Also, shouldn't we—"

You should not be here. The voice was deep and resonant, like all the movie versions of the benevolent, but extra snooty king when they deigned to talk to the lesser people.

Dexx put up his dukes, ready to fight.

The ancient elk spirit who had never chosen a human to bond with walked toward them, his head held high. But had been *forced* to bond with... *someone.*

That memory was locked as well. "Damn, scared me." A name came to him. "Mah'se. That's your name. I remember that much at least."

You should not be separated from your bond. You and Hat'tai should be one.

"Yeah, well, we're still working on that. I got some of me back."

Hattie twitched an ear. *There is a block working against our shift. That is why I called you here. Our fear is that the cub won't remember us when he exists in the other place.*

That was a strange way to say the *real* world.

Mah'se swung his head to look out over the plain, his majorly huge rack passing over even Hattie's head.

Part of him has been taken, Hattie continued. *Broken in the other place.*

How can he protect us as he swore to if he is broken? Mah'se asked.

Dexx opened his mouth to speak but recalled a vow he'd made the first time he'd bonded to his big cat, to protect the time before from the horrors of mankind. "I'm working on it," Dexx growled.

The elk sighed and looked at Hattie. *He should recall us when he returns to that other plane, but he* must *protect us from the twisted one.*

He had to be referring to Bussemi. Was that the reason Dexx'd made the choice all those years ago? Why he'd "stolen" Bussemi's knowledge or whatever?

You should leave.

"Okay, stop the world for this guy. My reality's a bit too inconvenient. Thanks for all your input, but if you aren't helping, you're hurting." Dexx made shooing motions.

Mah'se didn't move.

"Fine, hang out. But..." Dexx needed solutions. The real kind.

Hattie sat, then lowered her body to the ground, paws, in front of her, but intently watching the plain below. *Cub, rest while your mind heals. Mah'se will watch out.* She stared hard at the elk. *Because even the protectors need protecting sometimes.*

He dropped down and burrowed into her side, his hands

behind his head. She was warm and soft and— He became drowsy and before he knew what happened he fell asleep against Hattie's gentle growl.

Caught in the limbo as he was, he didn't dream.

Faint echoes of the pain from his brutal beating came through. Not enough to wake him up, but enough to be a low-level irritation. However, through this sleep, more of his memories filtered in and a small team of mind-elves rushed around organizing what came up. It was a little like cleaning up vomit.

As the memories surged forward, Dexx got a better sense of himself, but not just Dexx Colt, demon hunter extraordinaire.

Badass warlock shifter who kept those with powers on the side of fair. He didn't *understand* why his war witch abilities had been stowed away, but he did comprehend that he was sorely dampened for not having them.

At some point, he left the prehistoric landscape and slipped into the physical world. A cold pressure rocked him. Not roughly, but insistently.

He tried to open his eyes, but a wall of pain stopped him. "Uh, uh," he groaned.

The shaking began again. "Dexx," a soft voice whispered. "Wake up. Can you hear me?" The whispering was as gentle as the shaking, but he didn't know the voice. She was blessedly American, though. Accents were about to be his first red flag for bad guys.

"Please stop." The words came out as more of a wordless mumble, but in his head they were shouted.

Mercifully, the shaking stopped. "Can you stand? We have to leave."

Standing wasn't going to be super easy. His legs still felt on the mushy side of broken. "No." The word was a little stronger, but still more mumble than word. Bussemi really worked him over. He hadn't felt this bad when hed awakened after the "accident." His arms ached and burned. His knees still hung above the floor. His shoulders bore the lion's share of his weight.

"Drink this. It's a high protein, high energy drink. It'll help you recover."

"Hmm?" Whoever it was didn't understand the vast amount of broken bits in his body.

"High energy," the woman said as if it *meant* something. "With your shifter metabolism, it'll help the recovery process. I figure you need somewhere in the vicinity of six thousand calories. Maybe more depending on how long ago you ate. All you have to do is swallow. Damn. You're a mess, boss."

Boss? Didn't someone else call him that?

"The others are on the way out. You're the last, but I can't carry you. You have to help."

Dexx tried again, and his voice was stronger still, if only by degrees. "Who are you?"

"Ethel, dummy. If you don't mind, I'd like to play the name game *after* we leave. Michelle filled me in a little. You're Dexx Colt, demon hunter extraordinaire, and I'm the smartest forensics examiner this side of Abby on *NCIS*."

"How?" His voice was gravelly, but he couldn't trust anyone not named Dexx Colt at this point.

"Got a ride on one of Chuck's private jets. Boy, I'm never going commercial again. But I digress. *You drink.*"

The lip of a cup pressed gently against his mouth. His eyes still didn't work well enough to open yet. How in the hell did his lips hurt this bad? Bussemi was going to— no, the cardinal had proven how strong he was. If Dexx never saw him again, it would be too soon. Just his name scared Dexx more than he wanted to admit.

Liquid trickled into his mouth and he either swallowed,

or he'd choke on it. Peach tea poured down his throat. His favorite.

After the second shallow swallow, warmth spread through his chest and back.

His eyes opened and the woman in front of him was not what he pictured. She had blonde hair tied up in a messy bun and her pink boots warred with the lime green pants and off-pink coat. Or maybe not. She looked natural in the outfit.

More peach tea followed until he needed to breathe. He twitched his head up, and she stopped.

"Thanks." He *did* feel better, but he still hung from his hands chained to the ceiling. "Can you get me out of these?"

"Oh, of course. Stand up, and I'll get them off in a jiffy."

Releasing a long breath, he rose on legs that had been broken a dozen too many times.

Pressure let up on his wrists and the cuffs came away.

"Oh, if I had a nickel for every time I pictured you chained up in a sexy basement, not that this is a sexy—it's not." Ethel blinked rapidly and looked around. "Drink more of the tea." She handed him the cup.

Damn, what was in that drink? He needed to invest in it for real.

The torture room was empty except for them. "Rainbow?"

"On her way out with Tarik and Frey." Ethel's eyebrows rose as she looked at him. "Did you want to stay?"

"No. I really don't." Dexx still didn't trust his legs to carry him so he draped an arm over the woman's shoulders.

Ethel ducked under and took some of his weight.

They took two steps and someone came through the door in full tactical gear and body armor.

Quinn Winters' eyes went wide.

Damn it.

Quinn flicked the signal for, *They're watching*.

Ethel scooted behind Dexx as she recognized Quinn.

Great. He barely held himself up. He gave the under cover agent a two finger salute.

"What the hell do you think you're doing?" Her head dipped out the doorway, checking the halls.

"Leaving, but that asshole has stuff I need."

"You're dead!" Ethel breathed hard at Dexx's back.

Quinn turned a withering look at Ethel. "You only *wish* I was dead."

"Not true. *I* never wanted anything bad—"

"This is a bad time for this conversation." Dexx leaned against the steel gurney Rainbow had been strapped to.

"You should have already been gone," Quinn said.

"Kinda struggling with every bone in my body being broken."

She gave him a look that said that was valid.

"He knows someone on the inside helped," Dexx said. She had to know her cover was close to being blown.

Quinn licked her lips as if she was really considering it. "I'm taking this place down. I can't do that on the outside."

He stood as tall as he could. "Okay. Let's get started."

"Yes, let's." Quinn raised her baton, energy crackling at the tip.

"Make it look real."

Quinn took out her baton with a disgusted sigh. "Of course I will. There are two teams down the hall, but there's in the opposite direction of the exit. So, go to the exit. Don't pass Go. Just run."

"You got it."

She narrowed her eyes. "Don't get caught again?" She swung in one motion.

Dexx jabbed his fist forward, stepping inside Quinn's effective swing arc, recalling past life moves he'd never had in this lifetime.

She went down like a sack of potatoes.

Dexx dropped to his knees beside her and leaned close to her head. He slid his hand down the body armor to her belt. "Come with us," he whispered. "I can take you hostage."

"No," she breathed back. "I've got my reasons to stay. Take the information I copied for you."

Dexx opened her pouches, searching. "Where?" He didn't even know what he was looking for.

Quinn twitched her hand on her right side.

Dexx pulled her gloves off and tossed them to Ethel. "Put those on." He needed the footage to look like he plundered the body. He then opened a pouch and found a thumb drive. "This?"

"Yeah. You should have what you need there. It's more than what Michelle was able to put on her cloud drive. And it's protected so they shouldn't be able to erase it as long as you open it on a device that isn't connected to the net."

He palmed the thumb drive. "One more chance. Be my captive."

"Once, I would have been more." A ghost of a smile played at her mouth and her hips shifted a little.

Quinn was more than just super sexy.

"You have all you need. Contact me later."

Dexx tapped the inside of her wrist and unclipped her security badge as he stood. His head only swam a little. Ethel's brew was still working wonders. "Let's move." Dexx led the way out, walking more confidently.

Ethel followed right behind. "I normally don't understand what you're up to when you do it, but I'm completely lost. What just happened?" She kept her voice low as they checked the intersecting halls for agents.

"She told me they were watching. I had to put on a show."

"But... why is she *here*?"

"When she disappeared—" Which he didn't remember. "—she'd come here and she's working as a double agent. I don't know all the specifics."

"Oh," she said, her tone saying she understood, but didn't at the same time.

He opened his senses to determine if they were alone. Scents led him away from the torture chamber. And the way out. The halls stayed amazingly quiet. "What time is it?"

"What?" Ethel breathed hard even though they weren't running. "Oh, sometime after one, I think."

"It's going to be a trap." Dexx reached behind him to grab Ethel's hand. But what kind?

She didn't look like she could run very far if that was their only option.

He led them to one of the side exits, one that should take them to the library hall. He'd found a pretty good hiding spot behind a statue of an imposing man with a hand in his coat.

He stood at the corner in front of the doors. The last time he'd done this, someone had died. No. *Two* someone's.

"When we move, we move together, and you don't stop unless I stop you. Are we clear?" He put as much force into his words as he could, and still talk low.

"Crystal."

Dexx stretched out his senses, trying to feel if anyone waited for them. Nobody seemed to be out there. Everything was quiet as a church mouse, in a room full of hungry cats.

"Ready, go." He was already pulling Ethel along as he said the words.

She ran almost as fast as he did, fueled by adrenalin.

They closed in on the doors and skidded to a halt. He quickly passed Quinn's badge over the lock. The light turned green and the lock clicked. Dexx pushed the door open.

Sirens wailed and the alarm lights flashed. "Oh. Fkkk." It wasn't a word as much as frustration he pushed through clenched teeth.

Dexx ran, pulling a screaming Ethel in his wake. She got heavier and heavier the further they went.

"Run." Dexx commanded, slamming her with his primal will.

Ethel ran. The pull lightened and she kept up. All the way to the tall stone wall where the spotlight from the dorms caught up to them.

"Damn, not now." Dexx hunched over and laced his fingers together. "Ready for a boost? You get over the top and don't stop running until you get to America. Got it?"

"But what about you?" Determination settled like a stain over her face.

"Get *up.*" The wave of dizziness passed quickly, as she put her foot in Dexx's hands. He straightened pushing her upward. She flew up and caught the top of the wall and scooted over.

Sounds of fully suited and weaponized DoDO agents sounded in the distance. They would be close in just seconds.

Dexx jumped up.

He woke up in a park, next to a tree, Ethel staring out into the darkness.

"What—"

Ethel squealed as she turned. "Stop that." She slapped his bare chest a few times in one second. "You scared the devil out of me." She pulled in a breath and let go slowly. "Why didn't you shift before? I thought you couldn't."

"I… can't." He put a hand to his head, trying to remember what had happened after he'd leapt onto the wall.

"Well, obviously you can. You led me here. You and Hattie."

"I don't… where is everyone?"

"This way. I think." Ethel handed Dexx her coat that covered him, mostly. With the glance she gave him, she'd seen him this way more than once. Naked.

"Who *are* you?"

"Later. Now we find the team."

The *team*. Superheroes?

Finding the *team* took only as long as finding their abandoned warehouse.

Medusa waited by the door, her expression unfriendly. "*You* killed her." She punched him in the chest. "Killed them *both*." She punched him again.

Dexx staggered backwards as the remembered reality of Bruna and Doxy's deaths pummeled him. He deserved no less and a hell of a lot more.

Medusa glared once as a tear flowed silently down her cheek.

"Yeah." That was all he could say. He *had* killed them. His overconfidence. His need for the *kadu*.

She stiff armed him again and walked away.

He opened the door to the broken office and stepped in.

Ethel closed the door behind them.

Three sets of new eyes stared at him.

Dexx stopped.

Ethel didn't. She bumped into him, shoving him forward another step.

"Are you really back?" Rainbow asked in a small voice, wringing her hands slightly. She looked worried and smelled terrified.

Ethel answered for him. "Uh huh. It's really him."

The afro charged him, and before he could do more than lean back in defense, she had her arms around his nearly naked body, sobbing into his chest. "I knew you didn't mean it. I mean you just couldn't. What we went through, I knew you had a reason. You had a reason, didn't you? Of course, you did. I mean you're Dexx. You had a plan and we didn't see it at first, but you knew. The whole time, you knew."

Wow, Rainbow could talk *fast*. Must be her para-power.

He hugged her back, the action feeling normal, her slight form feeling familiar as if his arms remembered things his mind did not. Somehow, just having someone excited to see him was the best medicine. Too many lately hadn't wanted him around and he hadn't realized until that moment how much that meant to him.

"I'm not really myself yet. I can't remember who you are beyond your names. Any of you. But I'm glad we got you out."

Michelle looked at him like was the dumbest man on the face of the planet. "That was stupid, Dexx. Extinction level stupid."

"I *had* to try." He let Rainbow go, as she got herself under control sniffing back more tears.

The third woman he didn't know, but she had *all* the right curves. Frey was tall and blonde and fit to be a cover model.

She walked right up to him and hooked a fist to his mouth. "Fuck you. Fuck you and the horse you fucked before you fucked it. *Fuck you, Dexx.*" Fire lit her blue eyes, like real literal fire seemed to burn behind her eyes.

Holy Hannah, she hit *hard.* "I deserved that, I guess. I still don't know who you are. They wiped my memories. So if you're going to hit me again, hit me from that perspective."

"I must admit," Tarik said, rising to his feet. "I am thinking violence against you." He had Middle Eastern features that made Dexx think of Aladdin. Or Sinbad of *The Seven Seas.* "Can you explain yourself?"

"I can. But I'm *really* tired of going through it. Michelle." He tossed the thumb drive to her. "Quinn sends her regards."

"What?" Rainbow took a step back. "Quinn *Winters? That* Quinn? She died. When Mike Jones was killing all those people, and Tarik was stuffed with all the djinn. She died. There was so much blood."

Dexx held up a hand, *some* of those details coming back. "Didn't die. I don't know anything about that either, but she's working from the inside to take DoDO down. That's all I know." Exhaustion hit him hard as he flopped into the office chair. "I... met someone. I can't remember who she is, but—"

"Oo, Paige is gonna be pissed."

Good thing he'd already been sitting. The world rocked, finishing up with the room spinning.

"Are you okay?" Rainbow asked.

"It's a ward block." Michelle shuffled to the desk. "Roxxie said it could get worse until it kills him. Unless he can lift it himself." She grabbed his hand and put something in his palm.

His stone. One of the three. He felt a little better. At least the room slowed to a grinding halt.

"You didn't tell them?" Despite himself, a grin crept across his face.

"No time. And you're a lot of trouble we don't need. But you're our alpha. And we *need* you."

"Wait, what?" So there was a *lot* of ground to cover. "Can we spend like one *day* away from DoDO and get things straightened out? I need a rest. Looks like we *all* do. Anyone know where that angel is? Roxxie? And maybe a pair of pants? Or a blanket?"

They spent the next week getting to know each other again. Dexx felt flashes of his previous life but nothing so much that his bouts got worse.

Turned out Tarik was a djinn the assholes at DoDO had experimented on. At one time, he could have just blinked them back to America and away, but they'd done something to him and now he couldn't.

Roxxie hung near death, or at least she wasn't well. She'd pushed herself way too far, getting them all back, so she was out.

Rainbow Blu kept looking up to Dexx like he was a big brother, and Dexx took that as a good thing.

Frey had taken the memory loss as a personal insult. Apparently, they'd been good friends, but not as good as her and Tarik. They had a bond of sorts.

Ethel seemed to be the best off. She hadn't been captured by DoDO because she was one hundred percent pure human and way, way off anyone's radar.

Medusa kept their conversations to a minimum and business only. She said Furiel could not be reached.

That wasn't what Dexx wanted to hear, though. Especially not if Furiel was the demon Dexx'd entrusted to protect his stones.

Red Star took over the old grungy office, and actually made the place less gross. Ethel was working her way through the thumb drive Quinn had given them on a computer she assured them was hooked to nothing. Michelle acknowledged that a large portion of the information she'd been able to put on the cloud drive had either been contaminated or had been actually removed. He jabbed at her twenty-first century jokes, and she poked and prodded at Dexx's protection stone.

"There are so many layers of encryption," Ethel groaned, even though her eyes lit with the joy of a challenge. "And it's not all computer code. There're bits of encryption from old texts, dead languages. These guys are impressive."

"But you can get through it?" Dexx asked. He wasn't certain what he hoped to find. But Michelle had filled him in on what his not-quite-wife was up against in the states, and Michelle was hoping to find something to arm Paige with.

Which was great. It really was. But Dexx and the team were *here* and in a hurt locker. So, *he* was hoping to find something to take DoDO down, possibly for good. He wanted to find some weakness of Bussemi's, maybe?

"Paige needs something," Michelle said with a heavy sigh. "She's fighting a war on her own, practically. She needs some way to protect your twins."

Paige's name always seemed to trigger the memories that locked him up. But mention of the twins sent him even further.

Tarik caught him as he fell.

The headache went from the back of his head and streaked to the front. Nervous energy bubbled up and he trembled trying to use the energy looking for an escape.

"Those are getting worse." Tarik guided him to a chair and sat him in it.

"Yeah." Over the past week Dexx's visions became clearer whenever the memories came out. This time he remembered a blonde-haired girl with bright blue eyes and a troubled frown, and a toddler who glowed with angel light. "I have kids." He recalled two babies who had the ability to shift into any animal they wanted and tended to break the living room during naptime. "Four of them." His eyes focused on nothing as he saw their memory. "Oh shit. I have *kids*" He turned in the direction that felt like *home*. "We have to get back." He stood, or tried to.

Tarik held him down. Easier than Dexx would like to admit.

"They're in the states." Michelle looked reluctant. "They're safe. I hate to say this, but until we take care of this Bussemi guy, they're safer in her war than they are with you."

Ouch. That hurt.

"Whoa." Ethel broke in, backing up from her screen. Something didn't smell right. "Oh no."

"What?" Dexx rose, the dizziness passing as he walked, and shook off Tarik and Rainbow.

Michelle half-stood but went back to poking at the stone as Dexx steadied.

Ethel hovered close to the screen, tapping furiously on the keypad. "This is… *everything*. Or more than we've ever had before. Oh shit."

That was the first swearing he'd heard out of Ethel. "What?" He asked again, frustration taking over.

Her hands covered her mouth as horror filled her eyes with tears. "They're monsters. They're using paranormals as test beds for their new tech. DoDO is just the beginning."

"Beginning what?"

"Shit." Frey hovered over Ethel's back, reading the screen.

Dexx finally made it to a place he could see what was going on. She had several documents open.

"They're doing tests," Ethel said, as she continued to read. "They've uncovered ways to repress and *steal* paranormal abilities. They're trying to remove them and give them to soldiers, high-ranking people, people seeking power.

But—" Her breath caught in her throat as she swallowed. "Their extraction technique is brutal." She turned her wide-eyed stare up at Michelle. "And it starts with those collars."

Michelle's mouth opened as if she was about to say something, but then she shook herself. "I've gotta tell Pa—" She glanced at Dexx and then chucked her chin at him instead. "She needs to know."

Ethel nodded.

Frey kept reading.

Dexx didn't need to re-read what they were focusing on. Instead, he read through the file management window. One tab jumped out at him, in front of all the others. "Whiskey". The next one after that was labeled "Trash".

"That one." Dexx pointed to the file marked trash. "No way. Anyone who keeps a file marked 'trash' is hiding something important."

Ethel opened the link and more tabs lined up. The first was marked "USA" and the next was "History".

Ethel tapped the "USA" tab. A timetable opened on a spreadsheet, detailing events from the mid-nineties.

"Wow, that's a long time ago." Rainbow peered at the screen between Ethel and Dexx. "Did they even have computers back then?"

Dexx looked at her for a long moment. "Are you for real?" He could only shake his head when she nodded seriously at him.

"See here?" Ethel pointed to the screen. These are dates. Looks like they were archaeological digs. Here's one from Giza, another from Salisbury, La Brea Tar Pits, and one from Katmai National Park. The last entry was more than ten years ago."

Good thing Ethel could read the notes. They looked like someone had dumped a can of alphabet soup out and squished all the letters together.

He had a good idea of what they were after, though. *Kadu.* "But that's not all, is it? What's this one here?"

Ethel studied the columns and rows. "This is something else. I would have to have a frame of reference to decipher them. But these here—" she pointed a series of numbers and letters in red, "—these are birthdays, and death dates. None of them overlap. That's strange."

"Why?"

Frey leaned in. "Could be a family line. Those go back a long-ways. Longer than the *nineties*," she said sarcastically at Rainbow. "Valkyries can trace our origins to almost ten thousand years."

Michelle's voice wafted up from her study of the *kadu* digs. "Dryads go back a little longer, to about twelve, so there's nothing strange there."

Ethel tipped her head to the side, her eyes glued to the screen. "And sometimes there's a long gap in between the death and the next birth. The strange part is that some of these predate the Stone Age. The first date is... that's impossible."

Michelle picked her head up. "Yes, it is. There just wasn't much before then. The gods, mostly." She turned the rock over in her hands.

"Why?" The numbers were just numbers to him. And letters. Alphabet soup swirling on the screen.

Ethel twisted her head to look at him, then pointed at one set on the screen. "Because that would the earliest birthday in here, right in the beginning of the Stone Age. That's why I think it's impossible."

A memory floated up, and Dexx remembered a cold grass plain. A small fire burned in the night, with the noises of hunters echoing against the rough circle of rock outcroppings. Shadows moved in and lightning speared out from the far side of the fire to the darkness. A man stood there, his hands outstretched. He was short, but had a powerful build with small brown eyes that glared at him.

The great form of a massive dog landed just in the circle of light, his fur smoking.

Another form jumped through the shadows from the rocks above.

Not another wolf. This one was bigger.

A cat.

Light flashed in the office.

"Shit!" Michelle jerked away from the stone, her hand glowing as magick connected her to the stone arced away.

The light expanded and formed pictures on the walls. Vivid, real-life pictures superimposed themselves over the dusty office furnishings. It was the strangest movie projection of all time, but it matched exactly the memory Dexx saw in his mind

The man across the small fire held up a stone. Dexx's stone. He shook the rock, pointing at Dexx, then pointing out into the dark.

Dexx remembered a noise in his head, the projection was silent. He turned, and saw a large form bound out from the dark.

In an instant, huge paws smacked the man down to the ground and turned to Dexx, but the point of view changed, as though the camera was pressed hard to the rocks.

The person recording the memory was in trouble. The animal stalked around the fire swinging her head between the two. The fang-teeth came within inches of Dexx and she growled.

She?

Dexx *felt* the protection from the beast. She was protecting him.

She.

The man on the ground bled from deep gouges in his

side. He rose up to his feet, blood pouring from him as fire lit his eyes.

He lanced out his hand. A bar of pure light pierced the cat.

She let out a howl of agony and dropped to ground grievously wounded, but still alive.

Both Dexx and the perspective, reached out to the cat, touching the fur before rage overcame him.

He became the memory, moving in time with the vision on the walls.

Dexx's memory and the perspective moved simultaneously. His entire body clenched and the arms of the perspective flexed the same way.

The ground heaved. Dust flew up from the packed earth and shook loose pebbles from the rocks.

The sound had been deafening. Like ground zero of a nuclear bomb. Wool packed his ears, but that wasn't important.

Distantly, he saw the others back up and watch him and the memory projection.

When he and the point of view vision looked up, the man was gone, but the small rock was on the ground.

Without thinking, Dexx's arm superimposed on the perspective's arm and picked up the rock before rushing to the bleeding cat. The stone glowed in his hand and the saber-toothed cat relaxed. Dead or unconscious.

The vision flashed intensely then faded away, leaving the crusty office and five stunned people. Six if Dexx was included.

"I have never experienced what I just saw." Tarik recovered first. "I felt the era of that vision. I remember that time. A few thousand years after that, the djinn and the other demons were banished from this world."

"What was—" Rainbow swallowed hard. "Was that *Hattie?*"

Dexx stared at the wall where the vision had been, feeling the embers of the memory. "Yes."

"Spirits had form on the earth?" Ethel's eyes were wide.

Dexx relaxed his fists. The memory of his injured cat still had him angry. How could the emotions from a memory thousands of years ago still affect him, but he couldn't remember a wife he loved? Or his kids. He wanted to find Bussemi and punch him in the throat.

"*That man,*" Frey said hotly, "is alive. That man was our *torturer.* Older, bent by time, but it was *him.*"

The man at the fire, who had struck Hattie had been Bussemi? "*Fuck.* He said he'd known me from a long time ago." That they'd been friends? But more likely, Dexx was fucked up in the head.

Tarik blinked rapidly, taking his gaze to the ceiling. "There were rumors."

"What rumors?"

"Of the magickal humans doing things they should not be able to do."

"And if this was the same guy—" Bussemi, "—how could he still be alive? Some sort of Dorian Gray bullshit?" Magick and a demon deal.

"I cannot say," Tarik said, his horizontal pupils shooting to slits. But there might be some merit in your observation."

Well, if the demon deal *did* include a magick portrait to retain life, they could use that. Dexx turned back to the computer. "What else is on that thing?" He nodded at Ethel with her wide, disbelieving eyes.

She just stared.

"Please look at the screen. We're not done yet."

Ethel swallowed hard and nodded back. Her hands quivered as she pointed at the screen. "Well, this is probably an important tab." Ethel clicked on the one marked Whiskey.

"Likes his drinks, I guess." At least he could hope.

Ethel stared up at him for a few seconds, then turned back.

"You need to take this." Michelle held the stone with the markings on across it. "Take it, learn it, and unlock it. That magick is old. As old as my people and maybe older. That only responded to the calling, from the time when magick was wild and had less bounds."

Dexx didn't want it. He almost slapped it from her hand, but she held it out, the look in her eye like an insistent mother.

Slowly his hand rose and took it. "Okay. Got any suggestions on how I do that? It's not like there's a manual on these things. *He* said you can't even break those. Not easily."

"The only thing I can say is that it's up to you. There's nothing more I can do with it. Not even Paige could do what I did."

Dexx braced himself for the headache and the dizziness. Both came right on time, and with the images of the woman, this time with kids and blurry images of other people standing around her.

The rock warmed in his hand. Pleasant tingles of heat raced through his veins and spread through his back and chest and up into his head. The headache subsided and left the trace of the woman's image in his mind.

Paige.

Another image materialized next to her. This one was the cat that from the vision.

Hattie.

"*Damn it.*" The rock had *magick*. Another piece fell into

place. DoDO had never accepted anyone who wasn't a witch or elemental in their ranks.

Bussemi had known from the beginning.

The memory of what Bussemi had done scared Dexx to his core. Nobody had ever so thoroughly beaten him like that. Ever.

Bussemi's anger, his hatred, the sheer lunacy of the guy had done something not even his first demon hunt had. Dexx could and would avoid the man at all costs.

A knock on the door sent him into the air.

"Enter." Tarik calmly strode to the door even though he called them in.

Furiel walked through, somehow timid and boldly powerful at the same time. "May I come—" He stopped when he saw Tarik. "I am honored to meet you. I could not be sure you would… survive."

Tarik only inclined his head. "I was sufficient to the torture."

"Your eyes. The stories are true."

"They are."

The two were formal. Like two strange cats. Ready to claw and bite and carry on.

"Knock it off." Dexx passed in front of Tarik. "What do you want, Furiel? Seems you only show up when we don't really need you, disappear when we could use your help." Like when he was beaten within an inch of his life.

"Or before you even know you need the help. Some things you have to win on your own, or you become dependent. I am not all-powerful."

The truth. Huh. Well there's a first time for everything.

"You have seen your past, yes?"

"You spying on us?" Dexx went for a gun that wasn't on his hip.

"Not exactly. You have abilities we cannot duplicate, but

those are mostly due to your… transient nature on this plane. But I *do* know a small amount about that stone in your hand. Mainly, I was contacted by a mutual acquaintance and asked if I would keep that safe until you needed it."

"Liar." Dexx tensed as an overwhelming need to kill the demon overwhelmed him. He took a step back, reminding himself that in some lifetime, he'd entrusted this demon with protecting his stone.

"I do not think so." Tarik placed a hand on Dexx's shoulder. "I have lost some of who I once was and more during my incarceration, but I can see the truth. That ability has sharpened during my torture. He speaks the truth as he sees it."

That didn't mean Dexx could simply trust a *demon*.

"You operate exactly the same way, do you not?" Furiel released a pent-up sigh. "You will explain the truth as you see it. You would like to claim that all my kind are evil, yet there are two in front of you are not. Your truth to you is still valid even if the wider truth is not."

"Keep logic out of it. What proof do I have that you aren't working with that asshole?"

The look on Furiel's face called him an idiot. "You have your *shamiyir*, and your enemies do not. They are not here and are instead desperately trying to repair the portal you destroyed. Those are only *two* offerings of proof."

"How do you know the portal is still down?"

"I wouldn't even know how to explain it, but suffice it to say you and your Red Star team have lived up to your reputation even when you are not at your full strength."

Dexx was done irritated with so many memories so close and yet so far away. He didn't have the patience for this conversation, so unless the demon had arrived with a *reason*, Dexx was busy. He turned toward Ethel. "Tell me you've got something we can *use*."

Ethel opened her mouth to say something, but frowned at Furiel.

"Yes," Ethel said, tapping on the keys.

Tarik sighed. "Dexx, if you wanted to invest hours into understanding the most basic parts of our magick so you could understand how his words are true, then we can explain."

He didn't think he cared. "Would it help?"

"No," Furiel said.

Dexx sighed. "I need information we can use. Did you bring any of *that?*"

"Yes. I came to propose an alliance of sorts." Furiel sounded even more business than his formality usually made him sound.

"What's that? Dexx bit off the rest of what he was going to say, reminding himself that apparently *he'd* trusted demons in the past. He folded his arms and sat himself down to listen. "Tell me it's better than we do your dirty work for you and then get fucked."

"Quite the opposite." Furiel gestured toward a chair in askance.

Dexx shook his head with a shrug as if to say, "Whatever."

Furiel smiled tightly as he sat. "I help you as far as I'm able and *I* take the brunt of the consequences."

That was an interesting approach. "Bullshit."

"I assure you, I'm offering my assistance so you can see I mean what I say." Furiel shook his head. "Dexx, this arena is small compared to the greater resistance. This needs to be done and if I can assist with that now by taking a calculated risk, then that's what I will do."

"Then what? Self-sacrifice isn't in your make-up."

"We need you in the bigger battle."

That made sense.

"And I'm willing to give you an olive branch. Dexx," the demon said as if chastising a stubborn child. "Will you *not* accept my help?"

If the demon before him was a man, the answer would be yes. But he wasn't. He was a demon. Dexx had enough unknowns on his plate. He didn't know if he could survive another.

Furiel looked down at his feet for a moment. "Then I will leave you in peace," the demon said in quiet frustration. "But if you need my help, say these words: *Deas enror se Furiel.* I will be there in moments, so do not wait until it's too late."

Something about this guy made Dexx feel like he was being a complete ass, but… Damnit, but he needed a win. A real win. Dexx gave the demon a salute swung the door shut behind his retreating back.

Ethel put her hands in her lap, staring at Dexx. "Okay, if that's over, you'll want to see this. But just be warned. You won't like it."

Dexx let his head drop back and his arms fall limp. He set the *shamiyir* next to Ethel on the table as he leaned in to see the computer. What the fuck else could possibly make this any worse?

Picture files filled the screen, with more files on other tabs. Dexx saw himself on a street corner. Another picture had him sitting in a dive diner across from a woman. Paige.

This time, though, his world wasn't rocked.

More pictures. Him in Louisiana. The building where his "accident" had been. The same building with Paige and another man. The man looked like a Fed. He was talking with an old woman. The old bag of wrinkles looked like she could take care of herself, though. She had a certain something about her, but it wasn't on film. He just knew.

But there were more. Lots more.

Pictures of people being hauled off in handcuffs.

Pictures of what looked like war on a city street.

Pictures of people getting shots in their neck.

People in collars.

Death, destruction, mayhem.

The crappy thing was, he didn't know what this meant because his brain was still fragged. "Bottom line this for me. What am I not going to like?"

"First?" Ethel said with a sigh. "They've been watching you a really long time, like a creepy long time."

Which meant Bussemi had known he was the soul connected to the *kadu* for years. At least two. Maybe longer. "And?"

"DoDO's been contracted by the United States to enslave the paranormals they can't control."

That seemed like a bit of an overstep. "What are you—"

Dur anna esst arrun.

The voice was Bussemi's.

And in Dexx's head.

33

A buzzing began in his head, disorienting his vision and equilibrium. *Bring the kadu you stole from me back.* Dexx's head jerked up violently, but he covered it by coughing in his hand. He quietly excused himself from the office. Just outside the door, he fell to his knees. The buzzing became too much to stand. His head hung down over the floor.

"Get out of my head."

I do not think so. I have been patient long enough, little thorn. I want you to return my property.

The buzzing worsened, and Dexx's stomach clenched in the world's biggest cramp.

"They aren't yours." Dexx managed to say through his teeth.

Oh, I disagree. But it's been so long. We have finally been reunited, and you run away, just like you did before. When I first found out you succeeded at my efforts, I admit I may have gone a bit mad for a few years.

The asshole was enjoying this. Intruding in Dexx's head and enjoying the pain he caused. Because he was an ass hat.

Eventually, I came to the realization that I could affect the world. I didn't need you, but I always knew I would see you again, if I only waited long enough.

Dexx held his stomach, a burning sensation adding to the cramp. "Go... away."

Sure would be nice if that angel was around right now. Or the demon if he really *was* turning over a new leaf. But they weren't and he couldn't run. Where could he go that the voice in his head couldn't follow?

Fear tore at him. He clawed the ground trying to get a grip on something to help him get away, but his nail barely scraped dirt off concrete.

Hattie swelled forward, helping him fight the voice back with her will.

His stomach released enough for him to stand, though not completely upright. With her help, the buzzing reduced enough to see almost straight.

He wobbled toward the door at the far end of the warehouse. Where he might be going, he couldn't fathom, but he *had* to get away.

Running away wasn't *an* option. It was *the* *only* option. Run.

But not to save himself.

To save his team, the innocents behind him, who gathered around him. Like Bruna and Doxy, they'd end up dead just by being near him. Failure on failure piled on top of one another. Doxy, Bruna, Hattie, his *kids* and *wife*, all of it. He had to *run* to protect them.

Through the centuries I found potential, Bussemi continued like the worst villain ever. *Genghis Kahn, Alexander the Great, Ramses, Hitler, Mao. I made them all. I was the power behind the man. I won many times., But always there was someone who fought me from the shadows. It took lifetimes to discover who it was. Even if you never did. You and that* thing.

Hattie. Bussemi was referencing Hattie like she was thing and not a person.

You loved it more than your own family.

Dexx made it to the door and stumbled outside. The clouds had been driven back and the sun shone bright and cheery. Birds chirped and a passenger jet flew overhead with a deep rumble. Concrete turned rubble crunched under his feet too loud and far away at the same time.

"Not this time." He couldn't. He wouldn't. Paige—whom he didn't know in his mind, but did in his heart—drove him to challenge this man. To fight. To *win* so he could return to her.

But if he did, he'd—

No. He just had to win against this turd. Finally.

Yes, Hattie growled, but with a ring of caution in her voice.

Dexx stumbled along alternately shivering and holding his head, trying to shake Bussemi from his mind.

The cardinal wasn't going anywhere. *I can be forgiving. I have something you need. And you have something I want. Bring the missing kadu you stole from me and I will let you have yours. You can go your own way, and you will never see me again.*

Dexx'd learned that lesson.

Dexx stopped against another warehouse.

He heaved once, twice, then spewed all over the ground.

I give you my word. I can make it stop. Just give me what I want. You bring the stolen kadu to me and you live.

Dexx didn't think Bussemi intended him to *enjoy* his life.

Lightning cracked through the sky and speared the ground near Dexx. The light blinded him and the sharp thunder crack drowned out the cardinal, then… nothing.

The spot of afterimage cleared. Roxxie cradled him where he sat, wrapping one of her hands around his. She looked as dark and terrible as any demon.

"Are you well?" The fury and power in her voice made him glad she was on his team. She pulled him close to her. "I was so tired. I rested longer than I wanted. It's my fault he found you."

Now that he only had two voices in his head—his and Hattie's—and that strange rock in his hand, the disorienting buzz and the cramps faded. The strange warmth from the *shamiyr* turned to a tingle, but comforting and powerful. "We have to run."

"Where can go?"

"Aren't you supposed to talk me into facing my fears?" He hadn't wanted to admit the fear, but Roxxie sort of made it come out.

Dammit.

Roxxie smiled. She looked like the angel she was supposed to be. "Angels provide assistance. They don't force people into service."

Somehow that didn't sound right. "Then I say we put as much real estate between us and that bastard as we can get."

"I will be ready in two days. We will go then." She helped Dexx to his feet.

"You can't leave." Furiel appeared before them, his face contorted in anger. "You have to fight."

"Do you know how strong he is?" Dexx asked. "He kicked my ass. You want him so back, *you* do it. I learned my lesson. Until we know how to stop throwing bodies at him, I'm out."

Lightning danced in Roxxie's eyes. "I owe Dexx. I've learned to trust him over the years. We go when I'm ready to take us from here."

Furiel offered his hand, his voice fueled with frustration. "Then I pledge my power to you if you only confront them. You must bring the shift out."

"Hattie only comes when I sleep. And if that's my greatest power, we're fucked. He won."

"You stood up to an angel that nearly killed you on several occasions, a demon that almost destroyed three planes of existence, and you cower before a mere human?" Furiel stared at him confused.

"Yeah, well why don't you try being human and let me beat on you a while? Let me break your bones over and over. Snap 'em like sticks. Turn them to mush. Then you can go through the pain as they heal up, and do it all over again. Better yet, why don't you go as a demon go and just blast him?"

"You don't think we've *tried* that?"

Dexx pulled his lip up in a sneer. Anger and fear pouring out. "I bet an angel could do it too. Just spit ballin' here, but I bet the two of you together could smite the pesky human where he stands. I'm out, and if my team is with me, they're out too." But how in the hell was he going to keep them safe?

"You cannot ignore this. *Be* the *Shedim Patesh*. Your salvation is *there*."

Dexx turned and walked away. "You be the Shed Pot Ash. I'm done." He left them standing there.

He walked through the warehouse, down through the remodeled resistance fighter base and found his room. Not just his, Tarik, Frey and two more paras shared the barracks.

He flopped down on his bunk and closed his eyes. He needed to talk to Hattie.

The familiar swaddling darkness enveloped him immediately. Hattie and the plain materialized swiftly.

"I'm terrified, Hattie."

I know.

"They all need something from me that I'm not.

You are and always have been what they need. When you know who you are, you will be their alpha again.

"I don't want to rain on your parade, but that's gone." He

just wanted back to the states. Maybe get a real job. Do something safe. Like accounting. Maybe not that, perhaps something more like professional racing. Sure. That.

Hattie nudged his hand with her nose. *That looks like the last of the stones you made. What does it do?*

Dexx opened his hand for Hattie to inspect the *shamiyir*. How had it followed him to this place? *Couldn't say. Well, not really. Right now I think it's the thing keeping just the two of us alone in here.*

Hattie shook her head like shedding water. *The path to you turned thorny. I worried for a time, but the thorns went away.*

Dexx looked for a likely rock to sit on. *Yeah.* He *found me sort of. Climbed right in my head and buzzed my brains around real good.* He studied his *shamiyir*. "Everyone keeps telling me to do things. To fight. To go to war. To kill Bussemi. But…"

You feel broken.

He did.

You are special. We are special. We have lived this life more than once. We protect those unable to protect themselves. That is who we are.

"When something like this happened before, how did we get up and fight again?"

We took time to heal. Hattie sat down next to Dexx, her head way above his so he had to crane his neck to look at her. *When we could.*

"This feels worse than the times before." Not that he remembered a ton.

It is. It certainly is.

"Fine. Give me some space. I need to look at this thing." He held the *shamiyir* in his open palm.

In this light, the thing looked like a puzzle box. Thin lines that would twist the rock like a Rubik's cube. An experimental twist and the thing *moved.*

A piece spun, stopping when it merged with the other side. The lines glowed a soft amber.

So, he'd needed to study it in the time before? He twisted the rock.

Light flared out, enveloping him and his awareness. Wind battered him and heat seared his mind. His head pounded and threatened to split him like a melon. A rush sent waves of dizziness through him.

Something clicked home. Something else fell out of place. Something went right. Something else went wrong.

His eyes snapped open. It was all there. Dexx. Hattie. Paige. Leah, Bobby... all of them. What he did to his own team, to Chuck.

And he remembered Jackie. She sat alone in Portland, forgotten.

Like Paige who *wasn't* his wife. Not yet. He missed their text message conversations of silliness. His heart was cold without them. He missed his kids. He missed engine time with Leah or training time with Tyler or Lego time with Bobby.

He needed to call her.

His heart twisted. He couldn't. He'd been away for *weeks*. What was he going to say? "I'm sorry?" Yeah. He was. But he'd been the one to put himself in this situation. At least he was pretty sure he was.

He'd just show up in person. Surprise her with his arms.

Maybe he *should* call.

Fuck it all to fuck.

He had his memories, and they all said he was the biggest asshole ever. He had knowledge of being with Hattie over multiple lifetimes. Those faded to whispers in order to allow his other memories in.

"Hattie?"

Cub, Where are you?

He opened his eyes and saw his bunk. "I'm... awake. Right? I'm awake?"

You are, but I cannot see.

"You can't see what I'm seeing, or you can't see at all?"

I cannot see through your eyes.

"One step at a time, girl." But at least now he knew what he was doing. "Damn, it feels good to be back with... oh *fuck.*" He had his memories back, all of them, but he remembered where he was and why. But the fear of Bussemi was only stronger now. He had so much to lose. "I still gotta go. I can't even be on the same *continent.* Say we can go home and figure this out with Pea."

You must be the alpha. That is all we ever have been.

He didn't see how a cat was going to stand up to that steal giant o f a man. "I veto. We leave." Dexx felt a pressure in his chest, like a burp coming up, but it stuck and stayed where it was.

Hattie pushed forward but the block stopped the shift.

He pushed at it as well, but to no avail. He might have his memories back, but he wasn't a hundred percent... back. He was a shifter with no shift and without Hattie's strength, they were no match for Bussemi.

But with Paige by his side? "We go home, give Paige what we know, and figure this out together."

Cub. I hurt.

That...couldn't be good.

Dexx sat up on the bed. The rock didn't look any different. No, it *did.* The speckles on the rock didn't quite match up anymore. He pressed on the rock, giving it a twist.

Nothing. No movement.

It only moved in the time before.

I cannot move. Panic tinged Hattie's voice. *I cannot see.*

"But we're talking. That's okay, fat cat." He had no idea what to do. He needed Paige and Leslie and... Shit. He needed Leah. Damnit. "I'll see for us both. I got my wits back. Now we can leave this bullshit country to rot all by itself."

The door to the barracks slammed open.

Frey stepped inside before the doors swung shut. "Move your ass. Something's happening."

Dexx stood. "I have good news and bad news."

"Don't care. This is more important." Frey half turned to the doorway, obviously waiting for Dexx.

Dexx sighed. "Sure. Your thing first." Dexx brushed past her.

"Frey strode ahead, power walking. "DoDO and that madman are running a coup. First here, then the rest of Europe. Looks like they have a lot of backing from the states and the church."

"So, what are *we* supposed to do about it?" Taking out a demon, that was one thing, but overthrowing a government-size organization was way out of their league.

Frey spun on him, her face lashed with anger. "I knew you were a huge pussy. Just forget it. You aren't the alpha anymore. I felt it. I felt the shift. You don't have what it takes, so you can just be one of the grunts."

Dexx grabbed her arm before she could spin back around. "Hey. You better watch what you say. *I'm* still the alpha. *I'm* still the Captain of Red Star, and *I'm* going to require you show some damned respect."

Frey stared at him with her cold blue eyes. "You may have the *captain's* chair, but you don't have the *alpha* chair."

"Yes I do." Did he? *I still have it, don't I?*

Hattie didn't respond like he thought she would. *You* must *be the alpha.* She didn't sound as certain as she had in the past, though.

Not the answer I wanted. "I'm *just* trying to make sure we don't jump into a situation where we all get *killed.*"

"Prove it. Prove you're still my alpha."

Frey had always been the strongest willed of his team.

Dexx sent an alpha push her way. *Get moving. Take me to the others.*

Frey stood there, staring at him with cold eyes. "No? Go ahead. I give you permission. Push me."

Dexx stared back at her. He pushed like he normally did. There shouldn't be any resistance. She should be turning and taking him to the others.

She just stood there, staring, and apparently waiting.

Hattie, what's the deal here? Why isn't she moving in a snap-to sort of fashion?

Something is blocking us. Fear laced her words.

And his team was heading into a battle they had no business being in. *Well, move it the hell out of the way. I thought we were back, so what the hell is all of this?* Dexx inhaled a deep breath.

You must be the alpha.

Thanks for nothing, fat cat. "I'm not fully back up, okay? That doesn't mean I'm out of the game. I'm still in charge here."

She raised her chin. "I *know* you don't have it. You can buffalo the others, but *I* know. You lost your place."

Like hell he had. She turned on her heel and led the way.

Fear bubbled in his stomach. He'd become used to the power being the alpha lent him. Now he had to deal with a coup without it? He followed Frey and heard the noise before they hit the stairway. The buzz of activity was almost deafening.

Medusa met them at the door. "They're making their move, and we aren't ready."

34

D exx squeezed past Medusa into the actual communication hub, not Red Star's make-shift office. Ethel and Michelle worked at computer terminals of their own.

Michelle read information from her screen. "Police presence is minimal. The military is occupied without-of-country threats. Parliament is in session, so they're gathered all in one spot. Cardinal Bussemi is scheduled to speak today on tolerance and the church's position on the greater paranormal community." She shook her head. "They expect it to be a banner day, with the church condemning anything or anyone not 'pure human.' What's happening in the states is spilling over."

"Making war on the paranormals sanctioned and legal by quasi-legitimate governing bodies," Medusa sneered at Dexx.

What did *he* have to do with any of that? "What's going on in the states?"

Michelle looked at him like he'd fallen off the planet.

He kinda had.

"What happened with Sven made *international news,* Dexx."

Rainbow bit her lips and wrung her hands. "There's big heat coming down on Troutdale."

"And we're here," Frey added, her blue eyes narrowed dangerously.

"Bussemi is only going to make this worse," Medusa said.

"So what? Just move away. Go someplace better like the states or Canada." Why did everyone have to make things harder than they needed to be?

"Because you twat, they'll be voting to take away *all* rights." Medusa thumped her hand on her desk. "And that's there. The world is watching what we do, and they're likely to follow. They're already following your president."

"What happened?"

"The Registration Act?"

Dexx vaguely remembered that and...

Holy fuck! He'd seen *Paige* on the news with *his* babies. When he got home, he was gonna... Holy crap.

"Parliament is voting to follow the president's executive orders. That means taking away our rights to vote," Medusa counted on her left hand, "traveling and *speaking.* How long before the U.S. follows and votes to take away your rights? Is it really beyond your juvenile imagination to think they'll outlaw paranormals?"

"No?" Yes. Kind of. The government under *this* party? Yeah. Absolutely. He'd been *really* against this president and not because she was a woman, though Paige had gone head to head with him over that. No. He was afraid that this administration would overstep itself and trample all over their rights. Though, at the time he'd been thinking of his small collection of slightly illegal guns. But paranormal rights?

"Yank." Medusa rolled her eyes and turned to the activity in the room. "We have to stop the vote."

Something didn't add up. "I don't get it. How is this a coup? And how is a vote that goes Bussemi's way the same thing?"

"Because he's going to magick Parliament. He's set up, tested the theory. On you. According to his files, he used the modifier on you, and even though you broke it, these are mundanes. They don't have a chance."

"But I still don't— oh." Dexx being a shifter, a very powerful one he'd had the strength to fight against the memory modification.

Even if it would have eventually killed him.

Dexx shrugged. "Well, good luck. Let us know how it goes." Because if things were this bad here, he needed to be beside Paige as she took on the president, something that kinda actually excited his patriotic little heart. "We're leaving. Let's go guys." Dexx wound his finger in the air.

The entire Red Star team protested. Even Ethel who had almost no field experience.

What the hell? "I said let's move."

Rainbow quick-stepped to Dexx. "I mean, is that a good idea? They could really use our help. We could, you know. I think we'd be really good at it too. We just, you know—"

Dexx covered her mouth with his hand. "Pack. Your. Shit. We're going home. Look, if this shit is going on there too, then *that's* our battle. Not this one. When they come for us, we'll be ready. Anyone else have something to say?"

Frey tilted her head up and opened her mouth to speak and bought her hand to the back of her neck.

Dexx charged her, pulling the *ma'a'shed* from its sheath. He pinned her hand in place and put the silver-edged blade to the front. He whispered angrily in her ear. "We lost here. We go back to the states. We figure out what happened and fix it.

If we have cause and the ability, we come back. We'll hogtie that bastard and drag him through the streets, but right now, we're too beat up to go out and get more of us killed. You want to be a martyr in a hopeless cause, see what your death does. Nothing."

Tarik gently took Dexx's hand with the demon knife, and Frey's hand that held her sword, and pulled them away slowly. "We should not be fighting," he said quietly. "We have the duty to follow our leader, and he says to flee. We cannot afford to fight amongst ourselves."

Frey jerked her hand away from Tarik. "Coward." She stared at Dexx a few seconds, driving the point home and turned away. She gathered Rainbow and Ethel up and left.

"You have come down a long way, Dexx." Tarik looked as sad as when he learned Alma had died.

"Maybe." Or maybe he'd just had a double-sized helping of humility. He turned away and went up to the office on the ground level.

In two hours, they loaded up into a rickety old Mercedes work van and headed for the airport. Medusa watched them leave, an open sneer for Dexx. And sympathetic goodbyes for everyone else.

Dexx didn't care. He couldn't. He'd just remembered his team *and* that he *liked* these sons of bitches. He wasn't about to lose them like he'd lost Bruna and Doxy by being cocky.

"Boss?" Rainbow sat next to him up front.

The others were silent, piled wherever they could fit in the back.

"Yeah." The steering wheel was on the *wrong side* again, but nobody else was going to drive.

"Help me understand. Why are we leaving? Why *now*? Roxxie said to wait."

"This isn't our fight. There's another one at home. That's the one that counts for us."

Dexx's finger unconsciously rubbed the *shamiyir* in his pocket. The lines of the runes or whatever they were felt increasingly distinct from the rest of the stone.

Rainbow took a breath and stared at the floor. "I don't want to sound preachy, but would they want you to come home if you could fight to fix things here? I don't think there's *anyone* who can say they've seen you run from a fight."

"Not running away. Just running to the *right* fight." Hattie rumbled in his head. He also needed a better game plan for Bussemi. And taking the rest of his pack with him sounded like a great idea. The wolves. Leslie, Paige. Hell, maybe even Tyler. Okay, taking the tween into battle *wasn't* a great idea.

You ran once before. In our first bonding. You ran. Images came across the bond. The circumstances and the possibilities and the end result.

"Turn here." Rainbow held her phone up, watching the navigation guide them to the airport. "Too bad we couldn't see some of the sights. It's kinda neat how the currents feel different here."

Do you have a solution to Bussemi? Because going up against them when we're not at full force sounds like a death warrant to me.

She didn't answer.

Buildings and streets passed by and opened up to a wide plaza filled with pedestrians and traffic. A massive and austere building cropped up on the left. The clocktower gave it away as Parliament and Big Ben.

As he looked at the building through the traffic, he saw wispy white smoke rise from the corners. Natural smoke didn't curl and twist like that did.

He turned to Rainbow. "Did you take us this way on purpose?"

Her eyes were round. "Well, kinda. It's the fastest way—"

The *shamiyir* warmed in his pocket. "Damn it all to hell." The heated stone was almost searing hot.

"Wha—" Rainbow looked up from her phone to Dexx.

He pulled the stone from his pocket ready to throw it. The heat spiked and cooled to a comfortable hot potato.

A green flash radiated out from Parliament and rushed over the van, but bubbled around them. Every other person wasn't as lucky. The green flash passed through them.

The spell had the telltale markers of Bussemi's magick all over it.

"*Fuck.*" Dexx yanked the wheel at the roundabout and wove through traffic as quickly as he could whip that tired old delivery van.

He pulled to a stop and opened his door.

An explosion ripped through the street ahead of them.

Medusa led paranormals fighting and pushing forward.

DoDO agents fanned out, shooting conventional guns and casting spells, wiping out two and three at a time.

"Get out." He turned to his team. "*No* mundanes, got it?"

Michelle pierced him with her glare. "I've been a cop a long time, Dexx. I know the score."

"They don't fight me. I won't fight them." Frey slid the door open and pulled her sword from her pocket dimension. The sword gleamed as bright as Roxxie's *mavet ma'aka'el,* the sword version of the angel blade.

"Take out any DoDO agents you find. Dead is better than not."

Tarik nodded once, but he wouldn't be killing anyone. Not since he'd changed.

Ethel wouldn't be either.

Dexx grabbed her shoulder as she stepped out. "Where do you think you're going?"

"To…" She gestured to the gunfire. "…help."

"No, you're going to stay here."

Ethel began to protest.

"You have no experience fighting these guys. You'll be way too vulnerable." Like Bruna and Doxy had.

"But I—"

Dexx held up a finger. "Protect the van. We're still leaving as soon as we can."

Ethel tossed her head from side-to-side, upset and relieved. "Okay. Paige wouldn't make me stay."

"Yes, she would." He kissed the top of Ethel's head. "Keep the engine running." He ran after his team, pulling out his demon knife.

Frey was already hacking at anything that had black tactical gear and body armor.

Some of those could be actual police.

Dexx waded into the mass of black para-military figures, slamming his knife home and chopping limbs that got in the way. He had strength, better senses, and a little speed.

Michelle snapped her supple limbs at the agents like bull-whips. Each agent she touched was out of the fight. Most would live, though.

That worked for almost ten seconds.

DoDO had significantly changed the way they did things. Looked a lot like the way Dexx had intended his changes to work. They retreated quickly, behind already formed lines to regroup and fight defensively and offensively, alternating the lines.

They stabilized the field, then pressed their advance forward.

Damn. They had to choose *now* to implement his changes.

DoDO drove the paranormals back, forcing them away from Parliament.

Tarik and Frey worked together, keeping a space around them clear of any enemies. The two of them worked the defense—offense technique exactly like it should.

Medusa fought her monstrous tentacles whipping out, and sometimes connecting, but her effectiveness had minimal effect in the wide area as more and more DoDO agents erected barriers against her. She was being pushed back.

The vampires, too. DoDO had implemented some of Dexx's other tactics to deal with faster opponents.

"Fall back!" Dexx yelled over the noises. "Back!"

One glance told him that wouldn't be a good idea either. More agents were popping through portals into flanking positions. Where had the portals come from? Questions for another time.

"Shit." They had virtually walked into a trap. A public one. "Red Star, get back." He tried to get someone's, *anyone's* attention, but nobody was listening.

Tarik cast non-lethal magick. Bodies still flew through the air. Why did he have to be so nice?

Michelle took arms and heads and opened body cavities. She had the right idea. They wouldn't fight ever again.

Rainbow stood out in the open, gently swaying back and forth. She had her hands delicately raised, beckoning to DoDO agents.

One man, then another stood up, dropping their athames and guns, shuffling forward like zombies to Rainbow.

One by one, they disappeared just before they reached her. She had a make-shift trap for them. Sprays of water followed each person that fell into the manhole.

DoDO's lines began to waver, then they broke. The paranormals had only needed an opening. They pushed forward, the dozens, maybe hundreds of vampires in the lead with Medusa.

A woman stood on the far side of Rainbow. Cassandra. She held her wand out ready to cast. Yellow vapor began to form at the tip, gathering strength.

"Bow!"

Rainbow didn't move.

"Shitballs."

He cocked his arm over his head and threw the *ma'a'shed*. It sailed through the air with a ragged growl as it spun. The knife slashed through the wand and buried itself in Cassandra's throat up to its hilt.

Bright red blood spurted from the woman's neck, splashing to the ground.

Then the blood didn't escape. It arced weirdly from the ground and from the cut and splashed *into* the knife instead of spreading.

He raced to Cassandra and yanked the knife free. "Bet you'd take that portal now, wouldn't you?"

Cassandra's glossed-over eyes had no response.

Rainbow still stood in place, not seeing Dexx or *anybody*. Her eyes glowed with a blue light, casting her skin an aqua shade.

Her face became stretched and pale, her eyes sank and darkened to pits. She softly swayed like underwater plants. Or a dead body. She was a rusalka, after all.

More and more of the male agents rose, blank eyed. The single line turned into many lines. They all stepped into the waiting water, no longer splashing as water reached up to grab them to disappear beneath the surface.

A strange sensation pulled at his hand and twisted him around.

Another agent stood, casting a spell. This one used hand gestures.

Without thinking, his arm pulled back and flashed out.

The knife pinned the caster's arm to her chest through her heart. This time, no blood hit the pavement.

DoDO lines fell back and regrouped. More filed out of a portal to bolster the failing lines.

Now disarmed, Dexx had to dodge spells and duck behind rubble to recover his knife.

Bullets strafed the ground in front and around him as he dove for cover behind the dead agent.

A pinch-faced woman stared up at him with sightless eyes. Her skin looked pulled tight to her skeleton. Her hand was still pinned to her chest and cleanly sliced where the blade touched her.

Ma'a'sheds were *sharp*.

Her body was cold and gaunt like it had been dead a week.

Dexx yanked the knife free and felt heat. The sharp edge had turned the bright red color he remembered on his knife back home.

It buzzed with desire, longing to be used.

What was going on with this blade?

Visions assaulted his mind of Furiel standing beside him as they crafted several of these blades. This was made by *his* hand. And this was the first time it'd been blooded.

And it wanted more. It *needed* more.

They needed the blood of his enemies to bond further. He was more than happy to oblige.

Dexx leapt at the closest agent, nearly twenty feet away. There was no effort at all to fly through the distance to stab the man in the heart and give the blade a twist. The knife pulled the blood into itself and gained more power.

Red covered Dexx's vision. A sensation began at his hand with the knife and ran through his body, tingling with power. With nothing but a thought, the knife stretched and distorted until it was a split-bladed sword black as the deepest ocean with a blood red edge.

Dexx swung his *mavet ma'a'shed* through the plexiglass shield of the DoDO agent running up to reinforce his fallen brethren. The man's feet took one more step as the top his body slipped and spilled intestines all over the pavement. His arms skidded to a stop against rubble. His mouth made speaking movements and his eyes were wide in surprise. But there wasn't a drop of blood spilled.

The sword wanted more blood.

There was more to be had.

Dexx gave the man one final look and jumped impossibly far right into the middle of the reformed DoDO lines.

Three quick slashes with his sword, and they were all dead, pieces twitching in death.

Another magickal wave ripped through the air as another portal opened.

Dexx held his sword in front of him, splitting the magick before it could form. Tarik stood up from the bodies.

They'd made it to the Parliament building. "Are you okay?" Dexx nodded at Tarik.

"I am well. I am mostly protected from this magick, but humans are not. How are you?"

"I still have a few surprises." Maybe, just maybe, this was enough of a surprise to take out Bussemi. "You guys make sure everyone on our side is okay. Then come in. I have a feeling I'm going to need you."

That's all Dexx'd been waiting for. An advantage. "Let's see if we can kill this asshole." The *mavet ma'a'shed* screamed for blood.

Cardinal Bussemi's blood would do nicely.

Dexx walked through the doors hanging from their hinges.

35

Quiet. Inside, the place was too quiet. No DoDO agents, no guards, no anyone.

The sword vibrated in Dexx's hands, anticipating more blood.

What would happen if it didn't get the blood it craved?

The hallway in front of him opened up to the end, where the massive double doors were closed. Almost. One was propped open.

The smell of abject fear was slowly wafting away, replaced with a curious absence of nothing. There were people here, somewhere.

Dexx walked the length of the hall, keeping a close eye on the doors, but kept his ears and nose open. At least he still had his shifter senses even if they weren't as strong as they used to be.

Bodies littered the polished floor under large windows.

His vision shifted slightly, and soft glow lit people, dead and dying.

Dexx reached out to the door, cautiously pulling the handle.

The doors swung silently on well-greased hinges.

Inside, the entire House of Commons sat absolutely still. They weren't dead, just super calm and well behaved.

One lone raised seat sat at the far end of the hall with another calm person.

Dexx scanned the crowd.

Bussemi should be—

The Prime Minister stood. "The vote has been taken. You and your kind are not welcome here."

Dexx really didn't care. "*My* kind was trying to leave when *your* kind decided to start killing us. Where is he?"

The Prime Minister gestured to a door and another hall. Was this place made up entirely of hallways?

Dexx edged around the outside of the seated men, but none of them even twitched. "By the way, I see about fifty of *my kind* sitting in here."

That caused a stir.

Dexx didn't know if that was true, but he needed them to stop being creepy. He sidestepped through the door.

Right into what he expected earlier. Rank upon rank of DoDO agents dressed in full armor, all at attention. Facing something– someone further down.

Dexx stopped in the middle of his second step. *Oh, hells no.*

What is it, cub?

As one, every rank turned to the side, heels snapping sharply against the tile floor with a narrow corridor down the middle of the great hall. Then they stepped back with military precision to the walls.

"This is more like it." Dexx put the tip of the sword to the tiles gouging the floor.

Bussemi stood at the back of the hall, calmly leaning on his cane. The stick he had mercilessly beaten Dexx with.

"Brave. So very brave to come here. You always had no sense of survival. Too dumb to live."

"And yet, I'm still here." He hoped to hell this damned knife would be enough to take on this murdering son of a bitch.

The demon blade said it was.

Movement sounded behind him, and the scent of his team flitted to his nose.

Bussemi slashed his cane upward, a blue force ripping up the floor as it raced for Dexx.

He raised the *ma'a'shed* and sliced the arc in two. It felt like punching a rock barehanded. "Ow."

Bussemi's eyes opened wide. "Who gave you an unblooded *ma'a'shed?* All the better, it will take my call just as well as yours when I have your body."

It'd better not because Dexx was hedging a really major bet right now. "That's pretty sick, you know that?" Dexx held the *mavet ma'a'shed* in both hands, ready for the next strike.

"The words are new, but the false bravado is the same. You are but a shadow of what you once were. I have the knowledge from the beginning, and you are still ignorant of who you were."

Dexx needed to get closer. Just keep the old buzzard talking, and he might get close enough. He began to step slowly toward Bussemi, his team following. "They say the only stupid question is the one not asked. So here goes—" He just needed to waste time, and Dexx already knew the man loooooooved to monologue. "Who am I?"

"You are my oldest enemy. My oldest friend. You are my *brother.*"

Dexx stopped, rocked by the cardinal's words. He'd That *couldn't* be true.

One of the DoDO agents close to Dexx raised his wand, rushing forward as he cast a spell.

Frey slid past Dexx, her sword already moving with a short slash. The body fell to the floor with a sick thud, gore sliding around other agents.

Bussemi ran at Dexx, far sprier than he looked.

The hall broke into motion.

Dexx took the closest DoDO agents down before they had cleared their wands from their pouches.

Then it was block and parry.

Frey, Tarik, and Rainbow had his back, taking on as many agents as they could reach.

Lightning split the atmosphere in deafening spears. Luckily, the *mavet ma'a'shed* split those as easily as the bodies conjuring them. Some of the split bolts even managed to hit other agents.

Bussemi waded through his own people, using his cane to bat people aside. They didn't move when they stopped sliding.

Dexx had a rough circle marked out until Bussemi traipsed in. He swung his cane.

Dexx swung his sword.

The concussive rebound knocked everyone to the floor.

Dexx lost his hold on the *ma'a'shed,* and it skittered across the floor, burying itself in the wall. Moving was a bit difficult, being numb from hair tips to toenails.

Hattie howled in pain.

Bussemi lay on his back, not moving, but still holding his stick.

A few of the agents stirred, but they twitched more than made coordinated movements.

"Dexx," Rainbow whimpered.

"You okay?"

"We are fine," Tarik said. "Get up. Finish this. We have the agents. You have the ancient wizard."

Michelle writhed, her tree limbs swishing gracefully on the floor.

"*Fuuuuuck.*" Dexx managed to groan out. He rolled over, setting off stinging pinpoints to everything that touched the floor.

"That was not wise." Bussemi still had not moved, but his voice sounded calm and strong. He pivoted up without moving. It would have been comical if he didn't have fire in his eyes.

"Maybe you take the ancient wizard," Dexx muttered to the djinn.

"I believe I underestimated you." Bussemi breathed deep.

"Bet your ass, you underestimated me." Yeah, he really hadn't, but at least the blood blade was giving him a slight advantage. He just needed to retrieve it. Dexx rolled to his feet, alternating his feet as the stinging tingles faded away.

"You have made yourself more of a liability than a future asset. I can do what I need to without your body, without your power. I have all I need, and watching you die is as good an end as another. The *kadu* will give me what I want."

One or two agents began to make more deliberate movements, struggling to get up.

Dexx sprinted for his knife, dropping to the floor and skidding the last twenty feet as he dodged a bolt of lightning from the tip of Bussemi's cane.

True to his word, Tarik and Rainbow dealt with the rising mass of agents.

Dexx ripped the blade from the wall, commanding the blade to change. Nothing happened.

Shit! The curious buzzing was still there, but the blade stayed in knife form.

"Damn it." Dexx swung the blade into another blast of lightning, then Bussemi's cane turned into fire.

"Do you know what was like, being trapped in this body for *millennia*?"

Fucking Christ. The man was going to monologue *now*?

"The things I had to do to stop my aging, but never quite being able to regain my youth? The youth you got so many times without consequences."

"No, but I bet you're going to tell me." Dexx shifted his grip on the knife. When had his hand gotten so sweaty? What the hell was going on?

Was Bussemi doing something to him? Again? Using his *kadu* against him somehow?

"I made a pact. Torture every day. Thousands of years trapped in my own body, watching as *he* made plans, made his own deals, *furthered* his own agenda. Now it is *my* turn. I will be free of him. And I will take your lifeless corpse as my own."

"Boy, you have some issues." Dexx could have run if his feet would have moved.

An agent got his feet. He raised his wand, and... his head rolled off his body as Medusa whipped out a tentacle.

"Do you know what I find most amusing in all of this?" Bussemi asked, his face twisted in victory.

It was still a little early to be that cocky. "Don't think I care."

"When this is done, when I'm crushing the bones of your friends and bathing in the blood of your corpse, I'm going after your wife."

Dexx's veins ran cold.

"And then, I'm going to take those amazingly powered children of yours, and I'm going to drain them. I *will* have my youth back."

Over Dexx's dead body.

Hattie growled in agreement.

Bussemi sneered. "You *all die*." His eyes rolled up, and his face went slack. His skin glowed yellow, then brightened to orange, flames licking his chin from under his robes.

In a flash of fire, his robes turned to ash and revealed the leathery legs and torso of a demon. He stood tall. Much taller than he should have been and kept growing. The fire grew too. It became a mane of flames trailing over his shoulders, back, and arms.

The demon Bussemi dropped the cane and brought its hands together pulling a double-edged sword, flames, and runes marking the length of the blade and a nine-tailed whip also of—yup—fire.

"Sonofabitch." This wasn't a normal demon. Couldn't be.

Wings grew out of the demon's back, black and leathery, and its face changed to something of a cross between a dog and a lion.

The fight between DoDO and Red Star stopped. Every single person stared at the demon. More than one jaw hung open.

Dexx snapped his closed.

"Bahlrok," Medusa breathed, and went to her knees, her face hovering above the floor.

It drew in a breath and roared. Forge-furnace heat blasted from the beast's mouth, and the rumble shook the room. The bellow ended with a puff of superheated black smoke.

"*Sonofabitch.*" Things didn't look so good for the team. Running really *had been* the right move. Dexx shifted his grip on the *ma'a'shed* when he noticed a change in the vibration in the hilt.

The knife wanted to change allegiance. Before, the knife had felt like it had wanted Dexx to kill to feed it more death and blood.

Now it felt like it wanted *Dexx's* blood.

Hattie, I could really *use some help here.*

Hattie was silent.

Bahlrok brought its sword back for a strike. Flames trailed the white-hot blade.

"Fuck you, knife. You're mine." Dexx snarled at the demon and charged.

Three strides brought him close enough to leap up. Mid-swing, the knife shifted.

White-hot demon metal met pitch-black demon forged metal.

The room gonged like someone had rung the world's biggest bell, and forced Dexx and the demon back as though they'd been pushed... by a truck.

This time Dexx deflected enough to keep from being thrown to the ground.

The clash of swords brought the room back to life.

DoDO agents attacked.

Red Star Division defended.

Dexx learned a lot with his first two swings. Don't meet the blade head-on and be balanced *before* slapping blades together.

Dexx and the bahlrok had a *very* large open area to fight in, and it grew as the team increasingly picked off more and more agents.

Tarik was the first to clear a section away for Dexx. He called lightning, but it fizzled around Bussemi as though it lost power.

"Get behind it!" Dexx motioned Tarik and Michelle desperately. It wouldn't be able to counter spells if it couldn't see them. Right?

Rainbow stood midway in the hall and lashed out with a car-sized tentacle of azure water as Dexx went in for another swing. The room gonged again, but Dexx kept his footing better and managed to stay close enough for another swing as the demon was still getting ready. He slashed at the body of the Bussemi Demon, but the *mavet ma'a'shed* bounced off the chain mail.

"Damn." Dexx danced away from the swing, heat searing his eyebrows. He smelled smoke. *"Damn."*

Rainbow's water turned to steam, refusing to come within several feet of the demon. It never even looked in her direction, but a wrist-thick blast of lightning cracked through the water, hitting her square in the chest.

She flew backward and stopped moving, wisps of smoke drifting up.

Tarik kept his spell casting up, different elements with every cast.

Michelle cast spells of green magick in between snapping at the agents still standing.

Bussemi Demon batted them all down.

Michelle thrashed with her tree limbs, going for the demon's feet. She got one good pull, but as she did, a fireball formed and blasted her in the back. She fell, still.

Dexx dodged another three swings, searching for a better opening. He found one, scoring a hard hit on the arm that held the whips.

It bellowed again, more heat, more intense flames, and more hair singed on Dexx's head.

But the arms remained attached.

"Aw, dammit." Dexx backed up.

Frey stepped next to Dexx. "You won't win this by yourself. We go in on both sides."

"Fine by me. Go." He went in on the sword side. Frey went on the whip side.

They had done well. For almost ten seconds. The bahlrok, for all its size and slow appearances, moved way faster than it should have.

Dexx's skill with his swordplay increased but had nothing on Frey.

She was a true master, and although she seemed to get a

hit in every time she swung, they couldn't hit it anywhere that counted.

Dexx fought hard, as hard as he'd ever fought before. Not even Sven's horde of demons had much sword skill between them.

But Frey did. She batted the whips aside and hit arm, side, ribs, leg, ankle, all over the place, but nothing fazed Bussemi Demon.

Did this damned thing *have* a weakness?

Until they both got one hit in together. They slammed their blades into the chest of the bahlrok and it flew back like ropes had hauled on it. It roared again, spewing out fire and black smoke.

The whole building with Parliament, Westminster Abby, and the palace absolutely vibrated with the power of the anger in the bahlrok's roar.

"I think you pissed it off." Frey glanced at Dexx.

"Not me." He gave her a wink with a sideways smile. "That was you."

Bussemi Demon flapped its enormous wings once and flew over them, cutting off escape.

"That sucks." Dexx nodded to the door behind Bussemi.

"It's a good day to die. Who wants to live forever?"

Well, Dexx wanted to live at least another day, maybe two. He wanted to see Paige and the kids again. But this guy was too powerful, even for Paige. That was something he knew in his gut. If Bussemi decided to go after her and the kids? He hoped he and Hattie never reincarnated again because he didn't think he could deal with that. "Let's end this guy." Dexx charged the demon.

Frey followed.

They fought like demons themselves, parrying and striking, but not even Frey got another hit on the bahlrok.

They were slowing, and the demon didn't seem to have an end to his stamina.

"We're going to die," Dexx said, panting.

"Fuck him. We'll die trying."

A scream from behind the bahlrok caught all of them off guard. Even Bussemi blinked his flaming eyes several times.

"Damn it all to *hell.*"

Ethel hadn't stayed at the van.

"Deas enror se Furiel." Ethel's face went pale and her face slackened with paralyzing fear.

Dexx had never heard her so scared.

Two things happened so fast they were milliseconds apart.

A pure white light flashed from the Parliament, the scent of cleanliness overpowering the stench of the demon, and Furiel materialized in between the bahlrok and Dexx.

His eyes went wide with fear as he pulled a glass sphere from his coat and smashed it on the floor.

Their room went white, just before it went dark.

36

One day later, rain dripped down Dexx's hair and dripped on his coat. The skies were dark enough to make the afternoon look closer to night.

"She trusted you. The worst move she ever made, other than loving you. And you killed her."

Just as they were winning, Furiel stole them from the fight with Bussemi, the bahlrok.

Dexx leaned against a tree in the park across from Bruna and Doxy's shop. He owed them. "Yeah." He whispered. He didn't have to be told. Again.

Medusa leaned against the other side of the tree. "She never stopped believing you'd protect her. That you'd bring her through safe. She had the sight, you know."

"I have sight, too."

"No, you twat. *The* sight. She saw glimpses of the future and the past. Saw through the walls people put up. She saw right through to the core of a person, to who they really are. *That* sight. She was so giddy when she met you."

Dexx dropped his eyes. "I already feel like shit. You have to rub my face in it?"

"I do. Maybe that way she won't die in vain. *You* killed her. *You* said you would protect her. And now, my best friend is gone."

He got it. His cockiness had gotten a good woman killed.

Would it be what killed Paige, too? He had his memories back, and he had a lot more information about DoDO that could be helpful. They had an entire thumb drive to send to Paige.

And he knew he had his own personal villain, and there was something out there that could be used against him.

Medusa sighed. "She knew she couldn't keep you. She just wanted to have her time. Short as it was."

Dexx paused as pedestrians splashed through puddles to shops and through the park.

"*I* tried. Tried to buy her freedom. And don't you mean *them?*"

Medusa pulled in a shuddering breath and spoke slow. Careful. "Doxy was never truly alive. Bruna… split herself when she was younger. The result of bullying as a child. She *made* her own best friend. She—" Medusa stopped talking.

Dexx didn't need to turn around to *see* her crying. He heard her. Heard her heartbeat change and her scent turn musky with sadness, and the catch in her voice.

Medusa whispered, harsh words pummeling him like fists. "I want her death to *mean* something in a meaningless world. I want *you* to care for those who care for you. I don't mean pay lip service. I mean *really* care."

"Yeah, I get it."

"No. You don't. It's like…" She broke off and looked away. "It's like I'm speaking, and you're listening only because you have to."

"No. I have kids, you know. A wife. I have a family, and I know, *I really* know what it is to care." He did. "My oldest daughter—" Soon-to-be step-daughter. "—has gone through things I can't even begin to understand, but I try. Her mother went through just as much. And for everything I am or ever did, I always put them first." Which was why it'd pissed him off so damned much that Paige had taken the twins to D.C. after he'd said it was a bad idea. So pissed that *she'd* discount him, that he'd been reckless.

"Maybe you should have *listened* when she said no." Medusa meant Bruna.

But Dexx meant Paige. "Maybe."

The rain hid his own tears.

The twins had been a sweet pair, no matter where Doxy had come from. She'd cared too much for people by half. And Dexx way too much by far.

He pushed off of the tree to walk to the little bistro with tables outside. He popped the table umbrella open and sat on a drenched metal seat.

"Are you mental?" Medusa asked. "Everything's wet."

"We were supposed to go on a date." That whole time seemed so far away, and now that he knew that Bruna and Doxy were the same person, so many things started to make sense. Like when one would be wearing something and then suddenly the other was instead. Or the way the two of them spoke like they were the same person. "Two dates, actually. Neither one happened. So, this is for them."

"You are the stupidest Yank I've ever met. You're a fugitive, and you sit out here in the open?"

"They're watching the airports, not tiny little cafes. Besides, I think Bruna and Doxy liked a little recklessness in their men."

Medusa leaned her elbow on the table, watching it rain. "She also liked brains, which you clearly lack."

"Just sit." Dexx flagged a waiter who reluctantly came outside when Dexx refused to leave his seat.

He ordered the only American beer on the menu and did

the same for Medusa. When the waiter came back, he raised his glass and simply said, "Bruna. Doxy."

Medusa raised her glass but said nothing.

Three, maybe six beers in, the mood had lightened a little, and the rain had tapered off to a slight mist.

"Medusa. That's a helluva name. Did your dad hate you, or were you trying to compensate for something?"

She smiled sadly. "I'm a lilim. Well, a close cousin. I felt a little kinship with the gorgon because I was an ugly child. *Really* ugly."

"It barely shows." Dexx tipped his glass to her. "So, you went with a mankiller name. Okay, I'll go with it."

"Thanks. Because Gina or Terry or Sybil don't fit me. At all."

"I don't know. Sybil could. Just add a couple of personalities with your shapeshifting, and you'll have all your bases covered."

"What do you see when I let my other side out?"

What the fuck kind of question was *that*? Shit. He needed to ask that on the outside. "What the fuck kind of question is that?"

"I look different to everyone."

"I see. Well, I see an eight-foot-tall tentacle monster, that whips heads off men and women and whatever's close."

"I see." Medusa nodded with a sip of the beer.

"What are you supposed to look like?"

"Oh, no. I tell you, you tell a friend, and pretty soon, the villagers are chasing me with pitchforks and torches. I'd rather not."

"Can a third join you?" Furiel stood to the side, his jet-black umbrella sending drops of water splashing to the ground.

"Sure, why not." Dexx motioned to an empty spot, with no chair.

"Thank you." The demon magickally procured a dry seat.

Dexx leaned forward, his arms on the now-dry table. "Why pull us out of there? We were winning."

"You were *not* winning. That's what losing looked like."

"Looked like we were winning to me. Just found his weak spot. We were about to make him bleed out."

"You have never faced a creature like the bahlrok. They aren't your typical demon. Not even the great *Shedim Patesh* should take on a bahlrok with the expectation of living through it."

Good to know. "Can it be killed?"

"Not easily."

"Challenge accepted. What will Bussemi do now that he's been outed?"

A woman's voice from behind Dexx answered as he caught her scent. Roxxie. "He will likely pursue you. You destroyed his cover, and now many plans have collapsed."

"Have a seat." Dexx motioned to the empty spot opposite Furiel. "*I* didn't do that. Just tried to kill the fucker."

Roxxie sat on another magickally procured dry seat. "*I* did. But since he can't take his ire out on me, *you* will be the next best thing. Plus, he's hated you for a very long time." No rain touched her at all.

"And how long is that?" Medusa leaned forward. "He's got to be two or three times your age."

Dexx shrugged. "Let's just say it's been longer than that." He dug in his pocket and placed the *shamiyir* on the table. "Who wants to explain this first?"

Roxxie put her hand on his arm. "It's from the first time you walked the earth."

"I already know that. Skip to the part about what it does and how to use it." He had a *lot* of memories to flip through.

"It protects you. And other things. As for how these are personal. It's for *you* to find that out. You and Hattie."

"Perhaps *I* can shed a little more light on your past." Furiel reached inside his coat and pulled out a small stone bowl. A dark crack split from one edge to almost the middle.

"Hey—" A dark frown covered Dexx's face. How did you—"

The demon placed the stone on the table in front of him. "All I can say about this one is that it channeled magick."

Dexx moved his hand to grab it.

"I can't say what it will do now, however. Reuniting it with you may have—" Furiel tapped the table with his finger like he was still searching for the right word, "—explosive results."

"No *kadu?* You get this but not the important one?" It could still be used against him, and Dexx didn't like that.

Furiel shook his head. "Who said this one was not important? And sadly, no, I could not retrieve the *kadu*, or I would give it to you with this." He tapped the stone.

Dexx wasn't so big he didn't know when to be gracious. His unlocked memories let him know that Furiel had been instrumental many times in his several pasts. "Thanks."

Furiel nodded.

"Are you going to stay and help the paras here?" Dexx nodded to Medusa.

"This may be my place for the foreseeable future."

"Good. Make sure that you do. I'll be checking in on you from time to time." He pulled his glass up but cocked a grin at the demon before he sipped.

"I think I'll be watching too." Roxxie smiled.

"Perfect. How... sacrificial of you." Dexx sighed and took another drink. "I have another question, well I have a *lot* of questions, but how much did you know about what they were doing to me?"

"You were under the personal observation of a *very* powerful demon hiding in a paranormal hunter stronghold. I counted myself lucky to even do what I was able to for you. Things were even trickier when you took down your own people. I helped as far as I could. I made sure you found the *shamiyir*, and was not easy to do."

"Next time, just get me out of there so we can untangle the mess."

"Duly noted."

"Ugh." Dexx hung his head. "You got anything for me, Roxxie? Want to get any confessions off your chest?"

"Yes." She smiled in her pure way, and her scent never even flickered. "I may not have been as recovered as I let on. I misjudged the demon in Cardinal Bussemi. I'm also very disappointed in myself for my eyes being deceived as they were. He should not have been able to hide like he did in the church."

Dexx laughed at her confession. "Of course. Shame you couldn't erase the footage of me and my team *attacking* Parliament." They were now wanted criminals. Awesome. "We get to run until all this is forgotten or purged or whatever. I'd like to go home now."

"I regret I can't help with that this time. I *can* give Paige a message from you, though. It would almost be like you were there."

"Thanks." But he needed to talk to Paige himself. However, there was one more thing that needed to be dealt with. His connection with Hattie. "I need to get this *thing* out of my head, or I won't be any help to Paige."

Roxxie put her hand on his arm. Electric tingles shot through him. "That is still only something you can do. The bahlrok is *very* powerful, and for you to fight off *any* part of the spell says something about your ability. The answer is out there."

Dexx saw images flash through his head as she spoke.

Places he had never been but were familiar. He gave Roxxie a sharp look, but she only smiled at him.

Damned angels.

"Still don't know how we're leaving this island."

"Oh, that?" Furiel gave a dismissive wave of his hand. "That is not a problem. None of you will be recognized for a long time on any sort of surveillance. My treat."

How many times could they have used *that*? Dexx sighed again. "Thanks?"

Furiel smiled.

"What made you decide to bring Alwyn along?" Out of everything, Alwyn being transported from the fight *with* them was the most confusing.

"That was not my intention." The demon winced. "My spell focused on the alpha. I couldn't' cast that many spells at once, but if I cast one that linked the alpha and his pack, then that would serve just as well."

Alwyn had been in bad shape. Broken ribs, a punctured lung, and a broken leg. Roxxie had patched him up but had left some healing to him. He still hadn't woken up yet. She must have left a *lot* to him.

"Then, where do I start?" Dexx wasn't going to hide the exasperation in his voice, but nobody seemed to care anyway.

"Might I suggest something?" Furiel raised a finger.

"Not pushing me in the direction you want to go at all, are you?"

"My direction is parallel to your own for the moment. Many demons make alliances this way."

"I know. I've hunted a lot, you know."

"I do. I have more than a few acquaintances that you have returned."

"Yeah, I'll bet. So shoot. Where do I go that *isn't* home? 'Cause *that's* where I really want to be." But he couldn't risk it.

Not yet. Wherever he went, Bussemi *would* follow. They needed to get the information about DoDO to Paige, and he needed to find a way to kill Bussemi once and for all. This wasn't a great win. It didn't feel like it, anyway, but they *had* gotten information they wouldn't have had before. So, at least there was that.

Paige would understand.

Furiel studied Dexx for a long moment. "Take the djinn home."

Oh, fuck. What would Tarik have to do with all of this? "Then take Frey home and Rainbow and Ethel, right?"

"That may come." The demon shrugged. "But first go where the djinn rule and take this." Furiel held up the cracked stone with the strange runes engraved in it. He pulled out a silk bag and slipped it inside.

"What am I supposed to do?"

"You will know when you get there."

Right because that always worked so well in the past. "Just tell me what you know."

"For this to work, you must go in with only *your* expectations. This is *your* journey. I am only telling you where to start."

"What the hell? You agree with this, Roxxie?"

"I do."

"Not going to tell me about the *ma'a'shed* either, are you?"

"Not today. You have enough to deal with. Now would be a good time to start." Furiel rose from the table, followed by Roxxie. "May your quest succeed. I have some investment in it."

Quest. Like this was a bad sword and sorcery book with all the pretty prose. Blegh.

Roxxie smiled and laid a delicate hand on his shoulder. "I wish you a speedy return. I have faith in you. Outside of Paige, you are the most resourceful human I know."

"Get out of here." He really missed Paige. "You're going to make me blush."

The angel and the demon vanished.

"I'm leaving too." Medusa rose to her feet, the rain stopping. "DoDO is bollucksed but not dead. They are exposed, but they still have influence. Now we have an advantage we can use for equal rights."

"Good to have you on my team, Medusa."

She rose.

Dexx stood to take her hand. "If you get to the states, look me up. I might have a spot on the team for you."

"I may consider it. Fortune favor you, Yank."

"Take care of yourself, Limey." Dexx turned and walked away.

Back at the van, Ethel and Rainbow were talking quietly. Frey leaned against it, her arms crossed.

Tarik sat near with his eyes closed, his hands in his lap.

Michelle stepped out of the van.

"We're leaving," Dexx said. "Got some assurances we'll be good for a while. Good news, Tarik. I think we're headed on down to your neck of the woods."

Everyone got ready to get in the van, eager to move on.

Dexx stopped them. "I have something to say."

Five sets of eyes waited for him.

"Thanks. You came for me or stayed with me. You didn't have to do. I may not be your alpha right now, but I'm the luckiest leader in the world."

"Just get in the van." Frey challenged him for the merest second, then turned to get in the passenger seat.

Dexx sat in the driver seat, adjusting mirrors that didn't need adjusting. He *wished* he was headed home. He just hoped Paige would understand, but he couldn't lead Bussemi to their kids. They'd faced a lot together, but…fuck. Nothing like that. "We good?"

Frey nodded as she shut her door. "We are. For today, we are."

Dexx cocked a grin at her. "Wouldn't have it any other way."

One thing was certain.

He was going to find a way home and make Paige his wife. For real.

Paige dodged a lightning blast aimed at her head and frowned at her youngest daughter.

Rai grinned impishly, her eyes dancing with blue lightning. "You said."

Paige didn't disagree. She'd told Rai not to hold back in order to get a good feel of where she was, but she didn't want to *die* in the process.

Margo leapt in, her wolf teeth bared, her black coat rippling. Her paws landed lightly on the ground before she launched herself at Leah.

Paige kept herself from protecting her oldest daughter, but it took every bit of overprotective strength she could muster. Her job was to train these kids to survive. It wasn't to baby them or protect them. Her kids were going to survive.

Leah blinked her blue eyes once, and then a door opened between her and Margo, closing behind the wolf's puffy tail.

Before Paige could ask where Leah had sent Margo, the wolf leapt out of thin air closer to the rope bridge of the obstacle course. "Well done, Lee."

Ember fought with Ripley, who shifted effortlessly through the trees in her ghostly dog form. As a death dog, her shifted form was less solid and was a lot more creepy.

But Ember's fire was still able to singe her fur. Something about him being a rajasi and how his fire could light a soul on fire, which was part of the reason the rajasi had been eradicated even from legend a millennia before.

Lightening tagged Paige on the shoulder, sending her body into the rigidity of electric shock. Her muscles tightened, snot streamed effortlessly from her nose. She thought she was going to puke.

But this wasn't the first time her daughter had hit her like this, so she was practiced in the art of recovery. Paige shifted into an elephant, the body mass taking most of the effects of the electricity and dispersing it, and charged her daughter.

Rai squeaked and shifted into a hawk, flying away.

Paige wasn't going to let her get away that easily. She leapt into the air with her giant elephant feet, shifting into a gorilla—which was quickly becoming her favorite form—and reached, grasping her daughter's brown tail feathers.

Lightening wrapped around her thick-skinned hand as tail feathers released, and Rai continued to fly away, but this time as a true thunderbird.

Which meant that Rai was getting serious.

Paige shifted into a pterodactyl wishing she could shift into a dragon.

Paige overtook her daughter in four wingbeats, her claws outstretched.

Rai screeched, her wings shooting lightning.

Paige's dinosaur skin reflected most of that, but not easily. The pain of the electricity made Paige's wings quiver. She dropped in altitude before she could correct herself. But then she gathered the air under her wings and shot through the sky, intent on taking her daughter down. She didn't want to die in the sky. She wasn't afraid of the electric bolts shooting at her. She was afraid of the landing. She hated flying.

Rai turned in midflight, her wings going still as she called lightening from the very sky.

Paige had never seen her daughter do that before.

And she knew that if Rai hit her with that much electricity—

It was time to get to the ground. Now.

Paige turned tail and dove for the ground, hoping Rai would remember she was attacking her *mother* and that she should hold back. The ground came in fast—faster than she liked. She shifted into a gorilla as soon as she came close enough because she needed better control.

But was hit with the lightening mid-shift.

Paige didn't know what exactly happened after that. The next thing she knew, her bright-eyed daughter leaned over, her long dark hair spilling over her shoulders unbound.

Ember knelt beside her, his amber eyes dancing with worry, his hair a fiery wraith of energy.

Leah joined them, pulling her long blonde hair back into a ponytail with experience. They had wounded on this obstacle course quite often. "Mom, you okay?"

Paige tried to grunt, but moving was…hard. The world was trying to destroy her, and here were her kids, the perfect weapons of destruction.

Bobby came over and flopped down beside her head, his hands lit with a golden light. He placed his hands on Paige, and the light enveloped her, surrounding her with love and healing. Her muscles realigned and healed, bones she hadn't realized she'd broken snapped back into place.

It wasn't entirely pleasant, but after several moments, Paige was pain-free. The light disappeared and sound invaded.

"….sorry, Mom. I don't know what happened."

"—totally wicked!" Tyler's voice rang with his bardic power. "I've never seen anything—"

"—crap," Mandy swore as she raced over and tripped, tumbling to join them. "Are you okay?"

Paige knew Mandy well enough by now to know that she could have been asking about anyone being okay except for the person dying. She was unsurprised to see Mandy staring at Ember.

He frowned at her like she'd lost her mind and nodded, his head pulled back.

Margo walked calmly and naked toward them, her dark eyes taking Paige in, the scar on her cheek ticking. Her belly bulged slightly with her pregnancy. "Are you healed?"

Paige moved her arms, which was a little hard because the kids were crowded around her. "Seem to be."

"Dang, woman!" Ripley shifted into human form as she ran up fully clothed, a wild grin on her face. "That was impressive."

A large grizzly bear charged them.

Leah turned and slapped black energy at him with a frown. "Joe!"

He skidded to a stop, shaking his big bear head, and shifted into a tall, naked man. "I wasn't going to run you over, Lee."

"Yeah, right," Leah grumbled.

He'd done it before.

Paige held up a hand, feeling a bit like Frederic from *The Pirate Movie* in the coffin scene. "I'm fine, guys. If a demon couldn't kill me, my own kids can't." Which obviously wasn't the case. Her kids *could* kill her and almost had.

How scary was that?

She pulled herself to her feet, meeting Margo's gaze. "I

think the training went well." But she needed to be done for the day.

Margo grunted, resting her hand on her belly. "I agree."

The kids took that as their cue to get up.

"Perhaps a little too well."

Paige moved her legs, working the kinks out. "I don't know what broke in the fall, but I'm certainly glad we have a healer." An unexpected bonus.

Ripley broke out of Joe's cuddle with a smile on her lips and a hint of worry in her eyes. "You fell hard and in mid-shape. I think we found a weakness."

Which would be cool if they were preparing to battle shifter witches. But she guessed this was one weakness she just had to find a way to shield herself against.

Joe shifted back into a grizzly and wandered off with a roar of challenge.

Leah raised her head and turned toward him, then followed. The other kids trailed behind her with a mixture of excitement and something else.

Fear.

Rai's movements were subdued and she held back.

Paige grabbed her daughter's attention and flagged her over.

The girl's shoulders slumped even further, but she headed over.

If Dexx were here, he'd know exactly what to tell Rai, what to say to lighten the mood. But the last she'd seen or heard from him had been a news clip on the BBC, showing him and the Red Star Division taking down some big demon in Parliament.

What the hell was her man doing in England, taking down a government that wasn't even theirs? If only she could *talk* to him.

But he hadn't called, hadn't texted.

And hadn't come home.

"I worry they're too strong," Margo murmured, walking to the small shed and pulling out a robe.

Paige shook off her worry of Dexx—was he even *coming* home? Had she pushed too hard? They'd argued before he'd...Had he left? No. She couldn't go down that path. Dexx was handling something. He'd managed to send a bunch of information on DoDO. He hadn't abandoned them—her.

Back to the matter at hand. Paige worried about their kids too, but they were *her* kids and she wasn't about to admit out loud or to herself that they might be a danger to the world. "Then, we need to teach them how to control it."

Ripley tucked the corners of her lips in and blinked. But it was obvious from her wide eyes that she was thinking something sarcastic to say.

Paige ignored her and wrapped her arm—which still ached, meaning it had been one of the broken things—around Rai's shoulders, giving them a gentle squeeze. "You did good up there."

"I almost killed you," Rai whispered, her voice constricted and low as if a ball of tears was wedged in her throat.

An answering ball threatened to fill Paige's. "I gave birth to you, remember? You're not gonna get rid of me *that* easy."

"I heard your bones break."

"Well, yes. But you didn't *kill* me."

Rai stopped and pulled away from her. "What if Bobby wasn't here? What if I *had* killed you?"

Paige wished Alma was there to share some of her wisdom. What would she have said?

In that moment, Paige understood the position Alma had been in, being a strong witch in her own right, raising granddaughters who were stronger and more powerful than her.

But instead of being afraid of that power like Alma had been, Paige was going to show her daughter—all of her kids whether they were hers or not—that they didn't need to fear who they were. They simply had to hone themselves to do the most good.

She took her daughter's shoulders in her hands and waited until Rai met her gaze.

It took a while. Lightning danced in them, wild and unfettered.

Afraid.

Paige's heart twisted. She cupped her daughter's cheek. A handful of months ago, Rai'd been a tiny baby. And here she was in the body of a teen. She gathered Rai into a hug, wrapping one hand around the back of Rai's head and tucking her close. "Be the best you can be. Do the best you can do. Don't die and if someone tries to kill you…" Why was she quoting Malcolm Reynolds from *Firefly*? "You try to kill them right back."

Rai held onto Paige for a long moment.

Margo took in a deep breath, meeting Paige's gaze, her eyes saying they needed to be very careful, but also that she understood. She put her hand on Rai's shoulder, offering her silent support.

Paige smiled at the wolf gratefully.

Ripley bounced on her toes, looking uncomfortable. She reached over and patted Rai awkwardly on the back. "We have work to do?"

Paige pulled away and screwed on a Mom smile. "You did great out there. Be scared. That's okay. Fear will keep you smart. But don't hide behind it. Don't allow fear to be your excuse to hide from life. Your thunderbird fought too hard to be freed just so her human could keep her hidden."

Rai frowned for a moment, but then raised her chin. She nodded once and then turned to follow Joe and the kids who were now climbing over the obstacle course.

Paige and Ripley made sandwiches while Margo got

dressed in the main house. Then, armed with a light lunch, they all three piled in Leslie's SUV and drove into town. Ripley and Margo had business in town.

As did Paige. She was the "Secretary of Paranormal Affairs" in name only, but that didn't mean she got to slack on her "duties." The reality was that even if the position wasn't real—because only the president could assign it to her —there was a void there and a need *for* the position, whether it was granted a title or not.

When Paige stepped out, she was greeted by a young woman, Willow Mathews, who had taken point in controlling what got to her and what she handled on a daily basis. Willow had volluntaken the position of being her executive assistant and was the only reason Paige was able to survive this incredible shift of responsibilities.

She and Willow handled some boring details on their way to Leslie's shop. Margo and Ripley led the way, dealing with some of the people who came up to them seeking answers or needing to send in requests for help.

It annoyed Paige that she needed bodyguards and assistants because *this* wasn't the job she'd signed up for. She was a detective, not a leader. She was learning as she went as a leader, and doing that could get people hurt or worse.

But an hour later, she had found solutions for the handful of people who'd waited for her to come to town, and she'd dealt with all the things Willow had on her plate.

All in all, things were starting to run a bit more normally.

Paige walked into her sister's shop earlier than expected and with time to spare. That was new, and she didn't know what to *do* with her free time. She'd become conditioned to having each microsecond crammed full with world-ending doom.

Leslie looked up from her work at the counter, surprise shining in her green eyes, her dirty-blonde hair in a messy bun of messiness. Like seriously more than normal. Some women could pull off that look and make it look effortless and cool. Leslie made it look messy. "Is the world on fire?"

"Not currently." Were there branches in her bun?

Leslie frowned and glanced out her shop windows.

Paige had no idea what she was supposed to do in that moment. "Do you need help?"

"With what?" Leslie's tone rose with indignation and derision. "I'm sorry, baby sister, but I just put my shop *back* together for the last time. If it explodes one more time, I'm callin' it quits."

Paige held up her hand in surrender. "I just offered because I could maybe learn some stuff?"

"I don't have time to teach you." Leslie gestured to her shop. "This was stocked this morning. Look at it."

A few bars of soap remained here and there. The shelves where the lotions had been were bare. The wine was gone. Even the candles were gone. "Oh." Paige gave her sister a smile. "Well, that's good. Right?"

"Right. Yes." Leslie nodded with a disgusted sigh. "You want to help? Take this case." She set down whatever she was working on behind the counter and disappeared behind it. She came back up , whacking her head on something. She grunted but came back up without so much as rubbing her head, handing Paige a thick case file instead.

"You okay?" Leslie had a thick skull, but *that* thick? She'd hit it *hard*.

"Fine." Leslie waved off her concern. "Ghosts are appearing all over town. They're possessing people. They're putting people into comas. Someone's torturing them to draw their energy."

"The ghosts?"

Leslie gave her a look like she was dumb.

Well, she'd obviously missed something.

"They're torturing the people to *death* and them *making* them ghosts." Leslie's green eyes flared open, and her lips set in a tight line before she continued. "*Then* the ghosts are possessing people—maybe tryin' to get a message out? Don't know. The possessed people are falling into comas before the ghost can do anything. That's what I have."

Paige was certain there was more. Leslie was a wicked smart woman, but she was also the kind of person who needed to focus on what needed to be done, and it would be best if everyone else just left her alone while she did it. "You got the case because?"

"Red Star's missing." Leslie turned and headed to the back of the shop. "And you're busy, but now that you're here and you want to help, stay out of my shop and solve the case."

Paige blinked as Leslie firmly but resolutely shut the cloth "door" in Paige's face.

PRE-ORDER MIDNIGHT WHISKEY

Join us in *Midnight Whiskey* as Paige fights to gather an army so vast, Dexx's enemy won't be able to enter, even is the man she loves fails.

Pick up *Midnight Whiskey*:
https://www.fjblooding.com/pre-order-wwmr-book-3

Don't forget to leave reviews! Let us know what you think!

WHISKEY MAGICK & MENTAL HEALTH

Sign up to learn more about our books and receive this free e-zine about Whiskey Magick and Mental Health.
https://www.fjblooding.com/books-lp

ABOUT THE AUTHOR

Shane Wolfram lives in his hometown with his amazing wife F.J. Blooding. Frankie let him take over Dexx's story one deadline-ridden night and he's never looked back since. He hadn't quite realized what he'd be jumping into when he volunteered, but he's grown as an author and is enjoying the journey.

They live with his twin brother, his wife, their two kids, and during their long summer days, he gets to spend time with his two amazing daughters. He loves working on cars and letting my bestselling wife write his bios, newsletters, and articles for him while he crafts amazing Dexx books and naps with the cat.

Enjoy!

www.ingramcontent.com/pod-product-compliance
Lightning Source LLC
Chambersburg PA
CBHW061349190726
48288CB00005B/1655